For my parents, Liz and John, whose love story is still going strong forty years after my father tucked a diamond ring into the pocket of the new denim overalls he'd bought for my mother. And for my two sisters, Katie and Mary Beth. Who would have thought, after all the years of hair pulling and name calling that we would end up the best of friends?

For my husband, Doug, the love of my life and the best lead a romance writer could ask for. And our beautiful daughter Molly, one of the best writers I know—being your mom will always be my life's most meaningful work.

Diversion Books
A Division of Diversion Publishing Corp.
443 Park Avenue South, Suite 1004
New York, New York 10016
www.DiversionBooks.com

For more information, email info@diversionbooks.com

First Diversion Books edition April 2014.

Print ISBN: 978-1-62681-280-2
eBook ISBN: 978-1-62681-278-9

Worth the Weight

Dear Kelsey,
Keep up your own
writing and you will be
(the next published author
at work)! Thanks for your
support!
xo
Eileen

EILEEN PALMA

DIVERSIONBOOKS

Chapter One

Jack couldn't decide if adding a super-sized cup holder to the CC-XL Deluxe stroller would be jumping the shark. He had retrofitted the design of the original CC-XL to fit up to eighty-three pounds—well past the sixty-five pound limit they had introduced back in 2008. He designed a wider wheelbase and a deeper seat to fit taller, heavier kids, some of whom were probably grade school age. He tweeted that he was working on the prototype of an upgraded CC-XL and now he was getting requests via Twitter, Facebook and the Considerable Carriages website for larger cup holders and built-in snack trays. Jack was up most of the night, trying to figure out how to satisfy his customer base without making his company a target for Jimmy Fallon.

He was sprawled out on his couch, debating whether it would be more productive to nap for a few hours or make a Starbucks run when his apartment door opened. Diesel, his scruffy Jack Russell mix, jumped off the couch and assaulted the moving door with fits of yippy barks.

"What if I had been entertaining?" asked Jack with a raised eyebrow when his sister Harper walked in with her daughter, Lauren. They lived in the top half of Jack's brownstone, but gave themselves carte blanche to the lower floors as well. When Jack converted the building into a duplex, he had kept the bottom half and rented out the top to Harper and her family for a nominal fee. His business was doing so well, he hadn't really needed to charge them anything, but Harper's husband David, a career Marine, wasn't the type to take a handout.

"The odds of you having a woman over are pretty unlikely. Did I hear you watching *Straight Talk* last night?"

"Damn these walls are too thin," grumbled Jack. "Kate Richards from *KidFit* filled her time slot ripping on Considerable Carriages. I was getting tweets about it all night."

"It's great that she wants to keep children from getting fat, but in the meantime someone has to keep them all from outgrowing their car seats and tipping over their high chairs."

"Someone needs to tell Kate Richards that," said Jack.

"God, this place is a mess." Harper cleared the drained Red Bull cans and empty Moroccan Delight food cartons off the coffee table and carried them to the kitchen.

"Don't you ever sleep in your bed?" Jack's ten-year-old niece, Lauren, flung herself on the brown leather couch. He was still lying down, but she was just the right size to squeeze next to him and steal most of his crocheted afghan. Then, of course, Diesel jumped back on the couch and took over the few remaining square inches of cushion.

"Maybe I should start sleeping in my room, so you two won't wake me up next time."

"What's up with the hair?" Lauren looked at him with narrowed eyes.

"You're the one who told me to grow it out. I'm still at the in-between stage." Jack's thick hair curled into what his friends dubbed a Jew-fro, even though he was only half Jewish and had never set foot in an actual synagogue. But with a last name like Moskowitz, he may as well own it.

"Try using gel. That might help the situation." Lauren had inherited the same thick stubborn curls, but since she was a girl she had the luxury to grow her penny brown hair to her waist to make it work.

"I wasn't aware that I was having an actual hair 'situation'." But in the end, Jack knew he would take her suggestion.

"Harper, you have to see this!" Jack queued up the YouTube clip on his laptop.

Harper walked back in, wiping her hands on a dishcloth. She plopped on the couch by Lauren's feet leaving even less room for Jack. He sat up and played back the sound bite.

"Childhood obesity is at an all time high in this country, making this generation the first one in history predicted to have their parents outlive them. Our next guest, Kate Richards, host of ABC's *KidFit*, and *New York Times* bestselling author of *Mini-Munchies*, is here to tell us how to put a stop to this epidemic."

The former White House reporter turned talk show host, Lucy Barrows, stood and clapped as the canned theme music to *KidFit* played in the background. She still wore the dark suits and cultured pearls of the DC press league and her shiny brown hair grazed her chin in a sleek bob. In contrast, Kate Richards wore army fatigue printed yoga pants and a tiny camouflage tee shirt with the *KidFit* logo stretched across her boobs—not too original, but it was her trademark look.

"Hi everyone," Kate sang, over the audience's cheers as she settled into the oversized armchair in the living room style set.

"Let's cut to the chase," Lucy began as soon as she sat back down in the other armchair. "What's your biggest pet peeve?"

Kate shook her loose blond waves over her shoulder and for a split second Jack almost forgot she was the enemy. "One word—strollers!" The audience rallied.

"We have so many uber-fit moms, especially here in Manhattan, who love jog strollers. They throw their kids in, shove organic chocolate milk and cookies at them and cart them all over the city, getting their exercise in while their kids pack on the pounds." The audience roared in agreement.

"There's been a lot of debate on the news recently about a company called Considerable Carriages, which actually caters to overweight children," Lucy explained.

"Don't even get me started about that company. As we speak, they're designing a stroller to fit children who weigh up to eighty pounds! Which either means mothers are intending on carting around their sixth graders or this company is profiting from morbidly obese toddlers." Kate Richards' voice poured from the screen, thick and velvety like chocolate and Jack had to remind himself that she was actually spewing hatred for his company.

Lucy cut in. "I heard the company was originally founded because heavier kids couldn't properly fit in car seats. So, isn't Considerable Carriages actually keeping these kids from getting seriously injured in a car accident?"

"Lucy, we need to curb childhood obesity rather than accommodate and profit from it."

Jack snapped his laptop shut. "That's pretty much the gist of it."

"You're not the bad guy here. You aren't the one pumping these kids with high fructose corn syrup and fast food," said Harper.

"This kid in my class brings Ding Dongs for snack every day," said Lauren. "I bet he used to ride around in one of your strollers."

"That's not nice, Lauren." Harper chewed on her bottom lip to keep from laughing.

"This chick is profiting off fat kids just as much as I am, with her diet cookbook and kids' exercise show."

"Exactly, so let your publicist deal with her and just focus on your designs."

"The best way to deal with a bully is to ignore them," piped in Lauren.

"Or knock them out. But I guess I can't do that in this situation." Jack rolled his head around to get the kink out of his neck. "So anyway, what are you guys doing here so early?"

"Guess who's going to be the next face of Sunrise Granola?"

While Jack's grey eyes had always been described as wolfish, Harper's ice blue eyes were more Siberian Husky, which was what turned her somewhat average appearance into that something special that landed her commercial and print work. Most of Harper's teen modeling photos had landed in local circulars and catalogs, but as she got older she grew into her looks enough to play the cool young mom in commercials, making her the rare model who booked more work as she aged.

"Congrats! I guess that means you need me to keep an eye on Lauren while you do the shoot?" Lauren was already reaching for a Wii remote as he spoke.

"Thanks Jack." Harper started inching towards the door.

"Can I play the Wii?"

"Sure. Just let me sleep for an hour and then we can go out and do whatever you want." Jack rolled over on the couch and pulled the throw back over himself. "And hit the mute button."

Harper paused at the door. "Jack, you really should let me set you up with one of my friends. I hate to see you sitting home alone every Saturday night."

"I'm not alone. I just had a movie date with my favorite niece last week." Jack pounded his closed fist against Lauren's in solidarity.

"Seriously, Jack. You haven't had a girlfriend in ages."

"I'm sure I'll meet the right one soon enough. And when I do, you girls will be the first to find out."

"I know this model who just got divorced, well actually I think she's just separated, but she's definitely getting divorced at some point."

Jack caught Lauren's eye from where she stood out of her mom's line of vision. She mouthed no and waved both hands back and forth.

"No thanks."

As soon as Jack's heavy eyelids touched down, his phone played the theme to The Dukes of Hazzard. It was his business partner Matt's ring tone, a nod to their favorite show growing up due to their mutual admiration for muscle cars and Daisy Duke.

"Did you finish the design?"

"Hell no. I'm still on the fence about those snack trays." Jack threw back the afghan and gave up all hope of getting that nap. He got up and poured himself a mug of stale coffee and headed to the picnic table in his back courtyard.

"The public's asking for them," said Matt. "We might as well give 'em what they want."

"You think *Straight Talk* was bad? We go all out with this

and there's no turning back." Jack abandoned the aggressively bitter cup of brew on the table. He would have to make a coffee run soon.

"I already drafted a rebuttal for that conservative hag to read on Monday morning."

"I told you this would happen if we bumped the weight class up to eighty pounds. Lauren's in fourth grade and isn't even close to that."

"Lauren's a gymnast. Dude, she'll be in high school before she weighs that much."

"Bad example."

"How many times have we talked about this? We can't provide car seats to keep all those kids safe without the revenue of the strollers."

"I know. You don't have to keep hitting me over the head with it."

"Bottom line—there's no Considerable Carriages without the carriages. So quit being a pussy and finish the design."

When Jack came back inside, the TV was off, the Wii controller abandoned on the coffee table next to his sketches.

"Starbucks run!" Listening for Lauren's answer, Jack heard the tub filling in the bathroom.

"Finish up so we can walk Diesel and get coffee. There's a vanilla Frappuccino in it for you if you're ready in the next five minutes!"

Lauren opened the door, releasing wispy curls of steam into the hallway. "You can come in. I was just giving Diesel a bath."

Jack had always wanted a dog named Diesel and had every intention of rescuing a Pit-bull from the pound, but he made the mistake of bringing Lauren with him and had ended up leaving with a squirrely fifteen pound dog and christening it with the monster dog name.

Lauren was wearing one of Jack's denim Considerable Carriages button downs with the sleeves rolled up over her own clothes. The ends of her hair were wet from leaning over the tub. Sometimes she reminded him so much of Harper. Like when she used to give their geriatric Lab mix weekly bubble baths leaving behind a trail of wet fur and an empty bottle of Herbal Essences for their mom to find.

Lauren turned off the water and Jack pulled his wet mutt out of the tub, soaking his shirt in the process. "We just gave him a bath last week. Was he really that dirty?" Jack gave the inside of Diesel's ears a good rub down with the towel as Lauren held him on the bath mat.

"I forgot to tell you! Diesel got invited to a birthday party." Lauren handed Jack a damp piece of cardstock. The center had a picture of a black and white Boston Terrier with huge runny eyes and a pink polka dot bow wrapped around her neck. *Sarah Jessica Barker Turns One!* screamed the headline in a *Sex in the City* style font.

"Where'd you get this?" Jack flipped the invite over to view the party details, which included cake and a romp in the Chelsea dog park.

"The dog walker gave it to me a few weeks ago when she dropped Diesel off. She said it was from one of her other clients." Lauren rubbed Jack's white towel back and forth over the dog's hind end while he stayed surprisingly still.

"Why would some random dog owner invite Diesel to their dog's birthday party?"

"Sarah Jessica Barker's not just some random dog! She's Diesel's girlfriend."

"Diesel has a girlfriend?"

"Don't you ever talk to Pam when she drops Diesel off?"

"I've been too busy working lately to say much more than hi and bye to Pam. Speaking of which, I was up half the night working. The last thing I want to do is go to a dog's birthday party."

Lauren looked up at him with puppy Siberian Husky eyes. "I really miss Dad and he's still at that base where he doesn't have Internet or phone. This would really cheer me up."

Jack sighed. He couldn't take it when she pulled the "my dad is stationed in Afghanistan" card. "Fine, we can go. I just really need a cup of coffee first."

"You're planning on changing your clothes too, right? And

taking a shower?"

"The dogs aren't gonna care what I look or smell like," mumbled Jack.

But twenty minutes later, Jack was showered, his hair gelled into submission, and he had changed into a fresh tee shirt and a relatively clean pair of jeans. Lauren had changed out of her dog-grooming smock, so that she was now wearing those denim leggings she practically lived in.

"I have gymnastics at four. You can drop me off after the party." Lauren grabbed her gym bag off the banister and slung it over her shoulder.

Jack pulled the heavy wooden door of the brownstone shut and made sure it was locked while Lauren walked Diesel onto the sidewalk. It was one of those warm September afternoons that had a hint of the crisp cool air that would carry them into fall. Diesel quickly figured out where they were going and started tugging on the leash.

The Chelsea dog run was only a few blocks from Jack's brownstone, sandwiched between the North and Southbound West Side Highway, but the sounds of barking dogs overpowered the noise from the cars rushing past.

When they neared the fence, Jack was immediately approached by a heavy-set man juggling a clipboard and a pumpernickel bagel that was oozing vegetable cream cheese from the sides.

"Sorry, folks. The dog park is closed for a private party." The cream cheese was dangerously close to dripping on Jack's sneakers.

"We were invited." Lauren's voice edged with gloating as she pulled the invitation from her back pocket and handed it to the man. "This is Diesel, the birthday girl's boyfriend."

As much as Jack didn't want to go to the party, it was nice to get one over on this sorry excuse for a bouncer.

"Here're the camera waivers." The man handed his clipboard to Jack. "Fill out both forms and sign the bottom."

As Jack reached for the clipboard, he suddenly registered the three cameramen stationed throughout the small dog park.

Living in Manhattan, he was used to stumbling on movie and reality show sets, but so far he had been able to evade that type of notoriety.

"You know Mom's fine with me being on camera. Remember, I did that episode of *Law & Order: SVU*?"

"How could I forget?"

Chelsea Piers was home to the *Law & Order* crew and they had needed some young gymnasts in the background of a scene. Lauren eagerly participated and ended up with what may or may not have actually been her toes and part of her elbow in a shot, but she still jumped at every opportunity to brag about it.

"What're they filming?" asked Jack. But the man had already turned to the next party guest who had actually brought a gift bag. Jack wondered what was hidden beneath the hot pink tissue paper. Rawhide bones? Tennis balls? Treats?

"It's probably an Animal Planet show." Lauren shrugged her shoulders and ran over to the food table.

Jack had just finished unleashing Diesel when he spotted his dog walker, Pam. She was hard to miss with her bright blue ASPCA cap and matching tee shirt over stone washed Levis. Pam had lived in a rent controlled studio apartment across the street from Jack and Harper their whole lives and had been their babysitter when they were kids. She moved onto dog sitting not long after they outgrew her, which Jack tried not to take personally. Diesel started humping Pam's leg and she gently pulled him off and shooed him towards a game of chase with a Chihuahua and a Maltese.

Jack reached his arms out for Pam's usual motherly hug that smelled of Johnson's baby powder and liver treats, but she stopped him with one firm hand to the chest.

"Are you fucking crazy?" Pam jerked her head so vigorously that her hat almost fell off.

"Not the greeting I was hoping for." Jack was pretty certain this was the first time he had ever heard Pam drop the F bomb.

"What're you doing here?" Pam's whisper shrieks bordered on hysterical, as she frantically looked around the dog park.

"Aren't you the one who gave Lauren the invitation?" Jack's

heartbeat quickened as it became clear Pam was using her body to shield him from the cameraman closest to them.

"That was before *Straight Talk*, you numskull!" Pam smacked his arm. Hard.

"Would you stop hitting me and tell me what's going on?" Jack could feel sweat beading up on the back of his neck.

"Sarah Jessica Barker belongs to Kate Richards. She's part of Diesel's dog walking crew. Kate handed me a stack of invitations for her dog friends and I gave one to Lauren before Kate skewered you on *Straight Talk*." Pam's words fell out of her mouth in a breathless rush.

"Shit!" Jack scoped out the situation. In order to leave, he would need to tear Diesel away from his game of chase and grab Lauren without making a scene, and without the cameras catching anything. He had already signed off on the release, so if there were any drama it would end up on the next episode of *KidFit*.

"You need to get out of here, Jack! Right now!" Pam nudged Jack towards Diesel.

"Pam! Stay right there. I'll be over in a second!" Jack would've recognized that sound anywhere. Not many women had a voice with the power of an instant hard-on. Only this time her words weren't oozing silky smooth from his computer screen; they were coming from the cake table less than five feet away.

In person, Kate Richards was beautiful, and not in that overly Botoxed TV star way either. Her soft blond hair fell in waves down her back. The kind of hair most girls seared the beauty out of with a flat iron. And unlike most workout fanatics, Kate Richards had curves in all the right places. She was the kind of girl that could make you lose all sense.

"Fuck. That's my cue to go play fetch with Diesel and Lauren."

*"The most pure love I've ever experienced is from my dog. I could
lose my show, never write another cookbook and go bankrupt and
she would still think I was the most amazing human on the planet."*
Kate Richards, Dog Tales Magazine

Chapter Two

"You didn't have to miss one of Grace's soccer games for this
did you Pete?" Kate turned to the burly guy who had been
filming her since they shot the pilot episode at a Queens sound
stage four years ago.

"Grace didn't complain when I told her this would help
pay for that iTouch she wants for her birthday." Pete winked at
her and Kate was glad she had talked the *KidFit* honchos into
kicking in overtime pay for the crew.

Kate wasn't usually into big parties. She had celebrated
her own thirty-fifth birthday at her sister's dining room table
in Bronxville eating a Betty Crocker yellow layer cake with
chocolate frosting made by her eight-year-old niece. Kate
planned on celebrating her dog's first birthday with an afternoon
at the park and a treat from Buttercup's Paw-Tisserie.

But her publicist and default best friend Dana had seized
the opportunity to film an extra segment for the show. Now,
they had taken over the Chelsea dog park with the *KidFit* film
crew and tables of food (both people and dog).

Not that Kate should complain. Since she had turned her
life over to Dana, *KidFit* had been syndicated and her kid's diet
cookbook, *Mini-Munchies*, had made the *New York Times* bestseller
list in both hardcover and paperback.

"Let's get some footage of the kids playing with the dogs. You can add voiceovers about how playing with pets is a great way for kids to exercise, yada, yada." Dana wiped a smudge of dirt off one of her Christian Louboutin wedge sandals that Kate knew for a fact cost over five hundred dollars.

"That's actually a great idea." As soon as Kate agreed, Pete zeroed his camera in on a little boy who was playing catch with a Black Lab puppy.

"Just try to pan the camera away from the woman in the leopard print skinny jeans—not a good look for her." Dana looked beautiful even when she was acting ugly. Her cappuccino skin illuminated her regal cheekbones and high forehead. She was also one of those rare women who looked great in any shade of lipstick from bubble gum pink to traffic light red.

Kate cringed, but before she could interject, she heard a voice arguing with one of the cameramen.

"What d' ya mean private party? This is a public dog run. You can't take it over with your film crew!"

"We're done at four. You can come back then," said the cameraman, with the calm of someone who had dealings with irate New Yorkers on a regular basis.

"This is bullshit! Everywhere you go in this city, some jerk off is filming a reality show. I just want to exercise my dog. Is that really too much to ask?"

"This is going to ruin the rest of the footage. Someone needs to get this asshole out of here," hissed Dana.

"I have a better idea." Kate slid past Dana to the wrought iron gate.

"I'm really sorry we inconvenienced you. Why don't you and your dog join the party?"

The man froze, a drip of sweat running down the crook of his nose, "You're the woman from that kids' workout show right? My wife's gonna go crazy when I tell her I met you!"

"I'm glad your wife enjoys the show. It's my dog's birthday today and …"

Kate lost her train of thought when she heard a deep growl resonate behind her. The transparent hairs on her arm stood up at the guttural sound. She spun around just in time to see a German Shepherd with pointy teeth bared, ready to jump on her Boston Terrier. By the looks of things, Sarah Jessica Barker had just stolen a rope toy from a dog that probably outweighed her by a good seventy pounds. Kate stood rooted to the spot, frozen in fear, while her dog growled at her opponent with the ferocity of an animal five times its size. The shepherd pounced.

Suddenly, a man flew across the dog park in two great leaps, grabbing the hose from the community water bowl on the way and blasting the snarling dog in the snout with a powerful surge of water. The mini geyser was harmless to the large dog, but it distracted him from trying to tear Sarah Jessica Barker to shreds. The man dropped the hose, soaking the German Shepherd and a few innocent animal and human bystanders in the process. Then, he plucked the Boston Terrier from the ground and carried her high above his head to the corner behind the cake table.

It wasn't until her dog was safely ensconced behind the buttercream Louis Vuitton doggy satchel, that Kate could make her feet move.

The Good Samaritan cradled the feisty pup in a football hold. "Calm down you little trouble maker. You gotta learn when to pick your battles."

For a split second Kate forgot all about her dog, as she checked out the stranger who was hot in an unexpected hero kind of way. In fact, he looked an awful lot like Seth Rogen in *The Green Hornet*.

"Oh my God! Is she hurt?" Kate focused her attention back on her dog, as soon as she reached the cake table.

The guy squatted down on his haunches and set Sarah Jessica Barker on her feet. The dog's black and white fur was matted in flat clumps; her pink birthday bow wilted to the side. He ran his fingers through her coat, separating the fur to reveal strips of stark white skin. Thankfully there wasn't any blood.

"I'm no vet, but I think she's okay—just pissed off she didn't win that fight." He stood up and brushed wet fur coated hands on his jeans. His eyes drank in the bright afternoon sunlight and turned a translucent gray with whirls of steel blue in the center just like the one perfect marble Kate and her sister used to fight over when they were little.

"Thanks for jumping in. I just froze. I literally couldn't move my legs. That's never happened to me before." She could feel the latent adrenaline surging through her body while her heart beat in double time. Kate wasn't used to having a man save her.

"Don't worry about it. The water trick works every time." He ran his hand through his brown hair, the waves breaking free from their prison of hair gel. Kate had always had a weakness for guys with curly hair, ever since she saw Tom Hanks in *Splash* at the Yonkers 6 Cineplex.

"Do you think I should take her to the vet to be on the safe side?" Kate scooped up Sarah Jessica Barker in her arms so she could double check for injuries, but her dog immediately jumped to the ground and ran towards a scrappy brown and white dog.

"I guess that answers your question. She looked fine as soon as she spotted my dog."

"You're Diesel's owner?" Kate ran her tongue over her teeth, and said a silent prayer that she didn't have poppy seeds stuck in them from that damn mini bagel she had just inhaled.

"According to my niece, our dogs are one step away from registering at Bed Bath & Beyond."

"Good for Sarah Jessica Barker. It's hard to find a decent single man in this city." Kate scoped out the ring finger on the stranger's left hand and was relieved that it was completely naked.

Kate was torn away from drooling over the cute stranger when she spotted an over muscled twenty-something dragging his snarling German Shepard past them towards the exit.

"Hey! I asked you when you got here if your dog was aggressive and you said no!" Kate ran to the gate to catch them before they got away.

"Cujo seemed fine this morning when I picked him up." The dog snapped his jaw wildly in the air and the guy had to pull back on the leash with such force, thick veins popped up on his forearms.

"Where'd you pick him up from? A dogfighting ring?"

"I borrowed him for the party."

"What do you mean you borrowed him? And didn't the name give you a clue?" Kate was practically blinded by the sun reflecting off the rhinestones on his skintight black tee shirt.

The man-boy shrugged his beefy shoulders. "Uh, no." He stared back at Kate with a blank expression on his fake baked face, which was an unnatural shade of burnt sienna.

"Why would you borrow a dog for this party?" Kate knew there was no way the meathead wearing a trucker hat with New Jerzee graffitied on it was a *KidFit* fan.

"Ask your agent." The guy pulled the dog through the metal gate and Kate watched as he struggled to get the seething beast across 23rd Street.

"Don't you hate when people swear their dog isn't aggressive right before it takes a chunk out of another dog?" But when Kate turned around she realized her hero wasn't there to commiserate with her.

Kate would have to get down to the bottom of the mystery guest with Dana later. For now she just wanted to find the cute stranger and explain that she wasn't as bitchy as she came across. Really.

Kate scanned the small park and spotted her Good Samaritan over by the food. He was close enough for Kate to hear him talking to a girl who looked like she was about nine or ten.

"Come on, Lauren. Time to go." He rooted through the stack of leashes hanging from the gate and grabbed a thick blue one.

"We just got here!" The girl devoured a mini sesame seed bagel in two bites.

The man stepped towards the pack of dogs and called, "Diesel!"

"You can't go yet. I didn't get a chance to thank you." As Kate got closer, she realized the little girl had an almost identical set of unnerving blue-gray eyes as the man. Kate's heart sank as she realized he must have forgotten his wedding ring at home.

"No big deal." The man shrugged and started to back away,

but he ended up bumping into the buffet table so hard the mini-bagel tower collapsed.

"Sorry!" The man grabbed the bagels and started stacking them back up. "I'm such a klutz."

"Don't worry about it." Kate reached for a pumpernickel bagel that had rolled near the veggie platter. In an attempt to grab the same bagel, the man ended up wrapping his hand around hers and Kate felt an actual flutter in her chest. He kept his hand there for an extra beat before busying himself with the bagel display.

"You could take him out for dinner," the girl piped up. Kate was elated when she realized the cute stranger must be divorced; otherwise his daughter wouldn't be trying to push him off on a date.

"Lauren!" The man gave the girl the stink eye. "That's rude." Kate stifled a laugh. It must be embarrassing to have your kid set you up.

"You guys could bring the dogs!" The girl pulled out her iPhone and asked Siri where the closest dog-friendly restaurant was. Siri's computerized voice responded with a selection of fifteen neighborhood hotspots where dogs were welcome.

"Lauren! Kate probably has other plans."

"Sadly, the only thing I have scheduled this weekend is my dog's birthday party."

"Hi, I'm Lauren. And this is Jack Horowitz." The girl, who was right on the cusp of pre-teendom, reached out and wrapped Kate's hand in a surprisingly firm grip for such a tiny person. She was wearing a red tee shirt that said

> *Dear Math,*
> *I am not your therapist.*
> *Solve your own problems.*

"I'm Kate. Nice shirt."

"Thanks. Uncle Jack got it for me."

"I thought he was your dad." Single and no kids. It kept getting better and better.

Lauren erupted in a fit of giggles. "OMG! I can't wait to tell my dad you just said that."

"Her dad is way tougher than me. He's a Marine." Jack finally looked up from the bagel display and a faint dimple that was probably a remnant of childhood appeared in his left cheek.

"You seem pretty tough to me. Breaking up that dog fight today."

"It was nothing. Really." The guy pinched his thumb and pointer finger between his lips and let loose a piercing whistle. Diesel bounded over to them in milliseconds and Jack leashed him up.

"It was something to me." Kate locked eyes with him and smiled.

"We really need to get going." Jack unlatched the gate.

"My uncle has to drop me off at Chelsea Piers for practice later. He can meet you by the M23 bus stop at 5 P.M."

"The last thing I expected was to end up at dinner with a cute stranger tonight." Maybe Dana had been right after all about throwing such a big party for Sarah Jessica Barker.

Jack pulled his dog and niece through the gate. "Trust me. This was the last thing I expected too."

"Matt Klein and I make a great team because we share a vision to provide safe accommodations for overweight children. It also helps that we've been best friends since third grade."

Jack Moskowitz, strollersavvy.com

Chapter Three

"What the fuck, Lauren?!" Jack waited till they were safely out of microphone and camera range before tearing into her.

"What?" Lauren handed him the hot pink swag bag that was crammed with gourmet dog biscuits, organic dog shampoo and PCB-free dog toys.

"How could you throw me under the bus like that?"

"Be happy I got you a date. Now you don't have to worry about Mom trying to set you up with that loser friend of hers." Lauren pulled Diesel towards the crosswalk. The hyped up dog wasn't anywhere near as eager to leave the party as Jack was.

"And Horowitz? Seriously?"

"What? You totally needed a fake identity."

"Where did you even come up with that name?"

"You know that annoying boy who sits behind me in orchestra? The one who smells like Doritos? It's his last name."

"Thanks a lot."

"It was the closest thing to your real name. I figured you wouldn't forget it that way." Lauren tugged on the leash again. "Come on, Diesel. Quit being so stubborn."

"Either way, I don't need my ten-year-old niece setting me up on dates. I'm not that desperate—yet." Jack reached for the leash. "Give him to me."

"It's better than mom doing it. Trust me. That friend of

hers she was trying to get you to go out with is a total freak. She eats her hair—literally. They just had to cut it up to her chin at her last photo shoot 'cause the ends were so ratty."

"At least your mom didn't try to set me up with someone who just tore me apart on national television." Jack gave up on pulling the reluctant dog away from the park and picked him up.

"She didn't say anything bad about you. She was just talking about Considerable Carriages."

"Same difference. It's my company." Jack carried the wriggling handful of fur across the street.

"*You* don't even think you should make the new gigantic strollers."

"What? Why would you think that?"

"I heard you and Matt fighting about it last week."

"You shouldn't have been eavesdropping." Jack reached his elbow out for Lauren to hold on to while they crossed the street.

"I wasn't eavesdropping. You guys were being loud."

Jack shook his head.

"You were right. These strollers for super fat kids are a really bad idea," Lauren continued.

"It's not that simple." As soon as they hit the sidewalk again, Jack plopped Diesel on the ground and dragged him farther away from the dog park.

As they got closer, Jack noticed the sun resting above the bright blue Chelsea Piers Fieldhouse. He felt a vibration in his pocket and reached for his phone, unsure if he had an incoming call or it was the cars rushing by.

"Hey man, since we're going with the snack tray, we might as well add the large cup holder." Matt started talking as soon as Jack picked up.

"I'm still thinking through the concept."

"You better think fast. We need to do this before Maclaren beats us to the punch." Matt practically screamed over the Linkin Park blasting in the background.

"Listen, you're not going to believe who I ran into at the dog park."

"Not that dog walker I slept with? I think she's stalking me. I swear I saw her waiting for me outside my building the other day." Matt sighed as if he was annoyed, but Jack knew having a possible stalker was a real ego boost for his friend.

"It was Kate Richards."

"Did you tear her a new one?" Matt lowered his music.

"No, I saved her dog from getting attacked by a German Shepherd."

"You should've let that fem-bot's dog get eaten. Would serve her right." Matt's voice remained loud even though his music was barely audible now.

"Come on. It's not the poor dog's fault her owner has such a big mouth."

"Lemme guess. It was a MaltiPoo or a Shitzu."

"Actually, she has a really cool Boston. Anyway, I saved the dog and long story short, I'm supposed to meet up with Kate Richards for dinner."

"Why would she ask the evil fat kid stroller guy out to dinner?"

"She has no idea who I am."

"Bullshit! She blasted our company on *Straight Talk* less than forty-eight hours ago."

"That doesn't mean she knows who I am. You're the face of the company, not me."

"That's because I have the better looking face."

"No, asshole. It's 'cause you have the bigger ego."

"Jack Moskowitz isn't the most common name out there. That must've clued her in."

"That's why my genius niece decided to introduce me as Jack Horowitz, named after the stinky kid from orchestra."

"I still don't get why you agreed to go."

"Lauren said yes for me. And I couldn't make a big scene with the *KidFit* film crew there."

Matt was uncharacteristically slow with a come back.

"I just haven't decided if I should stand her up or if I should go explain who I am," continued Jack. "Did I mention she's pretty fuckin' hot when she's not talking about strollers?"

"Haven't you ever heard that saying about keeping your friends close but your enemies closer? You're going on that date."

*"Everyone always talks about the big sign that you've met THE
ONE. But what if I drive right past it and miss my exit?"*
Kate Richards, Late Night with Jessa Silver

Chapter Four

"Lara wants to know when she's getting the finished manuscript."
Dana was filling a black Hefty bag with the abandoned plastic
plates, cups and other party ware.

"Beginning of next week? I'm still playing around with a
few recipes." With the exception of a few Nylabone Frisbees
she couldn't resist keeping for Sarah Jessica Barker, Kate was
loading up a cardboard box with the presents to donate to
the ASPCA.

"Did you add the Greek yogurt cheese cake?"

"I'm still tweaking it so it won't taste so sour. That is pretty
hard to do without adding sugar."

"You better figure it out. Greek yogurt recipes are at the
top of Google search." Dana's eyes glazed over as she stared at
the unclaimed slices of cake. For a split second Kate thought
she was going to abandon her wheat-free, gluten-free, sugar-free
diet, but then Dana scooped all the pink polka dotted paper
plates into the Hefty bag in one swift motion.

"I will. Then I should be just about done with the
dessert section."

"Hurry up. Lara needs time to look it over before she turns
it in to Random House."

"I'm going as fast as I can. But I'm really feeling the pressure
to make it as good as the first book." Kate tossed a plush yellow

Checker cab on top of a rubber Statue of Liberty chew toy. All they needed now was an I Love NY doggie shirt and the ASPCA could set up a souvenir stand.

"Sequels of *New York Times* best-selling books almost always make it on the list, whether they're as good as the first one or not." Dana tied an awkward knot around the top of the trash bag.

"Are you saying this book isn't as good as the last one?" Kate was finally voicing the fear that had been nagging her every time she sat down to type recipes.

"Insecure much?" Dana raised her impeccably groomed black eyebrows.

"I used up all my best recipes in *Mini-Munchies*. I really had to stretch myself to come up with more." Kate hoisted the box next to the other two that were waiting by the dog park gate for the ASPCA rep to come pick up.

"Did you try them out on your niece and nephew again?"

"Most of them."

"Good, because they're definitely our target demographic."

Kate threw a rubber steak at her. "You're evil!"

"You're just getting the sophomore blues." Dana caught the toy and tossed it in the donation box.

"I hope that's it. Because right now I'm just not feeling this book." Kate grabbed a flattened Fresh Direct box and worked a little magic with some duct tape.

"You better feel it after you just cut a check for forty grand to your sister. What the Hell did she need all that money for anyway?"

"Property taxes."

"That's what she gets for living in that big ass house in Bronxville, the most expensive town in Westchester. Why should you bankroll that?"

"They put the house on the market as soon as Jen got downsized from Morgan Stanley. But no one's in the market for a big house on the hill right now."

"You better hope someone buys it or you'll be kicking in the mortgage payments next."

"We wouldn't be sitting here talking about my book if Jen and Todd hadn't loaned me the money to go to culinary school."

"Fine, that explains helping Jen out, even though you paid them back years ago. What about the five grand you just wired to dear old Dad? And I know he didn't pay shit for you growing up."

"Bad business deal," mumbled Kate.

"Meaning bad day at OTB. That man's never gonna learn his lesson if you bail him out every time some bookie wants to kill him."

"I told Pop it was the last time. He promised to check into that gamblers' rehab I found for him upstate as soon as they have a free bed."

"He probably just told you that so you would save his ass from whatever bookie was threatening to slice his balls off."

"He better be serious. Jen said she would kick him out for good if he doesn't."

"How much are you ponying up for rehab?"

"Enough to make me kick my cookbook revisions into high gear. By the way who was the asshole with the rabid German Shepherd?"

"I owed the kid's agent a favor. He's a reality star who needed some extra camera exposure."

"Next time you do someone a favor, just make sure it doesn't involve my dog getting eaten alive." Kate involuntarily shivered at the thought of what might have happened if Jack hadn't been there.

"Speaking of which, I can't believe you actually asked that guy out."

"I had a little help from his niece."

"It's about time you got back in the game. But with him?"

"Why not? Did you see those eyes?" Kate sighed. Compared to Jack's, even Bradley Cooper's eyes would be downgraded to merely ordinary.

"No, I was too distracted by his hair. Hasn't the man ever heard of a Keratin treatment?"

"I think guys with curly hair are hot."

"Well guys with spare tires are not."

"My last boyfriend had a six pack and look how well that turned out."

"If you're going to put yourself back out there, it might as well be with someone who at least looks like they've been to the gym in this decade."

"And you wonder why you're still single?"

Dana stayed behind and waited for the ASPCA rep to pick up the donations. Kate leashed up Sarah Jessica Barker and closed the heavy gate behind her. She held on tight to her eager dog at the edge of the West Side Highway as they waited for the light to change. But when the walking man in the pedestrian sign lit up, she let her dog drag her across the street.

As soon as Kate got close to the Chelsea Piers Fieldhouse, the wind from the Hudson River pushed at her face bringing with it the smell of hot cocoa and fresh hamburgers from the new organic food stand.

Kate walked Sarah Jessica Barker to the metal bench by the crosstown bus stop and sat down to wait for Jack. The tiny dog, exhausted from her birthday festivities saw this as an opportunity to take a nap. She curled up in a warm ball on top of Kate's feet and took two deep breaths before closing her eyes.

Kate spotted Jack and Lauren as they ran across the bike path cutting off a swarm of black spandex-clad riders. Lauren collapsed in a fit of giggles when they reached the other side unscathed. Jack looped Diesel's leash on the edge of the chain link fencepost and walked Lauren to a side entrance to the Fieldhouse.

When they reached the door, Lauren and Jack began a typical high five routine with the requisite hand smacks up high, down low, and around back. Jack towered over his niece, his hands looking like bear paws smacking into hers. Just when Kate thought they were through, Jack lined up his back with Lauren's, bent his knees in unison with hers and began walking down an imaginary staircase. They both sank their torsos lower and lower till it looked like they had strutted down a flight of stairs. As soon as Lauren and Jack reached the ground, they swung their hands out for a high five and pulled each other up into The Roger Rabbit, arching their backs and skipping backward a few times before giving each other the final high five. Jack may not look like he lived at the gym, but he definitely had rhythm.

A group of what had to be Lauren's gymnast friends, judging by their short, muscular physiques stood by the door waiting, not looking fazed in the least by Lauren and Jack's performance. Jack left Lauren with her friends and stood on the pier with an arm above his eyes to shield the sun, watching as they walked into the field house. He stayed rooted to the spot even when the glass door shut, keeping an eye on her till she made it down the hall. Jack unhooked Diesel from the fence and gave him a quick belly rub before heading back across the congested bike path to meet Kate, his unruly curls moving lightly in the steady breeze off the water.

"Thanks for waiting. I had to make sure Lauren got in okay." Up close, Kate could see a few gray curls fighting through Jack's reddish brown sideburns.

"That was quite the handshake back there." Kate nudged Sarah Jessica Barker to wake her up from her power nap.

"I was hoping you missed that." Jack leaned down to pet the panting dog on her head. The side of his pinky rubbed up against Kate's and the friction sent a tiny shock up her arm like a bolt of static electricity.

"No such luck."

"Lauren and I started that craziness back when her dad first deployed. Or at least the first time she was really old enough to understand."

Kate grasped the leash with both hands while Sarah Jessica Barker pounced on Diesel. The two dogs rolled around on the sidewalk playfully gnawing on each other's ears while continued.

"I used to drop Lauren off at preschool when my sister had modeling gigs. As soon as David left for Iraq, Lauren was petrified no one would come back for her. She got so worked up she would have an asthma attack. My sister tried everything the school psychologist suggested, but nothing worked. So, one day I made up this goofy handshake with hokey pokey moves and lots of jumping up and down. The secret handshake kept her distracted so she could let me leave. Over the years, it became our thing."

"Do you do that every time you drop Lauren off somewhere?"

"No. But David went back to Afghanistan a few months ago and it's hitting Lauren pretty hard. So we started it up again whenever I leave her at the gym."

"She's lucky to have you in her life." Kate had visions of Lauren wearing a cap and gown doing her crazy handshake routine with Jack behind the scenes of her high school graduation.

"Yeah, well we'll see how she feels when I'm chasing away the teenage guys with my aluminum baseball bat." When Jack smiled, the skin around his eyes softened into deep creases that gave Kate a warm cozy feeling. "You don't really have to take me out to dinner."

"Are you kidding me? You saved my dog's life! The least I could do is get you a beer and split a bucket of mussels with you at The Frying Pan."

"I'm sure you have much better things you could be doing tonight. Lauren won't know the difference."

"Seriously, I don't." Kate tried to keep the disappointment out of her voice as she suspected the guy was trying to dodge her.

"How could I turn down dinner at The Frying Pan? It's probably one of the last weekends it'll be open before they close for the winter." Jack walked Diesel toward the footpath and Sarah Jessica Barker eagerly followed.

"How long is your brother-in-law deployed for?" Kate kept the conversation going and tried to convince herself that this wasn't a pity date.

"At least another six months. It's been rough for my sister Harper and Lauren this time. He's stationed in a black hole of communication."

"They must live close by for you to help out with Lauren so much."

"They actually live in the top two floors of my brownstone. I live in the bottom two."

"My sister Jen and her family live in Bronxville and believe me there are times I am grateful to be separated by the Henry Hudson Bridge. Especially since my Pop moved in with them."

"Don't get me wrong. My sister can be a pain in the ass. But Harper, David and Lauren are the only family I've got."

They walked up the pier against the wind blowing off the Hudson River. The two dogs took turns alternately running ahead, sniffing things out, and then waiting for their owners to catch up. As they walked along the pier the sun touched the crests of the choppy waves on the murky Hudson River, while cars whipped past them to their right on the West Side Highway.

It wasn't long before they reached the large iron skillet that hung from a wooden frame at the entrance to the floating restaurant. They walked up a waterlogged wooden walkway to the barnacle encrusted red metal boat.

"It's okay, Sarah Jessica." Kate's dog froze as soon as she realized their path was moving. Diesel howled and nipped at her heels until she barked back and followed him up the path.

As they walked the length of the ship, they passed couples and small groups knocking back beers and sharing buckets of shellfish. The air smelled like fried fish and spilled beer, but the casual restaurant had an air of romance especially when you caught a glimpse of the bright sun sinking into the Hudson River.

Jack led them to an empty table towards the front. He tied Diesel's leash to the bar that ran along the side of the boat and Diesel quickly nestled himself into a ball under the table. Jack reached for the Boston Terrier's leash and tied her up as well. Sarah Jessica Barker snuggled up next to Diesel and licked happily at her paws.

"Food's on me since you saved me a hefty bill at the animal hospital. Beer, a bucket of mussels and a couple ears of corn sound good to you?"

"Perfect." Jack leaned back in his white plastic chair and looked over the side of the boat at the rocky waves, while Kate went to the bar and ordered the food.

She brought back two chilled bottles of Blue Moon Ale with thick wedges of oranges stuck on the rims. "Food should be ready in a few minutes." Kate handed Jack a beer.

He held his bottle up. "Cheers."

"To new friends," Kate clinked her bottle against his.

"You know the summer's over when there're so many empty seats at The Frying Pan." Jack tilted his bottle back and swallowed a few hearty chugs.

"So I'm assuming you know what I do for a living." Kate pointed to the white glittery letters that spelled *KidFit* across her camouflage tee shirt. "Wanna level the playing field and tell me what you do?"

Jack was silent long enough for Kate to worry that he was one of the many people out of work these days. The last guy she had been set up with had been unemployed. It didn't bother her that he had been out of work for six months. Money was not an issue for her. But the enormous chip on his shoulder as a result had made it too difficult to really pursue anything.

"Sorry, I got distracted by that gigantic boat over there." Jack pointed to a massive cruise ship docked a few feet away from them. "That thing looks like a floating mall. I freelance for dot-com start ups."

"People still make money at dot-coms?"

"Mark Zuckerburg managed to," countered Jack.

"I can't believe that just came out of my mouth! Can we please forget I said that?" Kate always managed to lose her filter when she was nervous. But to be fair, she hadn't known anyone who worked for a dot-com since the '90s.

Jack took a long pull of his beer. "Sure. I'm just glad I'm not the one who said the first dumb thing. No offense."

"None taken. This could be why I don't get asked on too many second dates."

The corner of Jack's mouth lifted into a lopsided grin, making that illusive dimple on his left cheek come out of hiding.

Kate squeezed some of the orange juice into her beer so that the sweet citrus mixed with the light barley. She leaned back in her chair and took a long sip from the cold bottle.

"What do you do exactly for dot-coms?"

"Too boring to talk about. But I assure you I make money

at it." There went that lopsided grin again.

A bell ringing at the counter interrupted them.

"Saved by the bell. I'll be right back." Kate walked to the bar and grabbed the food. She tried to catch a glimpse of her reflection in the aluminum mussel bucket to make sure her hair hadn't gotten too frizzy from the sea air. She vowed on the walk back to the table not to say anything else that could possibly insult the first date she been on since she became too famous for eHarmony.

"I hope I didn't pull you away from anything too important tonight." Kate plopped the food tray on the table and doled out the paper plates heavy with ears of corn slathered in melted butter and liberally sprinkled with salt and pepper.

"Nah. I had four hours to kill anyway. Might as well be here eating with you."

"Four hours?" Kate grabbed a handful of mussels from the bucket and put them in a neat pile on her plate next to the corn. She didn't know what had possessed her to order the messiest food on the menu.

"Lauren's on the gymnastics team at Chelsea Piers. She practices twenty hours a week. I'm on pick up duty tonight."

"Hope your sister realizes how good she has it."

"Harper and I made it through some awful shit together growing up. Our dad left us, and then our mom died. If that doesn't make two people stick together I don't know what would." Jack shrugged his shoulders and loaded up his plate with a stack of steaming mussels.

"Wow. How old were you guys when all that happened?"

"I was ten and Harper was a toddler when my dad left. How do you think Pam made a living before she was the Lower West Side's most popular dog walker?"

"Pam was your babysitter?"

"Yeah, which Harper doesn't like to brag about. I mean how does it look to have your former babysitter go from changing your diapers to walking around with a Pooper Scooper?" Jack popped open a mussel and sucked out the meat with a quiet slurping sound.

"I could see her point. Are you still in touch with your dad?"

"Nah. But he tried to track me down on Facebook last year. Can you believe that?"

"Did he send a message with his friend request?"

"Yeah. Something like—sorry I abandoned you and your sister in your formative years. Let's be online friends and write comments on each other's wall like nothing happened." Jack pulled his mouth into a wry smile. His top row of teeth was perfectly even and straight like an ad from the orthodontist's brochure. But two of his bottom teeth overlapped just enough to give Jack more of a bad boy smile.

"You didn't accept his request did you?"

"Hell no. And I have to admit it felt pretty good to click the ignore button." Jack wrapped his lips around the tip of the salty mussel shell and sucked the juice back before pulling back the fleshy meat with his tongue.

"So you didn't want to get bogged down with Farmville and Bubble Safari game requests from the man who left your family?" Kate crossed and uncrossed her legs and forced herself to pull her eyes back down to her own food.

"Go figure. Sometimes I wish my dad hadn't stuck around."

"Why?" Jack put down his bottle of beer. "If you don't mind me asking."

"He's a compulsive gambler." Kate didn't usually talk about her father, but something about the way Jack opened up to her made her feel like she could tell him anything.

"Holy shit." Jack kept his eyes on Kate's; not looking away like most guys did when she got serious.

"You know those baskets the church puts together at Christmas for needy families?"

"The ones filled with non-perishable food that could withstand a nuclear attack?"

"We got one. Every year of my life till I moved out." Kate picked up a mussel, but put it back down when she remembered that talking about her childhood always made her lose her appetite.

"So I guess you're not a fan of meat that comes out of a tin."

Kate laughed. "I ate my last Pineapple SPAM loaf the year I turned eighteen."

"Do you still see your dad?"

"Yeah. Every time he needs me to pay off some bookie."

"Shit. Maybe I was better off having my dad leave." Jack opened a foil butter packet and put the yellow square on his already dripping corn.

"How old were you when your mom died?"

"Freshman year of college and Harper was in middle school. Some crazy judge actually granted my petition for custody of her. I was the only guy at NYU reading *Are You There God? It's Me Margaret.*"

"No wonder you two are so close."

"Yeah, it's a regular Lifetime movie."

"I just realized I've been asking you one depressing question after the next. Having dinner with me is like a bad Barbara Walters interview. Next thing you know I'll be passing the tissue box."

"I'm the one bringing up my dead mother on our first date. Clearly, I haven't been told that sob stories should be saved for at least the third date."

"That's okay. I can come up with another sad tale, besides the whole gambling dad thing of course." Kate took a long sip of her beer.

"Oh really? Well you better lay it on me, so I don't walk out of dinner feeling like some douchebag on a therapist's couch."

"*Dining on a Dime.*" Kate answered without hesitation.

"You mean that show on Food Network with the guy who's covered in tattoos?" Jack picked up a slick ear of corn and broke through the niblets with his front teeth. A spray of corn juice landed on Kate's cheek. She didn't wipe it away.

"Tyler, the host, also happens to be my ex-boyfriend who stole my show idea. Dining on a budget isn't the most revolutionary concept ever, but I wanted to have a show where two people competed every episode to come up with the best recipes for a four-course dinner on a shoestring budget. The winner gets their kitchen remodeled. Tyler pitched the idea to the Food Network right after the stock market crashed and they thought it was the perfect show to air during a recession. He neglected to tell the producers the idea was mine." Kate took a sip of beer to wash away the biting acid of anger in her mouth.

"Did you take him to court?"

"I tried. I met with a copyright lawyer and tried to pull a case together. But I didn't have enough proof the idea was actually mine."

"It must kill you to see him on TV doing your show."

"It used to. I spent so much time and energy fighting with him that I reached a point where I wasn't going anywhere. But eventually I got my shit together and landed *KidFit*."

"You're the one with the show on ABC, so I guess you ended up getting the last laugh." Jack took a long sip of beer. When he pulled the bottle away, there was a thin layer of foam on his upper lip. He stuck out the tip of his tongue and licked it off.

"I guess that's one way of looking at it. All I know is between Tyler and my father, I've learned not trust the wrong people anymore."

"I try to avoid awkwardness at all costs, which could explain why I can't remember the last time I went on a date."

Jack Moskowitz, The Chelsea Chronicle

Chapter Five

Jack went to the bar to get more beer and when he came back, he found Kate on the phone. Jack noticed she had done something to her hair while he was at the bar so her beachcomber waves hung over her shoulders and framed her heart-shaped face. Kate had also applied a peachy shade of lip gloss that made her lips look even softer and fuller than before.

"I'll be there in ten minutes. Can you wait?" Kate's brow was furrowed.

Jack sat at the table and pushed the beer towards her. If he had known he was going to get the blow off, he wouldn't have sprung for the extra beers.

"My old roommate isn't feeling well and needs me to walk her dog." Kate took the beer. "Thanks."

"Now that's one I haven't heard before."

"I usually send Dana a 911 text from under the table if things are going bad. Then she calls me with a quote-unquote work emergency. But look at my call history—it's clean." Kate held her phone out to Jack.

"Don't worry; I won't call your bluff." Jack left the phone in her hand and took a swig of beer. Kate was actually a pretty cool chick when she wasn't talking about strollers. There was just the little issue that Jack was about fifty pounds and two super-sized stroller lines out of her league.

"You should come with me. Diesel probably knows her dog Morty because he's part of Pam's dog-walking crew. He's the cutest miniature black Schnauzer." As soon as Kate said Morty, Sarah Jessica Barker and Diesel picked their heads up. "See, I told you. Morty is buddies with these guys."

"Diesel has a friend that sounds like a Lower East Side delicatessen owner and a girlfriend named after a movie star. I'm learning an awful lot about my dog today."

"You guys want to go hang out with Morty?" asked Kate, in the tone usually reserved for babies and companion animals. Sarah Jessica Barker followed by Diesel, abandoned their cozy spots under the table and started tugging on their leashes. Diesel let out a sharp bark, while his female counterpart let loose more of a high-pitched wail.

"That answers your question. Where does this old roommate of yours live?"

"A few blocks from here on 23rd." Kate took one last more sip of beer while Jack tilted back the rest of his bottle.

As she walked close to him down the boat ramp, Kate brought with her a smell of crisp apples mixed with vanilla. They walked east on 23rd past the row of gated brownstones with the interlocking Wisteria and Lilacs looping up the walls. The quieter residential section took up only four blocks. As soon as they neared Eighth Avenue, franchises like The Gap, Citibank, and Dunkin Donuts took over with their stark signs, fluorescent lighting and pristine store windows.

Jack and Kate crossed over Eighth Avenue to that Indian eyebrow threading salon that always had someone handing out coupons on the corner. Jack had no idea what eyebrow threading was, but it sounded pretty gruesome to him. He was surprised to see Kate leading Sarah Jessica Barker towards the salon entrance. She couldn't possibly be dragging them all with her to get her eyebrows done first could she?

Jack followed Kate up the carpeted stairs towards the Bollywood music and the door covered with posters of Henna tattooed women with perfect ebony eyebrows. Just when Jack thought she was going to open the salon door, Kate headed further up to a steel bar covered door that looked like it belonged in a jail cell. She punched a code into the keypad and opened the door when a buzzer vibrated through the narrow staircase.

When Kate opened the door, Jack felt like he had passed through the mirror into Wonderland. They left behind the brown industrial carpet in favor of a black and white tiled staircase that jutted in sharp right angles forming double landings God knew how many levels up. The endless checkered pattern made Jack dizzy.

The dogs seemed to know the building from their daily route with Pam, so Sarah Jessica Barker led them all to the second floor with Diesel following close behind. As soon as both dogs reached the wide landing, they started barking and pawing at the door. Jack ran his fingers over the bronze Mezuzah hanging shoulder height on the right side of the doorframe, remembering his grandmother, the only observant Jew in his family.

"Just a minute," called a voice dripping in New York from the other side of the door.

Kate held the dogs back from the door as it was pulled open.

"Jack, this is my old roommate Mrs. Fink."

Mrs. Fink's black hair interlocked into coarse ringlets and was topped with an inch long skunk stripe of white roots. Her upper lip was segmented into deep lines, but with her wide-set chestnut brown eyes and broad smile, Jack could tell she used to be a looker back in the day. Mrs. Fink was wearing a black velour sweat suit with Juicy written across her sunken chest in rhinestone loops.

"Katie, you didn't tell me you were bringing a man over. I already took my face off for the night," said the woman, in a voice that seemed too deep for an almost skeletal woman who was at least a foot shorter than Jack.

"We were out having dinner when you called."

Mrs. Fink raised her eyebrows and nodded her head with a sudden smile.

"I couldn't just ditch him could I? Now let us in already." Kate gently nudged the woman over and led the way into the apartment that the dogs had already furrowed their way into.

"Hi, I'm Jack." Jack followed Kate into the overly warm apartment.

"Jack what? In my day, a man never introduced himself by first name only."

"Horowitz." Luckily, Kate was quick to answer. For a split second Jack had forgotten all about his alias.

"A Jewish boy? Why didn't you tell me sooner? All is forgiven," said Mrs. Fink, with a short wave of her arm.

Jack was about to tell her that he was only a non-practicing half-Jew, but she looked so excited he didn't have the heart to break it to her.

Diesel and Sarah Jessica Barker ran circles around Morty while he stood in the center of the ring barking his head off at them. Morty was a black Schnauzer who was moving his way out of the mini category due to overfeeding. His potbelly dipped low to the ground, making Jack feel bad for his short legs.

"Thanks for bringing the dogs. This is the most excitement the poor boy has had since we watched *The Bachelor* finale last night."

"You didn't tell me what was wrong on the phone." Kate raised her voice over the loud barks.

"I'm old, that's what's wrong," said Mrs. Fink. "Now can you get Morty out of here before he ruins another one of my good Orientals?"

"Jack, you want to grab our two hooligans while I get Morty?"

"Jack's going to stay here and keep me company."

"Don't start asking him a million questions." Kate shook her finger at the older woman. "Jack, if she gets too nosy, make sure you let her know."

"Sure thing." Jack followed Mrs. Fink into her living room, helped chase down the dogs and gave Kate all three leashes.

Jack could hear the echoes of all the dogs trail down the stairwell. He followed Mrs. Fink into her living room, which looked like the set of the Golden Girls with the rattan couch and arm chair that were covered in pastel floral cushions and throw pillows. The white lacquer coffee table was empty except for a crystal bowl of stale looking pale pink and mint green M&Ms and an 8 x 10 crystal framed picture of Kate wearing a white chef's coat and hat with her arm around Mrs. Fink. Judging by Kate's razor straight bobbed hair, and thinly waxed eyebrows, the picture had to be more than a decade old.

Mrs. Fink picked up the picture from the table. "This is my absolute favorite picture! That was when Katie graduated from culinary school."

"You've known Kate since she was in cooking school?" Jack was trying to figure out the mystery of this Felix and Oscar pairing.

"Where do you think the girl lived at the time?"

Jack looked around the room to see if he could spot any more old pictures of Kate. That's when he noticed the back wall that led into the dining room. It was lined from side to side, floor to ceiling with gilt framed wedding pictures. Jack walked closer to the peach wall, and saw that the pictures dated back to the sixties when the brides wore beehives and almost white lipstick. He trailed the rows from left to right, top to bottom, until he got to the most recent wedding photo of two men wearing matching tuxedos standing in front of City Hall.

"What's with all the wedding photos?"

"I'm a matchmaker." Mrs. Fink took her time making her way over to the wall of pictures. "These are all the couples I've set up."

"For real?" asked Jack. "I didn't think matchmakers existed these days except in off Broadway productions of *Fiddler on the Roof*."

"Haven't you ever seen *Millionaire Matchmaker*? That Patty Stenger has some chutzpa all right, but she's got the gift."

"How did you know you had it?"

"It was passed down to me. My mother, grandmother and great-grandmother were all matchmakers in the small town in Hungary where I was born. It skipped my two sisters though. One of them became a teacher and the other a nurse."

"How do people know about your services? Do you have a Facebook page or something?"

"Word of mouth. I have my own little six degrees of separation up here on this wall. Every single one of these couples was referred by each other, which means they are all connected to each other in some way."

Jack found it fascinating that the guy from the '80s with the tight Jerry curl was connected to the two men in matching white tuxes.

"Where have you been hiding? I've been trying to find the perfect match for Katie all these years and here you come along out of thin air. Poof, just like that." Mrs. Fink closed her fists super tight and then opened her knobby fingers wide like a witch casting a spell.

"We met at the dog park today. I saved Sarah Jessica Barker from being eaten alive by a crazy German Shepherd and Kate took me out for dinner to say thanks. End of story."

"How do you know that's the end of your story, Jack Horowitz?"

"I think you're mixing me up with one of your clients," said Jack, with a wink. "I'm not looking for love."

"Love doesn't only come when you're searching for it." Mrs. Fink pointed a hot pink fingernail at him.

"We just met." Jack shrugged his shoulders. "How did Kate become your roommate?"

"Home companion, not roommate. I keep telling Katie roommate sounds so common. She answered my ad in the Village Voice."

"Along with a bunch of lunatics I'm sure."

"You're telling me. I narrowed it down to her and a drag queen named Tess Tosterone."

"I could see how you ended up with Kate."

"Come in the kitchen. I have Zabar's."

Jack followed her into the kitchen, which like most Manhattan rent controlled apartments had the original pre-war washbasin sink and white wooden cabinets. There was also a silver specked white Formica table with orange vinyl covered seats from the *Leave it to Beaver* era.

Mrs. Fink busied herself putting on a pot of coffee and

setting out plates of cinnamon and chocolate rugelach. Jack sat down and was relieved to be wearing long pants since the chairs were the kind that your legs stick to when it's hot. And it certainly was warm in the stuffy apartment.

As soon as Mrs. Fink sat down, she went into rapid-fire question mode without mincing any words.

"How old are you?"

"Thirty-seven," answered Jack, without missing a beat.

"Any kids?" asked Mrs. Fink.

"Not that I know of," said Jack, and then immediately regretted it when Mrs. Fink raised one thinly plucked eyebrow.

"You're not one of those people who hate kids—are you?"

"Of course not." Jack stirred the coffee that Mrs. Fink had sweetened with a heaping tablespoon of sugar and real cream.

"Any relation to the Delancey Street Horowitzs?"

Jack took a huge gulp of coffee and instantly regretted it when the hot liquid seared his esophagus. He shook his head mid-cough.

"What about the Riverdale Horowitzs?"

"No." Jack cleared his throat.

"That's a relief."

"Why?" Jack was eager to get Mrs. Fink off on a tangent about the Riverdale Horowitzs. Anything to get her to stop grilling him.

"Long story." She put an extra scoop of sugar in her own coffee. "Then you must be related to the Coney Island Horowitzs, which means I know your Aunt Rebecca and Uncle Ephraim."

There seemed to be no end to the Jewish six degrees of separation. "My family's originally from upstate."

"Upstate? You must've had a Hell of a time finding a synagogue!"

"That's why you're not feeling well." Kate burst through the folding kitchen door trailed by all three dogs. "Zabar's is gonna be the death of you."

"We have company. I had to put out some nibbles." Mrs. Fink smiled in Jack's direction.

"You shouldn't have these kinds of nibbles in the apartment.

You need to take better care of yourself." Kate leaned down and unleashed all the dogs in quick succession.

"I'm fine. I just had one of my spells."

"Where's Regina?" Kate grabbed a tennis ball from under the kitchen table and threw it towards the living room. The three dogs raced out of the room to fetch it.

"Who knows? She never came home last night." Mrs. Fink used a pair of silver tongs to plop an extra cinnamon rugelach on Jack's plate.

"I told you she wasn't going to be reliable."

"She's my great-niece once removed and she needed a place to stay. Would you have me throw her out to live on the street with the gyro trucks and men selling Coach knock offs?"

"The least she could do is walk Morty and cook something healthy for you once in awhile. What'd you have for dinner?"

"A bagel."

"That's all simple carbs. I'll make you an egg white omelet. Your blood sugar's probably all messed up."

Jack watched while Kate pulled a carton of eggs, a container of Zabar's chive cream cheese and a packet of Lox from the fridge. She grabbed a skillet and started whipping together an omelet.

"Don't forget to add the capers."

"Do I ever forget the capers?" asked Kate, with an exaggerated sigh.

"You guys are like an old married couple," said Jack. "When did you move out Kate?"

"If it was up to me she woulda been out of here years ago. But Katie wouldn't leave till she found someone to keep an eye on me. This big shot TV star lived with me in my crappy apartment until about six months ago when I told her my Regina was moving in." Mrs. Fink sounded annoyed but Jack could see the smile that reached her eyes when she talked about Kate.

"I wouldn't have moved out if I knew you would be living on bagels and rugelach."

"I don't have a husband. A woman's gotta have some pleasure in her life," said Mrs. Fink, with a wink at Jack.

"I bet you miss Kate's cooking." Jack dipped his last bite of pastry in the coffee before putting it in his mouth.

"Oh, yes. I got to eat all of Katie's homework assignments when she was in cooking school," said Mrs. Fink. "But after two years, I could barely fit through the doorway."

"You're such an exaggerator," said Kate.

Kate brought the steaming omelet over to the table and pulled up a chair next to Jack. The three dogs kept themselves occupied in the living room chasing a ball around.

Mrs. Fink took her time cutting her omelet into dainty little pieces, before taking her first bite.

"By the time you get to eating that it'll be cold," pointed out Kate.

"Sometimes the best things in life are the ones you have to wait for," said Mrs. Fink, with a raised eyebrow.

"Enough with the proverbs. Start eating your food," admonished Kate.

Mrs. Fink took a small bite of her omelet and her eyes practically rolled back in her head with delight. She pointed her fork at Kate and said, "This girl here cooks like nobody's business."

They fell silent for a few minutes while Mrs. Fink worked on her eggs and Jack and Kate noshed on rugelach and drank the freshly brewed coffee. Mrs. Fink was halfway through her omelet when she dropped her fork.

"Katie, run in the bedroom and grab my calendar. You know the little free datebook the synagogue gave me when I sent in my donation?" said Mrs. Fink, with a definite sense of urgency.

"What for?" asked Kate, as she stood up from the table.

"I need to check something. It's either on my night table under the Nicholas Sparks book, or by my Mah Jongg set in the living room."

It was clear that Kate knew her way around Mrs. Fink's things because she returned to the kitchen before Mrs. Fink started grilling Jack again.

Kate handed the small black datebook to Mrs. Fink, along

with a pair of rhinestone studded reading glasses. The small black book reminded Jack of the one that Chase had given him when he set up his business account, but it was clear this calendar had all the Jewish holidays marked in red. Mrs. Fink flipped through the pages till she got to the current date.

"I knew it!"

"What?" asked Kate, echoing Jack's own curiosity.

"Today is Tu B'Av." Mrs. Fink snapped the book shut and looked over her reading glasses from Kate to Jack.

"Forgive me, but my knowledge of Jewish holidays is limited to Chanukah, Yom Kippur and Rosh Hashanah," said Jack.

"I've never heard of it either," said Kate.

"It's the Jewish Valentine's Day." Mrs. Fink pulled her reading glasses off, folded them closed and rested them on top of the date book.

"How can there be a Jewish Valentine's Day?" asked Kate. "Isn't the holiday named after a saint?"

"Maybe Israel's Hallmark stores realized how much revenue they were missing out on," said Jack.

"With cynicism like that, it's quite clear how the two of you have remained single all these years," said Mrs. Fink.

"All right. We're listening." Kate met Jack's eyes with a suppressed smirk.

"Tu B'Av falls exactly one week after the saddest day in the Jewish calendar to remind us that even in sadness, happiness will always follow. It is the day of love, when Jewish men are supposed to consider who they will make their wife." Mrs. Fink took her glasses off and closed her book. "It's a day filled with hope, romance and possibility."

"Have you ever made a match on Tu B'Av?" asked Jack.

"Of course, but it's never the same as two people meeting by accident on this day of love. That is true cosmic force."

"Don't you think you're laying it on a little thick?" Kate rolled her eyes towards Jack. "Now you know why I was scared to leave you alone with this one."

"What? Who says I'm talking about the two of you?"

"I guess that means the boy who stopped to talk to Lauren

at the dog park is going to end up marrying her one day. I better tell my sister to start saving up for the wedding," said Jack.

"Speaking of Lauren—what time do you have to leave to pick her up?" asked Kate.

Jack looked at his watch, "Now. Mrs. Fink, you were such good company I lost track of the time."

"Your niece is the little gymnast with those powerful eyes, right?" asked Mrs. Fink.

"How did you know?" Jack was amazed at this tiny aged mystic.

"She's made the rounds with Pam before. Pam slips her a few bucks to help out when there's extra dogs on the route."

"Oh, that's right. I think Pam does it more as a favor to my sister Harper than because she needs the help."

"Tell her I said hi, and I have some black and white cookies in the freezer for next time she comes over," said Mrs. Fink. "Katie, you can go too. I'm heading to bed now."

"Since when do you go to bed at 8 P.M.?" asked Kate.

"All right. You caught me. I want to watch *True Blood* in peace." Mrs. Fink stood up from the table, and gave Kate a hug. "Thanks for dinner."

Mrs. Fink then turned her attention to Jack. "I'm a hugger," she said, as she leaned in to give him an embrace. Jack could feel her sparrow like shoulder blades poking through her velour hoody.

"Where do you live?" asked Jack, as they headed down the dizzying staircase.

"Right by the dog park, at 23rd between 10th and 11th in the new building across from the U-Haul place."

"That's on my way. I'll walk you home."

"So what happened to Mr. Fink?" asked Jack. He held the door for Kate and the dogs. It had gotten much darker since they had been upstairs and the air had dropped a few degrees.

"There never was a Mr. Fink. Pretty ironic for a matchmaker, huh?" The dogs ambled after Kate pushing each other through the door.

"I guess it's no weirder than the teacher who has no kids or the housekeeper with the messy apartment."

"Mrs. Fink lost the love of her life when she was a teenager." Kate stopped walking for a minute to untangle the two dog leashes.

"He died?" asked Jack.

"You're a glass is always half empty kind of guy aren't you? His name is Abraham and no, he didn't die. But she had to leave him behind when her family moved here from Hungary. Mrs. Fink couldn't bear the thought of Abraham spending years pining away for her while he tried to save up the money to come here. So, she wrote him and said that she eloped with the neighborhood butcher."

"Sounds like the plot of one of those depressing films that they're always showing at the art house on 19th Street." Jack slowed down his walking to match the pace of the dogs that stopped to sniff every crack in the sidewalk.

"I know. It's awful. He got the news and was so brokenhearted that he took up with her best friend Bertie. They got married and had four kids."

"No wonder Mrs. Fink never got married." Kate was walking so close to him, that Jack could see the goose bumps popping up on her arm. His hand instinctively reached out towards Kate, and he had to pull himself back.

"Mrs. Fink says she never found anyone else who made her feel the way Abraham did."

"I bet she's always trying to set you up with somebody."

"That's the weird thing. I've known her almost half my life and she's never set me up. She always said the timing wasn't right."

Jack and Kate made their way past the dog park to the corner of 23rd Street and Eleventh Avenue inhaling the roasted chestnuts and smoked sausages from the street meat cart on the corner. They crossed the concrete driveway that was filled with U-Haul trucks, each with a different state captured in one solid image splashed against the side. A bug eyed Roswell alien stood for New Mexico, while loops of green hills dubbed the Serpent Mound were supposed to be a draw for Ohio. These advertisements did nothing to encourage Jack to visit either of these states.

The street was deserted as they crossed over to Kate's building, an old coat warehouse that had been broken up into ecofriendly luxury apartments.

"Thanks for walking me home."

The outside fluorescent lamp illuminated Kate and unlike most women, she looked more beautiful in the harsh light. Jack realized her hair was made up of at least fifty different shades of blond from pale wheat to vibrant saffron. And her eyes weren't light brown after all, but a liquid wash of tiger's eye.

"Is Diesel okay?" Kate pulled her eyes away from Jack's and turned to Diesel who had thrown himself in a panting heap against the wall.

"You okay buddy?" asked Jack. Diesel's tongue hung out of his mouth like a dried out sponge and his eyes rolled listlessly towards his upper eyelids.

"He probably needs some water. Let's get him upstairs." Kate pulled Sarah Jessica Barker through the revolving door, gesturing for Jack to follow.

The elevator whisked them upstairs at warp speed and Kate hustled them down the hall to her apartment.

"I'm just warning you. It's a bit of a mess in here. I wasn't expecting company."

As soon as Jack walked in, he knew Kate wasn't exaggerating. The apartment was clearly the quick pit stop of a very busy person. Workout clothes strewn across the couch, a jumble of high heels and cross trainers kicked off by the door, and a stack of unopened mail on the kitchen counter.

Jack grabbed a green cookie off one of the many baking trays strewn across the granite counter top. He sniffed it and couldn't help grimacing. "Is this some sort of a spinach cookie?"

"Gluten-free kale carob chip. For the new cookbook."

Jack shuddered and dropped it on the counter.

"That one cookie has as much calcium as a glass of milk. It's my ticket to the best-seller's list." Kate grabbed a hot pink bowl that said *Keep Calm and Eat a Bone* off the kitchen floor. She grabbed the sink's spray attachment to fill up the dish since the sink basin was overflowing with sticky cookie sheets and batter coated mixing bowls.

Kate plopped the bowl on the floor, unbothered by the water that splashed over the sides onto her gray slate floor.

Diesel and Sarah Jessica Barker lapped up the water in a chorus of grunts and snorts. It wasn't long before the two of them drained the bowl.

"Good boy! You look much better." Kate rubbed Diesel's back while he tapped his hind claws on the floor in rapid-fire clicks and clacks.

"You were right. He just needed a drink." Jack scruffed his dog's wiry head and grabbed the empty dog bowl.

Jack brought the bowl to the sink, careful to keep his hand far away from the blender with the mysterious blue liquid coagulating in it. He grabbed the sink hose and pointed it towards the water bowl. Icy water ricocheted off it and sprayed all over the front of Jack's shirt.

Kate tilted her head back in a fit of giggles.

"You think that's funny, huh?" Jack aimed the nozzle at Kate and soaked her, unintentionally creating a scene out of an '80s movie wet tee shirt contest.

Jack was distracted by the delicious under curve of boob made suddenly visible against Kate's moist shirt, when she wrestled the sink nozzle from him and seared a stream of water from Jack's chest down to his jeans.

"So it's like that huh?" Jack took a step towards Kate and she let loose another icy blast of water.

"You got me. I surrender." Jack raised both hands in the air.

"Fine." Kate nodded solemnly and reached over the dirty dishes to turn the water off. "Truce."

Jack grabbed a half empty Poland Spring bottle off the counter and doused Kate.

"You liar!" Kate shrieked and lunged toward him with the sink hose cocked.

Jack took a step back and tripped over Sarah Jessica Barker who was standing behind him exactly at knee level. Jack ended up sprawled on his back staring up at the modern chandelier fashioned out of tarnished antique knives and forks.

"Wow! We just met a few hours ago and now I've got you here in my apartment on your back." Kate reached her hand out and tried to pull Jack up, but slipped in the pool of water and landed right on top of him.

Kate's hair dripped in waves ending in upside down question marks as she leaned over Jack. A black droplet trailed from Kate's eyelash down her cheek and pooled in the heart-shaped bow of her full upper lip. She smelled like an apple orchard after an afternoon rain shower.

Kate exhaled a slow steady breath of air that pushed out of her barely parted lips and when Jack breathed in, he felt like she had burrowed her way inside him. Another drop of mascara laced water trailed down from Kate's eyes and Jack caught the black teardrop with the soft pad of his thumb. He left his hand resting on Kate's cheek and felt the ins and outs of her breathing.

Kate closed her eyes and leaned into Jack's touch, a small sigh escaping her mouth. Jack lifted his head just enough to catch Kate's lips with his. She tasted like cinnamon, sweet with a little exotic spice mixed in. They kissed deeply, without abandon and all at once stopped being strangers.

Suddenly, Lady Gaga's "Telephone" belted out from Jack's back pocket. Jack jerked back from Kate, the sound jolting him into reality. "Shit!"

"I never took you for a Lady Gaga fan. The last guy I made out with who was a Gaga fan was bi-curious. Please, tell me you're not bi-curious too because that was a total nightmare."

"What?" Jack shook his head and raised a finger to his lips. "That's Lauren's ring tone."

"Uncle Jack? Where are you? You're never late!" Kate backed away from Jack, while Lauren shrieked in his ear. Jack's wet tee shirt clung to his stomach and he felt suddenly cold when Kate withdrew her warm body.

"I'll be there in five minutes. Wait with Irina till I get there."

"Hurry up!" Lauren's voice wavered between outraged and anxious. "I'm the last one here."

"Poor Lauren! I'm sorry I...um, distracted you." Kate bit her bottom lip. Her wet shirt was bunched up on her bra, leaving the moist slick of skin leading into her pants on display.

"Totally worth it." Jack shoved his phone back in his pocket. "But I better get outta here."

Kate unlocked the door and held it open as Jack scrambled to get Diesel leashed up.

Kate stood in the doorway, her hair hanging in damp waves over her face and her eyes shining bright beneath her wet eyelashes.

Jack just needed to get to the elevator bank without looking back. That phone call was actually a wake up call. He didn't belong here.

Jack squeezed past Kate close enough to hear the soft breaths coming from between her parted lips. He could feel the heat radiating off her body.

Kate moved into the hallway and let the apartment door close behind her with a loud click. "Bye Jack."

The hallway smelled like Indian takeout and Jack could hear Fox news blasting from the apartment next door. He just needed to take one more step and hit that elevator button without looking back. One more step.

Kate lifted her hand in a wave. Jack grabbed her hand and pushed it up against the door, holding it at the top, his arm pressed into hers. Kate's chest rose as she inhaled one sharp breath. Jack pushed his other hand into the door for support. The center of Kate's eyes burned fiery orange as she locked her gaze with Jack's.

The air felt heavy between them. It was if they were magnets pushing away from each other when they got too close. Jack ran his fingers down Kate's hand to the delicate skin on her narrow wrist. Kate closed her eyes as Jack trailed his fingers from her wrist to the soft skin on the inside of her arm.

Jack pushed through the tension and found Kate's lips. Kate let Jack take the lead as he kissed her. In that moment, Jack forgot who he was.

Kate pulled away first, but her wet hair still clung to his

cheek. "You have to go." Her words came out in between short breaths of air. Kate kept her arm pressed up against the door as Jack slowly ran his fingers down her arm. He kept his eyes on hers as he stepped back until her hair moved off his face.

Kate slipped back through her door as Jack ran to catch the elevator. Jack spent the whole ride to the first floor catching his breath.

Diesel followed Jack down 23rd Street with constant looks back as if Sarah Jessica Barker was going to materialize behind them at any moment.

"Come on, Buddy. I know how you feel." Jack picked up his dog and carried him the rest of the way to the field house. He didn't know what he was thinking. Because there was no way he could ever find a way to make things work with Kate Richards. And that was no one night stand make out session either.

"What're you doing here?" asked Jack, when he found Matt and Lauren waiting for him by the gym entrance.

"Small Fry called me when you were late. What the fuck happened to you?" His best friend was wearing his going out trolling for chicks get up or what Jack liked to call his Divorced Dude Duds. Dark gray straight leg jeans, white designer tee shirt with a black velvet blazer and black Kenneth Cole slip ons. His sandy brown hair was freshly clipped and gelled into short spikes.

Jack smoothed down the front of his damp tee shirt. "Diesel and I made a pit stop at the dog park."

"Looks you were playing with the hose."

"Oh yeah." Jack looked down at his shoes till he was sure he could keep a straight face.

Matt pounded his fist against Lauren's. She had to jump up to reach the 6' 4" man's hand. "How was practice, Small Fry?"

"Awesome. I finally got my Giant." Lauren shimmied her feet in a close approximation of the "Dougie" for her victory dance.

"Didn't you get the Giant last week?" Jack had been hearing about the difficult bar move all summer.

"Yeah, but this time I did it without anyone spotting me."

Lauren's smile stretched from ear to ear.

"I knew you would get it," said Matt.

"What's the deal with the new dog leash?" Lauren stared at Diesel's leash with a bemused expression. "I mean *Keep Calm and Play Frisbee* is tots cute, but hot pink? Seriously?"

"Shit! I must've grabbed Sarah Jessica Barker's leash by accident."

"Did you get any dirt on the fem-bot?"

Lauren stared at Matt. "You wanted Uncle Jack to spy on Kate Richards?"

"Relax. You just worry about getting my tickets to the next Olympics."

"She was actually pretty cool. Someone I would want to hang out with again." Jack tugged on Diesel's leash. The dog had slumped against the snack machine and was starting to drift off.

Lauren raised both hands in the air in triumph. "I knew it!"

"I said she was someone I would want to hang out with again. I didn't say I was actually going to. It would never work for obvious reasons." Jack was quick to add as soon as he saw the look of horror on Matt's face.

"If you guys really liked each other it would." Lauren grabbed the leash from Jack and pulled Diesel away from the snack machine.

"She's much cooler in person than the woman who just ripped me a new one on TV."

"Did you at least spike her coffee with real sugar instead of Splenda or let Diesel hump her little show dog or something?"

"You're sick, man." Jack shook his head.

"This is why I should've been the one to go on this date tonight."

"Matt, there's no way Kate Richards would've gone out with you," said Lauren.

"Well there's no way she would've gone out with me either if she knew who I really was," said Jack.

"Salmon and brown rice for the adults, boxed macaroni and cheese for the kids. Forget that! Feed your children the same healthy dinner you prepare for yourself. It will expand their flavor profile and save you a lot of work in the kitchen."

Kate Richards, Bites from the Big Apple

Chapter Six

"Do you still have the paper lying around? Morty tore mine apart before I had a chance to clip my coupons." Mrs. Fink started talking as soon as Kate picked up the phone.

"I'll drop it off later when I walk Sarah Jessica. Is that the only reason you called?"

"I was also wondering if you tried the coffee at the new diner on 23rd yet?"

"Haven't had a chance to stop in there since you told me about it last night. Anything else on your mind?"

"Well, since I have you on the phone anyway. How did it go?"

"I might as well tell you since you're going to drag it out of me anyway. We ended up making out like a couple of teenagers."

"Of course you did. You two have more heat than the Burrito Deluxe at Salsa City."

"So much for playing hard to get." Kate sighed.

"Hard to get is for is for women who have more than a baker's dozen of fertile eggs left."

"You're such a wise ass. Now what do I do?" Kate stood up and stretched, abandoning what was hopefully her last set of cookbook revisions, since it was clear she wasn't getting off the phone with Mrs. Fink so quickly.

"You get to know him better. Did he give you his number?"

"Not exactly."

"What does not exactly mean? Is there some new way you young people are communicating these days?"

"I meant Jack didn't give me his number in the traditional sense. But when he rushed out of here, he accidentally took Sarah Jessica's leash and left Diesel's behind which just happens to have Jack's number embroidered on it." Kate rubbed her thumb against the raised beige numbers on the navy nylon.

"Haven't you learned by now there are no accidents?"

"If he wanted to talk he would've just asked for my number. Don't you think?"

"Maybe he wanted to let you make the first move. Either way it was nice to see you out on a date. Not every man is like that good for nothing Tyler."

"Don't get all dramatic. I've been on dates since Tyler."

"Business lunches with the suits from ABC don't count. Neither do those one night stands from that sex website of yours."

Kate released a long sigh. "EHarmony is hardly a sex site. And it only happened that one time years ago. That's the last time I tell you anything."

"I'm getting older you know and I'd like to be around for your wedding."

"You know the Jewish guilt thing doesn't work on recovering Catholics."

But every time Kate tried to get back into her editing, she heard Mrs. Fink's voice in her ear. Kate knew she wouldn't get any more work done until she called Jack.

Kate flopped on the couch where her dog was snuggled up against a pile of dirty laundry with a gamey smelling rawhide. Kate picked up Diesel's leash from the edge of the couch.

"What do you think Sarah Jessica? Should I call him?" Kate nudged the little dog up from her afternoon nap and was met with a wide yawn.

"I guess you're right. What's the big deal?" Kate took a

deep breath and grabbed her phone.

"This is Jack." He answered on the third ring and clearly didn't know who was calling him.

"Hi, it's Kate." When Jack didn't immediately answer she interjected, "From the dog park."

"Kate from the dog park? You need to refresh my memory. I met a few Kates at the dog park yesterday."

"The Kate that cut dinner short to take you to a little old matchmaker's apartment."

"Oh, that Kate. That was the best rugelach I've ever had."

"I don't give up the rugelach on the first date for everyone you know."

"Good to know. I was wondering if you did that for all the guys."

"Smooth move leaving your number behind on a dog leash."

"You must've been waiting by the phone all morning debating about whether to call."

"Hardly. Ball's in your court now." Kate swiftly hung up, making a calculated gamble that one, he would be smart enough to get her number off the caller ID, and two, he would call her back.

Kate tackled the dirty dishes while she waited for the phone to ring. She had been experimenting with cookbook recipes for the past few days so there wasn't a clean spoon or glass left in her apartment. Kate had cleaned out the blender from the Strawberry Symphony Smoothie, her cookie sheet from the Veggie Monster cookies and her Springform pan from her hundredth attempt to get the sour taste out of her Greek Yogurt Cherry Cheesecake when her phone finally pinged.

Jack Mobile: Lauren said 2 w8 10 mins so don't look like losr. Made it 9 mins 42 secs.

Kate Mobile: LMAO

Jack Mobile: Want 2 walk dogs on Highline next Saturday?

Kate Mobile: K

Jack Mobile: Then dinner outside at Cookshop?

Kate Mobile: Luv that place

Jack Mobile: Me 2. Let's meet at Chelsea Highline
     entrance.

Kate Mobile: K

Jack Mobile: Diesel's looking forward to his double date.

Kate Mobile: SJB is 2

"People assume the most pivotal moment in my life was when my mom died. But really, it was years earlier when my dad walked out on us. That was when I became the man of the house and learned what it meant to put everyone else's needs above my own."

Jack Moskowitz, forthebaby.com

Chapter Seven

"What's the problem?" asked Jack.

"Ironic tee shirts are so last year." Lauren wrinkled her nose and grimaced.

"You don't think it's funny?" Jack smoothed down the front of his shirt. The distressed white V-neck was embellished with a picture of an old school stereo tape. *Legal Downloads are Killing Piracy* was spelled out in raised velvet letters across his chest.

"Can I look through your stuff for something better?"

"Fine, but it's not that big of a deal."

"Yeah, right Uncle Jack. And I only hung up One Direction posters all over my room because Madison made me."

Jack grabbed a dirty sock off the floor and chucked it at Lauren.

"Whatever you do—don't open your big mouth next time you see Matt. I don't even know why I'm doing this. The last thing I need is him giving me shit."

"You know you like her Uncle Jack." Lauren balled up the sock and threw it right back at him square in the belly.

"What's the point? The minute Kate finds out who I am it's all over."

"Not if she gets to know how cool you are first. Just wait

to tell her who you really are till you know she really likes you back." Lauren held up a threadbare Chelsea Prep P.E. tee shirt. "Seriously? Haven't you ever heard of Good Will?"

Jack's back pocket vibrated.

Harper Mobile: Come out front ASAP. Don't tell Lauren.
Jack Mobile: K. B right out.

"I have to run Diesel out." Jack shoved his phone in his pocket and grabbed Diesel's leash off the hook by the door. Diesel jumped off the couch and grabbed the leash from Jack's hands.

"This might take awhile. Next time, don't wait till the last minute to get my fashion advice." Lauren pulled a stack of hastily folded tee shirts from Jack's bureau.

Jack leashed up Diesel, locked the door and ran up the brownstone stairs to street level, bracing himself for the kind of news Lauren would be censored from. Jack's sense of foreboding deepened when Harper wasn't standing on the sidewalk in front of their building. After a few roundabout glances, Jack spotted his sister crumpled up in a heap on the chipped green stoop two buildings down. Jack brought Diesel with him and sat down on the stairs next to Harper trying to block out the image of his neighbor vomiting there two nights ago. He could feel the cold stone through his jeans and heard a crunching sound as his thigh landed on an abandoned Doritos bag. Harper's ropelike curls blocked the parts of her face that weren't covered by her hands. Jack had a sickening sense of deja vu of the day their mom had passed. Harper had been at school and he had been the one who had to tell her. They both knew it was coming, stage four lung cancer moved like an express train but it was still a shock when it happened. Jack told her on the walk home from school and she had collapsed on the same stoop.

"David's helicopter went down today," Harper whispered, through shaky hands. Diesel planted his snout across Harper's lap depositing a long thread of drool on her jeans.

"Is he …" Jack couldn't finish the question.

"They're transporting him to a Marine hospital in San

Diego. That's all I know. I'm catching the next flight out of JFK. Can you watch Lauren for me? I don't know how long I'll be gone," said Harper, without stopping to catch her breath.

"Of course."

"And keep her distracted while I run upstairs and pack a bag. I don't want her to see me leaving and start asking a bunch of questions." Harper twisted the palms of her hands into her eyes. Jack wasn't sure if she was wiping the tears away or attempting to wake herself up from this nightmare.

"How am I gonna explain where you are?"

"You can say I landed a commercial in LA. Just don't tell her about David, at least not until I know what's going on with him."

"Come in and at least say good bye to her."

"Lauren's going to take one look at my face and know something's wrong."

Jack took in Harper's tangled hair and mascara-dripped eyes. "Don't worry I've got Lauren covered. Go take care of David."

Jack walked Harper back to their own stoop, relieved that she had given him the bad news in front of their neighbor's house depositing all the bad vibes there. Served the neighbor right since he was always letting his Rhodesian Ridgeback take a shit in front of Jack's brownstone. He let Diesel pee on the curb while he waited for Harper to go in the main entrance.

Jack ran his hand through his hair and took a deep breath. His stomach roiled in protest at the bad news. He headed straight to his bedroom where Lauren was surrounded by a pile of his tee shirts on the foot of his bed.

"This is so much worse than I thought. Do we have time to go to like J. Crew or Banana?"

"You think landing your own network show is hard? Dating on an island where the women outnumber the men three to one trumps that any day."

Kate Richards, The 411

Chapter Eight

"Heels or flats?" Kate turned so she could get a side view of herself in the mirror. Her cobalt blue jeans worked well with the pair of silver grommet covered black bootie heels, but it was probably a bit much for an outside dinner date with two dogs.

Sarah Jessica Barker looked up from her dog bed and cocked her head to the side with a distressed whimper.

"You're right." Kate kicked her heels into the pile of rejects and slipped into a pair of black peep-toe flats. She pulled on a white button-down and layered it with a black blazer. She left the top two buttons open and pulled on a delicate silver necklace that dipped low into her shirt. She was just rolling up the sleeves when her home phone rang.

"I know you're leaving any minute, but I was just reading this article in *The Haute Life* about first dates." As usual, Mrs. Fink spoke so loudly that Kate had to hold the receiver away from her ear.

"New *Haute* or from the old pile under your bed?"

"New. That girl is always leaving her stuff lying around." Mrs. Fink heaved a loud sigh.

"I keep telling you letting Regina move in was a mistake."

"You weren't the neatest roommate either."

"I kept my mess confined to my room."

"And the kitchen and bathroom. Do you want to hear the advice or not?"

"Make it quick. I don't want to be late."

"First dates can be a nerve-wracking experience. What to wear, what to say, even what to order at the restaurant can be…"

"Not the whole article. Just give me the highlights."

"Rule number one. Never mention your ex-boyfriend on the first date. It will make your date feel uncomfortable and he'll think you're still caught up in the past."

"Shit. I already did that."

"Why would you bring up that good for nothin' bum?"

"It just came up. What else does it say not to do?" Sarah Jessica Barker sat perfectly still while Kate pulled a pink turtleneck sweater over her little head. It was the perfect double date outfit for the little dog.

"Rule number two. Let the guy pay for you on the first date. This will boost his ego and make him feel secure."

"I screwed that one up already too. Shit, shit, shit. I'm already off to a lousy start."

"Who cares what this *Haute* lady says. Bet she sits home alone every night microwaving Lean Cuisine and watching TV with her ten cats," said Mrs. Fink.

"Then why'd you read me the article in the first place?"

"Don't worry about it. Just have a good time."

Kate spent the walk to the High Line fixating on what else might be on Mrs. Fink's check-list. Sarah Jessica Barker knew Chelsea like the back of her paw from her walks with Pam, and she practically dragged Kate up 22nd Street for no explicable reason.

"Interesting way to get to the Highline, Sarah Jessica Barker. But we'll go with it."

Kate stopped short when she heard her phone ring. "I don't need any more date advice. You already traumatized me enough with that awful article."

"You're going on a date?" Kate's sister Jen practically screamed into the phone. "With who?"

"Try not to act so shocked." Kate stopped in front of

a thick oak tree that looked like it sprouted from the warped sidewalk and let Sarah Jessica Barker sniff at it.

"Sorry. It's just been awhile. Hasn't it?" Jen's smug marriedness saturated the phone line.

"I met this really cool guy at Sarah Jessica Barker's party. You would've met him if you had come."

"No offense, but I could hardly have Ripley skip her piano lesson, and Hunter miss his Kumon for a dog's birthday party."

"Of course not. What was I thinking?" Kate watched as Sarah Jessica Barker scratched at the small patch of dirt surrounding the tree. Until Kate had her own kids, her life would never be as important as Jen's.

"So, anyway. What's the deal with Pop's rehab?"

"I paid the deposit. We're just waiting for a bed to open up. They should have one in about a week."

"Good cause Pop's working my last nerve. I caught him trying to play that instant numbers game at the Pizza Beat when he said he was going to the bathroom."

"I told you he could stay with me." Kate held her breath, hoping her sister wouldn't take her up on the offer.

"All his bookie friends still live in the city. He's better off here in Westchester." Jen sighed to let Kate know that her sacrifice was far bigger than Kate footing the rehab bill.

"As long as he doesn't hit up Yonkers Raceway."

"Shit. I didn't think of that."

"Just don't leave any cash lying around and don't give Pop your car keys for any reason. If he has no way to get around, he won't be able to gamble."

"Forget about Pop for the night. Just get out and have a good time."

Sarah Jessica Barker pulled on the leash and practically dragged Kate across Seventh Avenue. They had only walked a few steps when Kate spotted Jack hailing a cab at the corner of 8th.

"You're a piece of work Sarah Jessica Barker! You brought me to Diesel's house?" Kate looked down at her panting dog and couldn't help but laugh.

Kate was just about to call Jack's name when she realized he wasn't alone. As the cab grinded to a stop, a woman with Pantene commercial worthy hair pressed her face into Jack's shoulder.

"Fuck." Kate picked up Sarah Jessica Barker and ducked behind a red Escalade. Her heart pounded when she realized Jack must've been hooking up with some other woman right before he left to meet her. Never one to avert her eyes from a car wreck, Kate couldn't help but watch as Jack wrapped his arms around the woman. They weren't kissing but there was something very intimate in the way they wordlessly held each other.

Just when Kate couldn't take it anymore, Jack let go of the woman and opened the cab door for her. He guided her in the backseat with a gentle hand on the small of her back and then grabbed an overnight bag off the curb and put it next to her. He shut the door and gave the trunk two hard swats with his palm signaling the cabbie to take off.

Kate could feel her face dipped in red from humiliation as her palms broke into a hard and fast sweat. She thanked God she hadn't slept with him the other night. Kate needed to stay hidden behind the oversized SUV till Jack headed back inside. Then she would stand the bastard up.

Kate watched as Jack walked to a brownstone that stood out from the others on the block with its freshly painted tan bricks and shiny new windows decorated with boxes filled with burnt orange and red mums. The cement stoop was lined with ceramic potted mums and cabbage leaves that led up to a mahogany front door embellished with a hay and Indian corn wreath. The whole building exuded family and warmth, not what you would expect from a man whore who booked back-to-back dates.

Just when Kate thought she was in the clear to start her walk of shame back home, Sarah Jessica Barker jumped from her arms and ran across the street after Jack like he was her long lost owner. Kate raced after her, thankful that 22nd Street didn't get much traffic on a Saturday afternoon.

Jack scooped up Sarah Jessica Barker and rubbed her ears. "You just love to freak your poor mom out. Don't you?"

"You know better than to run off like that!" Kate scolded

the little Benedict Arnold and pulled her away from Jack mid lick.

Jack ran one hand through his hair and scratched the back of his neck with the other. "Listen Kate. I meant to call you."

"But you were too busy putting last night's date in a cab." Kate plopped her dog back on the sidewalk and kept a firm grasp on her leash.

"What?" Jack raised his eyebrows at Kate.

"Seriously? Do you really think I'm that stupid? I just saw you."

"It's not what it looks like." Jack looked in her eyes, but kept his voice low. "Really."

"So you didn't just sleep with some other woman right before leaving to meet me at the Highline?"

"Hi Kate!" Jack's niece pushed the downstairs door open with Diesel in her arms. The dog leapt from her arms and landed on the sidewalk right in front of Sarah Jessica Barker who yelped with wild delight. Lauren was close at Diesel's heels and held on to his collar so he couldn't get away, not that it looked like he would go very far.

"This is the other girl I double booked myself with." Jack shrugged his shoulders with that dimple pocked half smile of his.

"My mom had to fly to California to film a commercial. So Uncle Jack's stuck babysitting."

"That's great news about your mom. What kind of commercial?" Kate knew she sounded overly excited about someone she didn't know filming a commercial, but she didn't care. She was so relieved that Jack wasn't the player she had just spent the last tortuous five minutes thinking he was.

"Sunrise Granola." Lauren's smile reached across her whole face and a tiny dimple appeared on her right cheek, a mirror image of her uncle's.

"Let me guess. She's going to play the super mom who comes to the rescue with the Sunrise Granola bars after the kids lose their soccer match?" Kate had seen enough of those commercials to figure out their formula.

Lauren shrugged her shoulders. "Probably. She didn't have

a chance to tell to me about it before she left."

"I'm thinking she saves the day after a botched beach volleyball tournament since she's filming in California." Jack picked up Diesel and deposited him back in Lauren's arms. "Can you take Diesel back in the house for me?"

"Aren't you and Kate coming inside?"

"I'm sure Kate has better things to do than hang out with us."

"What's better than burgers and a *Glee* marathon?" Lauren waved both of her arms in the air like Jack was crazy.

"Hmm. She does have a good point." Kate's answer was met with a know-it-all smirk from Lauren.

"Why don't you bring Diesel in and feed him his dinner? We'll be there in a few minutes. I don't want the dogs fighting over the food."

"But Diesel's never food aggressive," started Lauren. Jack raised his eyebrows at Lauren until she grabbed the dog and hurried inside, closing the heavy door behind her.

Jack took a step away from the door. He leaned so close to Kate that his lips brushed against Kate's ear. "My brother-in-law's helicopter went down in Afghanistan." Jack whispered so low Kate barely heard him. He stayed for a minute with his lips near her ear before pulling away. Her ear felt hot from his breath.

Kate took a closer look at Jack. His eyes were pools of gray fear. She wrapped her hand around Jack's ice-cold fingers and pulled him away from the door. She led him up the stairs to the sidewalk and over to the stoop where they would be out of Lauren's earshot. Kate sat on the middle step and motioned for Jack to sit next to her. Sarah Jessica Barker took a flying leap up the stairs and raked her tongue across Jack's cheek with such force she almost knocked him backward. Jack scooped her up, settled her in his lap and massaged the top of her head. The dog settled on his lap, her tongue wagging in unencumbered delight.

"What happened?"

"We don't really know much. Just that David's helicopter went down and he's en route to a Marine hospital in San Diego."

"That's awful! How's your sister handling it?"

"Harper headed to the airport as soon as she heard. I have to keep Lauren distracted. Harper doesn't want her to know what's going on till she knows how bad it is." Jack absentmindedly stroked Sarah Jessica Barker's back, his eyes fixed on the dog's pink cashmere sweater.

"I'm so sorry, Jack."

"I'm the one who's sorry. I meant to call you, but I lost track of the time."

"Don't worry about it," said Kate. "I totally understand."

"I think I'm in shock. I keep expecting to wake up. I hope David pulls through this." Jack raked his fingers through his hair.

"At least he's out of the field and on his way to the hospital now. The doctors are going to do everything they can for him." Kate could see Jack's back muscles tighten as he took a deep breath.

"Helping Harper get over my mom's death was one of the hardest things I've ever had to do. I don't even want to think about the shape she'll be in if David doesn't make it."

"Get through tonight. Then you can figure out what to do next."

"Lauren has our whole night planned. She wasn't joking about the *Glee* marathon." Jack shook his head and smirked.

"Season one or two?"

"Two. We watched season one when Harper was in Canada filming a bit part in a Hallmark movie."

"Great. I've been dying to see the Britney Spears episode."

"You don't have to do this. I'm sure the last thing you want to do is help me babysit."

"Make mine a turkey burger, no bun, garden salad, dressing on the side." Kate stood up. "Why are you looking at me like that? You owe me dinner."

"She's gotta love dogs. And there's a big difference between someone who likes dogs and a dog lover. A real dog lover doesn't mind getting licked in the face."

Jack Moskowitz, Fido Magazine

Chapter Nine

"Ready to go in?" Jack took a deep breath and rolled his shoulders back trying his best to loosen the tight knot forming between his shoulder blades.

"Yes. Are you?"

"There's only one way to find out." Jack headed down the stoop and Sarah Jessica Barker followed leaping down four steps in one bound.

As soon as Jack pushed the door open, Lauren shouted. "Don't come in yet!" She was struggling to jam the CC-XL Deluxe prototype into the coat closet. Luckily, the girl did gymnastics because the damn thing was heavy.

Jack quickly shut the door. "Apparently, my idea of a clean apartment is not up to a ten-year-old's standards. I think we have to wait here a minute while Lauren does a quick straightening up."

"Tell her she can come to my place when she's done with yours."

Jack reached in his back pocket to check his phone, something he had done every ten minutes since Harper had left.

"What time was your sister's flight?"

"She left about an hour ago. I know I won't hear anything for hours, but for some reason I can't stop checking my phone."

"I know how you feel. My nephew Hunter had an

emergency appendectomy last year. I spent the whole train ride to Bronxville with my eyes on my phone. Meanwhile, he wasn't even done with the surgery until well after I got there."

"Okay. You can come in now!" Lauren called to them from the other side of the door, but rushed to open it before Jack had a chance to.

Jack was impressed – not only had Lauren gotten rid of the stroller, she had hidden the stack of sketches he had left on the coffee table.

Lauren ran over to Sarah Jessica Barker, just as Diesel slid across the floor to greet the little dog. "Where did you get this doggy sweater? SJB looks so cute!" Lauren stretched out on the floor between the two dogs petting them both at the same time.

"There's this amazing shop in the West Village called Neiman Barkus. I also got her the coolest little yellow rain coat with matching booties there."

"You would look so handsome in a sweater, wouldn't you?" Lauren rubbed Diesel's ears

"Hell no. There's no way I'm putting clothes on this dog." Jack made sure to use his best "putting my foot down" tone.

"Who's up for some dancing? You guys aren't the only ones who do a mean Roger Rabbit." Kate picked up a Wii dance game from the stack on the end table and tossed her pocketbook on the couch.

"You're looking at the Chelsea Prep 1988 breakdancing champion." Jack threw himself on the ground into a sloppy but recognizable windmill.

"Lauren, you didn't warn me that I would be up against such stiff competition."

"OMG, Uncle Jack! Stop doing that before you hurt yourself!"

Jack stood up and was hit with a wicked wave of vertigo. "I think I'll sit the first round out. Give you girls a chance to warm up before I kick some ass."

After multiple rounds of dancing to the most popular hits, Lauren and Kate were tied and Jack was deemed the biggest loser. They all worked up an appetite for New York Burger takeout.

"Uncle Jack, don't you think it's weird that Mom had to go all the way to LA to film a commercial?" Lauren dunked a long fry into one of the many small containers of special sauce that the burger joint was famous for.

"She would've frozen her ass off in a bathing suit here." Jack dipped his fry into the same container before taking a bite. "Mmm. What's this one?"

"Chipotle honey. Who eats granola at the beach? Wouldn't it get all sandy?" Lauren asked, with her mouth still full.

Kate shrugged her shoulders. "I guess it's no different than eating chips at the beach. Try this sauce—it's amazing." Kate tipped a small plastic container filled with light orange sauce towards Lauren.

Lauren coated her fry with the sauce before popping it in her mouth. "Mmmm! Must be the Creamy Horseradish."

"I don't care how many of these secret sauces you try. The best thing to dip a fry in is always going to be a milkshake." Jack popped the plastic lid off the takeout cup and skimmed the top of his frothy milkshake with a salt-coated fry.

"That's disgusting!" Kate's face wrinkled into a grimace.

"Don't knock it till you've tried it." Jack dipped another fry into his milkshake and popped it in his mouth.

"I dare you to eat it." Lauren leaned over the table and stared Kate down.

"I never back down from a dare." Kate grabbed the longest fry from Lauren's grease lined paper packet and dunked it into Jack's shake.

Kate took one look at Lauren and popped the fry in her mouth. "That's freakin' amazing!"

"Strawberry's even better." Lauren dunked one of her fries into her thick strawberry milkshake and passed it to Kate.

Kate put it in her mouth and had a look of intense concentration on her face before saying, "You're absolutely right."

Jack shook his head. "We're a bad influence on the fitness queen over here."

"You know *The Inside Scoop* would pay big bucks for a picture of this." Kate scooped another fry into Lauren's shake.

"I still think this whole thing is weird. Mom never gets called back to work on a commercial after it's wrapped." A deep crease appeared right between Lauren's eyes.

"That happens with my show all the time," said Kate. "I film something I think is perfect and next thing I know I get an email saying I have to come back to the studio."

"I bet they don't make you go all the way to California." Lauren took a bite of her bacon cheeseburger leaving a trail of grease on her chin.

"I wish my producer flew me to California." Kate's bun-less turkey burger looked pathetic next to Lauren's massive bacon cheeseburger. Jack titled his milkshake towards Kate and she eagerly dipped another one of Lauren's fries in it.

"Your mom's out there kickin it on the beach while the rest of us suckers are back here digging the sweaters out of storage."

"She better bring me back a cool souvenir." Lauren eyed Jack's take out container. "You done with those fries?"

Jack slid the container to her. "They're all yours."

"Save some for me." Kate reached over and grabbed a few from the container before Lauren could eat them all.

"Ha! If your show audience could see you now! They'll be replacing you with Jillian Michaels from The Biggest Loser."

"Keep the camera phones away and I'll be okay." Kate dunked another fry in Jack's milk shake.

"Guys don't forget about our *Glee* marathon." Lauren held up the DVD set.

"How could we forget?" said Jack. "I'm dying to see the Britney-Britney episode."

Lauren raised her eyebrows at Kate and burst into hysterics.

Kate stopped laughing just shy of choking on her food. "Seriously, I'm so glad I came here tonight. Lauren, I could use your help with something."

"What would you need my help with?" Lauren popped the last bite of burger in her mouth and leaned forward in her chair.

"I've been thinking of doing a new segment for the show. I want to spotlight child athletes from all different sports to help inspire my audience to try something new to get in shape."

Jack nodded his head. "That sounds like a good idea. Do you need Lauren's feedback?"

"Way cooler than that. Lauren, how would you like to be the first child athlete I film?"

"OMG! Yes, yes, definitely yes!" Lauren jumped up from her chair and Sarah Jessica Barker and Diesel looked up from their game of tug of war to see what all the excitement was about.

"Your mom just has to sign a waiver. I can email it to her so she can do an e-signature on it from California."

"Wait till I tell Madison and Jules!"

"I'm sure Harper will be fine with it." Jack jotted down Harper's email address on a New York Burger Co. napkin and slid it across the table to Kate.

"We could film you conditioning and practicing your routines at the gym. Then we can film a bit at home if it's okay with your mom. I want to feature one of your favorite recipes so we can show everyone how important it is to fuel your body with the right kind of food."

Jack wondered if Kate had invented this idea on the spot to distract Lauren. From her tone of voice it seemed as if she was making the plans on the fly.

"Did Uncle Jack tell you I was an extra on *Law & Order*?"

"Oh, you have acting experience! That's a definite bonus." Kate smiled at Lauren.

Lauren and Kate prepped for Lauren's show segment by trying out a few of Lauren's favorite smoothie recipes and taste testing them. Then Lauren modeled her extensive leotard collection so they could decide which one would work best for filming. They settled on her competition one—a sleek silver leotard with powerful swirls of metallic black and red dotted with sparkling rhinestones.

They filled the rest of the hours till Lauren's bedtime watching the promised *Glee* marathon. Settled on the couch between Kate and Lauren, Jack was so relaxed he was able to forget about David and Harper for ten minutes here or there. When it was time for Lauren to reluctantly go to sleep she asked to stay in Jack's guest bedroom so she would be downstairs near

Jack and Kate. Lauren ran upstairs to grab her pajamas and her favorite stuffed dog and waited for Jack to come tuck her in.

"I'll be right back." Jack called to Kate over his shoulder as he headed down the hall.

Lauren stood on the double bed and pulled down a framed article, adding it to the pile of picture frames stacked on the bed.

"Shit. I forgot all about this stuff." Jack grabbed the top matted black frame. It was a *Success Magazine* article from when Considerable Carriages first came on the scene. The illustration was an oversized stroller rolling up a hill that was actually a money graph. Lauren and Harper had framed a bunch of magazine articles about the company and given them to him for his birthday last year. Jack thought it was a douchebag move to fill his home with articles all about his company, but he hadn't wanted to hurt the girls' feelings. So he lined the walls of his rarely used guest bedroom with the framed articles.

"Quick. Just in case Kate comes in." Lauren grabbed the last frame off the wall and shoved it under the bed. Jack grabbed the pile off the bed and added them to Lauren's hiding spot.

Jack shook his head. "Something tells me you're going to be a handful like your mom was when you're a teenager."

"What kind of trouble did Mom get in? Tell me!"

"Your mom would kill me if I ratted her out. Now get to bed. You have practice in the morning."

Jack threw his hand up for a high five followed by a low five, a fist bump then a kiss good night.

"Don't turn out the light all the way," Lauren said, as she snuggled under the blankets.

Lauren was so mature in so many ways, but looking at her with her stuffed animal sleeping with the lights still on reminded Jack just how young and fragile she still was.

Jack dimmed the lights just a little bit and shut the door. He headed back to the kitchen where Kate had recycled all the takeout containers and was wiping down the table.

"You clean too?"

"Only other people's apartments. You've seen mine." Kate filled up Diesel's water bowl and both dogs came over and happily lapped it up.

"I don't know what I would've done if you hadn't shown up when you did." Jack grabbed two bottles of beer from the fridge. He popped the caps off and handed one of them to Kate.

"No problem. Although I think the yummy take out and that cute Mr. Schuester from *Glee* should take the credit for keeping Lauren distracted."

"Now I'm going to have bad '80s song remakes stuck in my head for the next week."

"Is that an actual backyard?" Kate looked out the small kitchen window over the sink that looked directly onto the postage stamp sized yard with Jack's picnic table that was covered with stroller designs and bids from the steel and tire companies.

"Yeah. I don't think you want to sit out there now though. A mouse ran over my foot right around this time last night."

"I'm not really the outdoorsy type anyway." Kate shuddered and plopped right on the couch. She tucked herself into the corner and both dogs hopped up and joined her immediately.

"I hope David's okay." Jack sat down on the end of the couch that wasn't occupied by Kate or the dogs and rested his foot on the coffee table.

"When do you expect to hear from your sister?"

"She texted me right before the food came. She made it to San Diego and was heading straight to the hospital. So I should hear something soon."

"Your poor sister. She must be a wreck."

"She's a mess. I wish I could be there with her."

"You're taking care of Lauren. She can't focus on David if she's worried about her daughter." Kate tilted her head back and took a long sip of her beer. She had the neck of a ballerina, long and sinewy with a small brown beauty mark shaped like a heart above the dip of her collarbone.

"I need a distraction. Tell me how you became America's kids' fitness queen."

"I feel like the star of a telenovela. Last week, the love of Kate's life stole her show idea and went on to marginal success on the Food Network. Kate is left heartbroken, single and directionless. Cut to commercial break and weepy music."

"Was this all before or after Mrs. Fink and culinary school?"

"After culinary school and while I was still living with Mrs. Fink, so she still boycotts the Food Network and attempted a Tyler Miller smear campaign with everyone she knows. Which explains why that show has abnormally low ratings in the Jewish community."

"Mrs. Fink is definitely not someone you want as your enemy." Jack reached over and rubbed Diesel's belly.

"But she's the best person to have on your team when life sucks. I had this amazing job at Pied a Terre as sous chef. But they fired me because I was a mess over the break up. The last straw was when I went a little overboard with the flambé in the Banana Flambé I served to *Time Out New York*'s food critic. They fired my ass faster than you can say escargot."

Jack winced. "That's pretty bad."

"Yeah, so then I could devote even more time to cyber stalking Tyler, being an insomniac and causing a Kleenex shortage. Mrs. Fink was at her wit's end. So she found a job for me."

"At ABC?"

"Are you crazy? She's a matchmaker, not a TV producer. She hooked me up with one of her couples. That's the thing with match making. These people feel like they owe her their lives—literally. So this one couple had a twelve-year-old son who had just been labeled obese from their family doctor. Mrs. Fink talked them into hiring me as the family chef and fitness expert to get him back on track."

"I get the cook part, but when did you become a fitness expert?"

"I taught Tae Bo and yoga at Gold's Gym to support myself in college and culinary school."

"So Mrs. Fink was the brains behind your whole operation?" asked Jack.

"Yes, which is why she has a pretty decent amount of *KidFit* stock. Which you would never guess looking at her apartment."

"That Mrs. Fink is such a character."

"Tell me about it! So anyway, I was less than thrilled to use my culinary experience on this spoiled Upper East Side kid. But Mrs. Fink guilted me into it."

"Let me get this straight. You didn't start out as some Save the Fat Kids crusader out to demolish high fructose corn syrup, Happy Meals and Play Stations?"

"Hell no. In fact, I distinctly remember telling Mrs. Fink I didn't go to culinary school to make fat free fish sticks for some rich spoiled brat."

"Holy shit! If your audience could hear you now."

"I know. I cringe just thinking about it. But I quickly figured out that I was damn good at getting this poor boy, Carter, was his name, motivated to eat healthier and to exercise. And it was amazing to see the results."

"So did Carter's mom happen to be an ABC exec who ended up hiring you for the show?"

"You skip to the last page of books don't you? No. Long story short, I became the kiddy Weight Watchers for all families east of Sixth Avenue. Someone from *New York Today* got wind of it, wrote up a story about me and next thing I knew I had my own show on ABC."

"That's some crazy shit." Jack whistled through his teeth and both dogs perked up.

"Sometimes I feel guilty. You know? Like I'm not exactly the person everyone thinks I am."

"I totally get that."

"I try to make the right choices every day. But every now and then I indulge."

Kate Richards, Mini-Munchies

Chapter Ten

"Okay, now that I shared my telenovela with you. It's your turn." Kate polished off the lingering bit of beer and put the bottle down on the coffee table.

"We're going to need more beers for my life story." Jack shook Diesel off his lap and headed to the kitchen.

He returned with the beers and handed one to Kate. "Seriously, there's not much to tell."

"Well you're this great funny guy, who's obviously very successful in the dot com industry." Kate spread her arms around the richly furnished and decorated room.

"That's true. But I'm sure you don't want to hear about my work in the Internet trenches."

"That's right. But I do want to know how such a great guy is still single at your age which I'm guessing to be what thirty four?" When Jack raised his thumb up Kate said "Thirty-six?"

"Thirty-seven," Jack said, and ducked his head sheepishly.

"What's the deal? Do you know how many of my friends sift through the endless divorced-twice-house-in-foreclosure-never-wants-kids profiles on eHarmony for a guy like you. Seriously—how are you still on the market?"

"You can only come on a date with your thirteen-year-old sister so many times before you start to scare women off." Jack shrugged his shoulders.

"I'm judging by the ten-year-old girl sleeping in your guest bedroom that Harper must be old enough to stay home alone by now." Kate raised an eyebrow at him.

Jack grabbed a throw pillow from behind his back and threw it at Kate. "You don't pull any punches do you?"

"I just tell it like I see it."

"Stephanie Riggins was the girl I probably would've married if my mom hadn't died. We started dating our junior year of college. She was actually pretty cool about Harper always hanging around. But she wanted to become a surgeon, which meant med school in Seattle and then an internship and residency God knows where. If I didn't have Harper I might have followed her, but there's no way I could've uprooted Harper like that."

"Let me guess—after that you learned not to get too serious?" asked Kate.

"Clearly you speak from experience."

"I totally get being in a place where you just can't go there with someone. But that was a long time ago."

"Yeah, and just when I thought I didn't have to worry about Harper she goes and marries David pretty much right out of high school and has Lauren while the guy goes on two tours to Iraq and another two in Afghanistan."

"It's her." Jack grabbed his cell phone and jumped off the couch. He picked up the phone and whispered a greeting as he peeked his head in the guest room to make sure Lauren was asleep. He carefully clicked the door closed before speaking again.

"Thank God!"

Kate settled back into the couch cushions while Jack talked to his sister. He was talking too low for her to hear anything, but at least she knew they weren't dealing with the worst-case scenario. Diesel hopped up on the couch with her and snuggled up to her legs. She pulled a crocheted throw off the back of the couch and wrapped it around her shoulders.

Despite the stress of the night, Kate wanted to stay in this homey townhouse with the overflowing bookcases and the coffee table jumbled with Wii remotes and DVD's. There was something comforting about being surrounded by the mess of a family.

Jack walked back to Kate and sunk into the couch leaving only an inch between them. Kate's legs warmed up from the heat radiating off Jack's body.

"By no small miracle, David's alive and has all of his limbs."

"How bad is it?" Kate could tell from Jack's wobbly voice that his brother-in-law wasn't completely out of the woods. She wanted to reach over and wrap her hand around his, but both his fingers were laced together supporting the bottom of his head.

"David had internal bleeding. But the doctors think they got it under control. It's his eyes that are the problem." Jack stood up suddenly and walked across the room.

"See those black and white pictures on the wall? David took all of them. A gallery on Sixth Avenue showcased some of his work right before he left."

Kate walked across the room to the long hallway where rows of black and white photographs lined the apple cider colored wall. Lauren with her curls slicked back and secured with slender ribbon extended into a perfect handstand on the high bar. Her toes pointed in the air like an upside down ballerina, but what stood out was the expression on her face, proud and determined. Lauren running through a rainstorm with Diesel nipping at her heels. Her hair hung down her face in rippled sheets and her mouth was wide open in laughter.

"These pictures are amazing. This one is my favorite." Kate pointed to the last picture in the series. It was of Jack with someone who Kate now recognized as Harper, her long dark hair a mass of interlocking waves. Her eyes were locked on Jack's as she listened to whatever he was saying.

"He better get his sight back." Jack turned back to face Kate, his dimple back in hiding.

"He's lucky to have you here to take care of Lauren and Harper."

Jack winced and grabbed the top of his neck. "At least I have till the morning to figure out what to tell Lauren." He rolled his head around and pressed his fingers into the loops of curls at the bottom of his head.

Kate gently pushed Jack's hand away and rubbed her fingers into the knots of tension.

"Whatever you're doing—don't stop," murmured Jack.

His breath came out in jagged edges as Kate moved her hands over Jack's skin. His breathing quickly became light and feathery like cotton candy.

Jack turned to face Kate, his voice low and husky. "Thank you for being with me tonight."

Before Kate could answer he placed both hands in the hollows of her cheeks. His hands felt almost rough like the smooth side of an emery board. Jack tilted Kate's face up so she was looking directly into his eyes, which had turned the color of an early summer lake. All at once Kate felt like she couldn't breathe.

"We can't do this now," whispered Kate, as she held onto Jack's gaze. Sarah Jessica Barker sidled up between them, planting her drool-covered snout on Kate's calf. Kate nudged the dog to the side with her foot.

"You're right. We need to stop." But Jack didn't take his hands off Kate.

"It's too soon." Sarah Jessica Barker moved back between them snorting and sniffling as she pawed at Kate's leg. Kate shook her off and stepped closer to Jack, filling the space between them.

"Too soon." Every nerve ending in Kate's body crackled as Jack buried his fingers in her hair and gently pulled her face closer. His lips were Chap Stick smooth as Kate met Jack's mouth with hers. Kate parted her lips and Jack's hands wrapped tighter around her hair as he opened his mouth. Jack's tongue trailed around hers with such detail and purpose, it made Kate wonder what he could do to other parts of her body.

Jack kept his lips pressed into hers, his tongue tracing patterns while he slowly pulled her blazer off first one shoulder then the other and dropped it on the floor.

Diesel picked up Kate's abandoned jacket and tried to initiate tug of war with Sarah Jessica Barker who was too busy trying to get in on whatever game Kate and Jack were up to.

"My fucking dog sucks at being wingman." Jack reached down and grabbed the jacket and threw it towards the couch, sending both dogs racing after it.

"You can't get too mad at him. He's the reason we met." Kate pulled Jack back into a kiss. He tasted like the French fry and milkshake combo; sweet and savory at the same time.

Jack worked his fingers over the top button of Kate's shirt, fumbling with the tiny button. "Shit. They don't make these things for people with sausage fingers."

"Let me." Kate hadn't had sex in more than a year. She wasn't about to let some buttons get in the way. She moved Jack's clumsy fingers and flicked each button open herself.

"What the fuck is someone as hot as you doing with someone like me?" Jack put his mouth back on Kate's before she could answer. Then he slid his hands over her shoulders so that her shirt fell to the ground.

Kate could feel her nipples standing erect in her black lace demi bra, her breasts full and round. Jack cupped both of her breasts in his hands and trailed his mouth down to her nipple. He pulled it from the bra with his mouth, sucking it with just enough pressure to make a shiver ripple up from deep inside Kate.

Diesel took that moment to hop off the couch and run towards them with Sarah Jessica Barker close at his heels.

"Fuck Diesel. I never took you for a cock blocker." Jack grabbed Kate's hand and pulled her down the hall. He grabbed a few biscuits off the cookie jar on the kitchen counter on the way and threw them at the dogs. Then he opened a side door Kate hadn't noticed before. He pulled her through the heavy wooden door, shutting it firmly on the whining dogs.

They stood in what looked like the main entrance of the townhouse. The only light came through the stained glass on the front door. Beams of dark red and warm orange shone through the long corridor.

The ceramic tile felt cold on Kate's feet and helped to cool off the burning heat that was coursing through her whole body. Jack pulled her over to the heavy wooden staircase. He leaned her back against the rungs of the stairwell and pushed his mouth deep into hers. Kate could feel the square shape of a spindle digging into her back. She welcomed the discomfort because it helped keep her from losing herself so completely right away.

Kate reached her hands under Jack's shirt and pulled it up over his head. Jack wasn't as fit as the guys Kate usually dated, but there was something very soothing about his softer stomach, like he was comfortable living in his own skin.

Jack reached back and unhooked Kate's bra. He slid it down, his lips following the trail of the strap as it fell to the floor. He moved his mouth back to her breasts, holding them both in his hands while he flicked his tongue back over her nipple making it stand back up at attention.

Jack moved his hands down to the front of Kate's jeans. He worked his hands over her zipper while Kate responded just as quickly with his. Kate had Jack's pants unzipped and pulled down while he was still trying to slide her skinny jeans off.

Jack stepped out of his pants and underneath all those ironic tee shirts and loose jeans Jack was wearing black cotton boxer briefs that barely contained him.

Kate was glad it was too dark for Jack to see how wide her eyes had gotten. All she could think was I hope it fits, followed by, this is a UTI waiting to happen.

Meanwhile, Jack still couldn't get her damn pants down. He had gotten the zipper open and had edged the jeans down her hips, but he didn't have a prayer in getting them over Kate's ass cheeks. No matter how much Kate worked out, she was always going to have curves.

"How the Hell do you get these things off? I'd have better luck figuring out a Rubik's cube."

"Start with the ankles." Kate tried to maintain her sexy pose propped up against the stairs while Jack tugged at the narrow opening at her ankles. She held onto the stair rungs as Jack pulled. He managed to get the pants a few inches past her ankle.

"I give up."

"Getting skinny jeans off is not a pretty sight. You might want to look away." Kate grabbed the top of her pants and jiggled and shook a little to loosen her body from the denim suction cup. She cursed herself for eating all those fries. She managed to release her butt from the denim prison and then had to yank them down quick—like ripping a large oversized strip of duct tape off her legs.

Jack kicked the pants out of the way and palmed Kate's ass cheeks pulling her into him. She could feel him through her lace thong, hard and thick. Kate reached over to try to pull Jack's boxers down but before she could get to them Jack was kneeling on the ground pulling Kate's thong down with him.

Kate reached back and held onto the rungs of the stairs while Jack moved his mouth down her body. He grasped her arms and held them up high while he used his mouth to move aside her smooth folds of skin and thrust his tongue inside her. He massaged her with his tongue until Kate thought she would scream then he sucked back her wetness while she clung to the stair rungs. Her orgasm came in a steady stream that he eagerly met with his mouth.

Just when Kate thought she couldn't take it anymore, she heard the unmistakable sound of the foil being ripped off a condom wrapper. Jack let go of her hands and slid his briefs down. Jack rubbed just his tip against her, gliding in her wetness. He rubbed himself back and forth over her until all Kate wanted was for him to be inside her, not caring that he might break her wide open.

Then Jack slowly pushed inside of her pausing each step of the way until she felt completely filled by him. He stayed there a minute asking, "Are you okay?"

"Oh God yes. Don't stop now."

Kate let go of the stairs and grabbed Jack's back. She lifted both legs off the ground and straddled him. She found his lips in the dark tasting her own saltiness, pushing her tongue into his to match the thrusts that she was now leading with the power of her legs strong and flexible from years of yoga.

Kate pushed herself into Jack clenching her muscles so he could feel her tightness. Jack let out a low groan. Then he picked her up and carried her to a small wooden table. He pushed off the pile of mail and newspapers and hoisted Kate up. She sat down feeling the cold wood against her skin as Jack pushed himself into her over and over. Each time he went farther inside of her. She came again this time in one big rush.

"That moment when you realize you're happy."
Jack Moskowitz, Facebook Status Update

Chapter Eleven

"Mmmm. Good morning to you too." Jack mumbled into the couch pillow that was pressed against his face.

"Finally, he's awake. I thought you were going to have to take me to practice." Lauren's voice carried from the kitchen along with the sound of silverware clinking against plates.

"What the…" Jack opened his eyes and found Sarah Jessica Barker lying on the end of the couch licking his toes. He shuddered and quickly slid his feet away.

"You want some coffee Jack?" Kate smiled at him from behind the kitchen counter. She held a pot of fresh coffee that made the whole first floor smell like hazelnuts.

"That would be great. Thanks!" Jack sat up and rubbed the sleep out of his eyes, as he took in the scene in the kitchen. Lauren sat at the kitchen counter with a stack of pancakes in front of her, while Kate poured a cup of coffee for Jack.

Jack and Kate had made their way back in from the hallway and stayed up for hours on the couch talking. He vaguely remembered starting to drift off while Kate was telling a story about getting in some argument with her sister in the third grade over a Cabbage Patch Doll. The argument somehow symbolized their current relationship, but Jack fell asleep before he found out the exact meaning behind it.

"Kate makes awesome pancakes. Come have some!" Lauren forked a slice of strawberry with a huge piece of pancake and shoved it in her mouth. She gestured for Jack to join them at the breakfast bar.

"Perfect timing, Jack. I have a fresh stack all ready for you." Kate flipped a pancake expertly from the frying pan onto a plate as Jack made his way over.

"Hey, sleepyhead. You taking me to practice?" asked Lauren, before shoving another mouthful of pancake in her mouth.

"Don't I always?" Jack reached his arms up and stretched with a loud yawn.

"I'm gonna go get ready." Lauren jumped off the stool and headed upstairs.

"But you didn't finish your breakfast," Jack called, to Lauren's retreating back.

"Don't worry. That was her third helping." Kate put a plate of pancakes in front of Jack. They looked darker than the Bisquick ones he usually made and had chunks of oats sticking to them. His Mrs. Butterworth's was noticeably missing from the table, with a bowl of strawberries in its place.

"Wow. Thanks for making breakfast." Jack scooped some fruit onto his pancakes.

"I figured you could use a good breakfast after such a stressful night."

"I don't think stressful is how I would describe it. But I definitely worked up an appetite." Jack grabbed the carton of milk off the counter and poured a stream of it into his coffee until it turned the perfect shade of light brown.

"Oh, I did too." Kate pulled a strawberry from the plastic package on the counter and took a large bite, her lips pressed against the moist fruit. If Lauren weren't right upstairs, Jack would've grabbed Kate and taken her right on the counter.

"Sorry I fell asleep on you last night."

"That's okay. I was pretty tired too." Kate had piled her mass of waves into some kind of bun on top of her head. A few stray curls escaped so that they grazed her neck. She was wearing those bright blue jeans with Jack's faded Chelsea Prep dodgeball team shirt with no bra. Jack gulped down some coffee.

"You ready Uncle Jack?" Lauren bounded into the kitchen

with a pair of warm-up pants thrown on over a leotard and her gym bag over her shoulder.

"Give me five minutes." Jack shoved one last forkful of pancake into his mouth and washed it down with more coffee. He ran to the bathroom and washed up and brushed his teeth in record time. All he could think about was getting Lauren to the gym so he could get back home to Kate.

"I'll stay here and clean up the breakfast dishes, while you guys are gone." Kate was already scraping Lauren's leftover stack of pancakes into the trash.

Jack shrugged his shoulders. "You really don't have to clean. But I would love it if you were here when I got back."

Jack and Lauren did their usual speed walk to the gym so that she wouldn't be late. As soon as Jack got Lauren out on the gym floor, he practically ran the whole way back home.

Sarah Jessica Barker and Diesel both jumped at the door as soon as Jack pushed it open. He leaned down and gave them both equal pets and scruffs on the tops of their heads. He pulled two thick rawhide bones from the kitchen cabinet over the sink and ripped the shrink wrap off both in record time. He wasn't about to let the two dogs get in the way again. He tossed one bone on each end of the couch and the two dogs raced to get one. They settled in to work on their bones, while Jack looked for Kate. He could hear the shower running in the downstairs bathroom.

Jack opened the door and a rush of steam pushed its way out. The bathroom smelled of his evergreen bar soap and Barbasol shaving cream, manly scents that were a sharp contrast to the curvy silhouette of Kate's naked body in the frosted glass shower door.

"Jack? Is that you?" Kate called over the sound of pulsating water.

"No. It's the Fresh Direct guy." Jack yanked his shirt off and immediately sucked his gut in. The queen of fitness had only seen him naked in the cover of darkness so far.

"In that case, come right in. I've always wondered what sex with the delivery guy would be like."

Jack didn't need to be asked twice. This was the scenario of more than one fantasy of his over the years. Jack dropped trou and opened the shower door. The warm steam wrapped around him.

Kate's blond hair rippled down her back like a mermaid. Water trickled over Kate's breasts, streaming down her stomach and dipping between her legs where she was waxed clean. The whole scenario was like something out of *Penthouse Letters*.

"Come a little closer and I'll help clean you off. You must be sweaty from delivering all those groceries." Kate pulled Jack under the warm water. She opened her mouth and water poured into Jack's. Kate tasted like his wintermint toothpaste as Jack ran his tongue over hers.

Kate moved the soap filled pouf across Jack's chest and down the curve of his stomach like he was some fitness God, not the kind of guy who lived on takeout and hadn't been to the gym since Clinton was in office.

Kate trailed the pouf down lower and the feel of her fingers playing peek-a-boo through the mesh was maddening. Jack was almost painfully hard beneath the layer of suds. Kate wrapped her fingers around him and moved her hand up and down while gently squeezing at the same time. The warm water showering down made Jack more sensitive to her touch and he had to press his hand into the shower wall for support.

Just when he couldn't take it another second, Jack grabbed the pouf from Kate and swung her around so her back was facing him. Jack lifted Kate's hair and moved his lips across the nape of her neck. He trailed the pouf up Kate's arm, his touch goose bump light. He moved his hand over her shoulder and in the dip between her breasts while he layered kisses from the back of her neck to the heart shaped beauty mark on her collar bone.

Jack slid his hand down and rested it right above the slick mound between her legs. Jack leaned over and kissed Kate while he brought the pouf between her legs, gliding it back and forth in the bubbles of soap. Kate groaned as she moved her body to meet his touch. There were so many suds, Jack couldn't see where Kate ended and he began.

Kate turned back around, pressed both hands into Jack's cheeks and brought his mouth to hers. Water rained down from the showerheads as they kissed. Jack lifted Kate up and she straddled him with those strong legs of hers. Jack pushed through the suds, the water causing friction as Jack moved slowly at first, just wanting to be part of her.

Kate dug her fingers in Jack's back, daring him to move further inside her. He pushed her up against the shower wall and moved until they became one person.

Jack found Kate's mouth again as water streamed down on top of them. They kissed each other in only the way a new couple does, with abandon and without wanting to pull away first.

When prickles of cold water started lacing in with the hot, Jack eased himself off Kate.

"Where have you been all my life?" Jack was well aware this line was about as cliché as it got, but he really meant it.

"Around the corner." Kate grabbed the shampoo.

"Here, let me." Jack took the bottle from Kate's hands and squirted a dime-sized amount in his palm. Kate leaned her head back while Jack massaged the lather into her scalp. He started at the top of her head and slowly worked his way down to the base of her head. Then he worked his hands over the layers of tangled curls.

"You're a man full of surprises."

Jack helped rinse the shampoo out of Kate's hair just when the last of the hot water finally ran out. Goose pimples lined her skin when Jack turned the spout off. Jack pulled one of the hotel sized thick white towels off the towel rack. He wrapped it around Kate and watched as she grabbed a hairbrush off the counter and pulled it through her knotted hair.

Jack wrapped the towel around his waist and opened the bathroom door releasing all the steam into the hallway. Sarah Jessica Barker and Diesel were snuggled up against each other with their bones, waiting right outside the bathroom door for their owners.

"You guys are too much." Jack stepped over the dogs and left Kate to get dressed.

Kate came out of the bathroom wearing the jeans from the night before and buttoning her white shirt. Jack thought she looked even better without makeup, her cheeks scrubbed pink and her eyes shining bright.

"Shit." Kate frowned and grabbed her phone off the coffee table.

"What's wrong?"

"I have eight missed calls from Dana. I better call her back." Kate slid her finger over the phone and held it to her ear.

"What's the matter?" Kate shoved her feet back in her shoes and grabbed her black blazer off the edge of the couch.

"Can't you just tell me over the phone?" Kate shook out her wet hair with her fingers and the waves instantly sprung into shape.

"Be there in ten minutes." Kate shoved her phone in her back pocket.

"Everything okay?"

"I hope so." Kate grabbed her bag off the couch. "I hate to do this. But I really have to go."

"We wouldn't want to keep Dana waiting, would we?" Jack pushed aside Kate's shirt collar and pressed his lips against her neck. Her skin was smooth and still a little damp from the shower.

Kate sighed. "If you keep doing that, I'll never get out of here." She pulled away from Jack. "I really do have to go."

Sarah Jessica bounded over to her playmate and nuzzled his snout with hers. He flipped over and she started pawing at his belly.

"These two are not ready to say good-bye to each other," said Jack.

"I'm not either." Kate reached down and leashed up Sarah Jessica Barker, much to her dog's dismay.

Jack stepped closer to Kate and wrapped his hands around her hips. He pulled her closer to him and locked his lips back on hers. Already, they had their own language.

Finally, Kate pulled away. "I'll call you later."

As soon as they walked out, Diesel ran to the closed door

and whimpered.

"I know Buddy." Jack leaned down and scooped up his dog and brought him over to the couch.

Jack grabbed his cell phone off the coffee table. As much as he didn't want to bring down his post-Kate high, he would have to call and check in with Harper while Lauren was still out of the house.

"Looks like the internal bleeding is under control. David woke up, but he was so groggy from surgery he thought he was still in Afghanistan." Harper started talking right away as if they were already in the middle of a conversation.

"When will they know more about his vision?"

"It's hard to tell, especially since he's doped up on meds and hasn't been awake for more than a few minutes here and there." Harper's voice had the ragged edge of someone desperate for sleep.

"He's a fighter. He's going to pull through this." Jack poured a mug of lukewarm coffee, grateful that Kate hadn't dumped the rest of the pot out.

"Oh, I know. The army heals the soldiers quickly so they can send them back in the field to get hurt all over again. The doctor had the nerve to say to me, don't worry Mrs. Feldman, we'll get your husband back in fighting shape in no time."

"That bastard. Remember when Mom was about to start chemo and the oncologist said, 'Good thing you're a makeup artist. At least you can stay pretty'? You think they would offer a sensitivity course in med school."

"Don't remind me about that tool. I was so sure I would get busted and end up in juvey for egging his car."

"What do you want me to tell Lauren?" Jack grabbed a plate of pancakes from the fridge and nuked them for thirty seconds. Then he doused them with good old Mrs. Butterworth's.

"Stick with the story. I need to know more about David's condition before I tell her what's going on."

"I can't keep lying to her. She's not going to trust me when she finds out." Jack pushed his fork through the thick stack of pancakes. He almost groaned out loud, the pancakes were so good. Kate cooked like she had sex. She paid attention to every little detail.

"Are you talking about Lauren or Kate?" asked Harper. "I heard all about your little sleepover. Lauren texted me as soon as she got up."

"Shit. I'm sorry she spent the night with Lauren here. It just happened."

"I'm not worried about Lauren. It sounds like Kate did a good job keeping her mind off me leaving. You're the one I'm worried about."

"Don't you have enough on your plate without worrying about my shit?" Jack poured a heaping spoonful of sugar in his coffee.

"I'm going out of my mind. Your screwed up love life is as good a distraction as anything else," said Harper, through a thick yawn.

"In that case—what the fuck should I do?" Jack scarfed down another huge bite of pancake.

"Please tell me you didn't actually sleep with her while she still thinks you're Jack Horvath?"

"It's Horowitz and yes, I did."

"Shit." Harper whistled through her teeth.

"Twice."

"Obviously you really like her or you wouldn't be so worried. How does she feel about you?"

"Judging by this morning, it looks like she's really into me too."

"Spare me the details," Harper cut him off.

"The problem is she likes Jack Horowitz, freelance dot-com start up specialist."

"You told her you work for dot-coms? What is it like 1997?"

"I know. It just slipped out and now I'm stuck with it."

"Well you can't tell her who you really are, yet. Give her a chance to get more attached to you first."

"Yeah, But she's just going to become attached to Bizarro Jack."

"That's bullshit. You're so much more than what

you do for a living. Show her who you are separate from Considerable Carriages."

"She's going to hate me when she finds out I lied to her."

"She'll hate you even more if she finds out right after you first slept with her. If you tell her now you'll have no shot."

"You think I have more of a chance with her if I wait longer to tell her who I am?"

"The more involved she gets with you the more likely she'll give you a chance and actually listen when you explain everything."

Jack nodded as if his sister could see him over the phone line.

"And for God sakes, don't tell Matt what's going on yet or he'll fuck the whole thing up."

"Shit. I didn't even think about Matt."

"I have to get back to David. Tell Lauren I'll call her later," said Harper, through another yawn.

Jack tried to work on the stroller designs, but it was pointless. All he could think about was Kate and the feel of her skin against his. He eventually gave up and left the townhouse to clear his mind.

Jack headed over to Chelsea Piers. Instead of going to the gym, he walked down the path to the Hudson River Skate Park. Nestled across from the Chelsea Piers Fieldhouse with views of the river, the skate park was always packed with young kids, teenagers and middle aged men who had been skating since the fad first hit in the '80s. Jack and Matt would have lived at this park if it had existed back when they were obsessed with Tony Hawk. But when Jack's mom died, he was so busy taking care of Harper that his skateboard had ended up under his bed with the dust bunnies and lost socks. Meanwhile, Matt still spent most Sundays with his skater friends doing ollies and flip-kicks on the cement hills and valleys of the skate park. Jack was pretty certain that this was one of the reasons Matt's wife Anne had left him last year.

Jack headed to the back of the park where the half pipe was. He knew that's where Matt and his friends would be since the younger skaters thought the half pipe was too old school and left it for the dinosaurs to dominate.

Jack made it to the U-shaped cement ramp just as Matt rolled himself down and launched back up again effortlessly, pausing at the top in mid-air with both hands gripping his board before coming back. From a distance, Matt still looked like a gangly teenager with his skinny black jeans and Vans sneakers. It wasn't till you got close and saw the gray sprouting through his goatee and the deep-set laugh lines that you could tell the guy was pushing forty.

Jack sat on the edge of the cement and leaned against the safety fence. He watched for a few minutes while Matt took a few more turns. He felt like a douche not telling Matt about Kate, but Harper was right. Matt hated Kate enough to fuck the whole thing up.

As soon as Matt spotted Jack, he grabbed his board in one hand and walked over to him. "Sorry about David."

"Thanks, man."

"I talked to your sister this morning. She sounded wrecked."

"It sucks that I can't be there with her."

"Harper's tough. She'll be all right." Matt had known Harper since she was a toddler and had appointed himself as her honorary brother, taking that role quite seriously when it came to scaring jerks off when she aged into the dating pool. Matt, was in fact, the only friend of Jack's over the years who hadn't at some point made a move on his sister.

"How's Lauren taking it?"

"She thinks Harper's in LA filming a commercial. Harper wants to wait till she knows more about what shape David's in before we tell Lauren."

"That makes sense."

Matt's two friends grabbed their boards and left the edge of the pipe to greet Jack.

"Hey, man. When you coming skating with us?" asked P-Dog, a heavily tatted up guy in his early forties who left his neck, hands and wrists ink-free for his gig at one of the biggest law firms in Manhattan.

"The last time I tried to keep up with you guys, I ended up with my wrist in a cast." Jack returned P-Dog's aggressive hand smack, followed by a thump on the shoulders.

"Jack's hands are money right now. I don't need him breaking his wrist trying to keep up with you assholes," said Matt.

"Long time, no see, Doc," said Jack, when Matt's other skating partner rolled up. Doc could keep up with all the teenagers on the ramps and skateboarded every day to the Upper West Side high-end animal hospital where he worked as a radiologist.

"Give me a holler next time you bring Diesel in for a check up so I can come out and say hi," said Doc.

"Can you get me an employee discount?" asked Jack.

"No, man. Those bastards in billing don't even give the employees an employee discount." Doc took off his black-framed Brooklyn style glasses and rubbed the lenses on his sweaty tee shirt.

"We gotta take off," said Matt. "This cocksucker's been avoiding me all week."

They left Doc and P-Dog to carry on their skating session and headed out of the skate park toward the West Side Highway.

"Did you see all the tweets we got after my rebuttal on *Straight Talk?*" Matt had dressed to the nines and charmed Lucy Barrows, telling her all about the outdated measurements of current strollers and car seats and how the company was created to keep kids safe.

"Hell yeah. We were smart to pick you as the company spokesperson back in the day. I would've frozen the minute that woman started talking."

"You suck at recon missions too. I can't believe you didn't find one thing out about the fem-bot I could use."

"Did you really think Kate Richards was going to open up and tell me her all her darkest secrets over a bucket of mussels at The Frying Pan?"

"Maybe not. We'll just have to find another way to take that bitch down."

"We've got enough shit going on with the new line. We don't have time to waste on revenge with Kate Richards."

"The design's almost done?" asked Matt, while they both

stepped off the path to avoid getting mowed down by a teenage girl who was texting and skateboarding at the same time.

"That was close," said Jack, as he jumped back on the concrete trail. "I gotta tell you, I'm still on the fence."

"You overthink everything. That's your problem."

"The bad press from this could be the end of us."

"That's what we pay the PR chick the big bucks for."

Jack walked next to Matt while he neatly wove patterns next to him on the path with his skateboard. They headed towards the dog park, which made him think of Kate.

"Did you know that eighty percent of the kids in LA are overweight?" Matt pulled a half-empty VitaminWater from his knapsack and chugged it, leaving drops of the bright pink liquid to bead up on his tee shirt.

"Do you really want our company to contribute to a stat like that?"

"There's a difference between causing a problem and being smart enough to make money from it." Matt tossed the drained drink container in the recycling bin on the corner.

"We went from making car seats for overweight kids to creating little couch potatoes who are going to be drinking super-size desserts and eating food off their snack trays while their parents cart them around." Jack felt that muscle tighten up in his neck again.

"These kids are going to be drinking Frappuccinos, whether we make the damn cup holders or not."

"It doesn't matter. The media's still going to tar and feather us."

"I have more at stake here than you do, Jack. I lost fifty percent of all my earnings in the divorce. And Anne still has ownership of anything we created while I was still married to her. By adding the cup holders and snack trays, we can completely revamp the CC-XL, rename it and she has no claim over any of the profits from it."

There was no arguing with Matt on that one. Jack couldn't imagine how he would feel if he had an ex-wife wipe out half of everything he had worked so hard to earn. To top it off, she had hired the biggest legal eagle in the Northeast and socked Matt with her legal fees as well those for the shark he had to hire for himself.

"All right. Let me work them into the designs and I can think this through some more while I go."

"While you're at it I was thinking we could add a pouch for handheld video games like the DS, and maybe some speakers that synch up to an iPod."

"Is your child having trouble squeezing into their stroller? That doesn't mean you should walk into Babies "R" Us and say super-size me. Instead, trade in that stroller for a different set of wheels—a tricycle!"

Kate Richards, The Daily Chatter

Chapter Twelve

When Kate returned to her apartment building, she found Dana occupying the creamy white leather armchair in the lobby. Even on a Sunday afternoon, Dana managed to look fresh and sleek. She took advantage of the approaching fall weather by resurrecting her black knee high boots and pairing them with the skinniest of dark rinse jeans and a crisp white button down. Her cinnamon dreads were pulled off her high forehead in a sunglasses adorned ponytail.

"Holy shit! You're doing the walk of shame!" As soon as Dana jumped out of the armchair, Kate remembered she had texted Dana a picture of her date night outfit.

"Shh." She headed towards the elevator bank with Sarah Jessica Barker following behind a little slower than usual finally worn out from her extended play date with Diesel.

"Did you really bring the damn dog on another date?" Dana pushed the elevator button and stared at Sarah Jessica Barker without making a move to pet her.

"It was Jack's idea. We were supposed to eat dinner outside and go for a walk on the Highline." Kate stepped aside as the sleek silver elevator doors opened and a female cyclist wearing fluorescent cycling attire came out of the elevator wheeling a racing bike.

"How did you get from dinner with the dogs to getting it on at his apartment?" Dana got loud again as soon as the elevator doors shut them.

"We never actually made it to the restaurant." Kate kept her eyes on the elevator buttons as she pressed the one for her floor.

"Holy shit! It's always the quiet ones." Dana smacked Kate on the arm.

"It wasn't like that. It's a long story."

The elevator doors opened and Sarah Jessica Barker led them down the hall to Kate's apartment. As soon as Kate turned the key, the dog jumped on the couch and settled against the pillow ready for a long nap.

"Good thing you didn't bring him back here." Dana gestured to the piles of clothes strewn around the room and then moved her arms back to the kitchen counter covered with dirty dishes. ""You would've scared him away for sure.

"I really need to get myself a housekeeper." Kate grabbed a few of the dishes and half-heartedly ran some water over them.

"What happened to that Swedish girl?" Dana wrinkled her nose and threw out the carton of soymilk sitting on the counter.

"She was too high maintenance. She actually expected me to straighten up before she came over."

"All housekeepers want you to pick up before they come." Dana stacked up the bowls and plates from the counter and started loading them right in the dishwasher.

"Well if I had time to clean, I wouldn't need to hire someone."

"I'll try to help you find a new one. But you better get them to sign a non-disclosure agreement. Otherwise, we'll end up seeing pictures of all this on *Gossip Matters*." Dana filled up the top rack of the dishwasher with all the coffee cups and water glasses. "I never would've taken you for a second date kind of girl." Dana gave Kate a look of newfound appreciation.

"Well, the first time it just sort of happened."

"How many times did you guys hook up?"

"Only twice. Once last night and once this morning. It probably would've happened again if someone hadn't rushed me back home." Kate raised her eyebrows at Dana.

"Trust me you'll thank me for it. I have huge news!" Dana's honey-glossed lips broke into a wide smile.

"What?"

"They want it!"

"Who wants what?" Dana had so many deals in the works Kate had absolutely no idea which one she was so excited about.

"*New York Today*! The editor loves the op-ed piece you pitched. Your *Straight Talk* appearance stirred up the whole stroller debate so she wants to run the piece while people are still up in arms about it. Especially since Matt Reynolds, the CEO went on and did a rebuttal interview."

"I queried them months ago. Are you serious?"

"The editor's going to email you some suggestions. They want you to submit it within the week, so it can run two Sundays from now."

""I'll get it done. I'll just pull an all nighter."

"Don't stay up too late. Those dark circles are going to be hard to cover."

"Relax; Paula can work her magic in the makeup chair tomorrow. Can you get Lara to wait another week for the cookbook manuscript?"

"Yeah. She'll be psyched about the buzz the piece will create for the new book. Oh, and the *New York Today* editor wants you to add some stuff about Considerable Carriages."

"I'll just need to research the company a little bit more. I was caught off guard on *Straight Talk*, to be honest."

Dana pulled a stack of papers from her oversized black crocodile bag. "I printed up some info for you. Matt Reynolds was all over twitter last week after he appeared on *Straight Talk* with his rebuttal statement."

"Was there anything about the add-ons to the new design? I heard they were doing super-sized cup holders."

"And snack trays and get this—handheld video game pouches and speakers that sync up to iPods. These strollers are going to be souped up better than my grandma's RV."

"The Sunday edition of *New York Today*! I'm shaking.

Look!" Kate held out her hand, which had a slight tremor from thumb to pinky.

"Channel all those nerves into your writing. And don't forget about the cookbook revisions!"

Kate was ready to delve into her article as soon as Dana left. She settled on the couch in between a pile of laundry that was waiting to be folded and Sarah Jessica Barker. She pushed aside her stack of magazines and unread mail and put her feet up on the coffee table.

But every time Kate started to read the research Dana gave her, all she could think about was Jack. Her lips felt swollen from all the kissing and it made her feel like his mouth was still connected to hers. She was just starting to doze off over her laptop when her cell rang.

"Diesel's been slumped by the door waiting for Sarah Jessica Barker to come back since you guys left," said Jack, as soon as Kate picked up the phone.

"Sarah Jessica Barker is sound asleep on the couch. Diesel wore her out." Kate put her laptop on the table and stood up to stretch, glad for the welcome writing break.

"Thanks again for breakfast. And for hanging out last night while I waited to see how David was."

"Any more news?" asked Kate.

"He's pretty sore from the surgery. But he's still too out of it to really get what's going on."

"In this case, maybe ignorance is bliss. He can't make himself crazy about his vision if he doesn't know he's supposed to be worrying about it."

"That's true. I remember talking to a doctor back when my mom was sick. He said sometimes nature helps protect us by making our minds less aware of what's really happening to our bodies."

"That's when you think there must be some higher power out there taking care of us."

"I usually don't get into these kinds of philosophical discussions without a few drinks in me," Jack said, with a light laugh. "So how did your meeting with Dana go? I'm dying to know what was so important that she had to drag you away."

"I'm writing an op-ed for *New York Today*!" Even as Kate said it, she couldn't believe it.

"Wow! You write too?" asked Jack.

"Before now—just recipes for my cookbooks. So, I'm a little freaked out I won't sound intellectual enough for a newspaper."

"An op-ed isn't about making yourself sound smart—it's about getting your opinion across to the masses. Not only that, I don't think sounding intellectual is actual criteria for getting printed in *New York Today*."

"Was that meant to make me feel better?"

"Sorry. What're you writing about?"

"What else? Childhood obesity."

"That's a pretty broad topic," said Jack. "What're you going to focus on?"

"It's too early to say. I'll be ready to talk, after I've made a little headway."

"You sure you don't want to try out a few ideas on me?"

"I can't now. I'm still thinking it through. Besides, I'm sure the last thing you want to talk about is fat kids."

"You know they always say it's impossible to edit your own work. It's good to get a second pair of eyes to look it over for you."

"That's what Dana's for. And Mrs. Fink, too. She thinks she's a professional because she writes the Mahjong club newsletter. I want you to see the perfect draft."

"I'll be off in a minute!" Jack called with his hand over the phone to muffle his yell. "Sorry about that. Lauren forgot about some project that involves collecting a bunch of sticks to make into a wigwam. Did I mention it's due tomorrow?"

"Where the heck are you going to find sticks in Manhattan?"

"Good question. Looks like I'll be busy for the rest of the night. Which is too bad because I can think of a few things I would much rather be doing with you."

"I would much rather be with you too. But it looks like I'll be pulling an all nighter myself."

"Mahatma Gandhi got it right when he said be the change you want to see in the world. My business partner Matt and I were both devastated by the senseless death of four-year-old Oksana Karev because there were no car seats to accommodate her proportions. We created Considerable Carriages to prevent another tragedy like that. We are delighted to award Better Beginnings Early Childhood Center with the Oksana Karev Scholarship fund so more children can be the change they want to see in the world."

Jack Moskowitz, Oksana Karev Annual Scholarship Gala

Chapter Thirteen

Jack headed upstairs to check on Lauren. They had barely finished that stupid wigwam in time to hand it in that morning. He needed to make sure she didn't have any other ridiculous time wasters due any time soon.

Jack heard Lauren's voice as soon as he made it halfway up the stairs.

"Now that I got my Giant, I just need to cast into a perfect handstand and my bar routine will be ready for the first meet."

Jack peeked through the crack in Lauren's partially opened door and saw Harper's face filling Lauren's MacBook screen from where it rested on her desk.

"I'm so bummed I missed seeing you get your Giant. Maybe Uncle Jack can film you on bars and email it to me?" Harper's face was pale and her hair hung in lank waves like it hadn't been washed in a few days.

"Why does he need to video me? Aren't you coming home soon?" Panic filled Lauren's voice.

"Filming's taking longer than I thought. I miss you so much Bunny."

"You're filming a commercial, not a movie. I don't understand why this is taking like a year and a day." Lauren leaned so far back in her chair that Jack was afraid she would tip over. He stopped himself from warning her so he could hear Harper's response.

"Aren't you having fun with Uncle Jack? I bet the two of you love not having me around with all my rules." Harper forced her mouth into a smile and Jack could tell she was trying to keep her tone light.

"Yeah, we're having a good time. Uncle Jack's always fun, but I miss you. We never finished reading Homecoming." Lauren held up the thick book and spread it out so Jack could see they were about halfway into the book when Harper had left. He hoped to God he didn't get stuck reading that book with Lauren. It had been boring enough the first time around with Harper.

"I'll buy another copy here, and we can do the next chapter on Skype tomorrow night after practice."

"And Uncle Jack doesn't know how to do my hair right for gymnastics. It keeps falling out of my pony tail and getting in my face."

"Something tells me you might be ready to do your own hair for practice. You could even use some of my special hair pomade—the one they gave me at the Frizz-Tamer photo shoot. Just remember a little goes a very long way."

"Can I also borrow some of your special hand lotion? My hands are a mess from the bars." Lauren held up the palms of her hands to the computer.

"It looks like you're getting another rip. Have Uncle Jack put lots of hemorrhoid cream on both hands and wrap them up before bed tonight." Jack had been shocked the first time Harper had covered Lauren's hands with the thick white cream. But the giant blisters and rips on the palms of her hand had shrunk considerably by the morning.

"I'm all out."

"You know what that means."

"Uncle Jack has to buy more! He is going to be mortified!" Lauren laughed for the first time all day.

"What am I going to be mortified about?" Jack opened the door and Lauren held up her blistered palms.

"You have to buy me more hemorrhoid cream!"

"Let's hope Kate doesn't bump into him on line in Duane Reade when he's buying that." Harper's face brightened as soon as she heard her daughter laugh.

"How's the shoot going?" asked Jack, with a pointed look.

"Slower than I'd like."

"Hang in there. Don't worry about us here. We're doing great."

"We have to go so I don't get stuck doing push ups." Lauren stood up and started rooting through her leotard drawer.

"I'll call you later to say good night. I love you Bunny." Harper blew kisses at the screen. "Love you too big brother."

"Love you too Mom." Lauren blew a kiss at the screen. Jack hadn't heard Lauren put up with being called her toddler nickname in a long time.

"I'll wait for you downstairs. But hurry up and get ready." Jack shut the door and headed back downstairs.

"Lauren!" Ten minutes later, Jack was still waiting downstairs.

"OMG, you don't have to yell. I'm right here." Lauren materialized from behind him. She had added a chunky silver necklace and dangly feather earrings to her leotard and legging ensemble.

"You're just going to have to take all that crap off for practice."

"Chillax Uncle Jack. You're all riled up today." Lauren pulled her gym bag off the bannister and grabbed the banana Jack held out for her.

"Well, don't blame me when we're late and you're stuck doing all those push ups."

"I can't wait till I start filming with Kate next week," said Lauren, the master of changing the subject. "She's so cool."

"That's one thing we can agree on today." Jack grabbed his

keys and phone off the coffee table and headed towards the front door.

Lauren leaned down and ruffled the top of Diesel's head on her way out. "Bye Fuzz Monster."

As soon as they got to the sidewalk, Jack spotted Matt skateboarding down the street towards them.

"Listen, don't say anything about Kate to Matt. He hates her because of the whole *Straight Talk* thing."

"You didn't tell Matt you're, like, dating Kate?" Lauren didn't try to keep the shock out of her voice. "OMG! He's going to be so pissed at you when he finds out."

"Watch the language! We've got a lot going on with the business. So, keep your trap shut."

Matt rolled up, his skateboard wheels scraping over gritty asphalt; a sound Jack had always associated with his best friend.

"What's up, Small Fry?" Matt bumped his fist against Lauren's in greeting. "You ready for that push up contest?"

"Totally! You're going down Skater Boy." Lauren poked Matt in the chest for emphasis.

"Tonight after practice?"

"I'm so on to you. You want to do it when my muscles are tired from a four-hour practice. No way."

"Fine. You pick the day I'm going to demolish you." Matt folded his hands across his chest and leaned down to meet Lauren's eyes.

"First thing Saturday morning," countered Lauren.

"You're killing me. You want to get me when I'm hung over."

"She's a smart one," said Jack.

"No, she's sheisty. Just like her uncle," said Matt.

"You all right man? You don't look so good," said Jack. His friend's normally all weather-tanned skin looked washed out and he was wearing the same black jeans and VitaminWater stained tee shirt from the day before. Lauren used the distraction to shoot off a text, but Jack was sure she was still listening with one ear.

"I've been up late every night this week working on an ad campaign for the line I'm waiting on you to finish," said Matt. "And Anne left me a really weird message last night and we've been playing phone tag ever since."

"What did she say?" Jack couldn't remember the last time Matt had talked to his ex.

"It was hard to understand her, because of all the crying. I think she said something about bad timing and needing to talk." Matt rocked back and forth on his skateboard.

"She was probably just drunk dialing. I'm sure it's par for the course once those divorce papers get finalized."

"Maybe." Matt didn't look convinced.

"Just don't let her play with your head. Remember—she's the one who walked out on you."

"She sounded way off."

"She's not your problem any more."

"Come right back after you drop Lauren off. We've got to nail down these designs tonight." Matt leaned his board to the side and popped it up into his hands.

"Use your key to get in," said Jack. "I'll be back as soon as I can."

Jack and Lauren walked to Chelsea Piers quickly, and Lauren missed the dreaded pushups with a minute to spare. As soon as he saw Lauren safely inside the practice area, Jack headed to the soda machines for a Coke. He stopped when he saw a crowd standing around the plexiglass windows that overlooked the ballet studio.

"What's going on?" Jack turned to face a woman whose torso was completely covered by the baby wrapped across her chest.

"Kate Richards is filming a Zumba class. My daughter was one of the girls they picked for filming." The portly woman smiled brightly at Jack and he wondered if her daughter would turn out to be one of the more athletic kids Kate liked to use as an example or one of the overweight ones that appeared on her show looking for help. Jack knew the show's formula because he had downloaded a few episodes to watch with Lauren. He had told Lauren it was to help her get ready for filming, but he had to admit it was so he could see more of Kate.

Jack was just tall enough to peek over the heads of the

mothers who were crowded around every available bit of viewing space. He spotted Kate directly in front of the studio-mirrored wall wearing camouflage dance shorts and a matching tank with the *KidFit* logo stretched across her chest. Jack could feel the vibrations from the music beat against his forehead as he leaned on the plastic window for a closer look. Kate jumped and bounced in time to the music while the kids followed. She did a sequence of moves quickly, and then slower. Then she stopped and watched the kids. Jack couldn't hear what she was saying, but Kate was all smiles as she went around the room coaching the kids individually.

"Isn't this amazing?" asked the baby-covered mom. "My daughter Trinity is the one in the front row with the hot pink tank top. The poor kid put on a lot of weight since she hit puberty and has been really down on herself. She wrote a letter to the show and Kate invited her to come film the Zumba class. We drove all the way from West Virginia for this."

"Your daughter looks like she's having fun."

"Oh, yeah. This is all she's been talking about for weeks. She can't wait to go back to school and tell all her friends about it," said the woman, as she turned back to the window.

Jack pulled his cell phone from his back pocket. "Sorry man, I gotta bail."

"You can't keep dodging me," said Matt.

"You can be such a chick sometimes. I just remembered I have to meet with Irina tonight."

"How long is that going to take?" asked Matt. "I can stick around and watch the game till you get back."

"What game?"

"I don't know. There must be some kind of game on."

"It's probably gonna take awhile. By the time I finish with Irina I might as well stick around till Lauren's done with practice."

"We have to figure this shit out like today." Matt's usually laid back attitude was getting more and more aggressive the longer Jack held out on him.

"Relax. We can deal with it in the morning. Just pick up some bagels and coffee from Delish on your way over."

"Jack, I need to know you're on board with the upgrades."

"Let me deal with Irina tonight, and tomorrow you and I can meet up. You put the scholarship stuff in my lap every year. Don't get pissed at me for dealing with it."

"You know that shit makes me uncomfortable. I can't stand seeing Irina cry. It's so creepy—like the time the Challenger crashed and even mean Mrs. Rothschild was crying about it."

"That's why I'm handling it. So quit giving me a hard time."

Matt exhaled loudly, tickling the hairs in Jack's ear through the phone line. "I'll be at your door bright and early, so we can straighten this shit out. And tell that punk niece of yours to be ready for me to whoop her ass."

As soon as he hung up, Jack tracked down Irina Karev, head of the Chelsea Piers Fieldhouse, in her overly air conditioned office. She was wearing a black tracksuit with Capri pants that cut off right at her protruding calf muscles. The former Olympic medalist was several inches shy of five feet but could probably bench-press Jack.

"Good to see you." Irina stood up and gave Jack a tight hug. "How's David? I haven't heard from Harper since yesterday's email."

"As of this morning he could see blurred shapes. He's a fighter. Where do you think Lauren gets it from?"

"Remember the time Lauren split the beam and came crashing down during sectionals? I thought she had broken something for sure, but that kid got up, blinked the tears back and finished her routine. She's tough as nails, that little one," said Irina, her voice tinged with the remnants of her Russian accent.

"That's what I keep trying to tell my sister. Lauren can take the truth."

"Everyone handles situations like this differently. Trust Harper to figure it out in her own time."

"Listen, the reason I came by is to go over a few things for the scholarship dinner."

"You didn't have to do that tonight," said Irina. "I could've stopped by your place when it was more convenient for you."

"I was here dropping Lauren off anyway." Jack shrugged

his shoulders.

"Did you get my email with the date and location and all of that?"

"Yeah, sorry I didn't write back. All the logistics work for me. I'm still finishing up my speech. I'll email it to you in the next few days so you can let me know what you think."

"I'm sure it will be wonderful like it always is," said Irina. "I never worry about your speech."

Jack grabbed a Post-it note from Irina's desk and jotted down a number. "This is what we're working with this year." He handed the note to Irina.

Irina stared at the paper, in complete silence and practically collapsed back in her chair.

"I was thinking there was enough to start a second scholarship. We already fund the kids to do sports here. But what happens when they get old enough for college? I thought we could start a second fund to help supplement the athletes who only get partial athletic scholarships to college. Like Rachel Winter from the gymnastics team last year."

That's when the dreaded tears came. In the years since Oksana's death, the tears didn't flow as early in the discussion or as much, but Jack always knew they were coming, and the stress came with not knowing when. Coupled with the fact that Irina shoved away all forms of comfort when she was crying made for a tense situation.

"Are you sure you and Matt can afford all this?" asked Irina. "This is a big jump from last year."

"The scholarship fund is made up of a percentage of our profits. We did better last year, so the percentage is bigger. I set it up that way day one."

"I think a second scholarship is a great idea. We should have a press conference with you and Matt."

"I don't know. The scholarship isn't about all of that. Besides, Matt would be the one to do the press conference. He's really the face of the company. I'm perfectly happy keeping a low profile these days."

"Maybe if you put yourself in the spotlight more, you

wouldn't still be single." Irina shook her finger at him.

"Speaking of which, I need a favor."

"You name it kid."

"I need to borrow one of the ballet studios for an hour or two. Can you arrange that?"

"When?" asked Irina.

"Whatever time Kate Richards finishes filming today. Can you tell me when that is and then set up a room for us?"

"Why, so you can booby-trap her?" Irina raised her thin, penciled eyebrows. "I know you're probably still pissed about that business on *Smart Talk*, but don't drag me into it."

"I owe her dinner."

"What? Are you dating Kate Richards?" shrieked Irina, breaking her usual unflappable composure.

"Quiet, Irina. I owe her dinner. Let's just keep it at that." Jack turned around to make sure he had shut the office door behind him when he came in.

"How the Hell did you get her to agree to have dinner with the CEO of her most hated company?" asked Irina, her Russian accent getting thicker in her state of shock.

"Easy. She doesn't know what I do for a living and I'm trying to keep it that way just a little longer. Till she gets to know me better."

"Oh, Jack. There is no way this is going to end well."

"Can you get me the room anyway?"

"Turn up the radio and dance around the living room. Shoot some hoops or take a walk around the neighborhood. The best workout buddy for your kid might just be you."

Kate Richards, The Breakfast Nook

Chapter Fourteen

Kate was surprised to find Irina waiting for her on a bench in the coaches' locker room after filming.

"How are you, Irina?"

"I would be better if my best boys' team coach wasn't leaving us because some movie producer thinks he's going to be the next Harrison Ford."

"Craig, right? Lauren told me."

"Speaking of Lauren, you guys are filming in Studio B next Monday. Can you take a look at it to make sure the lighting will work?" Kate felt like a giant in all of her five foot three glory when Irina stood up.

"I'm sure it'll be fine."

"Check it out now, so we'll have time to move things around if the space doesn't work." Irina headed out of the locker room without even looking to see if Kate was following.

Kate hurried to catch up. They wound their way down the noisy corridor past the throng of little girls wearing starched tutus over pale pink leotards.

Irina pushed her thick industrial key into the door and opened it. "This studio doesn't have windows to keep the dance moms at bay. Look around and email me if it doesn't work."

Irina was halfway down the hall when she called back, "By

the way, the door locks automatically."

Kate walked into the dark room and felt against the wall till her fingers rubbed up against a plastic light switch and the room filled with bright fluorescent light and the low grade humming that always accompanied it.

Surprisingly, the small dance space smelled like Christmas dinner at her sister's house. The center of the dance floor was covered by a red and white checkered tablecloth and plastic take out containers.

Kate approached the food and slowly lifted the lid off the biggest container to reveal a whole roast chicken sliced and covered in translucent circles of lemon. She leaned over the container, and wondered if anyone would notice a missing drumstick. Kate froze with her hand poised over the chicken when the side door to the ballet studio opened.

Jack walked in carrying a chilled bottle of white wine and two glasses. His hair was gelled into submission except for a lone curl poking its way from the pack.

"Jack?" Kate breathed in the knowledge that this was all for her.

"Dinner from Cookshop. Since we didn't make it there the other night." Jack put the wine and glasses on the tablecloth. He pulled a lighter from his back pocket and lit the two thick candle pillars that sat a safe distance from the feast. Then, he turned off the overhead light, so the room was lit only by the candlelight that danced and reflected off the mirror's reflection.

"No one has done anything like this for me." Kate swallowed the lump in her throat. "Ever."

"Then you haven't been hanging out with the right people." Jack's charcoal gray cashmere sweater turned his eyes the color of slick gray stones from the bottom of a lake.

Jack reached for Kate's hands and gently pulled her down to the ground. Kate didn't know what it was about Jack that made her want to let him take the lead. Kate was disappointed when he let go of her hands to serve the food.

He scooped a large spoonful of mashed potatoes onto a plastic plate, followed by a bunch of crisp asparagus stalks and several slices of juicy chicken. He put the plate on the tablecloth in front of Kate's folded legs.

"How'd you pull this off? Irina has a tight hold on these practice spaces."

Jack shrugged his shoulders and filled up a plate for himself. "I helped her set up the team website. She owed me one."

"You must've done a pretty good job. You don't even want to know how much Irina charges an hour for these rooms." Kate's body rippled in an involuntary shiver from the overly air conditioned room.

"Here." Jack stood up and pulled off his sweater. His undershirt untucked from his jeans and clung to his sweater and exposed his doughy midsection that fell over the waistband of his boxers. Jack pulled the sweater over his head and sheepishly tucked his tee shirt back in. The solar system floated over the stark black shirt in vibrant primary colors. The bright yellow words *BACK IN MY DAY WE HAD* NINE *PLANETS* hovered above Mars.

"You might want to rethink that. I'm pretty sweaty." Kate shook her head and held her hand up in protest.

"I don't mind."

Jack kneeled down and bunched up the sweater in his hands. He pulled it over Kate's head. The shirt was warm with Jack's heat and as the cashmere moved across Kate's nose she could smell his evergreen soap.

As Kate pushed her hands through the sleeves, Jack dipped his hand into the sweater collar and freed Kate's curls. His warm hands wrapped in her hair made Kate think of their night together. He locked eyes with Kate and she suddenly felt short of breath.

Just when Kate though Jack was going to move in for a kiss, he pulled his gaze away and pointed to the plate that was loaded with enough food for two people. "Eat up, before it gets cold."

"This smells absolutely amazing." With the warm sweater keeping the air conditioning at bay, and the smell of lemon and herbs filling the air, Kate felt all at once like she was home. Not that she had grown up in a warm home that smelled of lovely cooking, but it was the kind of home she had always wanted.

"There were so many people crowded around the ballet windows, I thought Madonna was back with her kids again." Jack filled Kate's wine glass and handed it to her. "You have quite the following."

Kate laughed. "All those parents were there to watch their kids, not me." She took a bite of chicken and realized just how hungry she was.

"I saw a few guys out there who did not look like dads." Jack scooped a bit of mashed potatoes with a piece of chicken and ate it with a look of pure delight.

Kate laughed. "Thanks for the surprise picnic. I was starving from all that Zumba."

"Try the mashed potatoes. Fuck the calories. These are the best mashed potatoes on the West Side." Jack brought a spoonful of potatoes to Kate's lips.

He kept the spoon there until she parted her lips, and scooped the smooth potatoes off with her mouth. There was something incredibly sexy about a man who wanted to feed her.

"You're right. They're amazing!"

"How's your article coming?" Jack smiled when Kate went in for another spoonful.

"It's been nerve wracking. I mean I'm used to writing deadlines from the cookbooks. But this is different—it's the Sunday *New York Today*." Kate took a sip of the chilled wine to wash down the warm food.

"Your cookbook already made their bestseller list. They should be honored to have you as a guest writer."

"How did you know that?" Jack didn't seem to run with the *KidFit* regulars and it wasn't like his niece had any reason to watch the show.

"A handy thing I like to call Google." Jack put an extra spoonful of mashed potatoes on Kate's plate despite her groans.

"You did not Google me!"

"No, but Lauren did. I heard all about the anticipation over the sequel to *Mini-Munchies*. It sounds like people are going to line up at Barnes & Nobles at midnight like they did with that last boy wizard book."

"Did Google also say that it took me three years to write the first book and my publishers gave me six months to write the second one?"

Jack whistled. "That's a lot of pressure."

"Sure is." Kate tilted back her glass for a long sip of the smooth wine. Her stomach warmed from the food. "Thanks for surprising me. You couldn't have picked a better day to blow me away like this."

"Sticking around the other night was the coolest thing anyone's done for me." Jack put down his wine glass and smiled at Kate till that dimple popped up on his left cheek and his eyes crinkled in the corners.

"Who knew take out from a burger joint and a *Glee* marathon would turn into the most fun I've had in a long time."

"I think the real fun started after the *Glee* marathon."

Jack reached over and took hold of one of Kate's dangling waves. He swept his hand from the top of her hair down to the bottom so gently; she could barely feel his touch. Kate didn't breath till his hand came out from the curtain of hair and he opened his palm to reveal a silver foil star in it. "Where did this come from?"

"Filming. Tweenage girls are all about the shiny factor."

Jack reached for Kate's hand and put the star in it, resting his hand on top of hers. His thumb pressed into her palm and she could feel their pulses beating together.

Jack leaned forward so he was close enough for Kate to see the auburn grains of five o'clock shadow waiting to sprout on his cheeks. He brought his mouth to hers. Kate kissed him back, and he tasted like comfort food.

The worries about her cookbook revisions melted away. In this moment, all that mattered was kissing Jack.

"Fuck. I can't keep my hands off you." Jack slid the sweater off Kate and threw it across the room, narrowly missing one of the candles.

"Someone might walk in on us."

"Good thing the door's locked." Jack sent goose bumps up her skin as he pulled her workout shirt and sports bra off.

Jack's mouth was back on Kate's and she was suddenly desperate to feel his warm skin against hers. Kate slid her hands up Jack's sides, ripped his shirt off, and threw it on the floor with hers. Kate ran her hands all over his chest and back, wanting to feel every part of him that was always hidden.

The mirrored walls multiplied their candlelit reflections so that Kate could see Jack from every angle as he trailed kisses down her neck. She watched as he moved his mouth lower and tugged her nipple with his teeth.

Jack reached his hand inside her workout pants and pushed aside her thong. He stroked her button tip with his thumb till she felt a warmth rush through her whole body. He pushed his other two fingers inside her and glided them in and out, while his thumb kept stroking her most sensitive part. Kate got wetter with each thrust of his fingers.

Kate undid Jack's belt buckle desperate to have him inside her. She pulled his jeans off and slid her hands under his boxers happy to see he was ready for her.

Jack gently pushed Kate down to the floor. She lay on her back while she waited for him to pull her leggings down an inch at a time. He started at the top of the pants then froze at her hipbones, while Kate writhed on the floor. She had never wanted anyone this badly before.

By the time Jack got her pants down to her knees, she was clenching the tablecloth and gritting her teeth to keep from crying out. He took his time pulling the leggings off one foot, then the other, bringing the thong off with them.

Jack pressed his hands into the floor as he lowered himself over Kate. He found her mouth again as he pressed just the tip of himself against her. She arched her back and clenched the tablecloth as she waited for him to push himself completely in her.

Then the door handle started to turn. It was like something out of a horror movie, happening in slow motion, while they both froze.

"Jack? Are you in there?" called a voice while the locked door handle moved back and forth.

"Matt Reynolds brought my mom funny movies and buttered rolls from the deli when she was going through chemo. He taught my sister how to ride a two-wheel bike. You can't buy loyalty like that."
Jack Moskowitz, Northeastern Entrepreneur Summit

Chapter Fifteen

"Shit!" Jack jumped up.

"Who is that?" Kate whispered while she used her hands to cover her most naked parts.

"Hold on! I'll be right out!" Jack pulled his jeans on and grabbed his tee shirt. He pulled his shirt and slipped his sneakers on at the same time.

Kate crawled on the floor till she had grabbed every piece of clothing that Jack had thrown all over the room. "The one time, I try something *Fifty Shades*-ish," she muttered under her breath.

Jack leaned down and kissed Kate, quick and light on the lips. "I'll be right back."

Matt's hair stood up in rain darkened spikes and his damp shirt clung to him, illuminating the faintest hint of a burgeoning beer belly which Jack had never noticed before. He held his skateboard under the crook of his arm so that the muddy wheels left a dark mark under his armpit.

Jack grabbed Matt's arm and steered him through the corridor to the hollow spot where the Coke machine used to be, so they would be away from the dance studio.

"What're you doing here?" hissed Jack.

"It was the only way I could nail your ass down."

"I said I would meet you first thing tomorrow," said Jack. "I'm in the middle of something right now."

"Because you're dealing with Irina right?"

"Right."

"Then, how come Irina's in her office while you're hanging out in a ballet studio with the fem-bot? What the fuck's going on Jack?" Matt who was normally a close talker tended to push the boundary even more when he was angry.

"Keep your voice down. We're just having dinner." Jack took a step back and wound up crammed against the wall.

"Are you really going to stand there with your crazy sex hair, reeking of pussy and tell me you were just having dinner?"

"You're the one who told me to get to know her in the first place, so don't give me shit about this." Jack smoothed down the top of his hair.

"Seriously? I can't believe you were just banging our archenemy in a dance studio! What the fuck?!"

"Keep your voice down."

"And why did you feed me some bullshit line about meeting with Irina?"

"It's a long story. I can't get into it here—too many people."

Matt dropped his skateboard by his feet and cradled both hands on top of his wet head.

"What's really going on?" Jack knew this was about more than just him and Kate. It was clear Matt had been in meltdown mode long before he stumbled upon them in the dance studio.

"Anne's pregnant." Matt's eyes darted back and forth from Jack to his own clenched fists and back to Jack again.

"Shit, I didn't think she was dating anyone else yet." It had been bad enough when Matt had come home from a day at the skate park to find most of his apartment boxed up with a two line Dear John letter sitting on top on the empty dog crate. Anne having a baby with someone else was sure to finish the poor guy off.

"It's mine."

"Are you shitting me?"

"We had killer breakup sex the day we signed the

divorce papers."

"Let me get rid of Kate. I'll meet you at your apartment in ten."

Jack watched as Matt sloshed down the hall. He took a deep breath and smoothed his hair back.

When Jack got back to the room, Kate was tossing their emptied take out containers into the large garbage can by the ballet barre. She had all of her clothes back on and her hair pulled up in that bunch of curls that made Jack just want to rip her clothes right back off again.

"Everything okay?" Kate leaned down and blew out the candles.

"This time I really did double book myself."

"You planned another romantic picnic for Studio C?"

"I have one of those can't miss—my future hangs in the balance kind of business meetings." The lie slipped clean and smooth off Jack's lips and he realized that lying was becoming second nature to him these days.

"Web site designing, romantic dinners, business meetings, what else do you do at Chelsea Piers?"

"I scheduled it before I found out about David. With everything going on I just…"

"It's okay, Jack. I get it."

Kate grabbed one side of the tablecloth and motioned for Jack to grab the other side. Her hands touched his as they both reached to grab the halved cloth. She held her hands against his as they folded the cloth together.

"Shit. I don't want to go." Jack dropped the folded tablecloth on the floor and grabbed Kate. As soon as his mouth touched hers, Jack wanted to rip her clothes back off again. He figured Matt could wait another few minutes, or ten or twenty, couldn't he?

Kate pulled away first, the reluctance written all over her face. "You better go. Call me later." She waved her hands around the room. "I'll take care of all this."

The skies had opened up, one of those quick volatile storms that resolved just as quickly as it started. The Hudson

River was still rippled with angry waves, and the harbored boats were pockmarked with bubbles of water on the wax-coated varnish. All Jack could think about on the five-block walk to Matt's was Kate and what he would've done to her if they hadn't been interrupted.

Jack used his key when Matt didn't answer the door right away. As soon as he walked in, it hit him that he hadn't been back since Anne had first left. Sun broke through the clouds and streamed in through the uncovered windows, illuminating the shinier space on the floor where the couch had once sat. The only piece of furniture left in the living room was the battered leather armchair Matt and Jack had rescued off the corner of Ninth and 23rd Street when Matt had first moved in. The chair had always been a bone of contention between Anne and Matt, so Jack wasn't surprised that Anne had left it behind.

Matt walked into the bare living room in a dry tee shirt and gray cargo pants, vigorously rubbing a towel through his water darkened hair.

"Hey man. How you holding up?"

"I feel like I'm having one of those weird dreams where you know you're dreaming but you can't wake yourself up. I am really awake right?"

Jack punched Matt in the arm.

"Dude! What the fuck?"

"You're awake."

"Bastard." Matt lunged for Jack, but Jack was too quick for him.

"This whole thing is crazy. You guys were trying for two years with no luck. Then one round of break up sex and Anne's pregnant."

"It wasn't really once. It was more like…" started Matt.

"I really don't need the details."

"I just don't get why it never worked before. I had sex with her every time that damn pee stick said she was ovulating." Matt plopped down in his chair and opened the mini black fridge left over from his time in the dorms. He pulled out two Heinekens and handed one to Jack.

"Remember that God awful fertility tea she bought from that quack in Chinatown? That shit smelled like dirty socks."

"You don't want to know what it tasted like." Matt shuddered.

"What about the book Anne got with all those poses that were supposed to help get her pregnant? I made a mental note not to try any of those."

"She got that book in the beginning, when it was all still good."

"It was great for a long time with you guys. Anne just lost her shit when she couldn't get pregnant."

"I knew we were in trouble when she started buying pregnancy tests at Costco. There would be four or five negative test strips lined up on the counter when I came home from work."

"Do you think she had sex with you to try one last time for a baby?"

"Hell no. It wasn't that premeditated. Trust me. I haven't seen pubes like that since the last time I checked out my collection of '80s *Playboy*s."

"Way too much information, man."

"She wants to raise the baby alone." The remnants of Matt's smile dimmed.

"What do you want?" asked Jack, before taking a long pull of his beer.

"Anne. The baby. All of it. I just need to prove to her that she should take me back. And that's not going to happen if we fuck up this new line and sink the business."

"Who said anything about sinking the business?"

"Says the guy who's been dragging his feet and whining like a pussy in between his sexcapades with the Ann Coulter of childhood obesity."

"My questioning the new line has nothing to do with Kate."

"But it has everything to do with Anne and the baby. She thinks I've been a drunk fuck up since she left."

"You kinda have been."

"Asshole! I got my shit together and nothing's gonna prove that to Anne like some kickass numbers with the new line."

Matt's hoarse voice was laced with desperation.

Jack brought his beer down to the dusty floor and sat down on his haunches. "The new line's solid. I'm in."

"Fuck yeah!" Matt shouted in a voice left over from his high school football days.

"We need to meet with the marketing team to make sure we go at this the right way." Jack took a long sip of beer. "I still have my concerns about the company's image."

"Whatever. Let me handle that. I need you to focus all of your energy on getting those designs done."

"The damn undercarriage keeps tripping me up. We need to use more metal this time around to support all the extra weight."

"You'll figure it out. You always do." Matt finished his last drop of beer and grabbed two more from the fridge. "Now that we got that straightened out, can you tell me what the fuck's going on with you and the fem-bot?"

"I don't know man. It just happened." Jack shook his head, thinking back to that day at the dog park. It was all over the minute he saw Kate. "And stop calling her that."

"I have a few other choice names for her. She-Devil, Anti-Christ, Skinny Bitch …"

"If only you were this creative with stroller names."

"How does it just happen with a bitch who's been bad mouthing our company to anyone who will listen? You know it just wasn't *Straight Talk* right? She's been on Twitter too saying all sorts of crap."

"She's cool as shit when she's not talking about strollers."

"Clearly she still doesn't know who you are. What the fuck does Kate Richards think you do for a living?"

"I told her I freelance for dot coms."

"The dot com bubble burst over a decade ago. She must be a total moron!"

"She had no reason to think I would lie to her. That doesn't make her stupid. It makes me a douchebag." Jack finished off his beer and cracked open the second one Matt had put in front of him.

"I just don't get it." Matt shook his head. "She's declared all out warfare on our company. What are you thinking?"

"I haven't felt this way about anyone since Stephanie Riggins. You know the one…"

"How could I forget the med student who got away? We're fucked."

"Tell me about it. I've gotten myself in deeper and deeper and as soon as she finds out I lied to her it's all over."

"You shouldn't have slept with her. Trust me, I never thought that would be coming out of my mouth. But she's going to be ripshit when she finds out you lied about who you were and slept with her."

"You don't have to tell me that. What the fuck do I do now?"

Matt stood up with a loud groan and stretched. He rolled a basketball out from under the couch and started rapid fire dribbling back and forth across the hard wood floor. He made it to the window and back four times before the downstairs neighbor thumped the ceiling with what sounded like a baseball bat.

"Those assholes from downstairs never leave the apartment! I can't take a shit without them complaining."

"I'm fucked. I'm totally fucked." Jack polished off the last sip of beer and let out a loud burp.

"Don't tell her who you are just yet. The more attached she gets, the harder it'll be for her to leave your ass when she finds out what a lying bastard you are."

"The hardest thing for a control freak to do is let go."
                    Kate Richards, Sportif! Magazine

Chapter Sixteen

"I just walked past the dog park and thought of you."

Kate could hear speeding cars on the West Side Highway competing with Jack's voice.

"Why Jack, you know all the right things to say to a woman."

"I have two words you're really going to love then." Jack was quiet for a minute. "Notice the dramatic pause there."

"All right. You piqued my curiosity."

"Sleep. Over."

"I think that's only one word. And I can't tonight. I'm scared I won't have this article done in time."

"Lauren's sleeping over at Madison's this Saturday night. Which means she'll be at practice all day Saturday and gone for the night."

"So does that mean we can go on an actual date?" As much as Kate liked Lauren, it would be nice to get some alone time with Jack. Especially because they needed to finish what they started at the ballet studio the other night.

"Yes. Maybe we can get really kinky and actually try the bed out."

Kate laughed. "You really do know all the right things to say."

"You better spend the rest of this week getting that article done so you can relax with me on Saturday."

"I plan on it. What are we going to do?"

"I have it all planned out. Wear workout clothes."

"Hmm. Are we going for a run together?"

"No."

"Barry's Bootcamp in Central Park?"

"No."

"Soul Cycle?"

"Hasn't a guy ever surprised you before?"

"I don't like surprises."

"You'll love this one. Trust me."

Kate spent the rest of the week finishing the article, reading it over and rewriting it. She was up all Thursday night revising it and finally submitted it Friday morning right before filming. Jack was busy working on a big job all week so he didn't have time to hang out either. They were relegated to texts, emails and phone conversations where neither one of them wanted to be the one to hang up first.

Kate woke up on Saturday morning dying to know what kind of date required workout clothes. She took a long hot shower and tried to let go of all the stress of the week. She was really looking forward to spending the night with Jack without any interruptions.

Kate pulled on her black Capri length running pants and a teal sleeveless workout top. She grabbed her black zip up hoodie and was ready to go.

Jack was waiting in the white leather chair by the front desk. He was wearing a fitted blue long sleeved workout shirt with long black spandex running pants and sneakers. He layered a gray tee shirt over the workout ensemble. The tee shirt had a big round Buddha in the middle with the caption *I Have the Body of a God.*

"Whoa. You really look like you're ready for a hard core workout."

"You're not the only one around here who owns actual exercise clothes."

"You're starting to freak me out a little here. Please tell me we're not going on one of those sixty-mile bike rides. The one thing I really can't do is ride a bike."

"The queen of fitness never learned to ride a bike?"

"My dad pawned our bikes to pay off a bookie."

"We're not riding bikes today. But I promise to teach you another day."

"That's okay. I'm perfectly happy doing activities that keep my feet on the ground."

"Then you might be a little disappointed with what I planned. Oh, and you really should pull your hair back."

Kate pulled the rubber band off her wrist off and pulled all her damp curls into a long ponytail.

"Follow me." Jack led Kate out the lobby and headed west towards the Hudson River.

"I knew we were doing something at Chelsea Piers. I'm just hoping it's not golf because I suck at golf."

"You couldn't be further off than golf." Jack chuckled. "And we're not going to Chelsea Piers. I spend enough time at that place already."

They walked along the Chelsea Piers complex, past the field house, bowling alley and golf range and continued walking downtown along the Hudson River. Kate stopped worrying about where they were going and just enjoyed the quiet comfort of walking with Jack.

Jack finally stopped in front of the ladders that climbed high above the city skyline where wooden trapezes hung from ropes, waiting for someone bold enough to come along and swing from them.

"Are you serious?"

"I bet no other man has ever taken you on a date at The New York City Trapeze School." Jack's dimple appeared as his mouth stretched into a wide smile. He looked so proud of himself that Kate tried her best to ignore the thumping in her chest.

"You are so right about that." Kate rubbed her hands together to get rid of that pins and needles feeling that always came when she was absolutely panic-stricken.

"It's exhilarating to get up there above everything."

"Wait. You've done this before?" The more Kate learned about Jack, the more she realized just how much she didn't know about this man.

"I took Lauren here for her birthday as a surprise. I figured I would just pay for her lesson and watch. But she begged me to try it with her."

"Just out of curiosity—what do you love about swinging in the air hundreds of feet above everything?"

"You'll have to try it to see for yourself. Trust me." Jack held on to Kate's hand and walked her to the entrance to the trapeze school.

Kate spent the next hour learning how to work her safety harness, how to hold onto the trapeze the right way and how to position her body. She was so busy learning how to use the trapeze that she didn't have too much time to be nervous.

After passing her safety test, Kate stood at the bottom of the ladder. Jack grabbed both of her hands. "Listen to me. You know you're physically strong enough to do this. You also have a safety harness and a net to catch you. You are not going to get hurt. This is really about just letting go."

"If anything happens to me, you better take care of Sarah Jessica Barker for me." Kate dropped Jack's hands and took the first step up the ladder. The wind pushed against her as she made her way up the narrow rungs. The higher she went; the smaller Jack looked below.

Gwen, a blond instructor with a pixie cut was waiting for her at the top. She reminded Kate of Peter Pan, especially when she did a few demonstration swings to show Kate what to do. "You ready?"

"Yes. No. Wait a minute." Kate stood on the small wooden platform and looked out over the West Side Highway. She breathed in and felt the wind wrap around her. She closed her eyes and calmed her breathing down.

"Come on, Kate! You can do it!" Jack looked absolutely tiny from where he yelled below.

Gwen handed Kate the trapeze, and the wood felt hard and cold in her hand. "Remember to thrust your hips out and kick your feet forward."

Kate stepped off the platform and felt the wind rush at her

face as she flew. Survivor instincts kicked in and she pointed her toes and thrust her hips out so that the momentum would swing her all the way to the other end of the net. Then, all at once she was rushing back to where she started, her body resisting the air around her. Kate felt a rush as she pushed herself back to the other side and threw her feet up and tucked them under the bar. Kate wrapped her legs around the trapeze and hung from it like a little kid on the monkey bars. She felt a rush of exhilaration, as she swung back and forth high above the city.

"Let go Kate! Let go!" Jack yelled from hundreds of feet below.

Kate let go of the bar and swung with her hands hanging down towards the net. She swung back again, suspended in the air. When the momentum started to die down she pulled her hands back on the bar and flipped off, landing on the net with her feet. The net dipped low to the ground as she landed then swung her back up.

"You did amazing!" Jack helped pull Kate back to the ground.

"That was the most unbelievable thing I've ever done!" Kate felt the endorphins rush through her like the time she had run the New York marathon. She felt all the stress rush out of her body at once.

"Get back up there and do it again!" Jack cheered on Kate as she went back up on the trapeze again and again until her arms were practically numb. Each time she got a bigger thrill out of it than the time before. "Okay, I'm finally done hogging the trapeze. It's your turn." Kate pushed Jack towards the ladder.

Kate watched as Jack climbed up the ladder with no obvious trepidation. He got on the platform and stood there for a second before grabbing the trapeze. He propelled himself forward, his legs together and toes pointed, then shot backward much faster than Kate had felt like she had gone. His legs wrapped over the bar and instantly he was hanging upside down.

Kate looked toward the other platform and realized Gwen had already climbed up while Jack was swinging. She jumped off the platform and swung toward Jack. Kate covered her eyes and peeked through her fingers, scared that they would crash into each other. But Gwen just soared right back towards Jack's platform. Synchronized, they both flew towards each other and Gwen moved her knees on the trapeze so her arms were suspended like Jack's. They both soared back towards their own platforms—mirror images of each other then, they flew back together.

Jack reached over and grabbed Gwen's hands as she leapt off her trapeze. Jack held on tight as Gwen flew with him, as if they were one body. Then Gwen tucked her knees in tight and did a back tuck off the bar. Jack was all alone now swinging back and forth. He let go of the bar and did a double back flip off it. He bounced and landed on his butt before pulling himself off the net.

"So, you've only done this like once or twice?" Kate asked as soon as Jack was back in her altitude.

"Give or take a few times." There went that lopsided grin again.

"What? Why didn't you tell me?" asked Kate.

"I wanted you to feel relaxed. You and I are going to do that now."

"What?" There went that pounding in Kate's chest again.

"You already know how to swing back and forth. Now you just have to trust me to catch you."

"Trust being the key word here."

"You saw me catch Gwen, so you know I can do it." Jack looked at Kate as if he just expected her to do it. As if there was not reason not to. He locked his eyes into hers and she just couldn't say no.

Kate climbed up the ladder, her hands shaking so hard that the rope ladder was trembling in anticipation with her. Kate focused on grabbing each rung and pulling herself forward further and further above the city.

She took a deep yoga breath before stepping on the platform where Gwen was waiting for her. Jack seemed miles away on his own platform when he smiled and waved at her. "You can do this Kate." Gwen held the trapeze in one hand.

"Jack will catch you."

Kate stepped off the platform and thrust her hips forward, shooting her body towards Jack's platform where he stood watching her. She pushed her legs forward as hard as she could so that the momentum allowed her to pull her knees up to the trapeze on the way back toward her platform. She wrapped her knees around the trapeze and dropped her hands off the bar. She swung back while Jack jumped off his platform. Kate flinched as he swung towards her but his body shot backward before he came anywhere near her. He wrapped his knees around his trapeze as he flew backwards. Then, he swung towards Kate with his arms reaching toward her.

"Grab my hands, when I get close!" Jack yelled as he flew in the air.

Kate flew away from her platform towards Jack, her hands reaching toward him. He flew toward her with his hands outstretched. "Now! Grab my hands!"

But Kate couldn't do it. She couldn't grab Jack's hands because that meant letting go of her own trapeze. She drifted towards him and shot right back. "I can't Jack!"

"Yes you can! I promise to catch you." He headed back towards Kate his hands ready to catch hers. She reached her hands towards him as she pushed her body forward. The tips of her fingers were just about to touch his when she pulled her hands back. "I can't!"

"Yes, you can. Just let go!"

They swung towards each other again. "You can do it! I'll catch you!" Jack yelled as he pushed his body towards her a determined look on his upside down face. He pushed his hands towards Kate's. She reached her hands towards his and grabbed on. Jack wrapped his hands around hers and grabbed on tight.

Kate held onto Jack with a ferocious grip and unwrapped her legs from her own trapeze bar. Jack held onto her as she swung with him, their bodies becoming one. "I have you Kate. I'm not letting go."

"The one good thing about my dad leaving when I was a kid is that he didn't have the chance to disappoint me when I became an adult."
Jack Moskowitz, rock-a-buy-baby.com

Chapter Seventeen

"That was amazing! I never thought I would be flying from a trapeze." Kate pressed her fork into her plate of seared tuna and pulled off a moist, flaky bite.

"You were a natural." Jack spun his fork around a spiral of angel hair and grabbed a small piece of shrimp before bringing the forkful to his mouth.

"I think you were the natural up there. How did you get so damn good at the trapeze?"

"I go whenever I need to unwind." Jack pulled off a slice of warm multi-grain bread and spread a thin smear of honey butter on it and handed it to Kate. "Clearly I need to unwind pretty often."

"I could see how you could get hooked. Talk about a great stress reliever!" Kate took a bite of the bread and closed her eyes with a look of pure contentment.

"The trapeze is great because all you can really focus on is what you're doing, so you're forced to let all the other stress go. You have to be in the moment. You should try it again sometime."

"Oh, I will." Kate was tearing into her mixed greens salad when her phone rang from its spot next to her plate. Kate picked up the phone and slid the touch screen bar over to decline the call. She put the phone back on the table, but her eyes didn't leave it.

"So, what were we saying?" Kate cleared her throat and looked up. Her eyes were dull when she met Jack's gaze.

"That you need to go back there again sometime on your own."

Kate looked back down at her phone as soon as she heard the message alert sound.

"Not sure who that was, but it looks like you're not going to relax till you see what they want."

"It's my dad who…" The phone rang again cutting Kate off.

"You better get that." Jack smiled at Kate to show her he didn't mind.

"What's going on Pop?" Kate leaned away from the table and spoke quietly. A line Jack hadn't noticed before appeared between her eyes.

"How much?" Kate's voice was low, almost a whisper.

"I said how much?" Kate spoke a little louder this time and shook her head. "I'm going to have to go to like three ATMs to get that much cash."

"Where are you?" Kate pressed her fingers into her temple.

"Put him on the phone. Just put him on the phone Pop."

"Listen asshole, I'm good for the money. I'll be there in twenty minutes. But if you lay one finger on my dad, you won't get a cent. You understand?" Kate's voice sounded powerful and strong, while her eyes welled up with tears.

"Not one finger." Kate hung up the phone and put it on the table.

"Kate," Jack started.

"I have to go." Kate closed her eyes for a second and when she opened them they were dry.

Jack signaled for the waitress to bring the check and he pulled his wallet out. "Where are we going?"

"We aren't going anywhere. I have to go pay off a bookie for my father. Trust me. You really don't want to get involved." Kate pulled her wallet out and counted the few bills in there. "Shit."

The waitress came over and Jack handed her his credit card as soon as she handed him the black pleather bill holder. "Are you kidding me? Paying off a bookie is number twenty-seven on my bucket list."

"It's just a regular day in my life." Kate stood up and zipped up her warm up jacket.

Kate was right. She had to use three different ATM cards to get enough cash.

"I get the feeling this isn't the first time you've done this," said Jack, after Kate withdrew the last thick wad of cash.

"And every time I tell myself it's the last." Kate added the new stack of bills to her left pocket. She had another stash tucked in her right pocket, and two more piles in both her pants pockets. The stack of money was too big to fit in any one pocket without attracting a mugger.

"What makes you keep helping him?"

"The last time I practiced tough love, he was beaten to within an inch of his life. So, now when my sixty-eight year old father calls and begs me to bring money so some bookie doesn't kill him, I come."

Kate flagged down a cab and instructed the driver to head East to Avenue A. She was quiet the whole car ride. Jack reached for her hand, but she clenched her hands in her lap and looked out the window.

The cabbie dropped them off in front of a dive bar with an old wooden sign that said Salerno's. The sidewalk was littered with smashed cigarette butts and the air was thick with secondhand nicotine trailing from the two men wearing paint splattered jeans and construction boots.

"Thanks." Kate nodded to the taller construction worker who opened the door for them.

Kate headed straight to the bar, weaving her way between the men crowded around TV screens with different games and horse races splashed on them.

Kate walked over to a painfully thin man who was leaning over a glass of melting ice at the bar. He wore a simple red tee shirt over jeans with no sign of a jacket to ward off the cool night. Jack thought it looked like the guy had probably been out placing bets since the warm daylight hours.

"You with him?" asked the young guy behind the bar. "Cause he's got like a two hundred dollar tab. I threatened to call the cops but he said he had someone coming."

"Did you buy the whole bar drinks?" Kate pulled a small stack of bills off the top of the pile from her warm up jacket pocket. "Good thing I thought to bring a little extra."

"He bought shots for everyone when he was up." The guy took the cash and wasted no time counting it. His eyes widened and he quickly pulled the extra cash off the top and pocketed it. "Thanks."

"I'm so sorry Katie." The man looked at Kate with bloodshot eyes. "It was a sure thing. I swear."

"It's always a sure thing with you, Pop." There was no reproach in Kate's weary voice.

"Who's this guy you got here with you?" Kate's father pushed his glass aside and sat up straighter in his stool.

"This is Jack. We were out having dinner."

"Nice to meet you Jack. Eddie Richards." Kate's father reached out his hand and Jack shook it. When Eddie stood up, he wasn't much taller than Kate. He had thick white hair with strands of fading yellow running through it and a red beefy face with jowls. His face reminded Jack of a bulldog, but his body was rail thin.

"Thanks for coming sweetie." Eddie smiled at Kate and Jack could see his silver capped molars.

"It's not like you gave me much choice." Kate lowered her voice. "I can't keep doing this Pop."

"It won't happen again. It was just one of those sure things that went south." Eddie turned his smile to Jack. "You know how it goes."

Jack didn't want to smile back at Eddie, because he certainly didn't know how it goes, but Eddie had that same contagious smile Kate did.

A tall heavy-set man wearing a blue, velour warm up suit sidled up between Kate and Eddie. His sneakers looked like they had been scrubbed with white shoe polish. "Hey, beautiful. You a friend of Eddie's?" The man reached over and patted Eddie on the back with his thick ham hock of a hand, his gold pinky ring twinkling in the dim bar lights.

"Let's make this quick," cut in Jack. "You the person who

Eddie owes money?" He wrapped his arm around Kate's back and pulled her back an inch or two.

"Who the Hell are you?"

"I'm the person who's about to help make you two grand richer."

"What the fuck you wearing?" The guy stopped and stared at Jack's workout clothes. "What kinda guy wears tights to a bar?"

Kate pulled wads of cash from all her pockets and pushed the money in the guy's hand. "Does it really matter what we're wearing?"

The man licked his thumb and then used it to rifle through the cash, counting as he sifted the bills. "Nah. I guess not."

The man patted Eddie on the back. "Nice meeting you Eddie. Let's do this again sometime."

"You might want to think twice about that," said Jack. "Eddie here is broke, and he just tapped out his personal ATM machine. So he's a waste of time."

The man shrugged, "Guys like this always find a game."

"Let's go, Pop." Kate put her arm around her father and guided him away from the bookie.

Jack led the way through the throng of people dancing and singing out loud to one of Meatloaf's greatest hits.

"I could've sworn it was a sure thing." Eddie almost shouted so he could be heard over the music.

"I know you did Pop." Kate sighed, as she nudged her father out the door.

"It's so dark out here. What time is it?" Eddie squinted up at the sky and looked around at the night scene spilling out on the streets around them. He shivered and rubbed his hands up his arms.

"It's almost eleven. Does Jen know where you are?"

"Your sister's gonna kick me out for sure this time. She doesn't like me getting home late and waking the kids up."

"Oh yeah, it's the waking up the kids part that burns her," Kate muttered under her breath.

Jack followed Kate and her father as they headed west.

"You can spend the night with me. I'll call Jen and

straighten things out with her if you promise to go to a meeting tomorrow morning."

"You're not gonna tell her I slipped right? She said the OTB thing was the last straw."

"Relax. I'll talk to her. But first thing in the morning we're going to a meeting at that church on West 4th Street."

"I hate the meetings there. That asshole who cleaned out his mother-in-law's bank account always talks too much."

"That's not why you hate the meetings there. It's because the leader always calls you out on your bullshit. You're going to a meeting there or no deal."

Eddie turned to face Jack. "This daughter of mine drives a hard bargain."

"Take it or leave it Pop." Kate cut in, her voice low but strong.

"Got time for a bite to eat with your old man first?" Like most addicts, Eddie looked like the only thing he really took the time to nourish was his addiction. Jack had the feeling that the guy hadn't eaten in at least 48 hours.

"There's a Gray's Papaya around the corner." Kate didn't wait for an answer and just kept walking.

"That's my girl." Eddie smiled at Jack. "She knows how much I love chili cheese dogs."

"When he loses. Bacon cheeseburgers when he wins." Kate's blond ponytail bounced against her back in time to her brisk walk.

Jack and Eddie followed Kate to the well-lit Gray's Papaya that was only a block away from the gamblers' den. Jack grabbed seats for them at the counter while Kate got on line. She turned around and smiled at Jack, but when Kate turned back towards the counter Jack caught another look at her in the mirror over the register. She stared straight ahead with her mouth pinched and her eyes glazed over. The girl behind the counter plopped a hot dog smothered in chili and bright yellow cheese sauce on the tray next to a large paper cup of grape soda. Kate took a breath so deep; Jack could see her shoulders move underneath her coat. Then she turned back around with a big smile on her face.

"Most people think addicts don't give up their vice because they love it. But really addicts hate what they do, and hate themselves for not having control over their addiction."

Kate Richards, Breathe Magazine

Chapter Eighteen

Kate walked her father down to the church basement rec room that smelled like sweaty kids and stale coffee. The folding chairs were set up in a semi-circle where a few men sat wordlessly spaced far apart from each other. All three of them looked like they had gone directly from the racetrack to the meeting. One of them sat hunched over with his head in his lap.

"When was the last time we went out to breakfast—just the two of us? Without your sister and the kids?" Eddie gestured around the room. "You don't need to be hanging around people like this."

"But you do, Pop." Kate backed toward the door. "I'll be outside on the stoop."

Eddie smirked at her. "Got your warning loud and clear, sister. Don't worry, I'm not gonna try and give you the slip."

A tall man with silver dreads that rivaled Dana's walked over to them. "Long time no see! How you been man?"

Eddie responded with a high five followed by a few hearty slaps on the back.

"I had to meet him in at some dive bar in Alphabet City last night with two grand to pay off a bookie." Kate wanted to make sure Eddie shared at that meeting whether he wanted to or not.

"One last hurrah before that in patient shit huh?"

Kate inched her way out the door, while the group leader walked her father to one of the metal folding chairs.

She walked back outside and planted herself on the stoop in front of the only door where you could enter or exit the church. She was no dummy, or at least she wasn't since that one time her she had dropped her dad off and he had snuck out to a card game with two other men.

She tucked herself into the corner of the stoop and pulled out her cell phone. "Hi Jen."

"I can't believe you bailed him out again!" Jen's voice was hushed and Kate could hear a soccer whistle tweeting in the background.

"You remember what happened the last time I pulled the tough love card. His jaw was wired shut for six weeks!"

"He's never going to stop as long as he has you to pay off the bookies."

"He's sick Jen."

"And he's never going to get better with you enabling him."

"He's at a meeting now. His sponsor's gonna meet him at Grand Central after."

"So you get to save the day once again while I'm the bitch who has to enforce the house rules."

"I told you this would happen if he lived with you. You don't have to let him stay. I can put him up somewhere."

"As much as he drives us crazy, the kids love having him around. Besides, you can't afford to cover his rent, pay off his bookies and pay for rehab."

"This was his one last binge before rehab. I told him yesterday they would have a bed ready for him by Monday. That's what must've set him off."

All of a sudden a dog ran up the stairs and jumped on top of Kate, licking her face and almost knocking the phone out of her hand. It took her a minute before she realized it was Diesel.

"Jen. I have to go. Pop will be on the 11:35."

"Okay. I'll text you to let you know he made it home."

Jack wore a broken-in pair of black cords with grey Converse low tops. The centerpiece of his royal blue tee shirt was a conversation bubble that said *Autocorrect is DUCKED Up.*"

"I'd love to know where you buy all your crazy tee shirts."

"Ironicteeshirts.com." Jack smirked through his Sunday morning stubble and Kate couldn't tell if he was kidding or not.

"Seriously, what're you doing here?" Kate picked up Diesel and snuggled him into her lap. She scratched the top of his head while he let out little grunts of delight.

"There's only one church on West 4th Street that has Gamblers Anonymous meetings on Sunday mornings." Jack handed Kate a takeout cup of coffee.

"Thanks Jack. I really needed my caffeine fix." Kate took a sip and it was exactly how she liked it. A little soymilk and a pinch of cinnamon. Jack must've remembered from when they grabbed coffee after her trapeze lesson.

"You look like you could use some breakfast too." Jack pulled two wax paper wrapped bagels from the bag.

"Thanks!" Kate unwrapped the glossy paper covering and found a warm everything bagel smothered in vegetable cream cheese. "You're always feeding me."

Jack shrugged. "What can I say? I like to take care of you."

"Sorry about last night. When you said sleepover, I'm sure my dad staying at my place was not what you had in mind."

"What would one of our dates be without some family member crashing it?" Jack settled next to the stoop with Kate. "How's your dad doing this morning?"

"Humiliated, remorseful, ashamed. Swears it was the last time." Kate took a bite of her bagel, relishing in the crunch of the chunks of vegetables mixed in the smooth cream cheese. There was nothing like a hot bagel on a sucky morning.

"I'm guessing you've heard it all before." Jack tore a piece off his bagel and handed it to Diesel who scarfed it right down.

"Hundreds of times. But as long as he feels bad the next day I feel like there's hope." Kate wrapped her hands around the cup of coffee feeling it warm up the tips of her fingers. Diesel settled his head down in Kate's lap.

"You're right. That means a part of him still wants to get better." Jack shrugged and took a bite of his bagel.

"I enrolled him in an in-patient treatment program upstate. He starts Monday." Kate took another bite of her bagel, surprised at how hungry she was. She hadn't even thought about food until Jack showed up.

"Ahh. I get it. This like when a drug addicts ODs right before they check into rehab."

"Exactly. I shouldn't be surprised. Is that *New York Today*?" Kate pulled the newspaper out of the Bagel Time bag.

"Yeah. I couldn't remember if your piece came out today or next Sunday." Jack pulled Diesel's leash to get the dog away from a piece of gum he was about to peel off the step.

"Next week. But I don't need an excuse to read the gossip section." Kate opened the paper and turned the pages smudging black ink on her thumb and index finger. "Reading trashy gossip is one of my guilty pleasures."

"Holy shit Jack! Listen to this!" Kate cleared her throat for dramatic effect. "Spotted: New York's favorite kids' fitness guru flying on a trapeze with a mystery man. Has our exercise princess finally found her prince?"

Jack didn't laugh like Kate thought he would. Instead he sat there with his mouth open, his last piece of bagel out in his hand ripe for Diesel to come and snatch, which of course he did.

"Do you have to look so horrified?"

"I'm sorry." Jack scratched his head and raked his fingers through his curls. "I'm just not used to being in the paper."

"This is nothing. The last blind piece about me went something like this: which kids' fitness expert was caught raiding the ice cream section at Trader Joe's? Will she eat her way to a cancelled show?"

Jack didn't laugh like Kate thought he would. He brushed the bagel crumbs off his lap and took a deep breath. "Kate. We need to talk."

"Hold that thought Jackie boy. My daughter here needs to get me to the train station." Eddie burst through the door at the head of the group of men coming through the doors. The men couldn't get out of the church fast enough, pulling packs of cigarettes out of their back pockets.

"Jack can we talk about this later?" Kate stood up and gave him a quick kiss. "Thanks for breakfast."

Eddie reached over and patted Jack on the shoulder. "You're a good man Jack." He turned to Kate. "You better hold on to this one."

"My absolute favorite book character of all time is Atticus Finch from To Kill a Mockingbird. *He was a hero because he did something he really didn't want to do because it was the right thing and no one else was brave enough to do it."*

Jack Moskowitz, Uncle of Lauren from Room 4B,
Chelsea Prep Book Day

Chapter Nineteen

"Hey kid—great job on the bars!" Jack bumped Lauren's chalk covered fist. As always by the end of practice, the white powder had formed handprints and abstract designs on her shiny leotard.

"Thanks. I worked on my Giant so I can do it for the show." Lauren leaned down and rubbed Diesel's ears. The length of Diesel's tongue hung out of his mouth as he panted in delight.

"Kate's going to be really impressed," said Jack. "Put your hoody on."

"It's too hot." But Lauren unknotted the neon green sweatshirt from the waistband of her mesh shorts and pulled it on when Jack raised his eyebrow.

"Can I have a snack?" Lauren walked towards the vending machine outside the field house.

"You need real food after a workout."

"Anything but Moroccan Delight again. I don't think my stomach can take it." Lauren wrapped her arms around her midsection and rolled her eyes.

"How about a burger?"

"Yes!" Lauren pumped both hands in the air and led the way to the organic food truck parked at the entrance to the pier.

"You hold onto Diesel. I'll get your food." Jack handed the leash to Lauren and the dog was more than happy to go with her. Lauren walked Diesel over to the open space by the water where they would have room to work on their new trick. Lauren had spent the past week trying to teach Diesel how to stand up on two paws and dance with her. She was hoping to get the act ready in time for the mid-year talent show at Chelsea Prep.

As soon as Jack got to the food truck he pulled out his phone.

"Can't talk now," panted Matt.

"Do you seriously have to answer the phone during sex?"

"I'm on the treadmill, Douchebag."

"It's not like that would've been the first time."

"I still haven't convinced Anne to take me back yet. And she's throwing up like every five seconds. What's got you all fired up?"

"*New York Today* ran a blind item about me and Kate."

"Shit. Did it sound like they knew who you are?"

"No."

"All right. That buys us a little time."

"Just enough time for me to tell her who I am. I'm heading over there later to tell her in person."

"You've gotta sit tight one more week, buddy. Just till after the press release."

"Who said anything about doing the press release this week?"

"We need to do the press conference before next weekend."

"Why?"

"Don't worry about it. I already set it up for Friday night. I was going to call you as soon as I finished working out."

"What are you going to show the reporters? A pile of crumpled up pieces of drawing paper?"

"You better pull some shit together before then. We need to officially announce our new line."

"I have to tell Kate who I am before our press release."

"We don't need the tabloids getting wind of this shit. It'll be a huge distraction from the new line."

"Kate's not going to the tabloids."

"Chicks are a whole different species when they've been scorned. How do you think Anne ended up with so much in the divorce?"

"That's different. I've only known Kate for a few weeks."

"Trust me, all women are the same when they feel like you screwed them over. Anne was perfectly reasonable about dividing assets till she found out I slept with that waitress from Tao. Next thing I knew she ended up with half of my half of the profits from our company."

"Shit. And you didn't even cheat on her. That was after you were separated."

"Exactly my point. She left me, then I finally move on and she couldn't handle it."

"Does she know about all the other women you've been with since then?"

"When was I supposed to bring that up? After she told me she was pregnant, but before I begged her to take me back?"

"Shit. How did we get ourselves in these situations?"

"Think about it. Not telling Kate means you have one more week for her to get attached to you."

"It also means I'll get more attached to her, and it'll suck even worse when she dumps my ass."

"You're not telling Kate who you are until after the press conference. I'll handle it like I usually do. You stay behind the scenes. Trust me man."

"I've got no problem being behind the scenes."

"We need to set up the website for pre-orders," said Matt. "Show our customers we're not fucking around."

"Pre-orders? I don't even have the final designs drawn up."

"Who cares? We just need to throw one good picture up there with a list of all the new features. Don't you remember when the new VW Bug came out? People were lined up to order them based on one sketch."

"I don't think that's entirely accurate."

"We just need one good computerized drawing on the site. The new stroller can spin around with some cool music playing in the background. Then we can have the countdown for when it hits the stores ticking off in the corner."

"I can pull something together by Friday if I don't take any time out to eat, sleep or take a shit. I gotta go. Lauren's food is up."

Jack layered pickles, ketchup and mustard on Lauren's turkey burger. He deposited a dollar into the tip jar and grabbed the burger, bag of Smart Chips and icy cold water bottle off the counter.

Jack turned away from the food truck and his stomach lurched when he didn't see Lauren and Diesel in the same spot where he had left them. He turned quickly back towards the field house and didn't see them there either.

"Have you seen a little girl with a small brown and white dog?" Jack turned towards a mom holding a wriggling toddler.

She adjusted the little boy higher on her hip with a slight hip bounce and pointed to the water. "I saw a little girl over by those benches. The blue ones by the water."

Jack turned around and spotted Diesel tied up to the bench next to the tour boat stand. He exhaled loudly when he spotted Lauren standing by the railing lining the water's edge.

"Thanks." He called over his shoulder and took off in a sprint.

Lauren stood with both hands on her hips, her left shoulder angled towards the camera, the Hudson River as her backdrop. It was the same modeling pose Harper used in a lot of her print work. At first, Jack thought Lauren was with one of her gym friends. They loved to get in goofy poses and take pictures of each other with their cell phones, iTouches and all their other gadgets. They were all obsessed with Instagram these days. But as Jack got closer, he realized a man he didn't recognize was taking Lauren's picture.

As soon as Jack got to Lauren, the man lowered his camera.

Lauren broke her pose as soon as she spotted Jack. "OMG, Uncle Jack! I'm going to be in a magazine!"

The photographer hastily hit a button and the lens slowly moved back towards the camera base. He took two steps away from Lauren.

"What magazine are you from?" Jack walked between Lauren and the man.

"He said he could get me on the cover of *Sportastic!*" Lauren shouted over the chatterings of the crowd standing on the pier waiting to board the day cruise boat behind them.

"He did huh?" Jack turned back towards the man. "Where's your press badge?"

"Forgot it at home." The man shifted his overabundance of weight from one sneaker to the other and smoothed his shock of dark brown hair off his perspiring forehead. He was of that undeterminable age—somewhere between thirty and forty-five. His tinted coke bottle glasses and untamed brown goatee made it hard to tell.

"Did you forget your release forms too?"

"They're on the kitchen table with my ID. This is what happens when I leave the house without my morning cup a' Joe." The man seemed to be attempting a light hearted chuckle, but it came out like more of a grumble.

"Show me the pictures." Diesel must have sensed something was wrong from his spot tied up to the bench. He stood up, his fur instantly rising in stiff hackles.

"You saw the picture I took. Just your daughter standing by the water. Thought a story about gymnasts would be good for the cover of one of the sports magazines."

Jack looked over at Lauren. Her leotard wasn't visible and for once she wasn't wearing clothes that said anything about gymnastics.

"Show me the fucking pictures, asshole." This time, Jack didn't give the guy a chance to respond. Lauren's food flew out of his hands in a rush of ketchup and flying lettuce and tomato as he grabbed the camera from the guy's hands.

"That's a three thousand dollar camera!" The guy lunged forward, but Jack backed away while pressing the LCD screen. It came alive with the picture of Lauren posing by the water. But Jack knew that was just the tip of the iceberg. He swiveled his body from side to side like a basketball player playing defense to keep the guy from snatching the camera back. He pressed his finger rapidly on the touch screen through four more pictures till Lauren appeared again, her back arched as she propelled her feet up in the air and away from the high bar. Jack scrolled through picture after picture of Lauren and her friends in their leotards, practicing in the gym and hanging out by the locker room.

"Give me my camera back! Before I call the cops."

"You're going to call the cops on me? You fucking pedophile! They'll lock you up for child pornography."

"She had her clothes on."

"You're not getting these pictures back you sick fuck."

Jack swung his arm back with the camera in it, and the guy clipped him on the corner of his left eye with a surprisingly hard punch. Jack leaned over for a split second before he felt his sneaker slip off the pavement as he was tackled to the ground.

"Uncle Jack!" Lauren stood rooted to her spot by the water shrieking like he'd never heard her before. Her screams were ear shatteringly loud despite the fact that she had both hands clasped over her mouth.

"I'm fine Lauren! Hold on to Diesel."

Jack pulled one of his arms out from under the guy's hands and acted like he was going to punch him in the face. As his opponent lifted his arms off Jack to shield himself, Jack took control and flipped him over, putting his high school wrestling skills to work.

Lauren unleashed Diesel from the bench and ran towards the crowd boarding the Spirit Cruise Ship. "Help! Some crazy guy is attacking my Uncle!"

Jack smashed his forearm into the guy's chest to hold him down, but the guy reached up and boxed Jack in the ear. Jack belted him in the face and felt the guy's head ricochet off the pavement, his nose splitting open and shooting blood onto Jack's arm.

Jack pressed his knee harder into the man's gut. "Can someone call the cops?" Jack yelled towards the hoard of tourists who apparently didn't want to get close enough to dirty their dress shoes.

"Not necessary." A uniformed cop, who looked like he had been interrupted mid-lunch break judging by the smear of mustard by his mouth, ran to Jack and the struggling photographer with his gun pointing right at both of them. "Both of you get on your stomachs and put your hands behind your backs."

Lauren ran over with Diesel who was erupting into aggressive growls. "Don't point the gun at my uncle! Point it at the crazy guy on the ground!" Her shrieks came out in high-pitched wales and tears were streaming down her face.

"Let go of him and get on the ground." A female cop who wasn't much bigger than Lauren approached Jack from the other side.

Frozen by the metal shaft an inch from his temple, Jack realized his hand was pressing into the guy's windpipe.

"This lunatic tried to steal my camera and jumped me when I wouldn't give it to him!" The guy forced his words out so that Jack could feel his Adam's apple dipping into his hand.

"He's lying! He pretended to be a photographer so he could take pictures of me. Uncle Jack figured out he was a pedo-something and was just trying to protect me!"

"Hey buddy—let go of his throat now. We'll take it from here." The female officer kept her voice low and calm.

Jack leaned his face into the man's before taking his hand away. "You come near my niece again and I will fucking murder you."

"On your stomachs! Now!" yelled the male cop.

Jack raised both hands to show he was done and rolled onto the ground. Black spots danced in front of his eyes and pounding rushed through his ears. He felt a gentle knee in his back as the female cop pulled both of his arms back and snapped the cuffs on him.

Jack spit out the chucks of gravel from his mouth and yelled to Lauren, "Call Matt!"

"Stand up." The female cop pulled Jack to his feet.

"You're bleeding!" yelled Lauren, pointing to the splatters of blood scattered across Jack's shirt Pollack style.

"It's the other guy's. I'm fine." Jack smiled at Lauren, despite the pounding in his eye socket and the pinch of metal pulling the hair from his wrists.

"Did you hear him threaten to kill me?" yelled the man while the officer pulled him to his feet.

"Nope. Didn't hear a thing. What about you Officer Nunez?"

"Nah. I didn't hear anything either. Maybe you hit your head or something on the way down."

"Why is my uncle in handcuffs? He didn't do anything wrong!"

"Don't worry. We'll straighten it all out down at the station." The female officer spoke in a soothing voice and smiled at Lauren.

"Looks like someone's making the evening news." The other officer pointed at the hordes of tourists who abandoned the ship to point their cameras at Jack.

"Shit. Can we hurry up and get to the station?" asked Jack.

"Sure thing. I think your niece has had enough pictures taken of her for one day," said Officer Nunez.

"When I was a little girl, I had the biggest crush on Bruce Willis. I've always loved the rough around the edges kind of hero."
                                        Kate Richards, The Haute Life

Chapter Twenty

Kate found herself having yet another meal in a Chelsea Piers ballet studio. Unfortunately, this time it was just take-out with Dana in between Zumba voiceovers.

"That *New York Today* mention was like a gift from the Gods! You got three hundred more Twitter followers since yesterday and this morning's *KidFit* episode had the highest ratings we've seen all season." Dana was on another one of her juice fasts. She sucked the cayenne lemonade through a straw and instantly puckered her lips before swallowing.

"I just don't get it. Why do all these strangers care who I'm dating?" Kate shook her head and took a bite of her grilled chicken and arugula Panini.

"With all these reality shows, people feel like they're entitled to knowing everything about their favorite celebrities."

"Jack didn't sign up for this."

"That's bullshit. You don't go out with a celebrity and think you're never going to end up in some gossip rag." Dana took another sip of her drink and practically crossed her eyes when she swallowed.

"Honestly, I don't think Jack really gave it much thought."

"What did he say about the article?"

"He didn't seem thrilled about it yesterday and I haven't heard from him since." Kate spoke through a mouthful of food and looked at the large clock over the ballet barre. She only had a few more minutes till the sound guy would come looking for her. "If he walks away from you because of two sentences in a blind *Today* item, then it's better to find out now that he can't hack it."

"He doesn't seem like the kind of guy who would walk away so easily. I'm hoping he just got wrapped up with Lauren." Kate washed down her last bite of sandwich with a huge sip of SmartWater. She stood up and brushed the flaky crumbs off her camouflage Lycra pants.

Dana pulled her iPad from her Hermes canvas tote. "Don't go yet. We have to see if *New York Minute* posted your interview."

"I hope they include footage of the kids doing Zumba." Kate sat back down, glad for the excuse to hold off getting back to work for a few minutes. Voiceover work could be very long and tedious.

"I liked when you were going over the diet plan with that really fat girl. I couldn't believe the shit her mother was feeding her!" Dana scrolled through the rows of little square apps till the page appeared on the finger-smudged screen.

"That must be the story. Look it's Chelsea Piers." Kate pointed to a frozen clip with the bright blue Chelsea Piers field house front and center. Dana clicked on the black arrow that floated in the middle of the building.

A statuesque woman stood on the pier, the wind fighting against the hair spray in her blown out blond hair. She was wearing a charcoal gray dress with a navy blue *New York Minute* windbreaker over it.

"I'm Gloria Mainstay with breaking news. A pedophile was apprehended today at the famed Chelsea Piers, where thousands of Manhattan's kids come to play." The camera panned out to the pier that was lit by the setting sun and dotted with skateboarders, and kids of all ages in various sports uniforms.

"Joey Rocco was witness to the arrest when he was waiting to board the Spirit Cruise ship for an evening cocktail party. Joey, can you tell us what you saw?"

A man in a three-piece black suit garnished with a red

on red patterned bow tie leaned towards the microphone and looked straight into the camera. "This creep posed as a magazine photographer to lure a little girl into taking pictures with him. He got into it with the girl's uncle when the uncle figured out what was going down. The uncle held the guy down till the cops got there."

"Mr. Rocco was quick enough to get the whole thing on video with his phone." The woman spoke while the screen lit up with grainy cell phone footage of two men arguing. Then the burlier man clocked the smaller one in the eye and tackled him.

"The bigger guy on top is the pervert." Joey Rocco's voice cut in over the video.

"Is that..." started Dana.

"Holy shit! It is!" Kate grabbed the iPad from Dana. It was hard to see his face on the blurry phone footage, but Kate knew that was Jack caught in the rough tumble on the ground. He was wearing the exact same outfit she had seen him in the day before.

"You can't really get a good look at his face, but who else wears tee shirts with such stupid sayings on them?" Dana leaned over Kate, her hand pressing into Kate's back.

"Both men were brought down to the precinct after this fight, but the only one detained was Timothy Rainard, a Staten Island man who was on probation after serving time for lewd and lascivious acts with an underage girl."

The tuxedoed man leaned towards the microphone and cut in. "We all told the cops that the uncle was just looking out for the niece. And they were fighting over the camera which had pictures of the little girl on it."

"That camera was later used for evidence to hold Timothy Rainard. The other man, who was unanimously called a hero by all the witnesses, was originally brought down to the station as well for his part in this fight. But after Mr. Rocco showed police this footage, it became quite clear that the man was just protecting his niece and himself."

"Can you believe the guy wants to remain anonymous? He's a freakin' hero!"

"I'm Gloria Mainstay and this has been a *New York*

Minute 'Quick Break'."

"I guess that explains why Jack didn't call you back."

"That is so scary! Poor Lauren. I hope she's okay."

"Sounds like it was a close call." Dana shoved the iPad back in her bag. "If the blind item writer only knew your mystery man was also *New York Minute*'s big hero of the day."

"Don't you dare! The poor guy probably just wants some peace and quiet."

"Jack saving all those kids at Chelsea Piers from a convicted pedophile actually bumps him up to almost your league. We would have to do some kind of makeover too before we leak the news. A keratin treatment and a good stylist would be a good start."

"Absolutely not!"

Dana stood up and slung her bag over her shoulder, expertly balancing the weight on six-inch stilettos. "Think about it. I have to get out of here. Mandy has her court hearing today and that girl needs someone to literally dress her or else she will show up looking like she belongs on a corner at Hunt's Point."

"I've thought about it enough. Leave Jack alone."

Kate picked up her phone as soon as Dana shut the door.

Jack answered on the first ring. "I've been meaning to call you."

"But you've were too busy being *The Greatest American Hero*."

"Shit! How did you find out?"

"*New York Minute*. Don't worry they kept you anonymous and you can't really see your face that clearly. But it was hard to miss the tee shirt."

"I'm trying to keep the whole thing on the DL. Lauren was already embarrassed enough."

"Poor kid."

"I literally wanted to throttle her and hug her at the same time. She actually thought that dirtbag was going to put her on the cover of *Sportastic*."

"How the Hell did that creep get close enough to photograph her?"

"I was distracted talking on the phone and picking up a

burger for her at the food truck. Next thing I knew she was posing for pictures by the water for some pervert." Jack exhaled slowly in long breaths that exuded guilt.

"Good thing you got to her in time!"

"I know. That piece of shit had pictures of Lauren and her friends in their leotards. You could tell by what the girls were wearing that he had been there several times over the past few weeks."

"That is so scary!"

"I know. I can't stop thinking about it."

"How's your face? Looks like you took a pretty hard punch."

"I have a pretty nasty shiner. But that's okay. It'll give me street cred."

"How's Lauren holding up?"

"Hard to tell. She was holed up in her room on Skype with Harper for awhile last night."

"Does she have practice after school?"

"Not today. Why?"

"Why don't I take her off your hands for a few hours?"

"You don't have to do that. Besides, she's grounded for life."

"Start her punishment tomorrow—for your sake. You sound like you really need a break."

"To tell you the truth, I do have a splitting headache. That guy sure knew how to land a sucker punch."

"Great. This will give me the chance to get to know Lauren a little better before the shoot anyway."

"Just don't bring up the photographer. She'd be mortified as she likes to say."

"Got it. What does Lauren like to do in her free time? Besides gymnastics of course?"

"Bowling," answered Jack, instantly.

"Okay. I'll pick her up in at 3:30 and we'll head over to Lucky Strike."

"How's your father doing? Did he make it back to Westchester okay?"

"Yes. My sister and her husband drove him right up to the rehab in Brewster. They took him a night early and stuck him on a cot somewhere."

"How long's he in for?"

"As long as he needs. So I better get off my ass and get this damn cookbook on the store shelves."

"Good thing for him you are a second chance kind of girl."

"Second, third and hundredth chance in this case. So, I'm a little burned out when it comes to everyone else in my life."

The rest of Kate's day flew by in a blur of voiceovers and editing. Before she knew it, she was on her way to pick up Lauren.

"OMG! Are you really taking me to Lucky Strike?" Lauren must have been watching for Kate, because she swung the door open before Kate had a chance to ring the bell.

"Yes, unless of course there's something else you'd rather do?"

"Duh, of course not. How's my outfit?"

"Perfect," said Kate. "A love for ironic tee shirts clearly runs in the family." Kate took note of the tee shirt Lauren wore layered over a purposefully weathered long sleeved white shirt. She had dressed the outfit up with a black lace flounced skirt, and black sequined flats.

Lauren smoothed the hot pink shirt down, which said *If gymnastics were EASY, it would be called FOOTBALL.* "Uncle Jack got this for me for Christmas."

"Of course Jack picked that out. Where is he?"

Lauren jerked her chin in the direction of the patio door. "On the phone."

"Okay. Why don't you get your stuff together and I'll go tell him we're leaving."

Diesel assaulted Kate, as soon as she slid the glass door open. He jumped as high as her chest greeting her with barks interspersed with whines.

Jack was sitting with his legs propped up on his weathered picnic table. He jumped up when he saw Kate, and scrambled to scoop up the scattered papers that covered the table. He stacked them all into one semi-neat pile and put them under a terra cotta pot of mums. He motioned for Kate to shut the door behind her.

Kate slid the glass door closed and got down on the ground so she could give the little dog the proper attention he was looking for—a vigorous belly rub with a lot of exaggerated praise.

"She needs to know what's going on." Jack's voice was hushed but clearly irritated.

"Two more days, and then I don't give a shit what you say; I'll fly her out there myself."

"Yeah, whatever. Love you too." Jack threw the phone down on the table and stretched his arms up into a long stretch.

"Harper?" whispered Kate.

"Yeah. She's driving me crazy."

"How's David?"

"That's the thing. He's doing better. They're pretty sure he's going to regain all his vision."

"Then why can't you tell Lauren?"

"David doesn't want to tell her till he finds out for sure about his eyes. But I think it's mostly because his friend didn't make it and he's having a hard time. They did three tours together."

"Your poor brother-in-law."

"I know. But I think seeing Lauren will make him feel better."

"It would be good for her too. Especially after what happened yesterday."

"I know. Part of me wonders if she would've been so eager to go with that guy if she wasn't missing her own dad so much."

Lauren slid the door open. "You coming with us Uncle Jack?"

"Nah. I can't show my face in the bowling alley after you kicked my butt so bad last time."

"That triple turkey was pretty awesome."

"She got such a high score, they announced it over the loud speaker."

"Yeah, it was me and this old guy who's been on the bowling team for like a hundred years."

"Your punishment is officially suspended for the next two hours. As soon as you get back I'll have a list of chores for you," Jack said, in an official sounding tone.

Lauren groaned, but she still reached over and gave Jack

a sideways hug followed by a complicated series of high fives.

Jack mouthed "Thank you" over Lauren's head.

Kate and Lauren took a quick cab ride to 42nd Street and left behind the bright sun of the afternoon when they entered the club-like atmosphere of the bowling alley. As soon as they walked in, Kate spotted the small clumps of people waiting to bowl. Kate felt like kicking herself for not thinking to call ahead for a reservation.

"We'll never get a lane," said Lauren.

"Don't worry. We'll put our names on the list and grab a bite to eat while we wait. I don't have to be anywhere. Do you?"

"No, I just figured you have a lot of stuff to do." Lauren picked a fleck of purple nail polish off her thumbnail.

"Right now the only thing on my calendar is an afternoon of bowling with you. Come on. Let's give them our names."

The girl at the reservation counter had two thick shanks of flat-ironed hair covering both sides of her face as she leaned over the reservation sheet. "The wait time is between forty-five minutes to an hour. I can give you a beeper, but it only works in the building or right outside, so you can't…" Her voice stopped in the middle of her monotone speech when she finally looked up and noticed Kate.

"You're Kate Richards."

"I bet that means you can bump us up higher on the list," said Lauren, with a conspiratorial wink at the hostess.

Kate had been in situations like this before and she usually didn't like taking advantage of her semi-celebrity status in this way. But it was written all over Lauren's face how cool it would be to cut the crowd.

"You are totally going to the top of the list. The last time we had a celebrity in here, a bunch of photographers came and next thing you know I was being interviewed for *Gossip Matters.*" The girl's left ear was pierced with a silver bar that ran from the top of her ear lobe through the cartilage at the bottom of her ear. Her right hand had a small silver ball stabbed in the meaty part of her flesh between her thumb and pointer finger. It made Kate nauseous to look at it, so she looked up at the girl's face.

"OMG! Was it Brangelina?" asked Lauren.

"When they come we just close down the whole place to the public. But that other time it was Selena Gomez and Taylor Swift."

"I bet Selena comes back with her boyfriend," said Lauren.

"If they're not broken up again." She came out from behind the counter and Kate was surprised to see this Goth girl was wearing a perfectly normal black skirt and fitted white button down shirt. "Follow me."

Kate could hear the groans of annoyance as soon as the crowd of people realized the people who were just walking in were getting a lane first.

"Sorry, reservation," Kate called, over her shoulder.

Lauren wrapped her small hand right above Kate's crooked elbow and giggled as they hurried to keep up with the hostess.

Lauren chose a neon green bowling ball for herself and a purple one for Kate. Kate had just finished adding their names to the computerized screen, when a waitress brought over a tray of food for them.

"On the house, Ms. Richards. We selected the healthier items from our menu for you and your friend." The waitress set the food on the table and Lauren beamed at the word "friend."

"Awesome!" Lauren took a coconut-encrusted shrimp from the plate.

"Thanks, so much," said Kate. "I'll be sure to mention some of these foods on the show."

As soon as the waitress walked away, Lauren said, "How come rich and famous people are always getting things for free?"

"Good question." Kate grabbed some sort of fish wonton. It was light and crispy on the outside but when she bit it into a burst of spicy flavor filled her mouth.

"Try one of these skewer thingies. They're spicy, but really good."

"So what do you like about bowling besides the fact that you're amazing at it?"

"My dad and I bowl together when he's home. He's in Afghanistan right now." She looked off to the side over Kate's shoulder, and her brightness seemed to dim. All Kate could think about was this poor girl's dad sitting in a hospital.

"Jack was bragging to me about what a hero your dad is. He must be a pretty tough guy to be a Marine."

Lauren jerked her chin up. "He is. When he's home we do conditioning together, like running, push-ups stuff like that. He says I help keep him in shape."

"I'm sure you do," said Kate. Her mouth was burning from that skewer. She sucked back a huge sip of water.

"My dad's an awesome bowler. He holds the record at the Chelsea Piers bowling alley. He's been away for nine months and no one has beaten him yet."

"You're pretty lucky to have such a cool dad. I really didn't have that growing up," said Kate.

"Yeah. This one time he took me to the Jersey Shore. Just me and him for the day to swim. It was awesome."

"Sounds like fun."

"Yeah. But I haven't heard from him in like weeks. So things pretty much suck right now." Lauren pulled the last of her pink drink through her straw till it made a gurgling sound.

"Just think of how surprised he's going to be when you tell him you're going to be on TV!"

"I know! I can't wait to tell him!"

"We tape four months ahead. But I can get you an advanced copy of the show in about two or three weeks. As soon as the tech guys have it edited and ready to go. That way you can send it to him."

"Awesome!"

"He's going to be so proud of you when he sees it."

"If he ever gets to see it."

"If I were a kid I would much rather be pushed around outside in the fresh air any day than ride around in the back of a mini-van. You don't get car sick in a stroller."

Jack Moskowitz, strollersavvy.com

Chapter Twenty-One

"Did you forget something?" asked Jack, without looking up from his laptop.

"To add to your collection." Matt tossed a tee shirt at Jack.

Jack grabbed the bright orange shirt off his keyboard. A series of black numbers splashed across the chest underneath large block letters that spelled out Property of Sing Sing Prison.

"You're such an asshole." Jack winced and covered his eye socket. "Shit, it hurts to laugh."

"Where's the model at?" Matt grabbed a handful of chips off the bag from the table.

"Out. Did you just come over here to bust my balls?" Jack grabbed the bag of chips back from Matt.

"If it wasn't for me and my quick call to our legal team, your ass would've spent the night in that cell with Timmy Two Fingers and Radio Vinnie."

"They were actually pretty cool. Radio Vinnie offered me a great deal on surround sound for the whole townhouse."

"Send him my way when you're done with him."

"Seriously, do you need to meet about anything? Because I'm trying to get this drawing done for the pre-orders. And it ain't easy when I can only see out of one eye."

"Just wanted to let you know you're an Internet sensation.

Guess people can't resist watching a good sucker punch."

"It was all those fucking tourists and their cell phones."

"How close are you to finishing the picture?"

Jack tilted his laptop towards Matt, so he could see the computerized drawing he was working on.

"Holy shit! That looks amazing!"

"It's not finished yet. I have to clean up the lines on the sides and finish the list of color choices."

"Hurry up. We need to do that press conference ASAP so we can ride the wave."

"Hell no. I wasn't fucking around when I told the cops I wanted to be anonymous."

"What the fuck for? You got some sexual deviant off the streets. You're a goddamned hero!"

"If my name gets out, so does Lauren's. Do you really think she wants all the other kids at Chelsea Prep talking about this?"

"Shit. I didn't think of that."

"Not to mention I don't want Kate finding out who I am this way. I need to find a really romantic way to tell her. I was thinking I could rent a cabin in the Berkshires where we can really get away from all this media shit."

"Yeah, and she can pull a Shining on your ass. Good luck with that."

"I need to have control over when and how I tell her, otherwise I'm screwed."

After a few more good-natured jokes, Matt left to give Jack time to finish the designs in between Googling weekend house rentals in Lenox, Massachusetts. He found the perfect Victorian house with gingerbread trim tucked in a thicket of Pine trees. All he has to do was get this press conference over. Then, he could pawn Lauren off on Madison's family for the weekend. Kate would have to hear him out if she was stuck in the middle of the woods with him.

Jack flipped the laptop shut and headed in to grab some more Advil from the kitchen. He popped three in his mouth and stuck his head under the faucet and washed them down with metallic tasting water straight from the tap.

"Did you see those people still waiting by the door when we left?"

"Yeah, I still feel bad we cut ahead of them on the list."

"I don't!" Lauren ran into the kitchen with Kate close at her heels.

"Sounds like you girls had a nice time."

"Ew. Your eye looks even worse than when we left." Lauren stood on her tiptoes and lightly touched Jack's cheekbone with her finger.

"You are looking a little gnarly there. Can you even see out of that thing?" Kate took a step closer to Jack and grimaced.

"Barely. But you should see the other guy."

"We had such a good time. They let us cut the whole line since Kate's famous and we got all this free food and I beat my high score but it doesn't really count since we played with bumpers."

"Since when do you bowl with bumpers?"

"Lauren took pity on me after I got my sixth gutter ball in a row."

"How come you never feel bad for me when you're kicking my ass?" Jack turned to Lauren who was already rooting through the fridge for a snack.

"It was Kate's first time bowling in like twenty years or something." Lauren peeled the foil lid off of a Greek yogurt.

"I can't believe you're still hungry after all that food." Kate shook her head and laughed.

"Your two hours is officially up and your punishment has been reinstated. Bring that yogurt out front. Pam should be here any second. I told her you would volunteer with her at Bark Haven."

"I have homework to do."

"You can do that after you volunteer. Then after your homework you can clean the downstairs bathroom."

"How much longer am I on punishment for?" Lauren spoke through a mouthful of yogurt.

"Till you do enough chores to make me forget what an idiot you were yesterday."

Lauren threw her head back in a huff.

"Now say good bye to Kate and get out front."

Lauren ran over and hugged Kate. "Thanks so much. That was awesome."

Kate wrapped her arms around Lauren and smiled. "I had a great time too. I can't wait to start filming with you."

Lauren's smile reached from ear to ear as she headed out of the kitchen. She called from down the hall. "Gotta go. I can see Pam through the window."

"Ah, do you hear that?" Jack took a step closer to Kate and breathed in her familiar apple and vanilla scent.

"I don't hear anything." Kate scrunched up her face in concentration.

"That's the sound of us having the place to ourselves." It wasn't a coincidence that Lauren was at the animal shelter with Pam for the next two hours. Jack lifted the mound of curls off Kate's neck and trailed light kisses from the base of her neck up to the soft skin under her ear.

"Let's see, my dad's upstate in rehab, Harper's in California, Lauren's at the animal shelter and Dana's in meetings all afternoon." Kate ticked the list off on her fingers.

"So, that means no one's around to interrupt us." Jack took Kate's hand and led her down the hall to his bedroom.

As soon as they crossed the threshold, Jack pulled Kate in for a kiss. When their lips touched, all of Jack's fears disappeared. He knew they would find a way to be together.

Jack slid his hands up Kate's stomach, only taking his lips off hers long enough to pull off her silky long-sleeved shirt along with her sports bra. Jack moved his lips down Kate's soft skin from her neck down to the soft dip of her breasts. Kate arched her back and sighed when Jack teased her nipple up to attention.

Jack slid Kate's pants and thong off in one swift motion. Then he rested both hands in the curves of her hips and threw her on the bed. As soon as Jack leaned over her, Kate grabbed him and started kissing him. Kate's hands ripped Jack's fly down while she kept her mouth locked on his lips.

Jack kicked off his pants and moved his mouth down between Kate's legs, desperate to taste her. Jack gently flicked his tongue back and forth while Kate squirmed. He thrust his tongue deep inside her while Kate moved her hips to meet Jack's mouth inviting him to explore deeper.

Then, Kate slid down Jack's body and took him in her mouth while he still had his tongue inside her. She held him and slid her mouth up and down while Jack fucked her with his tongue. She took Jack all the way inside her mouth and it took every ounce of effort not to finish. But Jack needed to be back inside her.

Jack moved his lips up her body as Kate released him from her mouth. He traveled up her navel and her impossibly perfect stomach back to her breasts again before sliding behind her.

Jack pressed himself up against Kate from behind and pressed his hands between her legs. His fingers glided over the wet slick between her legs and pushed inside her, getting her ready for him. He moved his fingers in and out while Kate sighed and squirmed.

He waited until Kate was gripping handfuls of blankets and groaning, then he moved inside her. Kate pushed back into Jack taking him deeper. Jack grabbed onto Kate's thighs as he pushed into her again and again until he felt Kate tremble and quake. Then, he finally let himself go.

Jack stayed wrapped up in Kate even after he went limp. He just didn't want to let go of her. Then Kate twisted back to Jack and found his mouth again. She held his face in her hands and kissed him. Jack wrapped his hands over hers and kissed her back until their lips were raw and chapped.

"We finally made it to the bed." Jack finally pulled away and propped himself up against the pillows.

"We barely made it to the bed." Kate leaned down and grabbed Jack's jeans and boxers off the floor. "Quick put these back on before Lauren gets home."

Jack pulled on his pants and tossed Kate's to hers. "I lose all self control when you're around."

"I know how you feel." Kate pulled on her pants and

looked at Jack.

"I'm sorry I was such a dick about the *New York Today* story." Jack traced the bottom of Kate's chin with his thumb.

"I know it caught you off guard. But being in the spotlight is part of being with me." Kate kept her eyes fixed on the bedspread.

"I just have a lot of shit going on with Lauren and work right now. I wasn't really up for more drama."

"You mean paying off a bookie and ending up in the newspaper was dramatic?"

"I think we're about even considering the shit with David and then my most recent stint behind bars."

"Let's remember to block out all the other bullshit when we're together. We can be in our own little bubble of non-drama."

"I really hope you remember you said that one day." Jack pulled Kate back in for another kiss.

They stayed wrapped up in each other right up until they heard Lauren bounding through the door. Once Kate left, Jack spent every moment over the next two days finishing up the designs. He just had to get through the press conference and then he could break the news to Kate. He even put down a deposit on a beautiful B & B in the Berkshires. Once the press conference was over, he could focus on getting rid of Lauren for a weekend and on getting Kate to go away with him.

Jack opted to stay upstairs in the Considerable Carriages loft office and watch from the live video stream while Matt led the press into the design studio for the conference bright and early that Friday morning.

Jack did most of his designs at the old picnic table in his backyard, but they had an ultra hip and modern art studio set up in the office for when he passed the designs along to the rest of the team. The studio was the perfect venue for the press conference with its sleek row of Macs and clear Lucite chairs.

Matt traded in his usual skateboarding attire for a look straight off the mannequin at Kenneth Cole's—literally straight off the mannequin. That was Matt's signature move, whip out the wallet, and ask for whatever outfit looked the best in the window display in his size. He only did that when he needed clothes for press releases or big meetings, the rest of the time he lived in Vans and Levis.

"Most people drive their brand new mini-vans and SUVs off the lot fully loaded with satellite radio, DVD players, cup holders and snack trays. Why shouldn't kids getting schlepped around in their strollers have the same comfort and amenities? Considerable Carriages is pleased to announce the CC-XL Deluxe, which comes fully equipped with an iPod charger and built in speakers, a flip up DVD player and to make eating on the go more convenient…snack trays and larger cup holders. We also responded to the great demand to raise the weight capacity up to eighty-three pounds."

The Smartboard behind Matt was illuminated with a computer-enhanced version of Jack's sketch of the CC-XL Deluxe stroller. Seeing the stroller on the gigantic screen, made Jack realize he was proud of his design. It hadn't been easy to include the extra support bars and wider base, while still keeping the sleek design that made their line so popular. Matt clicked on the stroller so that it changed from charcoal black to a bright orange. Jack had played around with the color template combining basic primary colors with their fluorescent counter parts to create bold colors. Parents could choose from Electro Orange, Purple Explosion, Paradise Pink, Limeade, or Bombastic Blue.

"Mr. Reynolds, what's your response to all the criticism your company has gotten in recent weeks regarding your contribution to childhood obesity?" asked a rail-thin red head woman in the front.

"We believe all children deserve safe accommodations whether they're riding in a car, sitting in a high chair or getting pushed in a stroller. We don't want children tipping back in their strollers, or being jolted out of their car seats just because they don't meet outdated size standards for these products." Matt looked right into the camera, his brown eyes clear and bright and his smile genuine and wide.

"How do you respond to Kate Richards' recent comments about Considerable Carriages on *Straight Talk*?" A balding man in a canvas safari vest leaned in close to Matt when he asked his question.

"I invite Kate Richards to visit us at considerablecarriages. com, where every hit means we make a dollar donation to Michelle Obama's Move Your Body campaign."

"I used to think I would choose true love every time. I remember watching Pretty Woman and thinking Julia Roberts is a hooker— so what? If Richard Gere really loves her, he should be with her. Now, I'm not so sure."

Kate Richards, Late Night with Jessa Silver

Chapter Twenty-Two

"You have to admit the design is great," said Dana.

"It pisses me off that I can't even call the damn thing tacky." Kate pointed her yogurt-covered spoon at the computer screen for emphasis.

"Watch it." Dana slid her MacBook across the table.

Kate sighed and dipped her spoon back into the layers of yogurt, granola and sliced strawberries.

"I just don't get it. You would think the designers at Considerable Carriages would've finished the development on the new design before holding a big press release." Dana took a sip of the green juice she had brought with her to La Yogurt Barre in lieu of ordering any real food.

"This is so weird. It's like they knew about my article and scooped me somehow."

"But how could they know you were writing about them?" mused Dana.

"Who knows?" Kate shoveled another spoonful of yogurt-drenched granola in her mouth.

"At least your piece is more relevant now." Dana clicked on the bright orange stroller in the middle of the screen changing it to the color of a grape lollipop.

"I guess so. All this does is prove me right."

"Exactly."

"I bet one of the interns at the paper sold me out."

"Probably. They don't get paid shit. A little info can mean bucca bucks." Dana took another sip of her drink, pulling chunks of unblended mystery vegetables through her straw. "How's your Pop doing at rehab?"

"They haven't kicked him out yet."

"He could set up a gambling ring with all the other losers there and they would still keep him because they know you're gonna foot the bill."

"For your information he's participating in group therapy and the counselors think he has potential."

"That's good. Seriously, I hope this works." Dana took one last slurp of her green drink and stood up.

"Heading out so soon?"

"Yeah. I need to go get a mani-pedi. I have a date later." Dana slid out of the booth and snapped her laptop shut.

"Where'd you meet this one?" Kate was constantly amazed at the number of first dates Dana went on.

"Dry cleaners. You can tell a lot by what a guy drops off. Armani, Versace. We're talking a stack of designer suits."

"That means the guy has money. But he could still be a total jerk." Kate thought about Jack with his broken-in jeans and his tee shirts with the silly slogans.

"I'll give you the scoop after dinner."

"First dates suck."

"Look at you talking like you're never going on a first date ever again. Things must be going really well with Jack." Dana took another thick sip of her shake, making gurgling sounds with her straw.

"I'm happy. For the first time in a really long time, I can honestly say I'm happy." Kate grabbed her cup of yogurt and slid out of the booth.

"I just don't get it. You could be with any guy in Manhattan and you pick some chubby guy who lives with his sister?"

"When I'm with Jack, none of the other bullshit in my life

matters. He gets me to loosen up."

"So that's it." Dana stopped dead in front of the door. "You've been walking bowlegged ever since that second date of yours when you and your dog did the walk of shame home."

Kate smacked Dana in the arm and pushed her through the exit. "Dana!"

"Holy shit!" Dana stopped on the sidewalk. "This explains what a good mood you've been in."

"I'm not going to lie. Jack is pretty gifted in that area."

Dana cut Kate off. "I knew there had to be more to this guy than meets the eye."

"But it's not just that. We have a real connection."

"Let's just hope that all that super sized sex hasn't made you put your blinders up. The last thing you need in your life is another *Dining on a Dime* fiasco."

"Whoever controls the media, controls the mind. Not sure if Jim Morrison was tripping on acid when he said this, but you have to admit the guy had a point. Wonder what he would have thought about Twitter and Facebook."

    Jack Moskowitz, Northeastern Entrepreneur Summit

Chapter Twenty-Three

"What is it with you and sleeping on the couch?" asked Lauren, as she moved Jack's legs over and sat next to him.

Jack tried to pull the blanket over his face, but Diesel jerked it away with his paw and scraped his tongue across Jack's stubble covered cheeks.

"I made you breakfast," said Lauren, in the same cajoling tone Harper used when she wanted something.

"What time is it?"

"Almost time for you to take me to practice. But if you're tired I could just walk by myself."

Jack sat up, "And have your dad pull out a can of military whoop ass on me when he comes home. No way."

Lauren pushed a plate in his lap. "Turkey, peperoni, mustard and pickles on cinnamon raisin bread."

"That's your favorite, not mine." But as Jack sat up, he realized he was hungry enough to eat just about anything.

"Trust me, you're gonna love it."

"What happened to eating cereal for breakfast?"

"We're all out. Besides, it's almost two in the afternoon."

"Shit. I've gotta teach you to make coffee." Jack took a large bite of the sandwich and chased it with some flat Diet Coke from the can on the coffee table.

"You're a disaster, Uncle Jack."

"I was up…" started Jack.

"Late working. I know, I know." Lauren shook her head back and forth.

"Thanks for looking out for me." Jack took another bite and wasn't surprised when it didn't taste any better than the first.

"Someone's got to take care of you with mom away." Lauren looked at her watch. "You've got ten minutes to eat and put on some clean clothes."

"Did you finish your list of chores?"

"Everything but cleaning up after Diesel in the yard. Ran out of time."

"Pretty convenient."

"Have you forgotten what an idiot I was yet? I hate being on punishment."

"Can't forget while I still have this." Jack pointed to the fading blue-black ring around his eye.

"When it goes away can I be off punishment?" Lauren took a step closer and examined Jack's eye.

"Fine. You never told me what you and Kate talked about the other day."

"Not you if that's what you're wondering. She told me about when she was a kid, and about filming the show and living with Mrs. Fink. All sorts of stuff." Lauren stole a small bite of the untouched triangle of Jack's sandwich.

"I'm glad you guys had a good time."

"When are you going to tell her who you really are?"

"It's complicated."

"Grownups always say that about stuff that's not really. All you have to do is tell Kate you were scared to tell her who you really were that day at the dog park…"

"I wasn't scared."

Lauren rolled her eyes. "Oh, please. We both know you were terrified."

"I wasn't scared. I just didn't want to make a scene."

"Whatever. But now she knows how cool you are."

"Like I said, it's complicated. I was thinking of taking her away next weekend and telling her then. That way I won't fuck up your filming this week."

"Good thinking! You don't want to tell her right before I have to shoot my scenes. That would be totally awkward!"

Jack walked Lauren to Chelsea Piers and found Matt waiting for him back at the townhouse. Matt was occupying himself by skimming his skateboard on the edge of the sidewalk. He made it as far as Mr. Sullivan's gray brick brownstone before his board fell off the rim of the sidewalk. Jack waited while Matt made his way back towards the building.

As soon as he made it to Jack he pulled a newspaper from his back pocket. "You have a chance to read your girlfriend's op-ed yet?"

"Shit. I forgot that came out today." Jack reached for the paper. "Wait. How'd you know about Kate's article?"

"Remember that intern I hooked up with at *New York Today* when Anne and I first got separated?"

"The tiny redhead with the huge tits?"

"That's the one." Matt smiled proudly. "Anyway, she's a features editor at the paper now. She gave me the heads up that Kate was using the article to tar and feather us."

"Fuck! She told me the article was about childhood obesity. But I…"

"You didn't think that might have a little something to do with our company since she just ranted and raved about us on *Straight Talk* a few weeks ago?"

"Give me a break! I've been a little preoccupied."

"Yeah, banging the fem-bot who once again tore apart our company in a very public forum."

"It's nothing personal on Kate's end. We're just on different sides of the issue."

"Good thing I found out about this in time to move the press conference up."

"That's why you rushed on the press conference? You should've told me asshole!"

"I didn't want you getting your hands dirty. Just in case for some asinine reason the two of you decide to make a go of it." Matt popped his skateboard up with on its side and leaned down to grab it. He made his way towards the brownstone. "Although, I'm not sure you're going to want to be with her after you read this."

"Fuck. This can't be good." Jack unlocked his door and led Matt inside. He settled down at the kitchen table and flipped through the paper till he found Kate's article. "Stroller Use and Childhood Obesity: What is it Really Costing Us?"

"Can you believe this shit?" Matt grabbed two beers from the fridge and popped the tops off.

"I can't believe I didn't see this coming." Jack grabbed one of the beers from Matt.

"You were too busy screwing her brains out to worry about her article. Let me give you the highlights."

Jack took a long chug of his beer while Matt started to read.

"It's no coincidence that the increase in stroller use for three, four and five year olds coincides with the rising childhood obesity rates in that age bracket. It is actually suggested that stroller use should be limited between the ages of two and three as it could hinder a toddlers' ability to learn to walk. So why are parents keeping their kids in strollers well past the pediatrician recommended age of three? Who's at fault here? The parent choosing to push their kid in a stroller well into their walking years or the company making the stroller with an eighty pound capacity? Considerable Carriages' revamped CC-XL Deluxe has an eighty-three pound weight limit, super-sized cup holders, snack trays and iPod docking stations. Priced at a cool eight hundred dollars, you can purchase this elite stroller and push your kid to their first day of middle school."

"At least we got some free publicity for the new model," started Jack.

"Wait, listen to this." Matt cleared his throat before speaking in a newscaster's voice.

"Considerable Carriages made *Success Magazine*'s list of top ten infant and child product companies with gross profits in the millions last fiscal year. Meanwhile, taxpayers are the ones footing the bill for the trillions of dollars childhood obesity is costing Medicaid and ChildHealth Plus."

"Is she insinuating that the same kids riding around in the eight hundred dollar strollers are the ones racking up Medicaid costs?" asked Jack.

"Good point. You think the *New York Today* editor would catch that lapse in logic."

"There is no coincidence that the increase in stroller use coincides with the rising rates of childhood obesity. Considerable Carriages is taking full advantage of that ratio by increasing their stroller capacity to eighty pounds. Now they're going to add snack trays, super-sized cup holders and handheld video game pouches. Is this company accommodating overweight children or are they actually creating them?"

"Is that the worst of it?"

"No, I think the part when she compares our company to big tobacco is pretty bad too."

"Jesus-fucking-Christ! I finally find a woman I'm really into and this is what she thinks of who I really am?" Jack threw the patio door open and headed back to the yard. He needed some fresh air.

"Anne doesn't think much better of me and she's having my baby." Matt shrugged his shoulders and tipped back his beer.

"She can't think you're that bad. You finally knocked her up."

"Oh yeah? Look what she just gave me." Matt pulled a thick paperback from his messenger's bag. "*The Complete Guide to Baby Care for Complete and Utter Morons.*"

"At least she wants you to be a part of the baby's life. I got nothing keeping Kate tied to me."

"Nothing but that enormous cock."

"This is where all our designing really takes place. We should've had the press conference here." Jack, desperate to change the subject, leaned back in his chair taking survey of his picnic table littered with empty beer bottles, take-out cartons and crumpled up pieces of paper. He couldn't talk about Kate with Matt.

"This is definitely where the real magic takes place."

"How many times have you actually created anything in the studio space?" asked Jack.

"The only thing I've ever created there is my little mini-me that's becoming perfection in Anne's stomach as we speak."

"Dude, you know there are security cameras in there."

"Exactly."

"The question on everyone's minds this week has been 'Who is the mystery man that's been spotted all over the Big Apple with Kate Richards'? Well, you are not going to believe who it is! Tune in to The 411 to find out who America's hottest kids' fitness guru is dating, and why she's been keeping him under wraps."

Craig Ashbourne, The 411

Chapter Twenty-Four

As soon as Sarah Jessica Barker nudged Kate awake Sunday morning, she ran to her apartment door and grabbed the Sunday paper. It had been amazing to open it up and see an article with her byline. She sat at her breakfast bar with a cup of coffee and read the article as if someone else wrote it.

At 8 A.M. on the dot, her landline phone rang. Mrs. Fink was the only one who still called her home phone. Kate received weekly warnings from the woman about the links to cell phone use and huge cancerous brain tumors.

"Katie, are you awake?"

"Would I be answering the phone if I was still sleeping?"

"Morty and I have been up since 6 A.M. I set the alarm so I could read your article first thing." Mrs. Fink sounded like she was talking through a mouthful of bagel, which was probably loaded up with cream cheese and lox.

"What'd you think?"

"Very good. I can't wait to show the Mahjong ladies later today."

"I wasn't so sure about the opening sentence. I feel like I came on a little too strong."

"You're a single woman living in New York City, of course you come on a little strong. You have to be one tough cookie to make it here."

"And the line about Considerable Carriages being compared to big tobacco? I added that at the last minute and now I'm not so sure about it."

"You're always too hard on yourself. This is just like when you were convinced you failed your Soufflé class final."

"Uh, this is a little more serious than that. I really hope I don't come off too bitchy."

"How could anyone think the woman who's been helping all those kids was a bitch?"

Kate sighed.

"What are you doing today to celebrate?"

"I was going to stick around the apartment and work on this child athlete series. We start filming with Jack's niece tomorrow."

"Why don't you come over to my place?" asked Mrs. Fink. "The Mahjong Club would love to see you."

"I have a lot to do today."

"Mrs. Katz can't make it. Her husband has another kidney stone. He screams bloody murder every time he goes to the john. We could really use an extra player."

"Why don't you ask the lady from downstairs?" asked Kate, not relishing an afternoon playing Mahjong and listening to Mrs. Levi give all the gory details of her granddaughter's birth, episiotomy and all.

"That lazy eye of hers makes Mrs. Feinstein nervous. She spends the whole game thinking the poor woman is cheating."

Kate sighed. Mrs. Fink's friendships had all the complexities of a high school clique. "Same time as usual?"

"Of course."

"See you later."

Kate spent the rest of the morning fielding congratulatory phone calls from family and friends. Before she knew it, it was time to head over to Mrs. Fink's.

As soon as Kate walked in the apartment she was overwhelmed with the scent of lemon Pledge and Murphy's

Oil Soap. Mrs. Fink took her turn to host Mahjong Club very seriously and made sure every surface was clutter free and shining before her friends arrived. Her dining room table was empty except for the mahogany box lined with genuine ivory Mahjong tiles that Kate had gotten for her many Christmases ago. All the ladies had all known each other since their early twenties, but they insisted on calling each other by their last names. Mrs. Fink said it was because they were classy women.

Mrs. Fink had ordered everyone she knew to read Kate's article, so all the women arrived full of compliments. Mrs. Cohen even brought her copy along so Kate could autograph it. Mrs. Fink's friends were at experts at making Kate feel like a rock star.

"I'm telling you, the girl is going to be on *The 411!*" Mrs. Fink's best friend, Mrs. Feinstein had been fifteen minutes late and now wanted to delay the game further by waiting for the *The 411* broadcast.

"Wouldn't Katie know if they were going to talk about her on the news?" asked Mrs. Fink.

"*The 411* hardly qualifies as news," said Mrs. Cohen.

"I saw it in the promo. It's all about you and that new boyfriend of yours." Mrs. Feinstein wagged a gnarled finger at her.

"Jack is going to be mortified when he finds out," said Kate.

"He must be the one who took her to that circus school," said Mrs. Levi. "I read about that in *New York Today.*"

"I bet Craig Ashbourne did some digging to find out who he is after that article came out," said Mrs. Feinstein. "That Craig is a smart one."

"Those dimples of his are absolutely scrumptious," said Mrs. Levi.

"Forget about the dimples! Have you ever seen a picture of him with his shirt off?" said Mrs. Feinstein.

"He's not as hot as Mr. Levi was back in the day. But he's a close second." Mrs. Levi winked at Mrs. Feinstein.

Kate turned on the TV just as the *The 411* theme music came on. The women noshed on egg salad, mini bagels and field greens while they sat through the first fifteen minutes of the tabloid television show. Mrs. Fink turned a deaf ear every time Kate warned her about the lethal amounts of cholesterol when you mixed eggs with mayonnaise. They were just about to give up and start the game when a stock photo of Kate in her *KidFit* gear popped on the screen.

"Everyone's been dying to know who took America's number one kids' fitness expert off the market, ever since the gossip maven from *New York Today*, dished about Kate's romantic date at NYC's trapeze school with a mystery man," said Craig Ashbourne. His tight black tee shirt showcased his almost comic book looking biceps and Kate was scared she would have to get Mrs. Levi's inhaler for her.

His co-host, a tall willowy blond wearing a royal blue Herve Leger bandage dress interjected, "Kate Richards has made quite a name for herself coming from virtual obscurity to getting the first ever diet cookbook for kids on the *New York Times* best-seller list, while taking ABC's show *KidFit* to number one in it's time slot. In fact, Kate's been so busy making a brand for herself that she was probably too busy to date until now."

"She's squeezing time into her busy schedule for a new man in her life and you are going to be shocked when you find out who it is." Craig shook his head at the camera and smiled so that both sides of his mouth were bookended with cheek pinching worthy dimples. Mrs. Feinstein gripped both ends of her armchair.

"I can only imagine the two most important things on Kate Richards' checklist are that the guy is in shape and he's gotta love kids," said the blond, as she held up two black licorice colored fingernails.

"That's what I thought, so you can only imagine my shock when I found out who Kate Richards is dating," said Craig.

"Don't leave us hanging like that!" His co-host rested both of her hands on her angular hips.

"Leave it to an intern to solve the mystery. Natasha was down in the editing room watching YouTube clips with the other interns, when she stumbled on this video."

The screen filled with Jack restraining the pedophile, his arm covering the guy's windpipe.

"Footage of this anonymous hero who helped apprehend a convicted pedophile here in New York City circulated on YouTube last week. After coming off a caffeine rush from multiple lattes our intern realized the hero is also the same man who's been spotted with Kate Richards. Further digging identified the man as none other than Jack Moskowitz, CEO of Considerable Carriages, a company that makes strollers, high chairs and car seats for obese children," said Craig.

"What?!" Kate shrieked. She dropped her scooped out bagel on the floor and Morty wasted no time snatching it up. She felt a chill running up her spine and her toes and fingers burned like they were being pierced with thousands of tiny needles.

"I should've known something was up when he said he was from upstate," said Mrs. Fink.

"Craig is quite the investigative reporter. He blew the lid off that whole Jon Edwards love baby scandal," said Mrs. Feinstein.

"Ah, *Gossip Matters* beat him to it," said Mrs. Levi.

"Shhh," said Mrs. Fink, as soon as Craig started talking again.

"A few weeks ago Kate Richards tore apart Considerable Carriages when she sat down with Lucy Barrows on *Straight Talk*."

The green screen filled up with a playback of Kate's appearance on *Straight Talk*. Kate cringed.

"Don't even get me started about that company. As we speak, they are designing a stroller to fit children who weigh up to eighty pounds! Which either means mothers are intending on carting around their sixth graders or this company is profiting off morbidly obese toddlers."

Then the green screen behind Mario lit up with a picture from Sarah Jessica Barker's birthday party. Jack was holding the dog in his hands, while Kate was petting her and looking for any cuts.

"The day after *Smart Talk* aired Kate and Jack met at the Chelsea dog park when Kate Richards threw a birthday party for her dog Sarah Jessica Barker," said Craig.

"Gotta love that name," said the blond.

"I guess Kate Richards is a *Sex in the City* fan. Guests at the party heard Kate ask Jack out on a date to say thanks for saving her dog's life," said Craig.

The grainy black and white photo from *New York Today* appeared next. "That first dinner must have gone well because ever since, the two of them have been dating for weeks in secret, sneaking off to neighborhood hot spots like The Frying Pan and The New York Trapeze School for dates," said Craig.

"This is definitely a case of opposites attract!" countered the blond.

The screen filled with the image of the same stroller Kate and Dana had just been looking at online yesterday. "Friday afternoon, Jack's company Considerable Carriages released this picture of their new stroller, the CC-XL Deluxe, which comes equipped with supersized cup holders, snack trays, DVD players, iPod sync up, and can seat children up to eighty-three pounds."

"Wonder how Kate feels about that?" said the blond.

"I think she made that perfectly clear in today's *New York Today's* op-ed piece where Kate compares Considerable Carriages to big tobacco," said Craig.

"Is there trouble in paradise already?" asked the blond.

"Stay tuned to *The 411* to find out. And log on to us at the411.com for up-to-the-minute updates about this latest celebrity odd couple."

Kate felt all the blood rush to her face and she swore she could hear her own heartbeat as it pounded against her chest wall. She tried to catch her breath, but she felt like someone was squeezing a plastic bag over her face.

"Don't just stand there! Get the girl some water!" Mrs. Feinstein yelled from her armchair perch.

Kate clawed at her turtleneck sweater. "I can't breathe." She felt like an elephant was sitting on her chest and blocking the air from getting in or out of her lungs.

"Grab a paper bag too!" Mrs. Feinstein yelled after Mrs. Levi who was speed shuffling to the kitchen.

"Everything's going to be all right. Just focus on slowing

your breathing down." Mrs. Fink was at Kate's side rubbing her cold sparrow fingers on Kate's back.

Kate dropped to her knees, desperate to catch her breath while the room spun around her.

"Breathe in this." Mrs. Levi handed Kate a brown paper bag.

Kate held the bag up to her face. It smelled like everything bagels and she could hear the faint sounds of stray poppy and sesame seeds rolling around when she moved the bag.

"You better get all those crumbs outta that bag or the girl's gonna choke!" Mrs. Feinstein yelled from the armchair.

Mrs. Fink grabbed the bag from Kate and shook it out till a stream of miniscule black poppy seeds and rice like sesame grains shook all over her rug. The dogs made a mad dash for the crumbs. She handed it back to Kate and held it on her face.

Kate breathed in and tried to ignore the maddening pain in her chest. She felt the warmth of her own breath hit her face as the bag collapsed in and then she breathed out inflating the bag like a balloon.

"Didn't she know?" mumbled Mrs. Levi.

"Sure doesn't look like it," stage whispered Mrs. Feinstein.

"That girl sure knows how to pick em," said Mrs. Cohen.

"At least this one was Jewish," said Mrs. Levi.

Mrs. Fink promptly canceled the Mahjong game for the first time in the history of the club and shooed the women back to their Lower East Side apartments. Mrs. Fink disappeared into the kitchen until she had brewed the perfect cup of hot tea with extra milk and just a pinch of sugar. She put the mug on a tray with a piece of dry white toast. It was the same thing she had brought when Kate broke up with Tyler, and the first day his show aired on Food Network and the night when Kate found out at the age of twenty-nine that her parents were divorcing and she had cried for hours like she was ten.

"I slept with him you know." Kate took a sip of the tea that tasted like an afternoon on the couch with the stomach flu. "More than once."

"Of course you did." Mrs. Fink settled into the pink chintz armchair with Morty at her feet.

"He told me he freelanced for dot coms!"

"Has anyone even done that since 1998?"

"That's what I said!" Kate ripped into her rough toast with her teeth.

"Maybe he told you a bad lie on purpose. You know like a Freudian slip because he secretly wanted you to figure out who he was."

"Or maybe he's just a moron."

"He's a man. Enough said." Morty perked his head up and Mrs. Fink leaned down to pet him. "Sorry Morty. That only applies to humans."

"I can't believe I've been sleeping with a man who lied to my face about who he is."

"He met you by accident with your crazy television crew everywhere. The poor guy was probably too scared to tell you the truth."

"There's no way he met me by accident. I bet he knew exactly who I was when he showed up at that party. For all I know he planted that German Shepherd, just so he could swoop in like the big hero and save Sarah Jessica Barker."

"Now you're getting carried away. This is real life, not some rom-com movie."

"Carried away? He could've told me who he was at any time over the past few weeks."

"I'm sure you didn't make it any easier for him."

"What's that supposed to mean?"

"You have a concrete view of what's right and what's wrong, and that can be hard for people who fit somewhere in the middle."

"How can you be making this my fault?"

"I'm not saying this is your fault. But you close yourself off so completely, it can be hard for other people to get in."

"Well, I let someone in all right. And look what happened."

Dana's face lit up her phone screen and this time Kate didn't hesitate to answer.

"What the fuck is going on?"

"Your guess is as good as mine."

"Kashi is threatening to pull their *KidFit* sponsorship."

"Shit!"

"Meet me at your apartment. I'll bring the Excedrin."

"I have to go." Kate stood up so fast she got a head rush.

"Where are you rushing off to?"

"Dana's waiting for me back at my place. We need to figure out how to put a spin on this."

"What about Jack?"

"Who cares about Jack? I need to save my show!"

"Don't worry about all of this," said Mrs. Fink with a wave towards the television. "It will all work itself out and you and Jack will find a way to be together."

"I highly doubt that."

Kate gave Mrs. Fink a quick hug good bye and grabbed Sarah Jessica Barker's leash. When she opened the building door, she was surprised by the sunshine that almost blinded her. She felt like she had been drowning in her sorrows for hours at Mrs. Fink's, but really it hadn't been that long. She walked back to her apartment on autopilot, not noticing anyone or anything around her. It was no small miracle that she and her dog made it home without being run over by a cab or bike riding delivery boy.

On another day Kate would've noticed the swarm of paparazzi camped out in front of her building. She would've seen their empty coffee cups and cigarette butts littering the sidewalk. But Kate didn't notice the burly men with their unshaven faces and hairy legs that ended in childish sneakers until she was almost at her lobby door.

"Kate, Kate, over here—smile!" they all shouted at different times in rising decibels.

"How long have you been sleeping with the CEO of Considerable Carriages?"

"What does your boyfriend think about the article you just wrote about him?"

"How could you go out with a man who makes money off overweight kids when you're supposedly trying to help them?"

The questions assaulted Kate in rapid fire mode. She took a deep breath and lifted her sunglasses, thankful that she had dressed up and actually put makeup on for Mahjong Club at Mrs. Fink's. She pulled her lips into her best camera-ready smile and turned to the photographers.

"Hi boys, great to see you today," she said, as she placed her hands on the edge of her hips and tilted towards the left so they would capture her best angle. She stood still while at least fifty flashes lit off in her face. Kate ignored all the questions till she knew they all got their shots.

"I'm sure you're all here because of that ridiculous story on *The 411*. When are those people going to hire a good fact checker?" She smiled and waited for a few of the men to pour out their guttural laughs.

"How do you explain all those pictures?" asked a man whose gray tee shirt had sweat stains at the chest and under the armpits.

"They were right about one thing. Jack and I met at the dog park when he saved my dog Sarah Jessica Barker from an over-excited German Shepherd. Smile for the cameras, sweetie." The paparazzi ate up the shots and Kate was sure they would be featured on the Celebrities and their Dogs sections on several of the sites. Anything to distract them from her and Jack.

"That doesn't explain the pictures of the two of you together," said another cameraman.

"Jack's niece Lauren is a very talented gymnast who is going to be featured on my show *KidFit*, which airs weekdays 4 P.M. on ABC," said Kate.

"Everyone's looking for a one percenter to lynch right now. A one percenter who's a hypocrite? It doesn't get better than that."

gossipmatters.com

Chapter Twenty-Five

"You look better than you did this morning. You can hardly see the black eye." Lauren gave Diesel's leash a little slack so he could run a little further ahead.

"You and I both know I still look like crap. You're just trying to butter me up to get your punishment shortened."

Lauren's shoulders almost reached her ears as she heaved a martyred sigh. "When's mom coming home?"

"Soon. And don't think your sentence would've been lighter with her. I had to talk her down from two months of grounding."

"I feel like she's filming a movie instead of a stupid TV commercial."

"Tighten up the leash while we cross." Jack waited for Lauren to pull back on the leash and grab onto the crook of his arm before crossing Tenth Avenue.

"Did you hang out with Kate while I was at practice?"

"No. I was working with Matt. Why?"

"You said you were going to call her to find out what time I have to go for filming tomorrow. Remember?"

"Shit. I totally forgot."

"Come on, boy." Lauren pulled Diesel to the aluminum water bowl that Jack always left in front of the building. He eagerly lapped up the water, thirsty from a quick romp at the dog park after Jack picked up Lauren from practice.

"You earned yourself a treat." Jack leaned down to tousle

Diesel's ears. Expecting the normal bark of excitement at the word treat, Jack was unnerved to hear a deep guttural growl erupt from Diesel.

"What's the matter buddy?" Lauren leaned down and cooed in Diesel's ears, but his fur stood up in stiff rows of hackles.

"Let's get inside." Jack pulled Diesel away from the water bowl. "Something out here must be freaking him out."

Lauren started up the stoop, but froze halfway up. "Who are all those guys?" She pointed towards the building across the street.

Jack looked towards the row of townhouses on the other side of the street. A group of men were hidden behind a double parked Fresh Direct truck. Their flashes popped bright white light at Jack and Lauren.

"What the fuck?" Jack dragged Diesel up the stairs so he could get to Lauren. "Get in the house Lauren!"

But Lauren remained rooted to the spot while the photographers darted across the narrow street.

"How long have you been sleeping with Kate Richards?" asked a man whose five o'clock shadow didn't do enough to cover his acne-scarred cheeks.

Jack tried to head the men off at the pass. "Look guys, I'll come out and answer all of your questions as soon as I get my niece settled in the house."

"Did you know Kate was writing an editorial about your company when you were wining and dining her?" asked a blond with cat's eye glasses.

"How long have you been sleeping with the woman who hates your company?"

"Did you know about the *New York Today* op-ed?"

"Do you fight about overweight children when you're together?"

The questions came in rapid fire with no one leaving any time for Jack to answer.

"Lauren, come on," said Jack. "We can go in your mom's entrance." He reached up the stoop for her hand.

"Is it true Kate's been helping you take care of her niece since her father's helicopter went down in Afghanistan?"

"It all started with Bennifer."
Dana Johnson, In Your Sight Public Relations

Chapter Twenty-Six

Kate shut the lobby door but it did little to drown out the reporters. Sarah Jessica Barker's claws tapped across the marble floor as she made a beeline for Dana. Kate always wondered what it was that made animals lavish attention on the people who couldn't stand them.

"Rich and I just had a little talk." Dana tossed a handful of dreads over her shoulder and winked up at the 6'5" Armenian guy who worked the afternoon shift. She moved her exquisitely outfitted foot away from Sarah Jessica Barker's sniffing nose.

"Don't worry Miss Kate. I will not let any of these sleazebags into the building." Rich poured coffee from his aluminum thermos into a chipped ceramic mug.

"Thanks." Kate was relieved none of her neighbors were around to witness this spectacle. Most of them still had a bad taste in their mouth from when the Knicks star and his new bride had moved in with a reality show camera crew.

"I call police but they say sidewalk is public property." Rich kept both eyes on the door while he took a sip of the steaming black coffee.

"Thanks for giving it a shot." Kate forced her mouth into a smile.

Dana whisked her upstairs through the service elevator to avoid running into the neighbors. Dana's phone rang as soon as the elevator door shut.

"I was just about to call you. I'm with her now." Dana mouthed "the network" while the person on the other line talked.

"Al, listen." But Dana's mouth snapped shut. This was the first time Kate had seen anyone cut Dana off.

"Give me a few hours and I'll have this whole mess straightened out." Dana paced back and forth in the small elevator. Kate clenched and unclenched her fingers while she waited for her show to get canceled.

"Fine one hour. Hold the sponsors off in the mean time. They'll take their lead from you." Dana shoved her phone in her bag and breathed out one long sigh.

"Dana," started Kate. But Dana held one finger up to her mouth and didn't say a word to Kate till they were in her apartment with the door double bolted.

"Why didn't you tell me?" Dana paced back and forth, her black Jimmy Choos leaving angry pockmarks in the thick white carpet. "I could've figured something out before the shit hit the fan!"

"I had no idea!" Burning acid moved up Kate's esophagus and a wave of nausea spread through her whole body.

"Didn't you think it was a coincidence that the guy you were fucking had the same name as the CEO of the company you were publicly bashing?" Dana stopped mid pace, her heel piercing the carpet threads.

"He said his last name was Horowitz and that he freelanced for dotcom start ups!"

"Your bullshit meter should've gone off right there!"

"Who would make something like that up?" Kate ran down the hall with Sarah Jessica Barker close at her heels.

"I think I'm going to be sick." Worse than actually vomiting was leaning over the porcelain bowl gagging and drooling with nothing coming out. Dana wasn't the holding- your-hair-back kind of friend but she did at least stand in the bathroom doorway.

"How could I be so stupid?" Kate groaned when the gagging subsided. She lay back on the cold tile bathroom floor in between a hairbrush that Sarah Jessica Barker had turned into a chew toy and a pile of ripe workout clothes. Kate tried to ignore the patch of dog hair under her arm and focused on the cool tile against her searing skin.

"He had me fooled with his stupid tee shirts and kinky hair, but that bastard was clearly way smarter than he looked. He has more skills than that crazy blond chick on *Revenge*." Dana shook her head and the tiny bells in her dreads tinkled, making an ironically peaceful melody.

A wave of dizziness washed over Kate as soon as she sat up. "You really think Jack's behind all of this?"

"So, it was just a coincidence that Jack met you at the dog park right after you ripped into his company on *Straight Talk*?"

"Our dog walker gave his niece an invitation. He couldn't have planned that." Sarah Jessica Barker settled down on top of Kate's laundry pile and started gnawing on the wooden handle of the hairbrush.

"Didn't that dog walker say she used to babysit Jack when he was little?"

"Yeah, but…" Kate couldn't believe Pam with her motherly hugs and pocketful of liver treats could have been part of anything so shady.

"He gave you a fake name!"

"Actually Lauren did and Jack went along with it. Mrs. Fink thinks he just freaked out with the cameras there and was scared to tell me who he was."

"How do you explain the media finally figuring out who your mystery man is the day your op-ed comes out?" Dana narrowed her eyes at Kate.

"I don't know. None of this makes any sense."

"Don't be so thick-headed. Jack orchestrated this whole thing to bring you down."

"I just need to talk to Jack."

"Why so you can give him more rope to hang you with?"

"He's not like that. We're talking about the kind of guy who helped raise his twelve-year-old sister while all of his friends were rushing fraternities."

"He's also the kind of guy who just Paula Deen-ed your ass!"

There was no comeback. Kate knew Dana was right.

"Can we continue this conversation in a room that doesn't have a toilet?" Dana walked away without waiting for Kate to answer.

Kate gingerly stood up and Sarah Jessica Barker trotted down the hall behind her with the hairbrush in her mouth. The wallowing would have to wait.

Dana was waiting at the breakfast bar with a dusty bottle of club soda she had unearthed from a mystery cabinet. A rush of air hissed from the cap as Dana unscrewed it. She poured some over a glass full of ice and pushed it across the counter towards Kate. "Drink this. It should help settle your stomach."

Kate gulped down some club soda. The bubbles burst in her mouth and burned her tongue as she pulled up a barstool.

Dana grabbed the bottle of Skinnygirl Margarita from the fridge and poured some over her own glass of ice. "Listen, I totally get that you're heartbroken over Jack." There was a dramatic pause as Dana flicked her wrist over to look at her watch. "But we've got forty-nine minutes to salvage your career."

"How bad is it?" Kate gripped the counter and steeled herself for bad news.

Dana pulled out her iPhone and scrolled through her iPhone. "Kashi is threatening to pull their commercials. That alone is enough to sink the show."

"What about our other sponsors?"

"Simply Organix, Nutri-Kids and Annie's are all threatening to pull their commercials and Whole Foods is threatening to renege on stocking the new snack bars."

"Why are they all jumping ship so fast? I haven't even come out with a statement yet!"

"No one wants to be the last one standing in these situations. Once Kashi threatened to jump ship, they all followed."

"I'm going to lose everything!" Kate finally stopped thinking about Jack.

"I'm not going to let that happen." Dana took a chug of her drink and then tipped the bottle over her glass. The girl had a surprisingly high tolerance for someone so small.

"Don't tell me this is the worst mess you've ever had to

deal with."

"The Wexler-Cohen underage sex video was pretty bad, and I got the girl a reality show out of it."

Kate breathed out. "So, there's hope?"

"All you need in these situations is a good PR person, and you've got the best." Dana pulled a stool up to the granite counter and got busy turning Kate's kitchen into a mini office. She pulled her MacBook and iPad out of her patent leather Coach bag and arranged them on the counter.

"This can't happen. Not now. Between Jen's taxes and Pop's rehab I pretty much blew through my savings." Kate had assumed the money would just fill right back up again once the snack bars started selling and the syndication checks started coming in.

"I just Googled the twenty-five most memorable celebrity meltdowns. Let's see if one of these could be our answer."

"I don't see how a recycled meltdown is going to help."

"We could pull a Britney. Announce you're bi-polar and you stopped taking your meds last month." Dana pulled up a picture of Britney Spears with a shaved head slamming an umbrella into a paparazzi's window.

"No one will trust me if they think I'm crazy."

Dana scrolled down to an old picture of Ellen Degeneres' wife when she was morbidly thin. "Ally McBeal curse?"

"Don't you think an eating disorder would shake my credibility even more?"

"That's true. Plus you're not skinny enough."

Kate glared at her.

"Did your dad ever hit you?" Dana zoomed in on that terrifying picture of the singer battered and beaten by her hip-hop boyfriend.

"Of course not."

"Well he does have a gambling problem. That could explain your poor choice in men."

"Leave my dad out of it. He's finally getting better."

"How do you feel about spending a few weeks at Cirque Lodge? Could be for drugs or alcohol."

"Absolutely not. My whole brand is built on clean living."

"You're not making this easy." Dana groaned and scrolled further down the screen illuminating one celebrity after the next in their darkest moments.

"Wouldn't it be a whole lot easier to just tell the media I was tricked by Jack?"

"In this industry crazy is better than stupid any day of the week."

"I really don't see how being lied to…"

Dana grabbed Kate's arm. "I got it!" She zoomed in on a close up of the middle Kardashian sister in a wedding gown standing with the professional athlete that would be her husband for only seventy-two days while the divorce proceedings would take six times as long.

"What the fuck Dana? First you want me to say I never dated the guy. Now you want me to marry him?"

"Not Jack, you idiot! The best way to distract everyone from Jack would be to announce an engagement to someone else."

"There's just one small problem. Where do I find a fiancé?"

"Leave that up to me."

"You don't really think I would go through with a fake engagement?"

"Do me a favor and take that high maintenance dog of yours in your room. I need some space to figure this out." Dana kicked off her heels and rubbed the arch of her left foot.

"Wait. You do realize this is insane!"

Dana held up a hand. "Just give a few minutes."

Kate headed to her room with Sarah Jessica Barker at her heels. She opened the door and was blinded by the afternoon sunlight streaming in from her floor to ceiling windows. Kate shuddered when she realized the reporters below probably had a bird's eye view of her bedroom.

Kate pressed her back against the wall and slid over to the window like a cat burglar. When she reached the end of the window she grabbed hold of her sage green drapes and covered herself like a childhood game of hide-and-seek. She glided with the window treatments across the window. As soon as the curtain moved, flashes from the cameras below glinted on the window. Sarah Jessica Barker jumped on the bed poised for attack against the paparazzi below.

"It's okay, girl. We're safe and sound up here." Kate climbed into bed with Sarah Jessica Barker and her laptop. She did what she should've been smart enough to do weeks ago. She typed Jack Moskowitz into her search engine.

Before she could even finish typing his last name, Jack Moskowitz popped up followed by Jack Moskowitz Considerable Carriages, and Jack Moskowitz and Kate Richards. Hours ago she had no idea who Jack really was and now they would forever be linked on a search engine.

Kate couldn't help herself. She clicked on the top story about her and Jack. It was on the blog of that D-List male social climber who garnered his real fame off a gossip blog.

In the biggest scandal to rock the best-selling cookbook industry since the world found out southern belle Paula Deen wasn't nearly as sweet as her Skillet Fried Apple Pie—Kate Richards has been linked to Considerable Carriages mogul Jack Moskowitz.

Kate just blamed Jack and his supersized stroller company for being behind the whole childhood obesity debacle. Wonder who's sleeping on the couch tonight? Or was that just a little Shades of Grey *style foreplay with this unexpected couple?*

Kate couldn't believe that five hundred and thirty-four people had already posted the article to their Facebook pages and another nine hundred and eighty-two had tweeted it.

The door flew open and Sarah Jessica Barker jumped off the bed and hurtled straight towards Dana.

"Don't even think about jumping on me. This shirt cost more than you."

Sarah Jessica Barker backed away slowly and climbed back on the bed.

"I Googled Jack and it was like opening Pandora's box."

"I told you to stop worrying about that bottom feeder. We need to focus on you right now."

Kate slapped the laptop shut and pushed it away like a plate of overeaten food that needed to be moved from temptation.

"Don't say a word till I'm finished." Dana had pulled all of her dreads into a pile on top of her head and secured them with Kate's hot pink scarf, so she looked like a tiny African princess.

Kate heaved a great sigh. "Yeah, yeah, yeah. I'm screwed."

"I'm just making sure you get it. Lara told me to hold off sending the *Mini-Munchies II* manuscript."

"Fuck!" Kate pushed her fingers into her temple to stave off the pulsating pain.

"It takes years to build a career and seconds to annihilate it." Dana had a small fleck of red lipstick on her front tooth, which only made Kate feel worse. "It took three days for Paula Deen's multi-million dollar dynasty to crumble."

"Enough about her already. What's the plan?"

"First, you have to agree to do everything I say. I'm talking one hundred percent here."

"I already told you I was on board. Now you're really freaking me out."

"Honestly if you were anyone else, I might have hit the door running."

"I thought you were the queen of PR?"

"We're not talking about rehab here Kate. This is so much worse."

"Just tell me the plan."

"I found you a fiancé." Dana clasped her two hands together and smiled wide enough for Kate to see Dana's one remaining wisdom tooth.

"What?"

"His name is Alex Lombardi, which makes the two of you Ali-Kat. The tabloids are going to eat this up!"

"I don't get it." Kate grabbed the bottle of Tums from her night table drawer and popped two in her mouth. They squeaked against her teeth as she broke down the gritty tablets with no water. "How did you find me a fiancé?"

"I have very discreet connections in the industry. This guy is looking for a way to get his name out there, so it's win-win for both of you."

"So, he poses as my fiancé and then what? The cameras follow us right to the altar? Then I get divorced seventy-two days later?"

"You don't have to actually marry the guy. You just have to be engaged for awhile, then have a very public break up."

"This is insane."

"We have to get the attention off you and Jack. If people believe you dated, your credibility is shot and all your sponsors will jump ship."

"Who is this guy anyway?"

"He's from *The True NJ*." At least Dana had the good grace to look down at the carpet.

"Was The Situation from *Jersey Shore* unavailable?"

"This was the most popular season of *The True* ever. Everyone loves Alex, especially right now since the finale only aired a week ago."

"How old is he?"

"I think he's like twenty-three."

"Are you insane?"

"Listen, the guy is a double threat. We've got the popularity from the show and cougars are the hottest thing right now."

"Cougar! I'm only thirty-five!"

"The Considerable Carriages CC-XL Deluxe stroller isn't even in the stores yet and sales for it are already equal to more than Bugga Boo, MacClaren and Peg Perego sales combined for this fiscal year. If that doesn't say something about childhood obesity in this country, I don't know what does."

David Storm, News 24-7

Chapter Twenty-Seven

"Dad's hurt?"

Jack headed up the stairs towards Lauren, slowly like you would approach a wounded animal. "I was going to tell you."

Lauren bolted down the stairs past Jack and Diesel and practically body checked the anorexic looking reporter who was making her way up the stoop.

"Lauren! Wait!" Jack dragged Diesel down the stairs and pushed through the crowd. Quick on her feet from all the gymnastics and the shot of angry adrenaline—Lauren was already halfway down the street by the time Jack's feet hit the pavement. Diesel barked and grabbed playfully at the leash as he followed Jack down the sidewalk.

Lauren's thick curls whipped across her back as she ran, the soles of her feet barely hitting the sidewalk. A child with the stamina of an elite athlete, powered by anger, Lauren could probably run the length of the city without stopping. Jack had visions of chasing her over the Brooklyn Bridge footpath.

"Lauren! He's okay. Please stop so I can tell you what happened!" Jack forced the words out over his labored breathing. He vowed to cut back on the take out and to start working out.

Lauren stopped on the corner of 21st and the West Side Highway. She turned her flashing gray eyes on Jack.

"Seriously. I'm about to have a heart attack here!" Jack stopped next to Lauren and leaned over to catch his breath. Diesel started chewing on Lauren's shoelace.

"If he's really okay, you would've told me what was going on."

"He is, I swear." Jack grabbed his side.

Lauren plopped down on the sidewalk and pulled her knees to her chest. Her hot pink sequined sneakers caught the setting sun and scattered pink lights on the white car illegally parked on the corner. Jack squatted next to her, while trying to avoid the questionable wet stain on the sidewalk. Diesel tucked himself in a ball on the ground next to Lauren, resting his head on her feet.

"Your dad's helicopter went down a few weeks ago. When your mom first found out, she didn't know how bad it was and she didn't want to freak you out."

"When she left to film the commercial?" Lauren smirked and used air quotes when she said commercial.

"Yes. The night that Kate and I hung out with you."

"So the reporter was right," said Lauren. "Kate probably made up the whole *KidFit* filming just to keep me from figuring out about Dad."

"No. She really does want to film with you." But as Jack said it, he wondered if she would still want to now. That was just one more thing he would have to figure out once he got Lauren to come back home with him.

"Like I believe anything you say." Lauren pulled at a long pink string on her athletic shorts.

"Do you want to hear what happened to your dad or not?"

"Whatever," said Lauren, but she stopped pulling on the string and looked up at him.

"Your dad got flown to a marine hospital in California as soon as the medics stabilized him. Your mom had no idea how bad his injuries were when she flew out to meet him."

"She should've told me so I could go with her with her." Lauren kept her eyes on the sidewalk with one hand absentmindedly petting Diesel.

"She didn't want you to be as scared as she was. Your mom was just trying to protect you."

"Sure, whatever. What happened to my dad?"

"He fractured one of his hands and needed surgery to remove his spleen."

"Does he like need a spleen transplant now? Because he can have mine."

"No, he doesn't need another spleen. It's like your appendix. Don't know what it does, just that you don't really need it."

"So then why didn't you just tell me what was going on?"

"Your dad's worst injury was to his eyes. When he first got hurt, the doctors didn't know if he would be able to see again."

"No!" Lauren's voice was deeper than Jack had ever heard it.

"Lauren, listen to me. He had surgery and the doctors are pretty sure your dad's vision's gonna come back."

"Pretty sure? Like fifty percent sure or like a hundred percent?"

"I think ninety percent."

"When will we know?"

"In a few more days. Your parents wanted me to wait to tell you until then, so you wouldn't be worried."

"I want to see my dad."

"I'll take you," said Jack. "I just need a day or two to get us tickets and straighten out this mess."

Lauren tucked her head into her knees. Her auburn waves of hair fell forward looping over her legs and trailing on the dirty sidewalk. Her shoulders moved quietly.

Jack sat down next to her and rested his arm across her shoulders. She shook it off. Lauren had her father's strong resolve. She cried it out for a minute or two and brushed herself off—ready to head back home. She stood up, wiped her eyes on the sleeves of her hoody and grabbed Diesel's leash without a word.

They snuck back through a small alley between two buildings on 19th Street where they could access the back of Jack's small yard. Jack hoisted Lauren up and she pulled herself over the wooden fence. Lauren was so small and muscular it was like heaving up a bag of bricks. Then Jack dangled Diesel over the edge till he felt Lauren grab the wriggling dog.

Then it was Jack's turn to get over the fence. He got a leg up on an old aluminum trashcan and was able to pull himself over the edge. He got his right leg over the wooden fence just fine with the exception of a thick splinter of wood that lodged in his thigh when his jeans got hiked up. But when Jack tried to get his left leg down, the hem of his jeans got stuck on the top of the fence and he landed in an awkward heap on the brick patio.

"OMG! Are you okay?" Lauren whisper shouted.

Jack nodded and held a finger to his lips. But when he stood up and put pressure on his foot a sharp pain radiated from his pinky toe to his ankle. He exhaled sharply and had to restrain himself from slinging a string of curse words.

Lauren put Diesel on the ground and walked over to Jack. She put her arm around his waist and motioned for him to lean on her as they walked across the small yard. As soon as they were in the kitchen, she helped Jack to the chair so he could collapse.

"Thanks."

"This doesn't mean I like forgive you or anything." Lauren pulled a bag of frozen peas from the fridge and tossed them to Jack. She had sat in the same chair with a frozen bag of veggies resting on a gymnastics injury more than once over the past few years.

"Lauren," Jack started.

"Whatever. I don't want to talk." Lauren turned swiftly on her heel and headed upstairs.

Jack leaned back in the old wooden dining chair that had been his mother's favorite. The scratched blond wooden rolling chair didn't exactly go with the rest of the apartment, but it felt like home to him. He wheeled himself over to the junk drawer and grabbed a roll of duct tape. He ripped off a long piece using his teeth and MacGyvered a make shift ice pack around his ankle.

Jack almost fell backward in his chair a second later when the glass patio door opened and Matt walked in.

"You scared the shit out of me. How'd you make it past the

reporters?"

"How many times did we sneak in past curfew? I can hop that fence in my sleep."

"I clearly lost my skills." Jack gestured to his jerry-rigged ankle.

"You did the same thing that night we snuck in after Tommy Rizzo's party. Hopefully it's not broken this time." Matt opened the fridge and grabbed two beers. He handed one to Jack and kept the other for himself.

"What the fuck? You don't answer your phone?"

"Ringer was off. My cover's blown huh?"

"Shut the fuck up! You've got reporters camped out on your front stoop and you don't Google yourself?"

"I was just about to. I had some major Lauren drama to deal with first."

"Here's the low down. The press figured out the fem-bot was slumming with you. They did a feature story about you guys on *The 411* and it hit all the gossip sites. This is going to make the front pages of all tomorrow's papers."

"Fuck!" Jack held the cold beer bottle against his head and rolled it over his temples.

"We've had over fifty thousand hits on our website in the past half hour."

"I have to call Kate."

"First, let me show you the *Gossip Matters* site. They did a huge story and mentioned the new stroller."

"I can't think straight till I talk to Kate."

"Not so fast Romeo." Matt looked up from the laptop, the screen casting a blue haze over his face.

"Just so you know I'm eating stale crackers and mint jelly for dinner since we have no food in the house!" Lauren's voice carried from the top of the stairs.

"What's up with the kid?"

"Some motherfucking reporter whose ass I would love to kick let the cat out of the bag about David."

"I told you there's nothing more dangerous than a pissed off woman. How do you think the reporter found out about David?"

"Summer flings never make it past August because that's when all your asshole friends come back from vacation and hate your new girlfriend."

Alex Lombardi, The True NJ

Chapter Twenty-Eight

"We're not in California and medical marijuana's only legal if you have a script for it." Dana grabbed her heels from under the breakfast bar and grimaced when she wedged her blistered heels in.

"Do any of your jerk-off friends actually have a script?" Dana held the phone with her left hand and used the right to untie the scarf that had been wrapped around her hair. She shook her dreads loose so they fell down her back in thick chords of chai.

"Was he actually in the car with you when you got pulled over? No? Then how does that help?"

"I'm on my way. I'll call a lawyer from the cab. Just keep your mouth shut till she gets there." Dana hung up the phone and shoved it in her bag along with her laptop.

"I'll be back in a few hours. In the meantime, work on clearing tomorrow's schedule. We have some major PR damage control to do."

"Shit! I'm supposed to film with Lauren tomorrow."

"Push it back a day. But don't cancel it all together. She's our cover for you spending time with Jack."

"Poor Lauren's been really looking forward to this."

"And don't call Jack directly. Just send the kid a text."

"I have to talk to him sometime."

"Not until I can figure out what you're going to say."

Dana was gone in a rush of perfume, a quick slick of lip gloss and an extra swig of her drink.

"Stay." Kate pointed a finger at Sarah Jessica Barker and stared her down when her doorbell rang five minutes later.

"It's probably Dana. And you know how she feels about you jumping on her." The dog responded with an eye roll and a yawn.

"What'd you forget?" Kate threw the door open and found a delivery man standing in her doorway, his black NY Burger Co. baseball cap shielding his face.

"I didn't order. It's probably for 3G."

"Turkey burger, no bun, fries and a chocolate shake." The rim of the baseball hat lifted and Kate found herself looking right into Jack's bloodshot and swollen eye.

"Are you insane?" Kate hissed. "The reporters camped out front are waiting for a shot like this."

"Hence the disguise." In addition to the deliveryman's hat, Jack wore a black long-sleeved New York Burger Co. shirt over his jeans. He propped a road bike complete with a thick industrial strength metal chain against the wall. "But if you're really worried, you should let me in."

Kate tried to slam the door, but it bounced off his leg.

"Fuck!" Jack fell to the ground and grabbed his ankle, without moving it from the doorstopper position.

"Seriously?! Like I'm stupid enough to fall for that?" Kate knew she hadn't shut the door that hard. There seemed to be no end to Jack's bullshit.

Jack groaned. "Paparazzi injury." He pulled up the worn hem of his jeans to reveal a swollen ankle wrapped haphazardly in an ace bandage.

"That's nothing compared to my paparazzi injury!" Kate pushed against the door, but Jack showed no sign of budging. "At least your ankle will heal unlike my career!"

The nosy hedge funder from across the hall poked her head out her door. Her recently filler pumped cheeks made the woman look like a squirrel with a mouthful of acorns. "You okay Kate?"

Jack raised his eyebrows and whispered, "Might wanna let me in."

"Everything's fine Alison. The delivery guy just tripped on his way in."

"Let me know if you need anything." Alison lowered her voice. "You know. With everything going on." She flashed what was supposed to be a supportive smile, but Kate was no fool. She knew the woman would sell her out to *The 411* without a second thought.

"Thanks Alison. I will." Kate grabbed Jack's arm and helped him up, glad he fell with his back to Alison's door.

Jack stood up gingerly, putting all his pressure on his right side. He loped in through the door doing a cross between a hop and hobble.

Kate shut the door firmly before hissing. "It's so easy for you to lie isn't it?" She poked at the NY Burger Co. logo that stretched across his chest.

"I had to see you." Jack reached for Kate's hand but she yanked it away. He leaned down to pet Sarah Jessica Barker, but she scrambled over to Kate and hid behind her legs. "Great. Even the dog hates me."

"She knows what loyalty is. Unlike you." Kate felt a spray of spit fly out of her mouth.

"You never would've given me a chance if you knew who I was." Jack put the grease dotted brown paper bag of food on the small table by the front door and took a small step towards Kate.

"You've been lying to me since day fucking one! You're the one who didn't give me a chance." Kate took a step back and almost tripped over Sarah Jessica Barker.

"This is not what it looks like." Jack winced and leaned down to rub his ankle.

"Really? Because it looks like you lied to get in my pants while you were plotting with that disgusting business partner of yours to take me down."

"I didn't lie to get in your pants. And from what I recall you were just as eager to get into mine."

"That's because I thought you freelanced for dot com start ups!"

"So that's what turned you on? Now I know what to use as my new pick up line."

Kate grabbed a throw pillow off the couch and chucked it at Jack. But he ducked and it hit the wall and slid to the floor in anti-climactic silence.

"Getting the media to out you as my mystery man the same day my article comes out! Good play Jack!"

"You mean the article where you compare my company to big tobacco and blame Matt and me for all the pediatric cases of Type II Diabetes?"

"I wasn't attacking you personally. I had no idea who you were when I wrote that!"

"Exactly—what kind of research did you do for this so called article? Do you really think *New York Today* would've run your story if you didn't have a hit TV show?"

"I did enough research to know that childhood obesity rates have skyrocketed since you started making your strollers!"

"Enough about the damn strollers! You and I have something separate from all this other bull shit."

"Bull shit? You call everything I worked my ass off for bull shit?"

"We can figure all this out."

"You stay busy figuring it all out while my sponsors jump ship and my show gets cancelled."

"Dana won't let that happen."

"Paula Deen's last cookbook never saw the light of day even though pre-orders had already landed it on the bestseller list."

"Are you saying being with me makes you as bad as being a racist?"

"Being with you makes me a liar and a hypocrite." Kate grabbed the galley proof of *Mini-Munchies II*.

"My manuscript was a waste of the last six months of my life because it's never getting published now." Kate tried to rip the papers but the stack was too thick and her hands had always been embarrassingly weak.

"Need some help there—tough guy?" Jack grabbed the papers from Kate's hands and shoved them on top of the fridge where Kate couldn't reach. "Do you seriously think your cookbook won't get printed?"

"Random House officially delayed going to print."

"Well, I'm sure they'll rush to print once Dana and my PR reps figure out a game plan."

"They all could have thought of a plan a hell of a lot sooner if you had told me who you were!"

"I tried, Kate. I was too scared of losing you."

"Well, now I could lose everything because of you!"

"This will all blow over as soon as the next post-adolescent Disney star gets arrested."

"My career is in shambles and you're cracking jokes?"

"This is not what I wanted."

"Then what *do* you want? Huh, Jack? What do you want?"

"You know what I want." Jack made it across the room in two clumsy hops, his eyes locked on Kate's the whole time.

"Don't do this, Jack. Just take your ridiculous bike and go home." Kate stood there for a minute with her eyes closed, thinking that when she opened them again he would be gone, an apparition ordered to disappear.

But Kate didn't protest when she felt him reach for her. Jack's hand covered her entire lower back from one side to the other as he grabbed her and pulled her into him. He trailed his hands up her back until his hands got lost in her hair. Kate kept her eyes closed and Jack sunk his lips into hers at first timidly, searching for her tongue with his, then more greedily. And in that moment, the only thing that mattered was being with Jack.

There were no little funny comments from either of them this time. On another day Jack would've been sure to crack a joke about hooking up with the delivery guy. Instead, it was so quiet you could almost hear the sound of clothes being ripped off.

Jack's hands were everywhere as he searched Kate's mouth for answers. Then he pulled her down to the floor. She could feel the itch of the wool rug scratch her skin, while Jack kissed her.

All she wanted was for Jack to be inside her. Instead he held her wrists as he ran his mouth down the most sensitive inside part of her arm. Kate was ready for him. She jutted her hips forward to meet him but Jack held her down and moved his mouth over to her stomach and then up to the underside of her breasts.

"Jack. I need you. Now."

Suddenly in one hard thrust he was inside her. But it wasn't enough. Kate needed him as far inside her as he could get. She took control, flipping him over till she was on top of him.

Kate slid herself down Jack till she felt him taking up all of her. She arched her back and rocked herself back and forth, feeling him move inside of her till she felt herself tremble and quake and release everything at the same time he did.

"Holy shit." Jack spread his arms wide and lay there looking completely spent.

Kate stayed there for a minute with Jack still inside her wrapped in the stickiness of their shared bodies.

Then, the doorbell rang.

"Whoever it is, go away." Jack pulled Kate back into him and kissed her.

"Kate? Are you in there?" The door pounded again and Kate pictured Dana using all of the strength in her ninety-five pound body to make the thundering noise.

"Shit. It's Dana. Get dressed." Kate whispered, as she climbed off Jack and scrambled to find her clothes.

"Hold on a minute. I'll be right there." Kate found her shirt and bra flung over the edge of the couch. Her yoga pants were under the coffee table. But her underwear was nowhere to be seen. If this wasn't an occasion for going commando, Kate wasn't sure what was.

Jack winced as he shoved his bum leg back into his jeans. "Everything else is bullshit."

Jack pulled his hat brim back over his face and nodded to Kate. She pulled the door open in what she hoped was a nonchalant way. "Sorry, I was just straightening out my delivery order."

Dana walked in the apartment. "I finished up as fast as I could with that dingbat client." She walked in and Jack started to head out.

"I hope you gave this guy a good tip. He looks like he can barely walk." Dana nudged her head toward Jack.

"Oh, I gave him a good tip." Kate said, as Jack hobbled towards the door. He turned the doorknob and was ready to go when he took one look back at Kate.

"Wait a minute!" Dana was at the door in a second. She stood on her tiptoes and yanked Jack's hat off. "You almost had me fooled with that crazy hair of yours undercover."

Jack stood there sheepishly with his unruly hat head. "I had to see Kate to explain."

"Looks like you did a lot more than explaining!"

"Dana, be reasonable. We had to talk things out."

"That's why your fucking dog has your thong in her mouth?"

"Drop that!" It was pretty hard to maintain her dignity while she fished her thong out of her dog's mouth with an audience.

Dana rushed over to the window and closed the curtains.

"You better hope those reporters down there didn't get a shot of that!"

"Who knew a guy that designs strollers for fat kids could be so cute?
If Kate Richards doesn't want him—I'm goin' for it."
Jessa Silver, Late Night with Jessa Silver

Chapter Twenty-Nine

"This is un-fucking-believable! I just spent the whole cab ride from Chambers Street coming up with a game plan, while you're back here fucking the guy who put you in this mess in the first place!" Dana threw her bag down on the armchair as Sarah Jessica Barker scampered behind Kate's back.

"In all fairness, I didn't set out to screw up Kate's career..." started Jack. He spoke in a low tone like you would with someone in an insane asylum. He found Dana to be the most terror-inducing tiny person he had ever come across.

"Are you ready to walk away from all of it? The show, the book, the packaged food?" Dana completely ignored Jack and focused all her attention on Kate who was awkwardly smoothing her hair down from the tangled mass of curls sticking straight up in the back of her head.

"We can fix this."

"I already told you how we're going to fix this. And it doesn't involve hooking up with this douchebag." Dana spun around to face Jack so fast her whipping dreads made an actual swishing sound. She fixed her hazel eyes on Jack. They were an eerie shade of orange and reminded Jack of the vampire teens from those movies Lauren always watched.

"I thought I had you pegged Jack. Revenge scheme—pure and simple. Carnage done, I move in to do damage control."

Dana stood with her hands on her hips, trying to look tough, but Jack could see her wobble a bit in her skyscraper heels.

"It's not like that." Jack stood still trying to put all his pressure on the one good ankle.

"Oh, I can see that. This is way worse than I thought. You actually have feelings for Kate!"

"Of course I do. I fell for her at the dog park." Jack pulled the baseball cap on his head.

"You did?" Kate smiled at Jack and he felt a sudden burst of hope.

"Of course."

"We don't have time for this star crossed lovers bull shit. There are hoards of reporters out front. Rich showed me how to access the service exit that will let us out on 24th Street."

"You better go with Dana." Kate pulled her tangled waves out of the neck of her shirt and secured them in a loose ponytail.

"Don't worry. We'll figure something out." Jack leaned in and kissed the top of Kate's head.

Kate's eyes were still closed when he finally pulled away. When she opened them, she didn't say anything. She just lifted her fingers in a half-hearted wave and turned away before Dana shut the door behind them.

Dana walked down the short hallway to the elevator bank and pressed the button. Jack wheeled the bike behind her. They entered the elevator wordlessly and Dana hit the B button.

"How long did you spend building your business Jack?" Dana tugged on his arm so he had no choice but to face those other-wordly eyes of hers.

"All in all—about seven years." Jack swallowed hard, certain that this was the wrong answer.

"Kate's got you beat. She spent her whole life climbing out of the hole her crappy parents put her in. And you might have just cost her everything!" Dana words came out in seething hisses.

"I had it rough too growing up. Don't act like I don't get it." Jack tried to keep his voice calm to show Dana they were both fighting on the same side.

"Oh poor Jack. Your dad abandoned you and your mom

died." Dana's voice was laced in thick sarcasm as she sneered at Jack. "Kate would have been better off in your situation. You've met Eddie haven't you?"

"At least he's in rehab now." Jack was desperate to get out of the airless elevator. As soon as the door jerked open, he stepped out. But Dana was right on his heels in the dark basement hallway.

"Do you know how Kate became Mrs. Fink's roommate?" Dana walked in double time to keep up with Jack.

"She answered an ad in the Village Voice."

"Mrs. Fink knew Kate from the bagel shop where Kate worked in between her shifts teaching Tae Bo at Gold's Gym. Early one morning, Mrs. Fink found her sleeping on a bench outside the dog park." Dana led Jack past the recycling area stacked ceiling high with collapsed Fresh Direct boxes.

"Kate was homeless?" As shocked as Jack was, a small part of him was also hurt that Kate hadn't told him. He had told her everything. That is except his real name.

"She didn't start that way. Kate worked her ass off and saved until she could move to the city. Things were going great until her dad suckered Kate into giving him her rent money after he got mixed up with a Chinatown gambling ring."

"She couldn't make rent one month and her roommates kicked her out?"

"They were pissed off enough about that. Then Kate let Eddie crash for the night and he ransacked the place. Stole every loose piece of change and jewelry he could get his hands on."

"Fuck! Why is it such a big secret?"

"Because Kate doesn't want to pull the whole I was raised by wolves shtick Bethenny Frankel uses."

"Kate and I can go to the press and…"

"And what? Tell them you're both in love and you're going to have lots of little fat babies who will ride around in the new CC-XL Deluxe?"

"You're the PR genius. I'm sure you can figure something out."

"Walk away Jack. If you really care about Kate like you say

you do—walk away."

"I don't think I can do that."

"Then you're going to cost her everything."

The service exit let him out on 24th Street, which was deserted. He hopped right on the bike welcoming the throbbing in his foot while he rode the few short blocks to NY Burger Co.

Jack slipped into the bathroom, where he changed his shirt and ditched the hat. He found Steve, the older brother of one of Lauren's teammates behind the counter frying up burgers. He waited till the kid turned around.

"Thanks buddy." Jack reached over the glass counter and handed the shirt and hat over.

"Did it work?"

"Yeah. These reporters have been hounding me. It was the only way I could get to the office."

"Cool."

"I left the bike locked up outside." Jack reached over and palmed the kid a fifty.

"Holy shit. Thanks man."

"No worries. Catch you later."

Jack was almost out the door when he heard Kate's voice. He whipped around at the buttery sound and wondered how she had beaten him to the burger joint.

But when he turned around, he realized that Kate's voice was projecting from the TV screen from a *KidFit* clip. Kate faded into the background as *The 411* host Craig Ashbourne stepped into the shot.

"Will Kate Richards' career implode as fast as Paula Deen's? Rumor has it that soap star and *Dancing with the Stars* winner Shana Stilton in already in talks with ABC to take over Kate Richards' place as host of *KidFit*. This comes on the heels of reports that Kashi, Simply Organix, Nutri-Kids and Annie's are all threatening to pull *KidFit* sponsorship after Kate Richards has been linked to super-sized stroller mogul Jack Moskowitz. Random House has also reportedly delayed printing of the long anticipated sequel to *Mini-Munchies*."

Jack didn't wait to hear the rest. He hurried out the door

before anyone spotted him. Then he spent the walk home doing what he should have done from the beginning. He Googled *KidFit* and read everything he could pull off his iPhone.

Jack spotted a small crowd of paparazzi camped out on his stoop as soon as he rounded the corner by his townhouse.

"Jack!"

"Jack! Can you tell us about your relationship with Kate Richards?"

"What made you fall for a woman who hates your company?"

"Did Kate tell you about the *New York Today* article?"

Once Jack walked to the top of the steps he knew there was no going back. He cleared his throat before addressing the crowd of reporters.

"Look I know my strollers aren't cheap, but they last. Basically, till you kick the kid outta the damn thing. Then, you use it for your next kid or pass it on to a friend. That means per family I'm probably only getting you for about eight hundred dollars."

"That's a lotta money Jack." A pudgy reporter wearing a backwards Yankees cap interjected.

"The real question here is just how much Kate Richards is making off childhood obesity? She's got that new *KidFit* meal and snack line right? Do you know how much it would cost one kid to go on her diet plan?" Jack paused for dramatic effect. He knew because he had done the math on the walk over.

"Five hundred bucks a month. That's not including her workout DVDs or diet cookbook. Kate Richards better hope there's no end in sight for childhood obesity. Between the two of us, she makes way more off it than I do. Don't let her make you think otherwise."

"So I guess that means you two aren't a thing?" The Yankees cap guy wasn't the brightest bulb, but at least he spelled it out for everyone.

"Money hungry narcissists are not my type."

"Alex Lombardi tried his best to dupe the throng of reporters camped outside Kate Richards' Chelsea apartment after she broke the news of her engagement to the reality star twelve years her junior. Our very own The 411 *reporter Dan Waite spotted Alex entering through the maintenance door in the small alley between Kate's state of the art eco-friendly building and the loft space next door. Though Alex said 'no comment' it was clear by the look on his face that he wasn't going to let a swarm of paparazzi get between him and his sweetheart. What will his fellow* The True NJ *alum and former girlfriend Tammy say when she finds out about this?"*

The 411

Chapter Thirty

"How am I going to work things out with Jack if I pretend to be engaged to some twenty-something Guido from Jersey?"

"Have you given any thought to seeing a therapist?" Dana wheeled around from her laptop.

"That's just rude."

"I'm absolutely serious. Don't you think there's some sort of connection to "the gambling man" here?" Dana made sure to over emphasize the air quotes.

"What does any of this have to do with my father?"

"The male role model you grew up with has spent your whole life lying to you and taking complete advantage of you. I don't think it's a coincidence that you keep falling for the same kind of bullshitter. First Tyler, now Jack."

"How can you even compare Jack to Tyler? Tyler stole my show idea and made a fortune off it."

"And Jack lied to you about who he was and potentially destroyed everything you worked so hard for. Honestly, I think Jack took much more from you than Tyler ever did. Tyler stole your idea. Jack stole your reputation and the career you spent years building."

"Jack and I can…"

"You and Jack can sail into the sunset after I'm done resurrecting your career. Until then, you need to stick with the plan and keep Jack out of it." Dana looked back down at her laptop.

"I can't let Jack think I was with him and Alex at the same time."

"Hmm, doesn't sound like something a money-hungry narcissist would say." Dana flicked her finger across her iPad screen.

"What?"

Dana cleared her throat and read aloud while she held her iPad out for Kate to see the article.

The battle of the bulge heats up as super-sized stroller mogul Jack Moskowitz slams kids' fitness guru Kate Richards for taking advantage of the smallest victims of our fast food nation by bilking them for hundreds of dollars a month to follow her fitness plan. Still think these two are an item? Think again, Jack says he doesn't bring money-hungry narcissists to the bedroom.

"Looks like Jack's out for himself. It's about time you were."

"But we just…"

"Had sex? When are you going to realize all that guy cares about is screwing you then screwing you over?"

"Fuck!" Kate's head was throbbing and her ears were ringing. She had put her money on the wrong horse for the last time.

"You want revenge? Go change."

"What for?"

"One of my anonymous tippers just put the word out that Alex would be trying to sneak past the reporters to see you."

"How's he going to know what to say when they start asking questions?"

"No comment works every time. Trust me, he's well versed in this type of stuff. How else do you think those reality shows have such interesting plots?"

Kate smoothed down the wrinkled Dave Matthews tee shirt she had been sleeping in since college. "What do I care what this guy thinks of me? It's not like we're really dating." "Yeah, but do we really need to scare him off?" asked Dana. "Hurry up and go change."

"Hmm, what does one wear when they meet their fake fiancé for the first time?" mused Kate, as she slid off the kitchen barstool.

"Dark rinse skinny jeans, black ballet flats, and a fitted white button down."

"How did you know…?"

"Every respectable Manhattan woman has those items in their closet. And while you're at it, sweep your hair into a messy ponytail and add a thick headband on top."

Kate's phone rang for what was probably the hundredth time that day, but this time she actually answered because she saw Lifelong Gamblers' Recovery Center on the caller ID.

"Get dressed while you talk," said Dana, when Kate picked up the phone. She made waving motions towards Kate's bedroom door.

"Hello. This is Valerie, your father's case manager from the Lifelong Gamblers' Recovery Center. Is this Kate Richards?"

"Please tell me my father hasn't gotten into trouble yet?"

"On the contrary. He's taking an active role in his recovery and thriving here."

"Oh good. You had me worried for a second there." Kate let out the huge balloon of air that had been trapped in her lungs.

"As we discussed when you registered your father, his treatment is going to be lengthy given the severity of his condition. We have confidence that we can get him in recovery, but it is going to take an indefinite amount of time."

"I'm aware of that. I want him to stay as long as he needs to in order to get better." Kate didn't know why, but she was getting a very uncomfortable feeling from her end of the conversation.

"In light of your situation, I just wanted to check in that payment isn't going to be an issue. I don't want to put pressure on you, but they're reporting on *Gossip Matters* that the *KidFit* execs are already thinking of replacing you with that reality star who won *Dancing with the Stars* last year. If you don't think you can handle these payments long term, it's okay. It just means we'll have to alter your father's treatment plan and…"

"Stop right there. Keep my father's treatment plan as is. Don't worry about the money. I've got it covered."

Kate hung up the phone and followed all of Dana's directions to a t and even added a fresh slick of lip gloss. Maybe Dana was right, she shouldn't look a gift fiancé in the mouth.

Kate actually had butterflies in her stomach when the doorbell rang. She didn't know why she was suddenly so nervous. It wasn't like anything real was actually going to happen with this guy.

As soon as Kate opened the door, her sinuses were assaulted by a wave of spicy cologne reminiscent of her days back in high school, when boys didn't get the whole concept of less is more.

The hulking mass standing in the doorway looked like an advertisement for body building shakes. His blond hair formed a three-inch high shellacked crown around his face, which was a disturbing shade of orange reminiscent of the Oompa Loompas from the original Willy Wonka movie.

"Hey, I'm Alex." He walked into the doorway so that Kate had to take a few steps back to let him through. There was something vaguely familiar about him, but Kate couldn't figure out what.

"Sweet place." He pressed his top teeth to his full bottom lip and let loose a wolf whistle.

Sarah Jessica Barker jumped off the couch and landed at Alex's feet with bared teeth and surly growls. She thrust her butt against Kate's legs in an attempt to shield her from their guest.

"It's okay. I'm not gonna hurt you." Alex leaned towards the dog and came very close to losing a finger.

"I'm so sorry. She's not used to having guys around the apartment." Kate scooped up her dog and held her tight while whispering stern but reassuring words in her ear.

"Clearly." Alex took two big steps back and cowered in the corner from the fifteen-pound dog.

Kate was impressed with Dana's coordination as she slipped both feet back into her stilettos and hopped off the barstool in one fluid motion. Even with her six-inch heels, Dana stood at least a full foot shorter than this modern Greek Adonis.

Kate recognized the look of appreciation as Alex reacted the way most men did to Dana.

"Wow." Alex let loose another piercing whistle, which was growing old quickly for Kate. She held tight to Sarah Jessica Barker's collar to keep her from jumping out of her arms.

"I didn't know managers could be so hot. You should see mine."

Dana actually giggled. "Lenny's not that bad since he got the lap band surgery."

"You have such a smokin' body, you should be the fitness expert." Alex locked eyes with Dana and smiled.

There was something very familiar about Alex's thick Jersey accent. Kate was trying to remember where she knew Alex from when she noticed his tee shirt. New Jerzee was spelled out in blinding rhinestone swirls across his massive chest.

"Un-freaking-believable! You're the asshole who brought that aggressive German Shepherd to the dog park!"

"Did you ever think that maybe your little dog started the whole thing?"

"What? You bring some rabid dog named Cujo to a dog park and you're going to blame my dog for the drama?"

"She don't seem so friendly to me." He smoothed down the front if his shirt. "Just sayin.'"

"This isn't going to work." Kate couldn't believe she had actually changed her clothes for this jerk.

"Lenny said that fat kid show of yours is gonna go off the air if I don't help."

"You mean to tell me you hired someone to pose as my fiancé who hasn't even seen my show before?" Kate couldn't believe Dana had kicked Jack out of the apartment in favor of this jackass.

"No offense, but I'm not a fat kid and I don't got any fat kids so why would I watch your show?" Alex's smile quickly disappeared as he spun around to face Kate.

"He does have a point." Dana's voice was bordering on cajoling.

"The less offensive term is overweight." Kate spoke through gritted teeth. She debated letting her dog out of her arms and dealing with the consequences later.

"Doesn't really matter what you call the kids as long as they watch your show right?" asked Alex, with an exaggerated wink at Dana.

"You and I are going to get along great." Dana flicked several ropes of dreads off her face with a flick of her hand, exposing her regal cheekbones and angular jaw.

"You really need to at least watch a few episodes of the show, so you know what the reporters are talking about if they bring anything up in an interview," said Kate.

"Did you watch *The True NJ*?" asked Alex.

"I was too busy watching *Jersey Shore* reruns," snipped Kate.

"This is an easy fix," said Dana. "Give me an hour and I'll have DVDs for both of you."

"But my show's not on DVD yet," said Alex.

"Don't you worry," said Dana. "I have friends in all the right places."

"You really are my kind of woman." Alex fixed a dramatic wink at Dana.

"We need to take advantage of this photo op." Dana walked over to the floor-to-ceiling window that overlooked 23rd Street.

"No, problem." Alex stood up and pried off his tee shirt and carefully draped it over a chair. His body was the same tangerine hue as his face but with accents on his abs and chest as if someone had outlined all his muscles with an orange sharpie. His skin had a thin sheen that Kate hoped wouldn't rub off on any of her furniture.

"What're you doing?" Kate could hear the shock and horror magnified in her own voice.

Before Alex had a chance to answer, Kate hissed at Dana, "What is he doing?"

Alex stood in front of both of them, doing some kind of flexing exercise with his pecks. The acrid smell of spray tan mixed filled the room and Kate understood the need for so much cologne. "What kind of photo opportunity were you talking about?"

Dana picked up his tee shirt, when she got close enough to hand it to him her eyes were chest level and she didn't seem bothered in the least by the smell.

"Of course Dana, didn't mean that kind," said Kate.

Dana stood frozen with his tee shirt in her hands.

"Right Dana?"

"Oh no. It's too early for that." Dana finally handed Alex his shirt.

Alex shrugged, "That's better for me anyway. I'm having a bad peck day."

"They look pretty good to me," said Dana.

"Can we get back on track here?" asked Kate. "I just want to get this over with."

"Okay. At first I was thinking you could stand in the window making out. But then I thought that would look too staged," said Dana.

"That would definitely be too much," agreed Kate.

"You both need to stand in the frame of the window and look into each other's eyes and pretend to be saying something really romantic and meaningful," said Dana.

"How am I going to pull off romantic and meaningful with some guy I've known for like two minutes?" asked Kate.

"You managed to do that just fine in those pictures of you and Jack from the dog park. These pictures have to be even hotter." Dana tore herself away from Alex's chest and looked right at Kate. "Or else no one's going to buy it."

"Don't worry, I got this covered," said Alex. "I had a lot of practice with Tammy last season."

"You mean that was fake?" shrieked Dana.

"Let's hope he does a better job being discreet this time

around, or I'm screwed," said Kate, even though it didn't look like Dana was listening to her.

"Relax, I've got just as much at stake here as you do. Do you know how much those *Jersey Shore* kids made in endorsements and spin off shows? We're talking millions," said Alex.

At least the guy was motivated, thought Kate.

"Do you want to practice a pose?" asked Dana.

"No, let's just do it," said Alex. "It'll look more realistic that way."

"Yeah, but how we end up there in the first place?" asked Kate.

"Why don't you go stand in the window and act like you're on the phone, and Alex can join you in the frame," said Dana.

"You better get rid of the dog first. She looks like she's gonna go straight for my balls the second you let her go."

"Maybe she just needs a chance to get to know you better." Kate took a step closer to Alex and the dog erupted in full sized growls.

"Or maybe not. Stick her in the bedroom so we can get this show on the road." Dana kept her voice sweet for Alex's sake, but she fixed her eyes on Kate to show her she was dead serious.

"It's okay Sarah Jessica Barker. We're going to look back a few months from now and it will be like this never happened." Kate tucked her dog in her bed against the mounds of pillows and resisted the urge to climb in and bury her head under the covers. She took a deep breath before heading back to the living room.

Kate walked over to the picture window and pretended to send an email. She tried to keep her eyes trained on the small phone keypad, but the late afternoon sun was reflecting off the cameras below and making her see spots. She was so busy trying to act natural that she didn't notice Alex till he sidled up behind her. He so tall that Kate's head rested against his chest muscles, which had all the comfort of leaning against a concrete wall. It made Kate miss Jack's softness.

Alex lifted Kate's ponytail off her neck and buried his face in the hollow above her collarbone. Kate wasn't sure if she should keep typing, but she didn't want to turn to face him for fear that he would try to stage a make out session. Right now they probably looked like a scene right out of a Nicholas Sparks movie.

"That's perfect," said Dana. "Kate look up from the phone, but don't turn around. Alex, wrap your arms around her."

Alex moved his face down her neck towards the small space of skin exposed from her slightly unbuttoned shirt. She felt his lips brush against her skin as he enveloped her in his thick arms.

"Perfect. Once these pictures get out, everyone will forget all about you and Jack."

Chapter Thirty-One

Jack quick-stepped to close in the gap between him and Lauren. She had spent the whole ten-block walk to Chelsea Prep at least a full sidewalk square ahead of him. All attempts at conversation were met with either complete silence or if he was lucky a mumbled one word answer.

"How bout a doissant?" Jack pointed to the white food truck that sold hot coffee and doughnut-croissant hybrids.

"It's a cronut. And no thanks." Lauren didn't turn around but she did grant him a flick her hair in his general direction.

"You never ate dinner last night."

"Not hungry."

"You drool every time we pass the pastry guy. Are you really going to pass up the one time I cave and offer you straight sugar for breakfast?"

Lauren shrugged her shoulders. Jack closed in on her when she was stuck waiting for the light to change at Ninth Avenue.

"Did you talk to your mom?"

"Why? So she could lie to me some more about how awesome filming on the beach is going?"

"I know you're mad at your mom and me right now, but shutting us out isn't going to make you feel better."

"The only thing that's going to make me feel better is seeing my dad."

"Let's shoot for this weekend. I just need to stay here the

rest of the week to finish these new designs."

The walking signal lit up and Lauren bolted across the street. She ran up the school steps without even a backward glance Jack's way. He had a feeling the days of the secret handshakes were officially over.

His phone rang as soon as Lauren walked through the double doors.

"You just missed her."

"Shit. Lauren declined all my calls last night. I was hoping she would be less pissed by now." Harper sounded like she was in the hospital cafeteria and Jack took that as a good sign that at least she was eating something.

"She's just like you that way. The more time passes, the madder she gets."

"I know. But I thought maybe by this morning she might be ready to talk."

"You did the same thing to mom. Remember when she finally told us she had cancer. You gave her Hell for not telling us sooner. The poor woman was dying and you wouldn't talk to her for two weeks."

"Poor Mom. I was horrible back then."

"You got your pay back now."

"Seriously, how bad is Lauren?"

"She hasn't eaten since lunch yesterday. I got her favorite salad with that peanut dressing from NY Burger for dinner and she didn't touch it. She even turned down one of those croissant-doughnut things from the truck by school."

"Shit. She begs me every time we pass the Break Fast truck and I never let her get anything."

"I know."

"Is there any way you can bring her here?"

"I'm planning on it. I just can't get away till the end of the week."

"Maybe it would be good for you to get away from all the reporters."

"I'm pretty sure California has its fair share of reporters too."

"Shit, we're both a fucking mess."

"I know. The pre-orders keep coming in and I don't have a test model even ready yet."

"At least this drama hasn't hurt your business."

"Kate's the one who got screwed over here."

"Flowers aren't gonna fix this one big brother."

"I don't think anything's gonna fix this mess."

Jack hung up with Harper and headed to the office. He rarely worked anywhere other than his backyard, but at least he had security guards at the office. He had caught two paparazzi trying to scale the fence yesterday and another one digging through the trash.

Harmonie, the college intern was already sitting at her desk typing away at her laptop when Jack walked in. Jack had a feeling she spent just as much time on her own Facebook updates as the company page, but Jack was getting used to this new generation who texted and Facebooked at work.

"Hey Harmonie."

"Hi Jack. You know you actually look pretty hot on TV." Harmonie finger-combed her blond highlighted hair extensions.

"Thanks. I think."

"Our social media's been blowing up since yesterday. I've been trying to keep up with it."

"Good. You know I hate that shit."

"Don't worry about it. I've got you covered." Harmonie winked and her fake eyelash stuck to her bottom lid for a second too long.

"I have to finish these designs. So try not to let anyone know I'm here."

"No prob. I'll keep it on the DL."

Jack closed his office door and got settled at his desk with his laptop. He got right to work on the new designs. Their presales in one day had already surpassed their first month sales with the last line.

He was listening to his favorite design music—the Beatles Pandora station and working through the most underappreciated part of his design—the undercarriage when Matt burst through the door.

"The undercarriage is a bitch this time around. The extra weight means we need heavier steel, which might drive the price higher than we originally budgeted. Which is a serious problem since all those people just pre-ordered at what could be a low ball number."

"Don't worry about it. I found these steel guys from Detroit who can save us a shit load." Matt laid a slim wooden box on the table and slid back the top to reveal a perfect stack of Cuban cigars.

"You know my mom died of lung cancer and she didn't even smoke."

"Quit being a pussy. Aren't you even going to ask what the cigars are for?"

"I'm assuming they're for our crazy pre-sale numbers?"

Matt pulled out a thin sheet of paper with the unmistakable black whorls of an ultrasound.

"It's a boy!!!"

Jack jumped up and Matt pulled him into a crushing bear hug so hard he couldn't breath.

"Congrats man! That's unbelievable!"

Matt loosened his grip and Jack could see tears at the corners of his eyes.

"We came so close to this not happening. Now, Anne has this healthy baby boy growing inside her. This is just insane."

"Just wait till we get him his first long board!"

"I was just thinking that. This kid's gonna ride before he can walk."

"Unless Anne has anything to do about it."

"I don't think she's gonna give a shit. I've never seen her like this."

"Fuck it. Give me one of those cancer sticks."

"A few puffs won't kill us." Matt pulled two cigars from the box and handed one to Jack.

Jack pulled the cigar to his nose and inhaled the sharp musty tobacco that smelled like an old attic. He put it in his mouth and Matt held the lighter up to the end while Jack pulled his breath in. It took a few puffs to get the thing lit. As soon as Jack really inhaled, his chest was caught in a paroxysm of coughing. He pulled the cigar away and grabbed the water bottle from his desk. Matt thumped him on the back with two big wallops and Jack stopped coughing.

Matt stubbed the cigar out. "Classy shit is wasted on you. Next time I have good news we're just going to have to do some shots."

The door opened suddenly and Harmonie walked in.

"Are you guys smoking blunts in here?"

"No. Just cigars. How would you know what blunts smell like anyway?" asked Matt, with an eyebrow raised.

Harmonie shrugged. "You can't walk in the West Village without getting a contact high."

"Matt found out he's having a boy!" Jack held up the box of cigars.

"Congratulations! That's awesome."

"Thanks. Now what were you interrupting our little celebration party for?"

Harmonie stood in front of Jack's desk finger-combing her hair with her jet-black nails. She opened her mouth then shut it again without saying anything. She reminded Jack of one of those fancy goldfish with a large head and tiny body gulping for air.

"Did you break the printer again?" asked Jack. "You know you just can't ram the paper in there like you always do."

"The printer's fine. But you really need to go on the *Gossip Matters* website."

"I don't know what else they could possible print about me and Kate."

"Oh...it's... It's not about you and Kate this time. Just Kate."

Matt grabbed Jack's iPad off the desk and was on the website in seconds.

Cover Story: *Kate Richards: How I Found Love When I Least Expected It: Kate Richards opens up to us about how she fell madly in love with twelve years younger* The True NJ *star*

Alex Lombardi, how Alex popped the question, and their dream wedding plans.

If it weren't for the picture, Jack wouldn't believe it. A ridiculously over muscled spray tanned guy with blond hair gelled up at least five inches stood in the middle of Kate's living room with Sarah Jessica Barker sitting at his feet and Kate in his arms literally. He held her in the air, her dangling legs ending in skyscraper black heels. Kate was barely recognizable with her wavy hair flat-ironed pin straight and hanging back in the air as she tilted her head back—the camera catching her mid-laugh. The gigantic diamond ring on her finger stole the shot. The square diamond in a platinum setting glinted in the light and took away all attention from Kate and her orange gladiator.

Jack looked at the iPad with Matt and Harmonie leaning over both sides of him.

"Thanks for letting us know about this Harmonie. We'll see you later." Matt walked her to the door and shut it firmly behind her before she could say anything.

"What the fuck? She never even mentioned having a boyfriend."

"Looks like you weren't the only one lying the past few weeks."

"Look at this guy. Does he even look like someone Kate would talk to let alone marry?"

"She obviously didn't think you looked like someone who would own a stroller company for fat kids."

"This just doesn't make sense." Jack scrolled down to read the article.

After speculation that Kate Richards, host of ABC's highly rated KidFit *was dating Jack Moskowitz, the CEO of Considerable Carriages, a company that manufactures high chairs, strollers and car seat for obese children, she came clean to* Gossip Matters *about the real man in her life.*

"I never thought I would be engaged to a man so much younger than me, but I knew the day I met Alex that he really was an old soul," Richards says of Alex Lombardi, best known for his role

as "The Instigator" on last season's The True NJ. *The ultra fit duo met at a spin class at the Equinox in Chelsea.*

"We started talking one day after class and I realized that we had a lot in common," says Richards.

"And I realized she was hot. Why else would I always take the bike behind her?" cuts in Lombardi.

The high-ranking TV star and best-selling author plans to get married in a classic wedding gown surrounded by antique roses and a harpist. She wants a small wedding with just close family and friends. But Lombardi has other plans in mind, with a five hundred person guest list and celebrity musician Danger Mouse mixing tracks at "the after party".

For the rest of this exclusive story pick up a copy of the latest Gossip Matters, *which hits news stands Friday.*

"You got played." Matt grabbed the iPad from Jack and quickly closed out the *Gossip Matters* website.

"This has to be some kind of mistake. I was just there last night. Trust me. There's no way Kate's with someone else." Jack grabbed the iPad back and Googled Kate. Sure enough there were several more stories about Kate and the orange meathead.

"Maybe she wanted you to find out she was engaged the same way she found out who you were."

"Or maybe that shady publicist Dana cooked this whole thing up."

"You think this is a fauxmance?"

"Her camp had to get the attention off me and Kate."

"Dude, how would she get this guy to pretend to be engaged to her? And why would she pick him in the first place? He's a tool."

"You don't know Kate. There's no way she could carry on a conversation with a jackass like that, let alone marry him."

"Dude, he's less damaging to her career than you are."

*"A Big John's moving truck was spotted outside Kate Richards'
building with Alex Lombardi supervising the crew. Alex's one
must have item? His spray tan machine."*

dirtylaundry.com

Chapter Thirty-Two

"Not happening," said Kate.

"You want everyone to think you're pulling a Kim
Kardashian?" asked Dana.

"Where's he going to sleep?"

"The couch is fine," said Alex. "I've been living with five
roommates in an Alphabet City studio."

"Remember to keep the curtains closed at night," said Dana.
"The last thing we need is a photographer getting a picture of
you sleeping in the living room."

"Plenty of couples get engaged without moving in
together." Just Kate's luck. Now she finds a guy who wants to
commit right away.

"The more the gossip sites have to print about Ali-Kat, the
quicker everyone will forget about you and Jack." Dana busied
herself scrolling through her iPad for a moving company.

"You don't need to hire movers," said Alex. "I don't really
have that much stuff."

"We won't catch anyone's attention without a moving van."
Dana handed him her business platinum card. "Pick up a few
things and have them delivered to Big John Movers. They'll cart
everything over here at once."

"Sweet!" Alex pocketed the card, quickly as if he was scared

Dana would change her mind.

"We really should set some ground rules," said Kate. "I mean if you and I are going to be living together."

"Yeah, like can you keep the pooch off my bed?" Alex looked pointedly at Sarah Jessica Barker, who was nestled into her corner of the couch with a slimy rawhide bone.

Kate opened her mouth and quickly shut it when Dana shot her a vicious look. She picked up the bone and tossed it over to the armchair by the window. Sarah Jessica Barker leaped off the couch and made a beeline for the chair.

"Also, can you like put your dirty clothes in a hamper or somethin'?" Alex stepped over the pair of Kate's underwear that Sarah Jessica Barker had carried in and abandoned by the breakfast bar.

"Kate's just been overwhelmed with cookbook editing. She's usually much neater than this." Dana scooped up the pile of plates and cups off the coffee table and brought them to the sink.

"There a gym in the building?" asked Alex. He moved from the bar stool to the couch as soon as Sarah Jessica Barker vacated it.

"No. But you should go to the Chelsea Equinox, since that's where you and Kate supposedly met." Dana rolled up her sleeves and started loading up the dishwasher.

"Right. I gotta write this stuff down so I don't forget." Alex pulled out his iPhone.

"You can't take notes in your phone. What if it gets hacked or stolen?" Kate tried to catch Dana's eye to make sure she also recognized what a moron Alex was, but she was focused on Alex who had spontaneously thrown himself down on the ground and started doing push ups as soon as he put his phone back in his pocket. Kate was beginning to realize this guy needed to be in motion constantly.

"Don't stress about the details. You just need to smile and look hot for the cameras," said Dana. "You can let Kate do all the talking."

"I think I can handle that," said Alex, smacking his hands

together mid push up.

Kate's phone rang. "It's Jack." A tingling sensation moved through her hands and she felt her chest tighten like it did back at Mrs. Fink's.

Kate took two deep breaths before picking up. "Hi."

Alex looked up and Dana scooted closer to Kate on the couch. Kate got up and walked into her bedroom where she could have some modicum of privacy.

"I guess congratulations are in order." Jack breathed loud and heavy into the mouthpiece.

"I should've told you last night." Kate shut the door firmly behind her as soon as Sarah Jessica Barker scooted in the room. "But I guess I was just acting like my typical narcissist self."

"Sorry about that. I wanted to make it clear we weren't together like that."

"Oh, you made it abundantly clear." Kate could hear her own voice slicing through the airwaves like a knife.

"What else was I supposed to say? That we can't keep our hands off each other?"

"You certainly didn't have to call me names and rip on my livelihood."

"If you and Dana had kept me in the loop, I wouldn't have had to say anything. Not a bad idea, but I don't know about her choice in a bogus fiancé." Jack's voice sounded confident with uncertainty bubbling up beneath the surface.

"Jack, my engagement to Alex is real." Kate was glad she couldn't see his face. She squeezed her hands together to relieve the numbness in her fingertips.

"Yeah, right. There's no way you would be engaged to some guy who got famous for being an asshole on a Jersey reality show." The uncertainty was gaining on the confidence now and there was a slight waver to Jack's voice.

"Those shows are complete fabrications. Alex isn't really like that." Kate popped two antacid pills and crunched them with her incisors as soon as they hit her mouth.

"Then how come you haven't said one word about him to me until now?"

"It's not like you were an open book with me either. At least you knew my real name!"

"You're kidding, right?" Jack's voice had an edge to it that cut through the phone line.

"Alex and I've been on and off again for awhile now. I met you when we were off. There was nothing to tell."

"And now?"

"This whole thing put things into perspective with Alex and me. I finally said yes to his proposal."

"You didn't have wedding plans on your mind last night."

"I'm sorry Jack. I don't know what got into me. Maybe it was pre-wedding jitters." Kate could actually feel her stomach turning at her own words.

"Pre-wedding jitters? Seriously?"

"I'm sorry for leading you on. But it can never happen again."

"Oh, don't worry. It won't." Jack's bitter voice sliced through the phone connection.

"Jack."

"I have to go."

Jack hung up. Kate pressed the phone to her cheek and held it there, not wanting to break the connection with Jack.

The sound of the doorbell broke the silence. Kate shuffled back into the living room not eager to find out who was waiting on the other side of the door.

"What're you waiting for? Answer the door." Dana sat back on the couch, her iPad in hand, while Alex continued his push-ups.

"Mrs. Fink! What are you doing here?"

"We got big problems Katie. *The 411* is saying you're engaged to that creep from *The True NJ.*" Mrs. Fink leaned on the Swarovski coated cane she reserved for walks longer than a block. There was a glisten of sweat on her upper lip and her left eyebrow was painted on a little crooked.

"Come inside." Kate reached out a hand to Mrs. Fink who shakily accepted it. She guided the woman into the apartment supporting her back as they walked. Sarah Jessica Barker knew Mrs. Fink well enough to trade in her typical jumps for sedate licks on the ankle.

Alex popped up mid push up to an instant stand at attention position and reached a somewhat sweaty hand toward Mrs. Fink.

Mrs. Fink backed away. "As if you didn't already do enough damage to that poor Tammy! What's going on here Katie?"

Alex walked over to Mrs. Fink and leaned down to her level. "You can't believe everything you read about me. Kate, tell your grandma how we met at the gym."

"Grandma? Is he kidding me?" Mrs. Fink pointed her bedazzled cane at Dana. "I should've known you'd be mixed up with this somehow."

"Mrs. Fink, why don't you sit down and I'll get you a cup of tea." Dana couldn't stand Mrs. Fink, ever since the time she told her she wouldn't find a man until she tapped into her own femininity. But you wouldn't know it by the way Dana smiled and spoke in a soft tone.

"Sit down and relax for a minute. You're going to have one of your spells if you don't calm down." Kate grabbed hold of Mrs. Fink's arm again and led her to the couch.

"I'm not going to calm down till you tell me why 'The Instigator' is sitting in your living room like he owns the place."

Alex walked over to the couch and sat down. "You see Mrs. Fink, Kate and I were taking the same spinning class at the Equinox down by Chelsea Market and I…"

"Enough, Alex." Kate held her hand up. "This isn't real. Dana got in touch with Alex's agent and asked him to pose as my fiancé just long enough to get the focus off Jack and me. Before you know it we'll be having a very public break up."

"All I need is for the old woman to leak this and I'm finished in this town." Alex stood up rolled his shoulders back with a resounding crack.

"I don't think you ever really got started in this town young man." Mrs. Fink jerked her head back and forth like a teenager in a schoolyard fight.

Dana walked back in with a cup of tea. "Mrs. Fink, we need you on board with this. For Kate. That means you can't tell Mrs. Finklestein or Mrs. Levis or anyone else you know."

"It's Mrs. Feinstein and Mrs. Levi. Don't you have any Jewish friends?"

"I don't care what you call them as long as you don't tell them about all this."

"Katie, I can't believe you think lying about being with someone like this is better than being with Jack. This just doesn't make any sense."

"I came this close to losing it all. The network was ready to replace me on *KidFit* and *Mini-Munchies II* was never going to see the light of day."

"There's always another way Katie. You didn't think this through." Mrs. Fink pounded her cane into the floor for emphasis.

"That's what I'm here for. No offense Mrs. Fink, but your secret powers were off on this one." Dana's face was frozen in a half smile; the sneer was all in her voice.

"Katie, I taught you to think for yourself!" Mrs. Fink's voice gravelly voice echoed through the apartment.

"Look where that landed me! I'm not letting another man get in the way of my success!"

"None of that success is going to matter when you're old and alone like me one day."

"While out walking his niece to Chelsea Prep, Jack Moskowitz reminds us there's nothing hotter than a millionaire who loves kids. That's hot in a Jonah Hill kind of way."

grapevine.com/photogallery

Chapter Thirty-Three

Jack headed up the street hoping when he picked Lauren up she would actually be on speaking terms with him. Diesel started barking and pulled him forward.

"Diesel and Jack! What a nice surprise!" Mrs. Fink gave Morty's leash some slack so he could climb all over Diesel. Today she was wearing leggings that made her legs look like black lollipop sticks and pink ballerina slippers a la Amy Winehouse. She leaned on a sparkling silver walking stick.

"Good to see you Mrs. Fink." Jack was a little nervous how she would react seeing as he hadn't seen her since Kate found out he was a big fraud.

"Get over here. You know I'm a hugger." Mrs. Fink took baby steps toward Jack and reached up to give him one of her warm hugs. Jack didn't want to squeeze her too hard for fear of breaking a rib. But Mrs. Fink gripped him tight followed by two hard smacks on the back.

"I'm sorry, I didn't tell you who I really was when I first met you."

"You Jack Moskowitz are a good egg and that's all I needed to know."

"Is Kate keeping you busy with wedding plans?" Jack tried to crack a smile but his lips wouldn't cooperate.

"Those two will never walk down the aisle. They would end up with little orange babies wearing muscle tees."

"The kids will probably come out fist pumping."

"I don't know what fist pumping is. But it sounds pretty painful for poor Katie."

Jack laughed for the first time since he had seen the *Gossip Matters* article. "I'm so glad I bumped into you. You know how to keep it real Mrs. Fink."

"Don't give up Jack. In all my years of match making I've never been wrong."

"You didn't technically set us up. We met by accident at the dog park."

"On the Jewish Valentine's Day and ended up at the best matchmaker's apartment in New York. Coincidence—I think not."

"When we see Kate's wedding photos on the cover of *US NEWS*, maybe you'll give up hope."

"You know Bill and Hilary Clinton."

"Not personally. But if you were the one responsible for setting those two up, that's not something I would brag about."

"Hilary's cousin Beth was in New York during Clinton's first campaign and one of her friends had a match making party. It was filled with all of New York's most eligible single people and they paid me to come and make some matches. I brought some of my most hopeless cases that night and they left with future spouses. It was amazing."

"Let me know if you go to another party like that."

"Anyway, as soon as I met Beth, I knew she was the perfect match for one of my favorite clients. The problem was he was working on George W. Bush's campaign. I told him to keep that little tidbit hush hush until he could get the girl…"

"In bed?"

"No, you animal. Get the girl to go on three dates with him. If she was still around on the fourth date, I figured she would've gotten to know what a great guy he was even though they didn't have the same political ideals."

"Did it work?"

"Let's just say it got a bit messy. Accusations about stealing campaign secrets, secret service agents going through my client's underwear drawer."

"Okay, this story isn't making me feel any better."

"Twenty years of marriage later, with four kids and an adopted Somalian."

"That's crazy!"

"I don't mess around when I make matches. You remember that Jack Moskowitz." Mrs. Fink wagged her crooked finger at Jack.

"Okay. I have to get going. Lauren's waiting for me."

Mrs. Fink reached up for another hug. "You're a good egg Jack. Just don't give up."

When Jack got to the school Lauren was sitting on the stoop alone reading something on her phone. Jack steeled himself for more of the silent treatment but Lauren jumped up as soon as she saw him.

"OMG! I'm so sorry Uncle Jack!"

"Glad to hear you finally feel bad for being so rotten to me."

"Oh, you're totally still in the doghouse. But I do feel bad about the Kate stuff. I mean how could she be engaged and not tell you?"

"Oh, that."

"It seemed like she really liked you. And 'The Instigator'? He's the worst. He cheated on his girlfriend from home with Tammy and then dumped both of them as soon as they left the Jersey house."

"How do you know all this?"

"I have *The 411* app on my phone."

"Enough about the Kate situation. Let's just get through filming this week and then we don't ever have to see her again."

"Are you sure she still wants to film with me? She canceled yesterday."

"Kate didn't cancel. She rescheduled till tomorrow. That's what she said in the text right?"

"Yeah, but…"

"But nothing. Kate's not dumb enough to pass up on

Manhattan's most talented gymnast just because her uncle fucked up."

"What're you going to say to her tomorrow? This is going to be totally awkward."

"That's the thing Lauren. Can Madison's mom take you?"

"What? Why?"

"I have a meeting on the East side tomorrow. There's no way I can make it back crosstown in time to take you to the gym." Jack had been relieved when the perfect excuse to avoid seeing Kate was dropped in his lap.

"You're like the president of the whole company. Can't you just reschedule?"

"I'm trying to take care of things so I can take you to California."

"So you're not going to watch at all?"

"Hold on, it's Matt." Jack held up his finger and grabbed his phone.

"You didn't book your flights yet did you?"

"No, why?"

"The steel guys I told you about are coming in from Detroit this weekend. They want us to show them the town; you know a real New York weekend, Scores and maybe see a Rangers game."

"You really expect me to stick around this weekend to take those guys to a strip club? Can't you entertain them without me? Bring Doc."

"I didn't close yet."

"I thought it was a done deal."

"Not quite. I can't tell if they're yanking my chain or not. We need to corner them and get them to sign on the dotted line this weekend."

"Shit. I can't get that undercarriage made without the extra steel. If we can't guarantee their lower price, we're screwed."

"I wouldn't ask you to stay if I didn't think we needed to double team them."

"I know. Count me in. Maybe Lauren can miss school on Monday and we can fly out then. I'll see what Harper says."

"Thanks buddy."

Jack turned back to face Lauren. "Lauren, I'm sorry. I really have to close this deal."

"You said we were leaving on Friday right after school!"

"I know, and I meant it when I said it. But Matt needs my help this weekend."

"My dad needs me too!"

"I know he does. And I wish I could take you there tonight. But I just can't get you there till Monday."

"I'm never gonna see my dad."

"You are. I promise we'll go as soon as I can get this work shit straightened out."

"Whatever."

Chapter Thirty-Four

"I know things are awkward with us, but that doesn't have to affect Lauren's filming." Kate spoke quietly into the phone, in case that nosy boys' coach was lurking.

"What're you talking about?"

"You guys were supposed to be here twenty minutes ago."

"I'm stuck in a meeting on the East side, so Lauren's taking a cab from school with Madison and her mother."

"Madison's that girl who's even smaller than Lauren with the super curly hair right?"

"Yeah. The one Lauren's always hanging out with."

"I saw Madison come in the gym a good half an hour ago with no sign of Lauren."

"Check the locker room. She has to be there." Jack sounded like he was trying to convince himself just as much as Kate.

"I'll go check right now. Stay on the phone, okay?" Kate cut through the ballet studio into the gymnastics area and made a beeline for the team locker room.

"I should've rescheduled my meeting. But I'm trying to wrap things up so I can take her to California…" Jack's voice trailed off when Kate burst through the team locker room door. The sound of hyped up pre-teen girls was hard to miss.

"Hang on. I'm going in."

A group of girls wearing unnaturally hued leotards squeezed around the hairspray coated mirror with brushes and rubber bands. But the majority of them were still in their untucked school uniforms hanging out on the bench watching a YouTube video on someone's iPad. As soon as one of the girls recognized Kate, a contagious hush moved through the crowd.

"Have any of you girls seen Lauren?"

One of the older gymnasts stopped wrapping her ankle, her roll of Ace bandage hanging off the edge of the bench. "Not today."

Kate looked through the crowded room until she spotted a swollen poof of tightly coiled curls trying to break free from an elastic. The girl was leaning into her locker and taking a lot of care organizing her pile of clothes. Kate gently tapped her on the back.

"You're Madison, right?"

"Uh, yeah." The girl answered with her head still in the locker.

Jack yelled into the phone resting on Kate's ear. "Is that Madison? Let me talk to her!"

"Relax, I got this covered." Kate rested the phone on the locker room bench.

"Madison, I know you're really busy organizing your locker. But could you take a little break?" Kate kept her voice low and friendly.

The girls on the bench abandoned the iPad in favor of the action right in front of them. Madison slowly pulled her head from the locker but kept her eyes averted.

"Lauren told Jack that you and your mom were taking Lauren to the gym today. Why did Lauren lie?"

"Maybe she mixed up the days or something. Lauren isn't good with that stuff." She kept her eyes fixed on the faded Gabby Douglas poster hanging over the lockers.

"You know what I think? Lauren wanted to go somewhere today and she used you as her alibi. Do you know what that means?"

Madison shook her head very slowly while keeping her eyes

fixed on the poster.

"That means if something bad happens to her it will be all your fault! So forget about whatever BFF code the two of you have and tell me where she is before she gets hurt."

The older girl put down her ankle wrap and said, "Madison, you better speak up if you know something."

Madison's lower lip started to tremble. "I tried to talk her out of it but she wouldn't listen!"

"It's okay Madison. Just tell me where Lauren is and I'll make sure she's okay." Kate's stomach tied up in knots and she tried not to think about child porn rings and the other dangers lurking in the city.

"P-p-p-Penn Station." Madison finally looked up at Kate, her eyes wide and her lip trembled.

"Penn Station! What the Hell is she doing there?" shouted Jack from the bench.

"Going to see her father," stammered Madison.

"How is she getting to California from Penn Station?"

"Bus to JFK," said Madison. "We Googled it last night."

"Thanks Madison. I'll have her text you when I get to her." Kate grabbed her phone off the bench.

"Fuck!" yelled Jack.

"It's okay. Penn Station's only ten blocks from here."

"It's rush hour, it's going to take me forever to get crosstown."

"I know. I'll get there and keep her safe till you can come meet us."

"You won't be able to catch a cab."

Kate knew he was right. "Good thing I've got my running shoes on."

Kate ran down the hall and luckily bumped into her key grip Louie. "Filming's off today."

"You still there?" she asked Jack.

"Yeah. I'm running to the E train," he puffed.

Kate ran straight to the taxi stand, which of course was vacant. The few cabs in this neck of the woods always got snatched up right away.

"No cabs. I'm hoofing it. Call me as soon as you're in Penn. Try to find a spot with cell service."

Kate ran as fast as she could up the waterway bike path. She threaded her way in and out of the speed walkers and bicycles. The whole run over she prayed that Lauren hadn't gotten on a bus yet.

She made it uptown to 33rd Street in record time, and then crossed two avenues to 8th as quickly as she could. She went in through the Big Kmart entrance, a place she had taken Mrs. Fink shopping more than once.

Kate ran to the first open cash register, hoping one of the cashiers could direct her to the bus terminal. Kate leaned up against the candy display to catch her breath.

A young male cashier with a pierced eyebrow and lip said, "I wouldn't do that if I were you."

Kate turned around and saw that the Reese's Peanut Butter cups had rat sized bites taken from them.

She shuddered and simultaneously tried to catch her breath. "Where do I catch a bus to JFK?"

The boy returned a text before answering.

"New York Airport Service. I think it's on the ground floor by the Dunkin Donuts."

"Thanks," Kate said and took off running through the Kmart exit that opened into Penn Station.

She knew exactly where the Dunkin Donuts was since Mrs. Fink always needed to take a bathroom break there. She followed the large blue signs for the NYAS. The dark hallway winded up a bit and when she got to the NYAS terminal was just a plexiglass enclosure with a few metal chairs. The digital sign above the entrance announced the next bus was in ten minutes. Kate spotted Lauren right away, her thick waves of hair cascading down her back, one brown UGG boot rested on the chair in front of her. She was playing what looked like Fruit Ninja, judging by the way she kept slashing her finger against her iTouch screen.

Kate stayed out of Lauren's sight and called Jack. It went straight to voicemail, which was good because that meant he was probably on the subway. So she shot him a quick text explaining that Lauren was okay and where they were.

Kate walked up to Lauren's chair.

"Is this seat free?"

Lauren looked up wide eyed, an ear bud falling out and getting tangled in her hair blasting Lady Gaga on the way down.

"Madison is so dead!"

"I forced it out of her. I practically tortured her."

"Pretend like you didn't see me. I need to get on that bus." Lauren shoved her iTouch in her bag and stood up.

"You know I can't do that. Besides, Jack is going to be here any minute."

Lauren slid down in her seat. "This sucks! I missed the last one by like thirty seconds."

"Do you really think you could've boarded a plane by yourself?"

Lauren held up a computer print out. "I have an e ticket and everything."

"I don't even want to know how you paid for that thing."

"My mom's emergency Visa. She keeps it in her underwear drawer under all the lacy stuff she never wears."

"You still don't have ID."

Lauren pulled a laminated card out of her back pocket. "USA Gymnastics ID."

"Wow! You thought of everything. I have to admit I'm impressed."

"Doesn't matter. I still won't get to see my dad today."

Kate didn't know what to say.

"I'm sorry I bailed on you. I didn't think you really still wanted to film with me."

"I rescheduled because of all this craziness, I didn't cancel."

"Do you blame me for not believing everything that comes out grown ups' mouths these days?"

"I could see your point. I do still really want to film with you. But maybe we should wait till after you go see your dad."

"Ok. I can't really like focus on anything else right now."

"I get that. But you know you can't just run away."

"I wasn't running away. I was trying to see my dad. I don't care if he wants me there or not. I know he needs me."

"Your dad's getting better. Everything else will be okay."

"Everything is a mess."

"You know I was at another bus station when I wasn't much older than you. Only I wasn't running to my dad, I was running away from him."

"Really?"

"Yeah. My dad has a very bad gambling problem. He had just lost another big game and I found out I couldn't go to the seventh grade formal because we had no money for a dress, or shoes or a ticket."

"That sucks!"

"Tell me about it! So I went to the bus station and then I realized number one I had no money and number two, I had no where to go anyway."

"So what did you do?"

"What could I do? I went back home." Kate shrugged her shoulders. "Just be glad that you have the kind of dad to run to. And know that he is going to be okay and so are you."

Chapter Thirty-Five

Jack ran back into the boardroom where the group of Harvard MBAs and Wharton grads was waiting for him. A PowerPoint projected from a sleek, silver MacBook Pro and hovered on the movie theater sized screen. The men in their Brooks Brothers suits and the bone thin women in their ankle-breaker high heels were all waiting for Jack to come back in the room. They had abandoned live conversation in favor of texts and emails on their Blackberries and iPhones.

Jack grabbed his own laptop from the spot at the head of the large granite table. "Sorry, we're going to have to do this another time."

One of the suits stood up. "If you just give us five more minutes…"

"Email me the rest of the presentation." Jack ran out the door without waiting for an answer.

He had worn a three-piece suit and a pair of dress shoes that only saw the light of day for the thrice-yearly black tie meetings. Considering he had a black eye and a wrapped up ankle he had thought it was even more important than usual to break out the suit. His feet slid across the newly polished floor and Jack wished he had run sand paper across the bottoms of his shoes like his mother had done before his sixth grade graduation.

Jack's meeting was in the "Lipstick Building", a pink oval office building literally shaped like a tube of lipstick, located right across the street from the underground tunnel to the E train. He half slipped, half ran through the lobby, and booked across the street, almost getting hit by a cab on the way. His ankle throbbed as he ran down the subway steps, but Jack managed to block it out as made his way towards Lauren. Jake made an enemy out of virtually everyone on the steps down to the E train, Jack landed on the platform with a crowd of people all waiting for the slowest train on the NYC subway system.

After listening to at least three sermons from the homeless religious fanatic and two songs from the guy who played Beethoven on an actual saw, the subway came and Jack quite guiltlessly pushed his way through the crowd onto the train and was thankful to find a seat so he could rest his ankle at least for the ride.

Jack forced his way out of the E train door as soon as it opened. He shoved past a throng of college girls and their oversized handbags and overflowing shopping bags.

He thanked the MTA Gods and the recent fare spike for the fact that he actually had cell service if he stood completely still on the platform as soon as he got off the subway.

Kate Mobile: Lauren fine. At NYAS bus terminal. Next to DD.

Right past Dunkin Donuts was a bus terminal that like most things in the city remains hidden in plain sight unless you actually need it for something that relates to you personally. Jack heard them before he saw them.

"That's a mushroom, not a cupcake."

"That brown one gets me every time."

"Look out for the white spots. Only the mushrooms have them."

Jack walked around the plexiglass. Kate and Lauren were facing the opposite way. Kate was playing a game on Lauren's iTouch that sounded like Scoops. She twisted her body to the right and left while she moved the iTouch. As Jack took another step closer, his dress shoes echoed in the small area.

Lauren turned around, one long curl falling in her face.

Jack dropped his laptop bag and ran over to her and picked up all sixty-six pounds of rock solid muscle. She wrapped her legs around Jack's torso and rested her head on his chest.

Jack looked up at Kate and mouthed "thank you". She smiled and backed away and gave them the illusion of privacy.

Jack squeezed Lauren tight one more time before setting her on the floor. "Now that the mushy stuff is over. You are in deep shit little girl."

Lauren looked up at Jack. "I know."

"Kate, can I have my iTouch back?"

Kate handed Lauren the iTouch and Lauren passed it right over to Jack.

He kept his hand out and raised one eyebrow at her.

She sighed and pulled her cell phone out of her bag and handed it to him too.

"Do you know what could've happened to you if Kate didn't get here when she did?" Jack reached up and loosened his tie and unbuttoned the top button.

"Child porn rings, muggers, pick pockets, kidnappers." Lauren ticked off each item on her fingers. "I know Kate told me."

"She did huh?" Jack looked at Kate who was pretending to be reading a poster on identity theft taped to the scratched plexiglass wall.

"Yeah." Lauren rubbed the edge of her UGG on the ground.

"I told you I was taking you to see your Dad."

"You also told me that Mom was in California filming a commercial."

"Have I ever let you down before? Have I ever left you stranded at school or the gym when your Mom couldn't come?"

Lauren sighed. "No."

"You know you can count on me. One lie doesn't change who I am. I have always been there for you and I always will be."

"I'm sorry."

"We'll talk about it more later. In the mean time, go tell Kate thank you for saving your sorry ass."

Lauren walked over to Kate. Jack stood there and ran his fingers through his hair, loosening up the curls from the gel.

Lauren walked over to Kate. "Thanks for saving my so…"

"Watch it Lauren." That kid made it impossible for Jack not to smile, even when he wanted to wring her neck.

"Any time." Kate leaned down to Lauren's level. "Remember what I said to you before. You're so lucky to have an uncle like Jack who drops everything anytime you need him and a mom and dad who care so much about you that they didn't want you to worry."

Lauren looked at Kate and nodded. "I know."

"I would give anything for a family like yours. When you have people in your life who love you like that, everything else will always work itself out." Kate wrapped Lauren in a hug and held on. "I'm a hugger."

When Lauren broke away, Jack pointed at the beaten up chair and said, "Sit and don't move."

He stared Lauren down till she was sitting in the chair before he approached Kate.

"I don't know how to thank you." Kate filled the small vestibule with her vanilla apple scent and it took everything in Jack not to grab her and kiss her. She looked like his Kate the old Kate; not the one who had been gracing the cover of every gossip rag with her orange hulk of a fiancé and her pin straight hair.

"It was worth it to see you wearing something other than a retro tee shirt and jeans." Kate smiled at him the way someone does when they're uncertain you will laugh at their joke.

"I clean up pretty good don't I?" Jack pressed down the front of his suit. "Seriously, thanks."

"I was glad to help." Kate tucked a curl behind her ear. "Your eye looks a little better." Kate moved her hand to Jack's cheek and then froze for a second before dropping her hand.

"I hope I didn't drag you away from shooting any more magazine covers." Jack's skin ached where she almost touched him.

Kate opened her mouth then closed it and just stared at Jack.

"If I didn't say it yesterday, congratulations."

"Umm. Thanks." Kate shuffled her feet and stared at the gum wrapper strewn floor.

"All right kid. You ready to go to Cali?"

"What? Now?" shrieked Lauren.

"Looks like the next bus to JFK gets here in four minutes." Jack pointed to the digital screen overhead.

"What about Diesel?"

Jack tossed Lauren's phone back at her. "Send Matt a text for me and tell him Diesel's all his till we get back."

"You didn't even pack anything," said Lauren.

"You look like you're all set." Jack pointed to Lauren's overstuffed backpack and barely zippered shut gymnastics bag. "And I can buy whatever I need once we get there."

Lauren jumped up "Yes!"

The bus horn honked three short blasts and the digital screen flashed BUS BOARDING NOW.

"We better get going."

"Lauren, don't give your parents a hard time for lying to you. The important thing is that your dad's getting better." Kate said, as she walked Lauren towards the bus.

"Okay. Are we still filming?" Lauren scuffed her boot against the pavement again.

"Call me as soon as you get home. We'll start filming when you're ready." Kate pulled out her phone and took a picture of Lauren.

"OMG, my hair's a mess!"

"You look great. Now your picture will show up when you call so I'll be sure to pick up."

"You better get on the bus and grab us seats in the front so you don't get car sick." Jack nudged Lauren towards the door.

"Okay. Bye Kate!" Lauren ambled up the bus steps with her two bags and disappeared behind the folding door.

"So I guess this is good bye." Kate's hazel eyes were

phosphorescent in the overly lit bus terminal as she stared at Jack.

"I guess it is."

"You could call me when you get there. You know, just to let me know that you and Lauren got there okay."

"Sure, I could do that. As long as your fiancé won't get pissed."

"Last call for boarding!" crackled a voice over the bus intercom.

"I better go," said Jack. He stopped halfway up the bus steps. "Bye."

Kate wriggled her fingers at him. "Bye."

The bus was empty except for two families who were sitting in the middle. Lauren was camped out in the two seats behind the driver, reading a book since all her electronic devices had been confiscated. She had thrown one of her bags across the front seat on the other side of the aisle to save room for Jack. She was probably trying to avoid a well deserved lecture, but there would be plenty of time for that on the five hour long plane ride when they would be crammed in next to each other.

Jack moved the bag over and sat down in the window seat that faced the bus terminal. He looked out the window. Kate stood on the platform. Jack hadn't noticed before but she was wearing a *KidFit* workout tank and Lycra shorts with nothing else over them. It had been cold that afternoon, with a strong autumn wind that had made Jack thankful to be wearing a three-piece suit. Kate must've rushed out of the studio without taking the time to even grab a sweatshirt for herself. As if she could read Jack's mind, Kate wrapped both arms around her stomach and rubbed them with her hands.

Jack rapped on the window with his knuckles. Kate dropped her arms right away and smiled. She held up a hand and waved until the bus pulled out of the terminal.

"Kate Richards was spotted running through the cold city streets in nothing but a sleeveless shirt and shorty-shorts. Was the queen of fitness trying to cool off after a hot night with reality star Alex Lombardi?"

thebackfence.com

Chapter Thirty-Six

Penn Station was crawling with available cabs, but Kate ran back to Chelsea Piers, her arms slicing through the wind. She welcomed the sharp wind blowing through her lungs. Her breath came out in gasps and her legs and arms were tomato red by the time she made it back to the gym.

As soon as Kate walked in the field house, she spotted Irina through the viewing glass adjusting the height of the vault. Irina caught Kate's eye and gestured for her to wait.

"Is Lauren all right?"

"Yes, thank God. I can't believe she thought she was going to fly to California on her own."

"Nothing that kid does surprises me. She's one tough cookie."

"You should've seen her sitting at the bus terminal like it was no big deal. She even had an e-ticket printed up for a flight to San Diego."

Irina shook her head. "She gets her gumption from Jack. I'll never forget when he was starting the company up. He's no-holds barred when it comes to business."

"You've known him since before he signed the deal with the devil?"

Irina's face immediately flushed. "He didn't tell you how he knows me?"

"No. I thought you knew each other from him bringing Lauren here all the time. Oh, and I know he helped you set up the website. Thanks to that I got a nice picnic dinner in one of your practice rooms."

"He told you I lent him the room because he helped with the team website?" Irina shook her head.

"Must be a pretty awesome website. I know how much those rooms cost an hour."

"Now that everything's out in the open, I might as well tell you." Irina pointed at the older girl Kate recognized from the locker room. The one who had helped get Madison to talk. She landed a flawless double back handspring on the beam, but it was clear from the coach's reaction that it wasn't quite good enough.

"See that girl there?"

Kate nodded. "She's the one who helped me get Madison to fess up about what Lauren was up to."

"And the one doing back tucks on the trampoline? And the girl running towards the vault?"

"Yeah. They're all on the team right?"

"Yes. And they're all here because of Jack. So are half the kids over by the rock climbing wall, half of our soccer, basketball and baseball players, and a third of our after school program."

"What're you talking about?"

"Every year Jack and his partner Matt donate a percentage of their profits to a memorial scholarship fund in honor of my niece Oksana." Irina's face tightened and Kate could see the band of muscles in her jaw lock.

"I had no idea."

"Oksana and Lauren were in the same pre-school class at Sunshine Day School and they also took the same gymnastics class here. The two of them became instant best friends. Jack got to know Oksana very well. He took the girls to class when Harper had to work and the girls played at his house together all the time. Oksana had an endocrine condition which made her very overweight. My sister tried everything, healthy diet, extra classes here, but there really was nothing she could do to keep the weight off. My sister tried to keep her in a car seat but she just wouldn't fit. Poor Oksana would get huge welts on her legs from where the seat rubbed in and she couldn't sit back all the way because her shoulders wouldn't go far enough back in the top part of the seat. So, my sister had no choice but to let her ride with no car seat. Seven years ago this May they were rear -ended by a tractor-trailer and poor Oksana went through the windshield. My sister survived but let me tell you she's like a walking corpse."

"Irina, that's awful. I don't even know what to say."

"Thank you. It still feels like yesterday sometimes." Irina took a deep breath and pinched the bridge of her nose.

"Jack started the company because of what happened to Oksana. You know not every heavy kid out there eats too many Happy Meals. And even the ones that do—it's not their fault their moms overfeed them. These poor kids should be safe on the road like everyone else."

"You're right. They should."

"Jack didn't tell you who he was because he was hoping you would get to know him first. Meanwhile, he hid the best part of himself from you."

Kate looked down at the floor. Shame crept up hot and moist from her feet and saturated her hairline.

"I guess it doesn't matter now anyway since you're engaged. It's not like he had a chance with you anyway. I'll see you later. I have to get back to the girls."

Kate grabbed her stuff from the locker room and headed for home as quickly as she could. As soon as Kate reached the corner of 23rd Street she spotted it. The Big John's Mover's Truck was crowded by a swarm of paparazzi.

"Kate!!"

"Over here, Kate!"

"How do you feel about Alex moving in?"

Kate tilted to the side so the photographers could get their shot. "Alex and I are very excited to get our life started together." She swallowed the bile that was shooting up her esophagus.

"Kate, what really happened between you and Jack Moskowitz?"

"When's the wedding?"

"Sorry guys. I better go help with the unpacking!" Kate flashed another gleaming smile towards the photographers then tried to walk through the crowd to get to the front door.

Rich was waiting at the door and as soon as Kate got close enough, he opened it just wide enough for her to fit through. Kate slid in the small space between and Rich twisted his key in the lock behind them.

"This is why I tell you to use the service door."

"I wasn't thinking. It's been one of those days."

"Want me to help you get upstairs?"

"That's okay. Thanks."

"Use second elevator. Moving men using elevator one."

Kate passed the first elevator. The doors were wide open and the elevator walls were covered with cushioned canvas to protect the walls from scratches. Two men were carrying in a spin bike that looked to be of better quality than the ones at the gym. Kate wondered first where he would put it in her apartment, and then wondered if Dana had gotten ABC to cough up the dough for all these props or if she was going to have a massive AMEX bill at the end of the month.

The elevator ride went far too quickly and Kate resisted the urge to get right back in it when the doors opened. A trail of packing peanuts led the way to her door, which was propped open with a twenty-pound dumbbell.

Kate's living room had been transformed into a personal gym. Her dining room table was mysteriously gone and in its place was a massive Boflex machine. The shelf under her coffee table was lined with steel weights of varying sizes. Her end table was replaced with a giant rubber man waiting for someone to come and punch him in the face.

"A little to the left." Dana was directing two moving men who were in the process of hanging a framed poster of the *The True NJ* cast with Alex front and center flexing his pecs, his chest bare except for a huge gold chain.

"Dana! You said a few things!"

"That's perfect," Dana said to the moving men before turning to Kate. She had a Louis Vuitton scarf tied around her dreads and had the sleeves of her white button down shirt rolled up. Her version of an outfit suitable for housework.

"You weren't supposed to be home till much later. You didn't give me a chance to fix things up for you."

"Fix things up? Are we supposed to eat off the Bowflex bench? And what is that gigantic rubber man doing in my entryway?"

"That's Century Bob. All the MMA fighters use him to practice their moves."

"I can't live like this."

"It's only temporary. We have to stage this right or the press will sniff you out like a dog in heat."

"We filmed the *Gossip Matters* story without any of this crap here."

"Yeah, but everyone wants to know what the next step is going to be. You have to live your life like a reality show. That's how people think these days."

"I already have cameras following me everywhere I go."

"No, I mean you have to think in terms of episodes. Episode one the press outs you and Jack for being together, episode two everyone finds out you're really with Alex and you're engaged, episode three he moves in. You've got to up the ante every time or else you'll lose people's interest."

"Don't I want to lose their interest? At least in my personal life?"

"They lose interest in you, your brand disappears."

Alex walked out of the bathroom carrying a folded *Maxim*.

"You might not want to go in there for awhile."

"Alex, I can barely walk in here without tripping over a piece of workout equipment."

"I was thinking the same thing. We really need a bigger place." Alex used the bottom of his trademark black rhinestone dotted tee shirt to wipe a fingerprint off his framed poster.

"We don't need a bigger place. Nobody told you to move

in the whole body builder section of Dick's Sporting Goods." Kate tried to keep her voice low since the movers were near by, and her voice ended up coming out in a scary whisper scream.

Alex pulled up his shirt, releasing that horrible fake tan smell into the air and flexed his ab muscles. "I gotta keep myself in check. This is why my season had the highest ratings out of all the *The True* shows."

"Why can't you work out at Equinox like we talked about?"

"I need to work out in the privacy of my own home. These posers have been watching me at the gym to try to figure out my routine."

"We're in talks to get Alex his own workout show. We need to keep his secrets under wraps." Dana smiled up at Alex.

"If we get a bigger apartment, I can turn the extra bedroom into my workout room."

"We're not going to be together long enough to move!"

"You have to hang in there long enough to make this look legit. Getting a bigger apartment would definitely add to your credibility." Dana directed her comment at Kate, but kept her eyes on Alex's stomach, which he had left uncovered as he absentmindedly fondled his left pec.

"Where do you want this?" Two men held up the stationary bike.

Kate walked down the hall to her room, doing her yoga breathing on the way. Thankfully her room remained unchanged. Poor Sarah Jessica Barker was huddled on the bed among the throw pillows.

"I know exactly how you feel." Kate climbed into bed and snuggled up to her dog.

Sarah Jessica Barker jumped back when Kate's phone rang.

"Thanks." Jack sighed. "You're a good friend whether you want to be or not."

"Oh, I could really use a friend right now."

"I'm in as long as The Instigator doesn't kick my ass."

"I'll protect you. How's Lauren?"

"Good now that we're booked on the next flight to California."

"Are you still in the doghouse?"

"I'm working my way out of it. Her mom on the other hand is in for it when we get there."

"Does Harper know you're coming?"

"Yeah. But Lauren wouldn't even get on the phone with her."

"They'll work it out."

"I hope so."

"Call me or text me to let me know you guys got there okay."

"All right. I better go before Lauren buys out the gift shop."

"Jack?"

"Yeah?"

"Nothing. Have a safe trip."

Dana walked in without knocking and pounced on the foot of the bed like a cat.

"I know this is a little overwhelming."

"You call my entire apartment being taken over a little overwhelming?"

"I told them to leave your room alone. Right now Ali-Kat is trending at number one."

Kate sat up. "Did you know why Jack started his company?"

"Yeah. Some little girl died in a car accident because she was too fat to fit in a car seat."

"Don't you think that would've been helpful information to share with me?"

"I thought you knew."

"I had no idea. That information wasn't in any of the research you gave me."

"Would that have changed anything?"

"I would've focused my article on something other than Jack's company maybe."

"Clearly he's lost sight of why he started the company and he's catering to the Fast Food Nation crowd now."

"Did you know he donates a big percentage of the profits to charity to help kids get in shape?"

"Big tobacco pays millions of dollars a year for anti-smoking ads."

"How soon till the moving men get done? I have a splitting headache."

"Another hour or so. Clear your schedule for tomorrow morning. We have to register."

"What? I just got engaged!"

"Relax, it'll be fun. Oh, and I got you a huge order of fettuccine carbonara from Chelsea Market. Eat as much as you can. We really want you to have carb face in the morning."

"Carb face? What?!"

"It's like a carb hangover when your face gets all bloated the next day after you overdo the bread basket. Oh, and wear a baggy shirt."

"You can't be serious!"

"Nothing gets the baby bump rumors started faster than carb face and a peasant top. How do you think Jen Aniston ends up on the cover of all those magazines every month?"

"Jack Moskowitz leaves on a jet plane after Kate Richards reveals she's engaged to reality star Alex Lombardi. Will the CEO of Considerable Carriages mend his broken heart in the land of sunshine and starlets?"

thedailychatter.com

Chapter Thirty-Seven

Jack gently nudged Lauren who had been sleeping on his shoulder pretty much the whole flight.

"Are we there?" Lauren didn't bother to open her eyes.

"You're the only person I know who could sleep through that turbulence." Jack knew Lauren hadn't slept through the night since she heard about her dad, so he was relieved to see her fall asleep shortly after take off.

Lauren pulled the window shade up and their eyes were assaulted with bright, unfiltered light bouncing off the tarmac below. Jack rolled his shoulder back and rubbed it with his hand. His ankle was throbbing, despite the bucket of ice the flight attendant had been nice enough to give him and he was still wearing the suit from the day before. Jack swung his laptop bag over his shoulder and grabbed Lauren's bag from the overhead compartment. Then they made their way into the slow moving line of people getting off the plane.

"Your mom's waiting for us. Don't give her a hard time."

"She should've told me about Dad. I would've been here weeks ago."

"That's not the point. You guys need to be there for each other right now.

"I would've been there for her and my dad if only someone had thought to tell me what was…"

"Mom!!!" Lauren dropped her bag and took off at a sprint into the terminal. Lauren threw herself into Harper so hard, Jack thought his sister was going to fall backward, but she held strong. Lauren held on tight to her mom's waist and Harper leaned down and rested her chin on top of Lauren's head.

"I missed you so much!" Harper broke away from the hug first and leaned down to look at Lauren.

"I missed you, too. Can we go see Dad?"

"Let's get some breakfast for you and Uncle Jack first. You guys must be starving."

"I'm not that hungry."

"Speak for yourself, Small Fry. That airplane food didn't cut it." Jack walked over to his sister. She had a smile on her face, but it wasn't fooling Jack. Her masses of curls looked like they hadn't been brushed in days and were pulled into a matted ponytail. Harper who usually didn't bother with makeup when she wasn't working had coated her face with some kind of cover-up that was a shade too dark and ended at her chin so that her neck was a ghostly hue underneath it. Jack pulled Harper into a hug and he could feel her rigid back muscles relax for a minute till she pulled away and straightened herself up.

"Come on. Let's get something to eat. Dad's still sleeping and he really needs his rest to get better."

Harper drove them to a diner that was a few blocks from the hospital. It was filled with doctors and nurses who looked like they had either just gotten off the night shift or just about to start the morning one. A thin woman wearing Winnie the Pooh scrubs sat in front of an untouched muffin staring into space with her eyes glazed over like a zombie. A group of baby-faced guys wearing wrinkled scrubs and shiny stethoscopes around their necks devoured plates of pancakes in between loud tales about saving the victims of a massive car pile up on the highway.

"You think that was enough to get you through till lunch?" Jack pointed to the massacred short stack, curls of dried up egg yolk and fatty bacon discards on Lauren's plate.

Lauren took a gulp of orange juice before answering. "I have a granola bar in my bag just in case."

"A few weeks away and I almost forgot how much you eat!" Harper had ordered black coffee and two slices of rye toast that she had barely touched. Jack thought back to how hard it had been to get her to eat when their mom was sick.

"That was the best omelet I've ever had." Jack pushed his plate away so he wouldn't be tempted to eat even a few more bites and anger his already protesting stomach.

Lauren reached her fork over to pirate a few bites from his plate. "California food rocks."

Jack slapped a stack of wrinkled bills on top of the check and stood up. "Ready to go back to the hospital?"

"I hope Dad's awake."

"I'm sure he's sitting up waiting for his two favorite girls."

Harper slid out of the booth. "Thanks for breakfast, Jack."

"Thanks, Uncle Jack." Lauren followed her mom out of the booth.

The diner was only a few blocks from the hospital, so they decided to get a little fresh air and walk over there before they were trapped in the world of disinfectant and recycled air for the day. Jack's ankle was feeling much better from the Aleve Harper always carried in her bag. Lauren walked a few paces ahead of them, texting Madison on the way.

"Thanks for bringing Lauren. I'm such an idiot for listening to David."

Jack shrugged his shoulders, "Hey, you did exactly what your laid up husband asked you to. Most people wouldn't call you an idiot for that."

"I should've known seeing Lauren would help and I also should've realized she could handle this."

"Stop worrying about things you can't change and just be happy that we're here with you now." Jack put his arm around Harper's shoulder and pulled her into a side hug.

"Sometimes I don't know what I would do without you." Harper took a deep breath.

"Stop getting all sentimental on me. I can't take it on a

full stomach."

Harper punched Jack in the arm and pulled away to look directly in his face. "So how come I had to hear from the nurses about Kate and that juicehead?"

"You had way more important things to worry about than my drama."

"When I said you needed a girlfriend this wasn't what I had in mind."

"Trust me, things didn't go how I planned either."

"How are you going to fix this?"

"I'm not." Jack kicked a small stone gently in front of him.

Harper grabbed Jack's arm. "Hey, look at me for a second."

"Quit getting all dramatic on me," said Jack. "This is where Lauren gets it from."

"I heard that," said Lauren, without bothering to look up from her phone.

"I saw those pictures of the two of you together. I've never seen you look so happy." Harper fixed her steely blue eyes on Jack's like a game of chicken. He looked away first.

"Kate really likes Uncle Jack too," Lauren piped up.

"Reality check—she's engaged," Jack was quick to point out.

"There's no way Kate's gonna marry The Instigator! That would be so gross!"

They reached the hospital entrance and Lauren's giggles stopped. She closed her eyes and took a deep breath.

"How bad is it, Mom? Tell me now so I don't freak out in front of Dad." Lauren stood tall with her shoulders back and her hands clasped in front of her like she did when she was standing before the judges at a gymnastics meet. This was her go-to position when she was nervous.

"Dad's improving everyday and he's going to be in even better shape when he sees you."

"I think Lauren needs to be prepared for what he looks like." Jack thought back to his mom lying in the hospital bed, with tubes connected everywhere and the oxygen tubes going into her nose. He still had nightmares about it.

"Dad has a cast on his arm, which he's been waiting for you

to sign and decorate. And he's going to be wearing sunglasses because his eyes are still very sensitive to the light. He also has some bruises and scrapes, a really bad one of his face. But nothing too scary, I promise."

"Okay. Let's go." Lauren led the way through the doors of the hospital.

The lobby looked like any other hospital except there were a lot of people in army fatigues, including the doctors who wore camouflage scrubs under their white coats.

"This is Dad's room. Uncle Jack and I will wait out here."

Lauren's chest rose as she took a deep breath and she steeled herself before turning the doorknob. Jack squeezed her shoulder and she went in while Jack and Harper looked through the window so they could go right in the room if Lauren needed them. Harper didn't say that was the plan, but she and Jack didn't always need to put things like this into words.

David was wearing thick, dark sunglasses that obscured most of his face, but Jack could see abrasions and cuts in various stages of healing poking out from around the sides of the lenses. He also had one particularly angry looking gash on his forehead that extended under the glasses and down his cheek. He was wearing a hospital gown and a cast that went from the tips of his fingers up to the top of his elbow. His black Semper Fi tattoo dipped into the cast, so that only the Sem was visible. He had tubes running from different parts of his body to machines and bags under and around the bed.

"I'm here now." Lauren approached the side of the bed with David's good arm. She gingerly took his hand, careful not to touch the tubes coming out of it.

"Lauren?" David's voice came out thick and groggy from a pain killer induced sleep.

"It's me." Lauren spoke softly.

David inched himself gingerly up to a sitting position. "There's my pretty girl."

"Can you see me?"

"Not all the way. But enough to see how beautiful you've gotten since I left."

"I missed you so much, Daddy." Lauren stood on her tiptoes and gingerly leaned over the bed to hug David.

"Is that all you got? Don't worry, I'm not gonna break." David gestured with his good arm for Lauren to climb up on the bed.

Lauren slipped her sneakers off and climbed into the space next to David. She seemed fine for a minute, but as soon as he slipped his good arm over her, she broke down.

Harper was through the door in seconds. She leaned over Lauren and wrapped her arms around David.

Jack took a step back from the window when he realized his breath was fogging up the glass.

"Ali-Kat blew up the Bloomingdale's wedding registry today. Their wedding date is listed as June 26th. Do you think it's a real date or are they just trying to throw us off the trail?"

theinsidescoop.com

Chapter Thirty-Eight

"Give me the gun!" Kate tried to wrestle the scanner from Alex's hands.

"Hell no!" Alex clicked the scanner gun over the bar code on the black diamond encrusted cuff links.

"You do understand that we're not actually getting any of these items since there isn't going to be a wedding?"

"Alex has the right attitude. We have to make this look as authentic as possible." Dana trailed her fingers on a white ceramic watch.

"Authentically speaking—I would never marry the kind of guy who would register for six hundred dollar cuff links. Not to mention, I don't think you even own a shirt that requires cuff links Alex!"

"Where's the men's section?" Alex craned his head to get a better view of the fluorescent-lit aisles.

"People don't register for clothes and I'm pretty certain they don't register for jewelry either."

"Relax, and let's just move on to the bed and bath collection." Dana guided Alex forward with her hand lightly touching his back. As soon as he was ahead of them Dana ran the scanner back over the cuff links and made them disappear off the registry.

"Let's start with the bathroom. Since your apartment already appeared in *Gossip Matters*, people know that you have black and white decor. So let's stick with that." Dana walked over to the display with a crisp white shower curtain embroidered with oversized black peonies.

Kate's phone vibrated. "I have to take this call. Can you guys handle this?"

Kate headed over to the bedding section and hid behind a display of feather duvets.

"Did you make it to California okay?"

"Yeah. We're at the hospital now."

"You don't sound so good. Is everything okay?"

"Actually, life's pretty fucking good. Nothing puts things into perspective like seeing someone you love get a second chance at life."

"How is he?"

"David's putting on a tough front for Harper and Lauren. But you can tell he took a pretty hard hit. Anyone else might not have made it back alive."

"Thank God for Lauren and your sister he did."

"I know. It makes me realize none of this other petty bullshit matters."

"I know exactly what you mean." Kate looked over at Alex and Dana who were comparing identical looking black towels.

"Are the paparazzi still camped out in front of your building?"

"Yeah. It's only gotten worse. But at least when you come home they shouldn't be waiting for you."

"I hope not. I'm getting too old to be hopping the fence."

"How's your ankle?"

"One of the nurses saw me limp in here and she keeps trying to talk me into getting X-rays."

"You might as well. You're stuck there anyway."

"I don't have time for tests. I have to go find somewhere quiet to work on the new line."

"Did you see the SNL sketch?"

"Oh, yeah. It was real hilarious."

"You have to be able to laugh at yourself sometimes."

"Easy for you to say. Kate Hudson pushing Bobby Moynihan in a baby carriage? A hot actress pretends to be you, while the guy best known for his Drunk Uncle impersonation plays me?"

"Well, he definitely has the right hair."

"You are such a wise ass."

"Irina told me about the scholarship fund."

"Too bad she didn't think to tell you that before you ripped me a new one in *New York Today*."

"Seriously, I wish I could take it all back."

"Ever heard of a retraction?"

"I already tried."

"Seriously?"

"I called the *New York Today* editor this morning and asked if I could write one."

"No dice?"

"Apparently it's far more interesting for a TV personality to tear someone down than to admit they were wrong."

"But were you wrong really?"

"Don't you think I am?"

An overstuffed human length pillow pelted Kate in the head. She stood up and there was Alex pointing the scanner gun at her.

"You better not give me shit about what I registered for while you're kicking back over here."

"Is that Alex?" asked Jack.

"Yes." Kate glared at Alex and pelted him right back with a slew of throw pillows followed by a desperate shooing away motion with her hands.

"Did he just say something about registering?"

"Yeah, we're at Bloomingdale's."

"I better let you get back to that."

"It's okay. What were you about to say?" Kate ducked from the onslaught of feather bolster pillows coming at her.

"Nothing more important than wedding plans. Bye, Kate."

"You asshole!" Kate whisper screamed as soon as she hung

up the phone.

"I'm just saving you from yourself."

Kate ducked when Alex picked up the pillows from the floor, but he just popped them back on the display racks.

Dana materialized with the registry woman who looked like she had been working at Bloomingdale's since they penciled in wish lists in marble notebooks.

"I can't take you two anywhere. These two are such pranksters. I'm not going anywhere near these two on April Fool's Day."

"Ah, young love." The woman clutched a clipboard to her chest and beamed at Kate and Alex.

"Kate's funniness was the first thing I fell in love with." Alex stacked the last pillow back. Then, he leaned over the aisle and literally plucked Kate up in his arms and pulled her over the rows of pillows and planted her at his side.

"You two are the most fun couple I've worked with in awhile. You should see some of the couples that come in here. I always think to myself, if you can't agree on Farberware or Creuset how are you going to work out the bigger issues in life?"

"Matt Reynolds, the other CEO of that famous stroller company made it rain money last night at New York's famed SCORES strip club. Guess he's celebrating the hundreds of thousands of dollars in pre-sales from the CC-XL Deluxe."

dirtylaundry.com

Chapter Thirty-Nine

"You look like a new man," said the nurse behind the counter. She wore camouflage scrubs and a kind smile.

"I had to get out of that suit. Thank God for the gift shop. Have you seen my sister and niece?"

"I talked them into going to the cafeteria for a little food. I thought Lauren needed a break. It can be overwhelming for kids to see their parents like that."

"I totally get that."

"Have you had a chance to visit David yet?"

"No. I wanted to give the girls a chance to see him on their own."

"He's awake now. I bet he would be happy to see you. We got to know David really well and the one thing that helped him keep it together was knowing that you were back home taking care of his daughter."

"Thanks. I needed to hear that." Jack smiled at the nurse and headed to David's room.

He opened the door and David popped awake from a light sleep.

"Harper?"

"No, man. It's me."

David gingerly edged up the back of the bed to a semi-sitting position.

"Hey buddy. Sorry. It takes me a few minutes for my eyes to adjust."

"I've been growing out my hair. But I didn't think it was long enough for you to mix me up with my sister."

Jack walked over to the bed. Up close the scratches and cuts on David's face looked angry and raw. His brother-in-law who was on the shorter side, but had always been a wall of solid muscle, looked small and vulnerable in his hospital gown. His wheat blond hair that Jack had only ever seen in a buzz cut was long enough to comb to the side, so Jack could see how fine it was—almost like a toddler's hair before their first hair cut. David turned his head toward Jack, but Jack couldn't see his eyes through the dark lenses of his wrap around shades.

"Thanks for taking care of the girls while I've been gone, especially Lauren these past few weeks."

"Lauren's the easy one. Harper's the handful."

"Tell me about it. She's driving the doctors and nurses crazy. Nothing's good enough for her. Either they wake me up by checking on me too much or they haven't been in to check on me enough."

"She did the same thing when Mom was sick. The doctors would duck and run for cover when they saw her coming."

"That was before the Internet. If she quotes from WebMD one more time, I think the doctor's gonna lose it."

Jack laughed. "At least you know they're going to have all their bases covered."

"Yeah, they just want to get me better so they don't have to deal with my crazy wife anymore." Even without actually seeing it, Jack could tell David's smile reached all the way up to his eyes.

"Now they've got Lauren to contend with, too."

"Thanks for bringing her."

"She didn't give me much of a choice. She would've been here whether I brought her or not."

"I should've let Harper tell her sooner what was going on. I wasn't thinking straight."

"Sounds like you weren't ready to see her yet. You made the right decision keeping her away."

"See all this shit?" David lifted his casted arm and waved at all the wires and tubes coming from all the different parts of his body. "It's nothing."

"Doesn't look like nothing to me."

"My best friend Mike didn't even have enough pieces of him left to send home to bury. This is nothing."

"Were you with him in the end?" asked Jack.

"Yeah, but it happened so quickly. There wasn't anything I could do to help."

"At least he probably didn't suffer."

"That's what I told his mom. I also told her he wasn't in any pain, but that was a crock of shit. I can still hear his screams whether I'm awake or dreaming."

Jack immediately thought about something horrible like that happening to Matt right in front of him and realized his brother-in-law was in much worse shape from his grieving than from his physical injuries.

"What can I do to help?"

"Stay. I need to know the girls are taken care of while they're here. I just can't right now."

"Anything."

"We brought you fro-yo!" Lauren announced as she burst through the door, while Harper stayed in the hallway with a doctor cornered against David's window.

Lauren ran to the bed with a cup draped with a perfect spiral of chocolate and vanilla swirl draped with coconut shavings.

"That's my girl! You got my favorite." David reached for the frozen yogurt with his good hand, but didn't make a move to eat it.

"You're not eating."

"I'm sorry sweetie. I'm just not that hungry."

"You're never gonna get better if you don't eat."

"Hey Lauren. I got you a new tee shirt." Jack reached into the plastic shopping bag from the commissary and tossed the new shirt to Lauren.

"Awesome! Look Dad!" Lauren held the shirt against her chest. It was a white tee shirt with a pair of boots smack in the center that said, *"Your dad may wear suits to work, but mine wears combat boots."*

"You have to wear that to school when you go back home to the land of finance guys." David cracked a smile, but he put his frozen yogurt on the night table.

Lauren popped in the bathroom for a minute and came out wearing her new shirt. "Thanks Uncle Jack." She immediately noticed the abandoned dessert and picked it right up.

"Come on, Dad. You're getting way too skinny. You need to get better so you can beat your old record at the bowling alley. I didn't tell you but that old guy—you know the one who reeks of cigarettes and has the horseshoe tattoo on his arm? He beat your old score."

"Rex beat my score? As soon as I get back, we need to go rectify that." And he reluctantly opened his mouth while Lauren shoved a spoonful of frozen yogurt in.

"Fine. I'll eat. But let me feed myself. My arm's broken not amputated."

"See you guys later. I have to get some work done."

Jack left them in the room and scooted past Harper who was harassing the doctor about the high incidence of MRSA in broken limbs post surgery. He squeezed her arm and kept walking so he wouldn't get caught up in that conversation.

"How's my dog doing?" Jack asked, as soon as Matt picked up the phone.

"How about how's my business partner doing on his own trying to entertain the steel guys?"

"I'm sure they dragged you kicking and screaming to SCORES."

"Actually, it's not the best timing. Anne's staying over."

"When did that happen?"

"She's warming up to me. The last thing I need is for her to find out I went to SCORES while she was sitting at home eating crackers and drinking flat ginger ale."

"Shit."

"When're you getting your ass back here?"

"I don't know. David needs me to hang out for awhile."

"Shit."

"I know. But maybe I'll get more work done here without the press hounding me."

"Stay strong. Call me if you need anything."

Jack decided the best place to get his work done was in the maternity ward. It had great Wi-Fi, comfy chairs, and a big screen TV. Nowadays everyone and their mother literally hangs out in the delivery room, so he had the whole place to himself.

Jack hopped himself up on free coffee and used the buzz to figure out the last of the damn undercarriage designs. Jack heard voices coming down the hall. He hurried to put his ear buds in so whoever it was wouldn't get any ideas about sitting and chatting with him. This little impromptu cross-country trip was already setting him way behind.

"You mind if I change the channel?"

"Go for it." Jack looked up from his laptop.

A man in his early thirties dressed in military fatigues pushed a stroller into the waiting room. The carriage housed a long and lanky boy who was dressed in a camouflage tee shirt with brown cargo pants that fell an inch or two above his Converse slip-ons. His head was tilted to the left as if the muscles in his neck couldn't support it and his flaccid legs hung over the edge of the stroller supported by what looked like the flat aluminum top from an instrument stand.

"It's *SpongeBob* time." The man wheeled the boy to a spot directly in front of the TV. Jack noticed that the make shift foot stand wasn't the only modification made to the stroller. There were also homemade armrests covered with fleece SpongeBob material. The back of the stroller had a mini California license plate that said Eddie's Ride.

The man settled into one of the hard backed chairs with posture that rivaled Lauren's. Jack made eye contact with him and nodded his head in greeting.

"Hey," said Jack.

"Your wife having a baby too?"

"Nah, my brother-in-law's laid up from a helicopter crash. Just hanging out down here while my niece gets some alone time with her pop."

The man shook his head. "I lost a buddy that way. Hope he recovers soon."

"Sorry to hear about your friend. My brother-in-law was pretty lucky. He should make a full recovery."

The man kissed two fingers and held them up towards the ceiling, "From your lips to God's ears man."

"You waiting on a baby?"

"Born last night. Beauty named Eliza. Eight pounds, five ounces." The man beamed from ear to ear.

"Congratulations!" said Jack. He turned to the boy, "You're gonna love being a big brother." The boy who looked to be anywhere from five to eight kept his eyes fixed on the screen and his frozen face showed no signs that he had heard Jack.

"We've been with them all morning, but it's *SpongeBob* time. What can you do?" The man shrugged his shoulders.

"Hey, I'm Jack." Jack stood and walked over to the man and gave him a smacking high five turned into a hearty handshake.

"Martin, and this is my son Eduardo."

"Nice ride." Jack kept his voice low so he wouldn't disrupt Eduardo's show.

"Thanks, I made the changes myself." Martin smiled cautiously as if he wasn't quite sure if Jack was being sarcastic.

"The music stand for a foot rest is pretty original man." Jack noted that the dimensions were almost perfect.

Martin shrugged. "The military teaches you to make do with what you got."

"What's that stuff under Eduardo's feet?"

"It's black rubberized flooring. You know—the kind that comes in squares to put under workout equipment. It helps Eduardo grip his feet."

"Ingenious," said Jack. He leaned down and ran his fingers over the tire tread. "Where'd you get these wheels?"

"I got a buddy who owns a tire plant. I asked him to make me something shock absorbent. Eduardo has sensory issues so when we hit a bump it feels like an earthquake to him."

"Sorry to be so nosy but I work in the industry."

"You make stuff for kids with special needs?" asked Martin.

"No, I make strollers. Ever heard of Considerable Carriages?"

"The fat kid strollers?"

"I don't really like to refer to them that way, but yeah. Do any of Eddie's classmates or friends have souped up strollers like his?"

"You should see the kids getting carted to Sunday funday at the rec center. No offense, but none of us have money for one of your strollers."

"Can I ask you a question without offending you?"

"Depends what it is."

"How come Eddie's in a stroller instead of a wheelchair?"

"Wheelchairs are for people who can't walk. My son can walk, but he needs a break sometimes because he has low muscle tone and some other issues. A lot of his friends are the same way. They can do some walking, but when they get too distracted or they can't keep up, they ride in a stroller."

"That makes a lot of sense."

"My wife is also mad tiny. Pushing the stroller is way easier than lugging around a wheelchair."

"If I were to make the ideal stroller for Eduardo, what features would it need to have?"

"You thinking about making strollers for kids like Eddie?"

"It would take a lot of research to get it right."

"I got some time. What do you need to know?"

"Kate Richards and Alex Lombardi kicked off Columbus Day weekend with dinner at Cipriani 42nd Street, where it is rumored they plan to hold their wedding. Alex dined on the Braised Veal Shanks Cipriani, while Kate ordered the Sea Bass with Artichokes. Wonder if these two items will make it on the wedding menu?"

thebackfence.com

Chapter Forty

"First comes love, then comes marriage, then comes the baby carriage. Or will the baby carriage make an appearance first? Kate Richards wore a peasant blouse over leggings for a Sunday afternoon walk through Chelsea with her adorable dog Sarah Jessica Barker. Was the famous kids' fitness guru hiding a baby bump under that oversized shirt?"

thewatercooler.com

"Production halted at the KidFit set today as everyone from hair and makeup to the directors and producers gathered to give Kate Richards a bridal shower. The newly engaged star was reportedly so surprised, she burst into tears as soon as she saw the crowd gathered to celebrate her upcoming nuptials to twelve years younger reality star Alex Lombardi."

therumormill.com

"Kate Richards and Alex Lombardi, otherwise known as Ali-Kat were rushed to the front of the famously long line at NYC's Magnolia Bakery for a private wedding cake tasting. They left the packed Greenwich Village cupcake shop filled up on Hummingbird,

Red Velvet, and Banana cake. According to the star-struck counter girl, Kate was leaning towards the Red Velvet while Alex loved the Hummingbird. Either way their wedding guests are in for a treat!"

grapevine.com

"Kate Richards and Alex Lombardi made an appearance at the New York Public Library Halloween fundraiser last night dressed as their doppelgangers Barbie and Ken. Kate and Alex raised an astounding seventy-five thousand for literacy when they auctioned off a week of Mother-Daughter personal training and nutrition sessions given by none other than the super couple."

nytoday.com

"Over three thousand jobs were saved at P & G Steel as brothers Paul and Gabe Riccio inked a deal with Considerable Carriages to provide steel for the new CC-XL-Deluxe stroller. According to Paul, the company was weeks away from closing up shop and filing for Chapter 11 bankruptcy when they signed on the dotted line."

detroitnews.com

Chapter Forty-One

"Considerable Carriages wins the tenth annual Classy Award for most Philanthropic Business of the Year. Co-CEO's Matt Reynolds and Jack Moskowitz donate a whopping twenty percent of their profits to The Oksana Karev Scholarship Foundation annually. Because of their generosity, thousands of inner city children attend private schools and participate in numerous after school athletic programs. CEO Jack Moskowitz, made famous for his rumored fling with KidFit host Kate Richards, maintains that it's not that big of a deal."

bizjournals.com

"Just who is this Jack Moskowitz? He was trending at the top of the Google search engine for a good twenty-four hours until everyone found out he wasn't really dating Kate Richards. Now it's like Jack who? Meanwhile, I would love to hear a little more about this CEO of a multi-million dollar company who also happens to be single and Jewish."

Jessa Silver, Late Night with Jessa Silver

"When I saw the lines of people wrapping around Union Square

at 3 A.M., I thought for sure the latest X box was out and they were all waiting to snatch it up at Best Buy. But Holy shit was I wrong! All those freaks were lined up to get into Babies R' Us for the latest model fat kid stroller from Considerable Carriages. What is this country coming to?"

Morning Joe, The Morning Joe Show

"If only we all could have a dog walker like this! Looks like Alex Lombardi keeps in shape by running with his fiancé Kate Richards' adorable Boston Terrier. Alex pounded the pavement from Chelsea to Central Park with Kate's beloved Boston Terrier playfully nipping at his heels the whole way."

thegossipmill.com

Chapter Forty-Two

Kate heard Dana's laugh as soon as she got off the elevator. It was hard to believe it had been almost six weeks since Alex had taken up residence in her apartment and Dana had become a constant presence. Kate dreaded entering her own home and becoming the third wheel.

Alex was hanging from the push up bar he had suspended from her hallway closet door. Of course he was shirtless. All of Kate's coats were laid over the armchair so Alex could fill the empty cavern with his hulking body. Alex was so tall he had to keep his knees bent as he lowered his body towards the ground.

"Don't you have a better place to do that?"

"You don't have any other door frames near a TV." Alex pulled himself up to the bar until his chin touched it. His muscles stretched and pulled in his chest, his biceps and forearms segmented so that you could see every muscle and ligament.

"Except for your bedroom, but I knew you would have fit if he worked out there." Kate spun around to see Dana sitting at the kitchen bar, her laptop open. Her chair was positioned so that she had the perfect vantage point for watching Alex's workout regime.

"Don't you have other clients who need you?" Kate grabbed Sarah Jessica Barker's leash from the hook by the door. Usually the sound of the metal leash clip clunking against the hook made her dog jump up and run for the door, but she stayed on her new dog bed resting her head in her paws.

"You're the most fucked up one she has right now." Alex popped off the chin up bar and headed right for the kitchen.

"I can't argue with that." Dana smiled at Alex but froze when she caught Kate's glare.

"Which one is for post workout?" Alex asked, while he hung on Kate's fridge door. He opened it wider and Kate saw the shelves were completely full of those garish colored bottles of juice drinks Dana usually drank when she was on one of her fasts.

"Spicy lemonade." Dana took a sip from her own bottle, which was filled with some sort of thick beet juice concoction. It looked like she was drinking blood.

Alex grabbed a bottle of the clear yellow drink and chugged it. Kate didn't get favoring drinks the color of bodily fluids over actual food.

Kate jiggled the leash. "Come on, Sarah Jessica." Kate walked towards her dog with the leash, but Sarah Jessica Barker didn't even lift her head. Usually, she jumped up and bounded for the door when it was time for her afternoon run.

"What's the matter with my dog?"

"She's just tired from the run," said Alex. A bead of sweat trickled down his pecs towards his belly button. Kate looked away.

"What run?"

"She went with me." Alex tilted the bottle back to get the dregs of lemon pulp from the bottom.

"Wait a second. You took my dog for a run? The same dog you refuse to let on the couch or anywhere near you?"

"Dana told me to." Alex shrugged and made a clean shot with the bottle in the recycling bin.

"Check this out." Dana handed her iPad to Kate. Her home screen was opened to a picture of Alex running shirtless with

Sarah Jessica Barker close at his heels.

"Is that over by Central Park?" asked Kate.

Alex hopped off the bar. "Yeah, I always run crosstown."

"Don't you think that's a little far when your running partner has four inch legs?"

"She was fine. You gotta to learn to chillax." Alex shook his at Kate like she was insane.

"This is the money shot. *Grapevine*, *The 411*, *Dirty Laundry* and *Inside Scoop* all had it on their sites before Alex even made it back to the apartment."

Kate picked up Sarah Jessica Barker and headed to her room. The poor dog was so sore she didn't move an inch in Kate's arms.

"Why does it look like a ninety-nine dollar David's Bridal sale in my room?" Kate yelled down the hall. There were rolling racks on each side of Kate's bed lined with white, cream and ivory chiffon and satin creations. Her heavy iron curtain rods were lined with more dresses, while the remaining few lay across her bed covered in garment bags.

"Kate Spade, Vera Wang, Badgley Mischka, Cynthia Rowley, Diane von Furstenberg, Marchesa, Oscar De la Renta." Dana appeared in her room and spread her arms wide, announcing each name as if she were hosting the Oscar's. "The designers have been sending them over all day."

"Holy shit!" Kate knew she should appreciate the tens of thousands of dollars worth of original designer dresses draped across her bed, but all she wanted to do was push them to the floor so she could hide under the covers.

"I've been waiting for you to get home. We have got to try some of these on." Dana pulled a Kate Spade garment bag off the bed. "I've been eying this one all day."

Dana grabbed a crisp white spaghetti strap dress that had a full skirt covered in swirls of taffeta flowers.

"Go ahead. Try it on." Kate didn't have to say it twice. Dana slipped out of her sweater dress and stepped into the layers of white.

"Zip me up." Dana held the bodice over her tiny sternum

and waited while Kate pulled the zipper up the back.

"Put some of those silver clamps down the back so we can see what it would look like if it fit." Even the sample size was too big for Dana. She pointed to a clear plastic bag of clamps sent over with the dresses from one of the designers.

Kate pulled piles of fabric back until the front of the dress hugged Dana's boyish frame. She cinched the back and when Kate looked up she was surprised to see the layers of material gave the illusion that Dana actually had some curves.

"Wow. You look amazing!" Kate let herself get caught up in the moment as she admired her friend.

"Your turn. Try on the silk sheath from Cynthia Rowley."

"I'm going to be trying on enough dresses at the photo shoot tomorrow." This was the first photo shoot in Kate's career that she was actually dreading.

"Fine. I guess I'll have all the fun."

Dana looked like a little girl playing dress up in her mom's clothes while she plopped on Kate's bed, her tiny body swathed in a swirl of satin and chiffon. She threw herself against the pillows and pulled her feet up to her chest and grabbed her ever present iPad off Kate's night table.

"Okay, we have requests coming in from all the reality shows. *Say Yes to the Dress, A Wedding Story, For Better or For Worse, Whose Wedding is it Anyway?, Bridezilla,* and *My Big Fat Fabulous Wedding.*"

Kate just stared at Dana.

"Okay, if you don't want to go that route, I've got just the show for you. *Project Runway!*"

"*Project Runway?*"

"The contestants would compete to see who could design you a dream wedding dress and a tux for Alex that would go with it. How cool is that?"

"Oh yeah—real cool. I make these poor kids work hard designing outfits for a wedding that's never going to happen!"

"Oh please. Have you ever seen that show? It's full of a bunch of cutthroat designers who couldn't give two shits about you or your wedding. All they care about it is getting to the big finale at New York Fashion Week."

"You never told me a reality show would be part of this deal."

"I had no idea! What about *Top Chef?* Same deal except everyone would be trying to come up with the best wedding menu. Or *Cake Boss* for your wedding cake?"

"Do I need to keep reminding you that there isn't going to be a wedding?"

"But you need to act like there is. That way when Alex dumps you, everyone will be sympathetic."

"It's really hard to sit here and have this discussion when you're dressed like you belong on the top of a three tiered cake."

"It's probably my only chance in life to wear a thirty thousand dollar wedding dress. Come sit, I bet one of these shows is on now." Dana shoved aside a chiffon mermaid style dress and patted the bed.

Kate climbed on the bed, knowing there was no getting rid of Dana till she at least watched one of the shows and pretended to consider it. She could always tell her no in the morning.

Dana grabbed the remote and flicked the TV on. "How do I get your channel guide?" She flicked past a cooking show, an old *Friends* episode and the only living daytime soap left on the airwaves.

"Wait! That's Jack." Kate couldn't believe it. There he was on *Straight Talk*.

"He's with some military guy. Is that his brother-in-law?"

"I don't know." Kate grabbed the remote from Dana and turned the volume up. "Shhh."

"Considerable Carriages CEO, Jack Moskowitz made the news last month when all the gossip sites linked him to *KidFit's* Kate Richards. We all know now that those rumors were false since Kate Richards and her fiancé Alex Lombardi were here just last week talking about their wedding plans. But Jack's here to talk to us about something that really is near and dear to his heart, strollers for kids who can really use them. He's here today with Marine Sergeant Martin Sanchez and his son Eduardo." Lucy Barrows had her bob scooped back into a tight French twist and she was wearing a gigantic strand of creamy white pearls.

The camera zoomed in on Jack. His hair had gotten longer and his curls were smoothed down with gel which Kate knew wouldn't last for long. His silvery blue shirt brought out the gray whirls in his eyes and made them almost hypnotic.

"You know I have to start off by saying something about those rumors. Have you taken a good look at Kate Richards? I have to say I'm really flattered that people would even think I'm in the same league as her." The audience fell into light laughter.

"So you're saying nothing was going on with the two of you before Kate got engaged to Alex?" Lucy Barrows leaned forward, her hands clasped in her lap.

"Do you really think Kate would take a second look at me when she was dating a guy in his twenties with an eight-pack? Kate and I got to know each other because my niece Lauren is doing a segment on *KidFit*. By the way, one day you'll see Lauren in the Olympics taking home the gold in gymnastics."

"Now that we have that straightened out. Let's find out who your friends are." Lucy cut in with a bright smile.

"This is American hero Sergeant Martin Sanchez. He's served one tour in Iraq and two in Afghanistan. He brought his son Eduardo with him today."

The camera panned around the live audience who were standing on their feet and applauding. Then it zoomed in on Martin's son Eduardo who was staring straight ahead, his jaw slack and his eyes blank.

"How does it feel to get a greeting like that?" Lucy asked over the roar of the audience.

"It feels great. Especially because I have a lot of buddies back in the Marine hospital watching today while they heal up." Martin sat ramrod straight in his chair, his head perfectly aligned with his spine.

"Isn't that where you and Jack met?" asked Lucy.

"My brother-in-law David was in the hospital recovering from a helicopter crash," started Jack.

"I'm sorry to hear that."

"We were pretty lucky. For a while there we didn't know if he was going to lose his eyesight permanently. But he's going to be okay and he's coming home soon."

"That's great news," said Lucy . "Now tell me how you and Sergeant Sanchez met."

"I was in one of the waiting rooms working on my stroller designs when Martin came in pushing Eduardo in this totally souped-up stroller. I was so impressed with the modifications Martin made on Eduardo's stroller that I had to talk to him about it."

"What kind of changes did you make?" Lucy rose from her chair and headed over to the stroller.

"I put shock absorbent tires on so Eddie won't feel all the bumps, special padding on the arm rests and a bigger foot rest to support his legs better." Martin walked around the stroller pointing out the features while the camera zoomed in on them.

"Of course I had to wonder why I never thought of any of those things!" Jack smacked his forehead and the audience broke into laughter again.

"Does this mean Considerable Carriages is going to start making strollers for kids with special needs?" Lucy asked as soon as the audience died down.

"Yes, but I need a little help with that. I hired Martin as my personal consultant, but he explained to me that every kid with special needs requires different accommodations."

Martin cut in. "Some kids could use softer seats with extra cushion, while others need firmer, more structured ones. Some kids need textured arm rests to help with OT issues while others need smooth ones like Eddie has."

"So we're asking everyone out there who could use one of these new strollers to log on to considerablecarriages.com to let us know what kind of modifications your own kid might need, so I can make sure to include it in my designs." The camera zoomed in on Jack as he spoke.

"Are we talking about special order, custom made strollers?" asked Lucy.

"Yes. I want every parent out there who has a kid with special needs to be able to personally design the stroller that would work best for them," answered Jack.

"That sounds like it would cost a fortune." Lucy Barrows' collarbones jutted from her black dress as she grimaced.

"That's why I have one of my execs working with the insurance companies to see what we can get covered. We're making so much off the new CC-XL Deluxe that it will offset selling these strollers on a sliding scale."

"Thanks for coming in today to tell us about this, Jack. For all of you at home, log on to the *Straight Talk* website where we have a link to the Considerable Carriages webpage." Lucy stood to signal the interview was over. The audience cheered as the theme music played and Lucy leaned in to talk to the little boy.

"Why couldn't he have thought of this when the two of you were together?" asked Dana.

"There's a bottled water shortage across Manhattan as warnings of an out of season hurricane that will rival Superstorm Sandy came from The National Weather Service. Evan Marks, manager of the 53rd Street D'Agostino said the last four cases of bottled water flew off the shelves hours ago. Poland Spring has scheduled extra deliveries to Manhattan. Let's hope they can get their trucks over the bridges before the storm shuts them down."

New York Minute

Chapter Forty-Three

"That book report's not gonna to write itself." Jack looked up from his computer, which was propped on the picnic table. The sky was clear without a cloud in sight despite all the hysteria about the soon to come hurricane. He wasn't taking any chances after they had no power or heat for twelve days and ran out of bottled water and food during Hurricane Sandy. The generator was ready to go, and they were fully stocked with bottled water and whatever packaged food Lauren loaded the cart with at Whole Foods. Now they just needed to wait for the storm.

"Homecoming's totally impossible to summarize in one page." Lauren flipped through the book without reading a single page.

"Nobody told you to pick a four hundred page book to review. I would've done one of those Ramona books."

"Those are for like second graders." Lauren rolled her eyes and snapped the book shut.

"Well you better figure out how to write a review on this book or get cracking on another one. I told your mom you would have this shit done by the time she gets back from the rehab place with your dad."

"I can't believe Dad's coming home in two days!"

"That's why you need to finish. So you don't have to waste your time doing this crap when he gets home."

"Ugh, school sucks!" Lauren groaned, but she flipped open her own laptop and started typing.

"Why the long face, Small Fry?" Even though the reporters had long since abandoned Jack's front stoop, Matt had gotten into the habit of scaling the fence rather than simply walking through the front door.

"One word—school."

"Keep it up. You need to get educated so you can work for us one day. We don't hire stupid people."

"Except Matt. He's our one exception." Jack ducked as soon as he said it, and narrowly missed one of Matt's lethal kidney punches.

"Keep it up and you'll be peeing blood."

"You two are so immature." Lauren rolled her eyes.

"I'm not the one who got left back." Jack took a step back with both arms blocking his kidneys.

"I wasn't left back. I have a late birthday, dickhead."

"Seriously, man. What're you doing here? I thought you were visiting your sister in Westchester." Jack saved the spreadsheet he was working on and closed his computer.

"Didn't want to get stuck with her and her douchebag husband when the big storm hits. You got any bottled water? They were all sold out at D'Agostino and Food Emporium."

"I have an extra case under the kitchen counter. It's all yours. You don't want to run out of water with a pregnant woman in the house."

"Yeah, if Uncle Jack and I run out of water we can always drink soda."

"I bet you'd love that." Matt slapped a folder down on the weather beaten table.

"Oh no. Please tell me these aren't more changes to the damned steelworkers' contract." Jack reached for the manila folder.

"Forty-five hundred square feet, center hall colonial, six bedrooms, five and a half baths, finished basement, subzero fridge, fenced in yard."

"I'm confused."

"Ball to the walls!" Matt let out a loud warrior cry that Jack hadn't heard since their days playing cowboys and Indians back when it wasn't politically incorrect to call it that.

"Are you drunk?"

"No man! It's called being high on life."

"You're really freaking me out." Jack opened the folder and pulled out a glossy picture of a traditional looking white house with black shutters and a shiny red door with a brass doorknocker. The bright green front yard had crisscrossing lawn mower tracks and a white walkway lined with groomed antique rose bushes.

"You're looking at a real, honest to God homeowner!" Matt pulled out an official looking paper and pointed to his signature across a dotted line.

"They don't have houses like that in the Lower West Side. Where the fuck are you moving?"

"Scarsdale."

Lauren pulled the paper from Jack's hands. "OMG! This is like a mansion!"

"Aren't you the one who always says Westchester's for douchebags?"

"Well, than I'm one happy motherfuckin douchebag because I have a fifteen year fixed APR mortgage for 529 Red Robin Lane."

Jack grabbed the paper back from Lauren. "This doesn't look like a house you'd be caught dead in."

"But it's a house I could live in with Anne and the baby." Matt smiled serenely.

"How do you know she'll go with you?"

"Because this is my big Kris Kringle moment here."

"This is the weirdest conversation I've had with you since we did shrooms that time at the Thanksgiving Day parade."

"What're shrooms?" asked Lauren.

"Don't you remember Miracle on 34th Street? The real black and white one, not the shitty remake." Matt cut Lauren off and shook his head at Jack.

"Yeah. We watched it with my mom when she was going through chemo."

"Hello? I still don't know what shrooms are." Lauren waved her hands wildly at them.

"Pipe down, Small Fry. That was the last time I saw it too. To be honest, it made me kind of sad to watch that movie because it's always reminded me of your mom. But Anne really wanted to watch it the other day, you know with Thanksgiving coming up. Anyway, all the little girl really wants is a perfect house, with a perfect yard in the suburbs. She cuts out a picture of just the right house and shows it to Kris Kringle and says if he's really Santa Claus, he'll find a way to get the house for her."

"And in the end she gets her dream house and she knows Kris Kringle made it happen because he left his cane by the fireplace!" Lauren piped in. "What? You think you two are the only people in the world who've seen that movie?"

"Well, Anne had never seen it, which is insane. Anyway, we watched it together and she was crying by the end." Matt smiled sheepishly and Jack knew he must've been crying too.

"Dude, of course she was crying. It's a sappy movie and she's pregnant."

"I know. But I'm telling you she was crying because that's what she wants. The house in the burbs and the perfect family."

"You just spent millions on a hunch? What if she doesn't come with you?"

"She'll come." Matt looked just as determined as when he secured their bank loan for the business.

"You should totally drive up there with her. Pretend you're going to Westchester to see one of your friends' new houses. Walk around with her and wait until she keeps admiring how nice it is and then tell her you got it for her." Lauren waved her arms around as she talked and her voice got louder with each sentence.

"Good thinking, Small Fry! Clearly, you don't take after your uncle in the brains department."

Lauren grabbed Matt's arm. "OMG! Wait, I have a better idea! Instead of telling Anne you got the house for her—you need to leave something of yours by the fireplace!"

"Holy shit! You're a fucking genius!!" Matt put both hands on the top of his head and shook it back and forth with an ear-to-ear grin.

"The question is, what?" asked Jack, finding himself getting into this plan despite his reservations about Matt leaving the city.

"One of my Yankees caps?"

"Everybody who lives in New York has a Yankees cap. You have to pick something that could only be yours." Lauren raised both hands in the air in exasperation.

"The new stroller?" suggested Jack.

"She's pregnant! Do you want her to think you're saying her new baby is going to be fat?" Lauren did a perfect handstand on the line of slate stones lining the yard, and landed back down on two feet seamlessly.

"That's it! You're a genius!" Matt grabbed Lauren and swung her around in a circle.

"What did I say?"

"Our sonogram picture! I can put our sonogram picture on the mantle!"

"OMG! That's such a good idea!"

"Don't all those things look the same? How's she going to know it's yours?" Jack didn't want to burst anyone's bubble, but those gray and black swirly pictures were completely undistinguishable from each other.

"Anne put it in a homemade frame. Do you know what this means for you buddy?" Mat swung around to face Jack.

"I'll finally have to learn how to drive?"

"If you really want to be with the fem-bot, you have to have your own Kris Kringle moment."

"The most romantic scene of any movie has to be in Titanic when everyone knows the ship is sinking and they're all going to drown in the icy abyss. That one elderly couple get into bed, the husband cuddles up next to his wife and they just stay like that, holding each other while the ship goes down."

Kate Richards, Straight Talk

Chapter Forty-Four

"Beautiful!"

"Absolutely gorgeous!"

Kate's strapless dress was banded in hundreds of thick white ribbons that crisscrossed and cinched in tight at her waist leading to a full skirt of the finest silvery- white gossamer. She looked just like Cinderella in the Disney cartoon she and Jen had watched a million times when they were kids because it was the only VHS tape their dad hadn't pawned.

Kate clutched her American Beauty bouquet and smiled through the clicks of the cameras flashing at her from four different angles. The overly fragrant flowers were plugging up her sinuses and the bright lights were making her feel hot and nauseated.

"How does it feel to be our June cover girl?"

Kate kept her smile for the next ten rapid clicks of the camera, and then held up her hand.

"The June edition?" Kate could barely get the words out. Her mouth was so dry her teeth were sticking to her upper lip.

The *Beautiful Brides Magazine* editor slid her thick Armani glasses on top of her flat -ironed hair. "Most people would kill for the June cover. I mean we're talking A-List over the years—Drew Barrymore, Jessica Biel, Reese Witherspoon."

"I know, I know. I'm sorry." Kate silently ticked the months off on her fingers. Seven months. Seven more months of pretending. She tried to take in a deep cleansing yoga breath, but the metal boning on her corset dug into her ribs.

"Kate's a little overwhelmed. You can understand—her first time trying on wedding dresses." Dana took a break from giving the photographer pointers to sooth the editor's ego.

"Oh. I didn't realize this was Kate's first time. You should've brought her mother." The editor's voice softened while her Botox frozen face remained expressionless.

"Her mom was scared to come out in this weather. The bridges will close if this keeps up." Dana looked pointedly at Kate to make sure she knew to play along. As if Kate was dumb enough to tell the editor that her mom wasn't the wedding dress shopping kind of mom anyway.

"It's all those suburban soccer moms driving around in their mini-vans. Global warming's gonna be the end of us all." The editor put her glasses back on and scrolled through the pictures from the shoot on her iPad.

"Kate's looking like her blood sugar's getting a little low. Do you mind if she takes a ten minute break?" Dana looped her arm through Kate's and acted as if she was supporting her. Meanwhile, Kate knew if she really leaned all her body weight into Dana, they would both instantly drop to the floor.

"We had takeout sent to the dressing room. But make it quick. I promised the crew we'd wrap before the storm hits."

Kate was off the makeshift stage before the editor could change her mind.

"You're supposed to look like a happy blushing bride, not like someone going to their own funeral!" Dana turned on Kate as soon as she shut the dressing room door.

"June? Seriously, Dana, June!" Kate grabbed a Poland Spring bottle off the dressing room table and chugged it in breathless gulps.

"If we pull the plug on this too soon it won't look authentic.

Besides, the June cover is huge!" Dana fluffed her dreads in the light bulb brightened mirror.

"I can't last another seven months!"

"Yes you can. Get your shit together and don't come out of this room till you can put a smile on your face and fake it for the cameras."

Dana opened the door, then paused in the doorway, "And don't eat too much. We'll never be able to squeeze you in the Badgley Mischka."

As soon as Dana shut the door, Kate felt her heart quicken to a staccato double beat while she struggled to catch her breath. She felt like she was suffocating under the layers of ribbon and tulle. She desperately wanted to rip the dress off. The problem was it had taken two women to fasten the hundreds of seed pearl buttons on the back.

The smell of food from the grease-coated bag on the makeup table overwhelmed Kate. Her stomach grumbled under all the dress layers. She hadn't been able to stomach any breakfast before the photo shoot.

Kate opened the brown paper bag and inhaled the unmistakable fragrance of hamburgers and French fries. She pulled the lukewarm fry packet out of the bag, and almost dropped it when she saw the red NY Burger Co. emblem on the white wax paper. Kate reached back in the bag and pulled out an aluminum wrapped burger and a tall cold takeout cup. She knew as soon as she saw the condensation beading up on the sides that it was a milkshake.

Kate looked up at the ceiling. "Seriously?"

Kate clutched the fries to her chest like she did with her bible on her first communion. "Is this a cosmic joke? Or is this a sign? Because seriously I just don't know the difference anymore."

The dressing room walls felt like they were closing in on Kate while the rows of lights in the makeup mirrors glared in her eyes and made her overwhelmingly hot. The sound of her phone broke through the ringing in her ears.

"Fuck. This is all I need right now." Kate grabbed the phone when she saw it was her dad's treatment facility.

"Hello?" Kate steeled herself for the worst; her dad got kicked out of rehab or escaped and went on a bender.

"Katie?" Her father always spoke too loud on long distance calls. Kate had to hold the phone away from her ear.

"Pop? What's wrong?" Kate leaned against the wall; the layers of dress forming a barricade so all she could feel were steely barbs of crinoline scratching her legs.

"What'cha doin' next Saturday?"

"Pop, I'm not up for another family counseling session." The last two times Jen had stormed out and Kate left with a massive headache. Not to mention, all her father's therapists wanted to talk about were her wedding plans.

"Screw therapy. You need to get me the Hell out of Dodge."

"Dad. I'm not breaking you out of rehab." Kate collapsed to the ground in a pile of white.

"Who said anything about making a run for it? I'm graduating!" Her father's voice boomed into the phone.

"What?"

"Dr. Lanslow said I'm ready for out-patient." The word out-patient dripped in pride as Kate's dad made his announcement.

"This doesn't mean you're healed you know." The first image that popped in Kate's head was her father hitting up the closest OTB.

"Yeah, but it means I get one last chance to fix things with you and Jen."

"Oh Pop." Kate sighed.

"You're a good egg you know that?"

Kate held the phone and just breathed.

"You didn't give up on me. Even when everyone else in the world did."

"Pop?"

"What's up Buttercup?"

"Nothing." Kate stood up and smoothed out the layers of her dress. "See you Saturday."

Kate pried the lid off the take out cup and revealed a swirl of melting vanilla ice cream and milk. She pulled a long salt-dusted fry from the packet and inhaled the scent of fried goodness. Kate skimmed the fry over the top of the milkshake. She closed her eyes and relished the sweet and salty bite. Then she reached for another fry and didn't stop until the only thing left in the fry packet was a grainy layer of salt.

Kate licked the salt off her lips and opened the door and checked first to make sure no one was looking before she snuck down the hall and pressed the elevator button.

"Can I get something for you Ms Richards?" Kate hadn't noticed the editor's assistant because she was so thin her skin had taken on a translucent glow.

"No thanks. I'm just meeting my assistant down in the lobby. I'll be right back."

Kate just needed to get downstairs to the wide open lobby where she could breathe. Being in the enclosed elevator didn't help, nor did the crush of people that piled in and around her dress on the fourteenth, seventh and fourth floors. No one seemed shocked to see a lone bride in the elevator. They were too busy mumbling about when the subways would stop running, and which Duane Reade still had batteries in stock.

Once that door opened, Kate knew there was no going back. She felt all the other people rush out of the elevator around her before taking that step into the open.

Kate stood in the middle of the lobby and just breathed. She inhaled until she thought the tiny bodice buttons would pop and then exhaled till she got all the trapped air out. No one stared at her; they were too busy looking out the windows to survey the powerful storm.

Kate stood and listened to the whistle of the wind and the rush of water pouring down the windows. The intertwined blocks of glass rattled at their stainless steel seams. She didn't know how long she had been stuck in the windowless studio, but it was long enough for the hurricane to descend.

"What the fuck is going on?" Dana practically ran out of the elevator as soon as the doors opened.

"I can't do this." Kate didn't know she was going to say it till the words spilled out of her mouth.

"We're almost done. They just want a few more shots of

you in the Badgley."

"I don't just mean the photo shoot."

"You just need to hang in there a little longer." Dana licked her thumb, and then pressed it from the edge of Kate's mouth to her chin. "Is that ice cream on you face?"

"This shoot is for a cover that won't hit the stands till June! I can't wait that long."

"Fine, I can ask them to use the shot of you with the dark red roses for the February cover."

"I really didn't think this all the way through."

"Bravo wants to film the wedding. We'll get you the holiday *Beautiful Brides* cover, then schedule a New Year's wedding. Alex can leave you at the altar. You can make it till January."

"I can't." Kate lifted the layers of dress and headed towards the door.

"Wait! Where are you going?" Dana's voice overtook the rumblings of wind.

"To find Jack!" Kate leaned all of her weight into the rotating door. But the wind was on Dana's side.

"Wait! What about the wedding dress?"

"Tell them to send me the bill!"

Kate's dramatic exit was stuck on the slow motion setting. She was able to get the door moving, just enough to start to squeeze through. But the hard part was fitting the mounds of tulle and organza into the telephone booth sized glass compartment.

"You're committing career suicide!" Dana pounded on the glass with her fist. "Kate!"

The one good thing about the claustrophobia inducing door was that once it finally moved enough to accommodate her huge dress it locked Kate into a sound proof barrier that muffled Dana's voice.

Kate pushed against the door, and it didn't take more than a second for her to panic when she realized it wasn't moving. She was vacuum sealed in the airless space. Kate picked up the layers of tulle and pressed them up against the glass to shield her hands in case the glass broke and pushed as hard as she could. She twisted her neck around and was grateful to see Dana still standing there. Kate couldn't hear what she said, but it was obvious she realized that Kate was stuck. Dana was pressing as hard as she could to get the door moving, but she just wasn't big enough to give the door any momentum.

Kate tried to calculate how soon the air would run out. She pictured herself suffocating in a rotating door while wearing a wedding dress. She could only imagine the newspaper headings that would bring.

All of a sudden the door started to move. Someone had come in the rotating door from the outside and as soon as Kate felt the door inch forward, she moved with it. That's when she heard the unmistakable sound of fabric tearing. The top layer of tulle from the dress' skirt was stuck in the bottom of the door and it stayed behind as the door rotated. But all Kate cared about was getting out of the glass box. She pushed at the door and didn't stop until she got to the sidewalk all in one piece— minus the first layer of her dress. Thank God she picked the one dress from the unknown designer to run away in.

Kate turned to look through the glass to let Dana know she made it through unscathed. But all she could see was a hulking mass standing in the lobby completely obscuring Dana except for the bit of bright red high heel sticking out to the side. He must've been the one who was strong enough to get the door moving. Then the large man turned a little to the left and Kate couldn't mistake the orange face. Their bodies weren't touching, but there was intimacy in the way Alex looked down at Dana. Alex had been worried about the storm and hadn't wanted them to leave for the shoot. Now, Kate knew why.

The first thing Kate noticed when she got out of the building was the sky. It was dark as night even though it was only 10 A.M. Clouds hung low in the atmosphere like deep bruises and thick raindrops pelted down between balls of hail.

The sidewalks were empty, all the people having rushed for refuge in the foliage covered shops that lined the streets of the flower district. Kate took cover under the umbrella-like leaves of a large banana tree while she looked up and down the streets for a cab.

Sirens and the eerie screeching of the wind were all Kate could hear. She spotted a cab coming up 28th Street and she ditched her shelter and ran to the curb, shielding her face with her arms against the assault of hale. Kate stuck her hand in the air, but the cabbie kept moving, his eyes fixed only on the flooding road ahead of him.

A sandwich board advertising "$20 mani-pedis" flew across the street and crashed into the glass window of an exotic flower shop. The howl of the wind was so deafening Kate couldn't even hear the glass as it shattered. She covered her head and ducked, narrowly missed flying shards of glass. Kate felt like she was on the set of a high budget disaster film.

Kate knew there was no way she was going to get a cab to stop. She would have to run. Good thing she had already ditched the Ferragamo heels for flip-flops. The only problem now was the heavy multi-layered hoop petticoat underneath her dress. The lacy bottom layers had already soaked up the icy rainwater like a sponge, weighing Kate down. Kate reached under the layers of tulle and organza and untied the drawstring top of the petticoat. It felt so good to pull the petticoat down and step out of it. The wind lifted the petticoat up and the medieval contraption floated down the avenue like one of the Macy's Thanksgiving floats. Kate's dress hung off her body like a deflated balloon, but at least she could run now.

The wind was in Kate's favor as it pushed her towards Eighth Avenue. The heavy bi-layer veil did nothing to shield her head from the rain. It was like running with a window screen clamped into her hair but it was secured so tightly Kate had no time to take it out.

Despite the balls of hail hitting her on the back, and the rain streaming down her face, Kate finally felt like she could breathe. Kate headed uptown on 28th Street and felt like she was in an urban obstacle course race as she dodged rolling garbage cans, shielded her face from flying debris and ran through inches of ice cold water.

Suddenly, Kate stopped short even though her feet were

still moving. It felt like someone had grabbed her dress and yanked her back. Kate had been running so fast she hadn't noticed the gigantic stroller abandoned on the sidewalk. Kate was both relieved there wasn't an overweight kid stuck in it and aggravated to see her dress was snagged on a piece of white plastic jutting out from the stroller. Kate's hands were so numb from the cold water and so fatigued from holding up the heavy layers of wet dress that she could barely make her fingers work to try to free the dress.

"You had to go with the snack tray didn't you Jack?!"

The wind roared in response and Kate came very close to meeting an untimely death by stroller. Luckily, she wasn't knocked unconscious when the steel contraption lifted just enough to slam back down on the rest of her dress. Kate was now pinned down by the steel frame of the new CC-XL Deluxe.

"I am not going down like this!" Kate thought of the mountain climber who was trapped by a boulder and had to amputate his own arm using only a dull pocketknife. She could do this. Kate blew warm breath onto her frigid fingers then rubbed them together as hard as she could to wake them up. She gritted her teeth and used every bit of strength she had to pull at the wet crinoline until she felt it tear. Kate pulled and pulled layer after layer of crinoline and silk until only two shreds of organza remained of her beautiful princess skirt. The rest of the skirt swirled and flapped in the wind firmly stuck to the abandoned CC-XL Deluxe stroller.

Kate would be eternally grateful to Dana for talking her into wearing thigh length nude SPANX to the photo shoot. Otherwise she would've been running through the streets of New York in a thong that was only covered by jagged layers of wispy lace.

Kate ran until her feet were numb and the unscathed top of her dress was soaked through. The townhouse looked different, almost like it was ready for battle with its heavy wooden shutters closed over the windows. Then Kate saw Jack leaning out to protect that last one.

"Real success is knowing what you want and having the balls to go for it."

Jack Moskowitz, Success Magazine

Chapter Forty-Five

The newscasters had talked of nothing for days but the upcoming hurricane. Jack was ready. Except for the damn windows. He forgot to cover them till the hail hit, bouncing off the glass panes as hard as golf balls at the putting range. He started with the ground level windows and worked his way up.

Diesel tucked himself into a ball between Lauren's karaoke machine and her violin case. He would have felt much safer in the cover of Jack's claw foot bathtub where he waited out most thunderstorms, but the dog sensed impending danger and would not leave his owner's side.

"Hang in there, buddy. This is the last set." Jack pushed aside the jumble of throw pillows, books, and stuffed animals and climbed on top of Lauren's window seat.

"Hey! Watch out for Mr. Fluffy! He's geriatric." Lauren pulled the threadbare brown teddy bear from under Jack's sneaker.

"This would be a lot easier if you didn't have so much crap lying around." Jack moved aside the mound of Lauren's old Cabbage Patch Kids and planted his feet firmly on the oak window seat.

"Do you think Mom and Dad will still make it home this weekend?" Lauren tucked Mr. Fluffy under the polka dot covers in her twin bed.

"I'm sure everything will be back to normal by then."

But as Jack watched the wind rip the striped awning off the brownstone across the street, he wasn't so sure.

As soon as Jack unlatched the window, it flew up carried by a gust of wind. Jack leaned out the window and quickly reached for the shutter, hoping the wind wouldn't change direction and force the window back down on top of him guillotine style.

Luckily, the hail had been replaced with goldfish sized drops of rain by the time Jack started on the third floor windows. He relished the splashes of water on the back of his neck and enjoyed the shock of cold on his warm skin. The city noises had given way to an eerie quiet as all the people had emptied the streets to take shelter wherever they could.

"Jack!" A voice floated up on the gusts of wind. "Jack!"

Streams of water poured down Jack's head onto his face as he looked down and saw a blond woman standing on the sidewalk in front of his townhouse. She was wearing a wedding gown on top with nothing on the bottom. Jack wiped the stream of water from his eyes with the back of his forearm, thinking the storm was conjuring some kind of half naked bride mirage.

"OMG! Is that Kate?" Lauren dropped Mr. Fluffy and jumped on the window seat and shoved herself next to Jack to get a better view.

"Jack!" This time the wind carried her voice and there was no mistaking it for anyone other than Kate.

"Where's the rest of her dress?" Lauren leaned her head out the window to get a closer look and Jack grabbed her and pulled her back in.

Jack didn't even bother with the last shutter; he let the window slam shut and ran to the front door.

"Stay here!" Jack ordered Lauren, as he tried to open the front door. The wind pushed against the centuries old door causing a vacuum seal. Jack threw all of his body weight into it and was able to force it open in the short lull between bursts of wind. And there was Kate standing in front of his town house—wearing a mutilated wedding dress.

Kate looked like a bride on top, in a strapless white ribbon wrapped corset thing. She even wore a delicate silver tiara attached to a long veil spilling over her wet waves of hair. Her flip-flops were black with New York City sludge and she had mud splattered up her calves leading to some kind of weird flesh-colored bike shorts. But for the first time in Jack's life he understood how someone's beauty could take your breath away.

"Kate…" Jack started, but Kate didn't let him finish.

Kate rested her hands on his cheeks, and Jack's whole body tingled as she gently pulled his face to hers. The rain sluiced down on them and Jack reached his hands under Kate's veil to grab onto her hair. Kate's hands were everywhere, first his face, then the back of his neck, then wrapped in the folds of his wet tee shirt.

Jack didn't know how long they stood there wrapped in each other. But it was long enough for his lips to feel bruised and swollen and his clothes to hang heavy with water. It was excruciating to unlock his lips from hers, but he had to. Jack took a step back and was instantly filled with remorse.

"Please don't say anything yet." The rain ran in rivulets down Kate's forehead and pooled on her full bottom lip.

"Kate, I …"

"Please. I need to say this." Kate pushed her shoulders back and stood up straighter. She smoothed down the two shreds of white lace that remained of her bridal skirt.

"Wait. I need to know why you're here now wearing half a wedding dress with those creepy shorts. Did you just pull a Runaway Bride that somehow involved tearing your dress to shreds in front of everyone?"

"No! I was at a photo shoot for *Beautiful Brides* and I just had to get out of there. You wouldn't believe what I snagged my dress on."

"Kate…"

"I'm falling in love with you Jack. I have been all along."

"Forget falling. I'm there already."

Jack didn't know who reached first, but they fell right back into each other, their kisses less violent and slower this time. Jack lifted Kate up and held her there suspended in air with the rain falling around them as they kissed. Then the hail came back.

"Maybe we should head inside." Jack rested Kate back on the ground, but kept his hands draped on her hips.

"I thought you'd never ask."

"What about Alex?" Jack couldn't stop himself. He had to know what happened to the creepy orange bastard. Jack wrapped his fingers around Kate's icy ones and pulled her towards the townhouse.

Kate stopped just shy of the stoop, and stood in a pool of murky water. "I'm not with Alex."

"So, you kinda did pull a Runaway Bride." An oversized chunk of ice pelted Jack right between his two eyebrows.

"I was never really with him." The wind lifted Kate's veil and pushed it over her face. She left it there.

"I don't get it." Jack ran his fingers through his hair, shedding shards of ice.

"Dana came up with the plan. I just had to pretend to be with Alex long enough to get the attention off you and me." Kate shoved the veil back, but the wind pushed it back over her face.

"Let me get this straight. Dana thought being with The Instigator was better for your image than being with me? And you agreed?"

"Jack, you have to understand. This has been killing…"

"I understand completely." Jack cut in. "Being with some hard partying reality star half your age is better for ratings than being with a guy who makes strollers for fat kids." Jack's anger seared through the cold rain and wind.

"You're the one who put me in this position!"

"So I was a complete asshole for lying, but it's okay for you to create a sham engagement?"

"I feel horrible about it. This has been torture for me!" Kate pushed the veil off her face again and when the wind tried to force it back over her she ripped it right off the tiara. The wind lifted the veil right out of her hands and carried down the street.

"You actually let me think you were with that meathead! You lied to me for months!" All this time Jack had felt bad for lying to Kate, meanwhile his lie paled in comparison to hers.

"You left me no choice!" Kate moved to the side just as a thin branch cracked off the Juniper tree.

"That's bullshit. There's always a choice." Jack grabbed Kate's arm and pulled her out from under the tree.

"Well I'm here now. Choosing you." Kate's eyes looked just as stormy as the air around them as she held Jack's gaze. She wasn't backing down.

"It's too late." The words fell out of Jack's mouth before he could stop them. But once he said it he knew it was true.

"It can't be too late." Kate grabbed Jack's hands and held them tight. "It's not too late Jack. We can fix this."

"I can't do this." Jack yelled to be heard over the fire truck sirens that wailed in the distance.

"You're with someone else?" Kate dropped Jack's hands.

"No."

Kate inhaled. "Oh, good. You really had me worried there."

"Kate, this isn't going to work."

"We can figure it out."

"You inspired me to be a better person and I did. I finally got my own shit together. This new line is the first thing that's not about what Harper or Lauren or even Matt need."

"I get that. I can be there for you. Maybe I could even help you come up with some ideas for it."

"Kate, the minute the news hits that you broke things off with Alex to be with me, I'll have a media circus camped outside my stoop all over again. That will take away from everything I've worked for."

"They'll only stay until the next Disney star gets arrested. Remember when you said that to me?"

"Kate, I'm serious. I can't do this." Jack never thought he would be the one saying no.

"Can't or won't?" Kate backed away from him slowly. Then, in a split second she turned around and bolted.

"Wait!" But Jack's words were lost in the rushing wind. Kate was a blur of white in between the drops of heavy rain mixed with pelting balls of hail.

The bottoms of Jack's feet were numb as he trudged back up the stairs. He barely touched the brownstone door when the wind pushed it open.

"Where's Kate?" Lauren stood in the doorway holding two large beach towels. Diesel sat at her feet looking up at Jack expectantly.

"Gone." Jack grabbed one of the towels from her. Only when he wrapped himself in the faded Barbie towel, did the violent shivers move up from his feet.

"What?" Lauren followed Jack down the hall towards the bathroom. "How could you let her leave?"

"Not now Lauren. Not now." Jack suddenly felt a hundred years old. He rubbed the towel over his wet hair

"Are you really letting Kate go?" Lauren grabbed Jack's arm. "Seriously?"

"It's not going to work with us." Jack shook off Lauren's freakishly strong grip. "It never was."

"Yes it will!" Lauren's shrieks echoed through the hallway. "You guys are meant to be."

"It's not happening, Lauren."

"But she came here in a mangled wedding dress! For you!"

"It's too late."

"Don't you get it?" Lauren threw her arms up in the air and shrieked.

"Get what?" Jack knew there was no running away from Lauren. She would follow him around till she got the last word in.

"This is your Kris Kringle moment!" Lauren's eyes were wide as she spread her arms wide open. "Go to her!"

Jack ran back to the front door. It took every ounce of strength he had to get the damn thing back open. He looked down the street. Kate was already a block away although she probably would've been a lot farther if she hadn't been wearing flip-flops.

"Hurry up! Before she gets away!" Lauren snatched the towel back and shoved Jack towards the door.

"Kate! Kate!" Jack didn't know if she couldn't hear him over the storm or if she was ignoring him. He hopped down the stairs two at a time and landed in the calf deep puddle at the bottom of the stoop. He started up the sidewalk, which was now an obstacle course of broken branches, rolling soda cans and soggy newspapers. He ignored the phantom pain in his ankle and the chafing of his wet jeans on his thighs as he tried desperately to catch up to Kate.

"Kate! Come back!" Jack chased her past the boarded up newsstand, and the shelves of wet produce outside the Korean vegetable market. He was gaining on her but she sped up, taking advantage of her clearly superior conditioning. That's when Jack was certain that she could hear him shouting.

Just as she was trying to cross Eighth Avenue, Kate's foot slid ahead of her body and she skidded off the curb. She slid across the slick street and landed in a heap on top of a manhole cover in the middle of the avenue. A cab was barreling towards her, the driver clearly blinded by the surge of water gushing down the windshield. There would be no way he would see Kate, or expect a person to be planted in the middle of Eighth Avenue in the middle of a hurricane.

Jack ran into the street and slammed his body into Kate with football player force and shoved her onto the sidewalk just as the cabbie swerved out of the way unleashing a string of curse words from the open window.

"Um, you can get let go of me now." Kate's voice was muffled under Jack's body.

Jack had thrown himself on top of Kate, covering her whole body with his in case the cab jumped the curb. His arms were wrapped tightly around Kate, his face burrowed into her shoulder. He loosened his grip, but didn't get up.

"Kate Richards, I'm never letting you go."

Epilogue

"The Lower West Side's favorite matchmaker Mrs. Fink finally made her own match just days shy of her eightieth birthday. Mrs. Fink reconnected with her childhood sweetheart at a West Side Jewish Center fundraiser, sixty-five years after falling head over heels for Abraham Weinstein in their native Hungary. Mrs. Fink bonded with the widower over brisket and matzoh ball soup and walked down the aisle with him less than two weeks later. Mrs. Fink is rumored to have a hand in more than one hundred successful marriages including Tom Hanks and Rita Wilson, Jennifer Garner and Ben Affleck, and Ellen DeGeneres and Portia deRossi."

The Chelsea Chronicle

"Roll out the red carpet for this bouncing baby boy's stroller, but don't worry it doesn't have to be a supersized one, yet. CEO and Co-Founder of Considerable Carriages Matt Reynolds and his on-again wife Anne welcomed a new baby this morning and named him Jackson after Matt's business partner and lifetime best friend. Maybe Maximillian would've been a more appropriate name considering Considerable Carriages is neck in neck with Apple on Forbes' top businesses list."

Craig Ashbourne, The 411

"Jack Moskowitz's niece Lauren Feldman might steal his girlfriend's thunder. Rumor has it that the pint sized turbo athlete was such a hit on her guest role on KidFit, that producers have asked her to star in the show alongside Kate Richards on a permanent basis."

insidescoop.com

"Dana Johnson and Alex Lombardi first made headlines when their affair sidelined Ali-Kat's much anticipated nuptials. Watch this May-December couple go from public enemy number one to America's sweethearts in their reality show Tying the Not, airing on Tuesday nights right before my show."

Jessa Silver, Late Night with Jessa Silver

"Westchester better make some room because Considerable Carriages is moving its supersized division there for CEO Matt Reynolds to head up. Reynolds moved to Scarsdale in time for the birth of his first child with wife Anne. Meanwhile, back in Manhattan, Jack Moskowitz will head up the new line of strollers called Considerate Carriages, which will accommodate children with special needs. According to Moskowitz, the profits from the Considerable Carriages line are enough to allow the Considerate Carriages line to be sold on a sliding scale basis."

Success Magazine

"Spotted: an engagement ring on Kate Richards' finger. This time around her sparkler was noticeably smaller than the Neil Lane bauble featured in her Gossip Matters cover story with ex-fiancé Alex Lombardi. But this ring's sentimental value more than makes up for its meager carats. Jack Moskowitz proposed to Kate Richards with a ring handed down to him by his maternal great-grandmother. The antique white gold ring has made it through two World Wars and the Great Depression, so Jack thought it was a good symbol of his commitment to Kate."

happilyeverafter.com

Acknowledgments

"There are two kinds of teachers: the kind that fill you with so much quail shot that you can't move, and the kind that just give you a little prod behind and you jump to the skies." Robert Frost. Thank you to my writing teachers and mentors Patricia Dunn and Jimin Han for all the little prods along the way.

Thank you to my beloved writing group Ahmed Asif, Marlena Baraf, Jacqueline Goldstein, Nancy Flanagan, Rickey Marks, Nan Mutnick, and Ines Rodrigues. And to my writing friends Pari Chang and Susan Kleinman, thank you for your limitless support.

David Donnelly, Katrina Brown and Sweet Orefice, thank you for creating a positive writing community at The Writing Institute at Sarah Lawrence College, the place where this book was born and grew up. Thank you to the Romance Writers of America/New York City, Inc., a supportive professional organization for people who love to write about love.

Thank you to my editor, Mary Cummings, and the rest of the amazing team at Diversion Books: Sarah Masterson Hally and Brielle Benton.

To Eric Ruben, my fabulous agent, thank you for helping this book breathe life outside the confines of my laptop.

Stephanie Lia, my forever friend, thanks for sticking with me since the days of braces, teased hair and sneaking out in the black Camaro. To the Graviers, Tatarians, Burrowes, Coplans, Lathams, and Dawsons. Thanks to all of you for believing in me. Your families have become extensions of my own.

Special thanks to Julie Latham for planting the seed that grew into Considerate Carriages.

Thanks to the Kinderhook ladies, for being the first book club to read this book. And to my two Bronxville book clubs for being so supportive. Thank you also to all of my Junior League of Bronxville friends who have offered me endless encouragement.

Thanks to my talented photographer cousin, Syrie Moskowitz, who squeezed in my photo shoot in between jaunts around the world.

To my Frisbee catching wonder dog Rufus, who didn't leave my side for fourteen years and to my eternal puppy Oscar, thank you both for being my favorite writing buddies.

To the keepers of my heart, Molly, Tommy, Connor, Riley, Reagan, Maddox and Mason. Thanks to my mother-in-law Betsy for treating me like her own daughter and for taking Molly on all sorts of fabulous adventures so I could write. Thank you for always being there for me. Thanks to Tracy for reading early pages and to Jon for making fun of the risqué scenes. Thank you to my brothers-in-law Bond and Paul for learning to deal with the loud and opinionated Moskowitz girls and to my sisters for always being there.

Thank you to my mother for handing me my first *Writer's Market* and saying "This is your chance to become a writer," when I was too sick to teach anymore. Thank you to my father, my hero, for all the times you rescued me, whether it was when the prom limo driver bailed or when you drove twenty-four hours round trip to bring me home from Ohio when I was sick.

Finally to Doug and Molly, thank you both for giving me my happily-ever-after.

CPSIA information can be obtained at www.ICGtesting.com
Printed in the USA
BVOW05s1739220414

351281BV00002B/10/P